Flicker

Zoe Moon

Published by Zoe Moon, 2024.

This is a work of fiction. Similarities to real people, places, or events are entirely coincidental.

FLICKER

First edition. November 11, 2024.

Copyright © 2024 Zoe Moon.

ISBN: 979-8227871299

Written by Zoe Moon.

Chapter 1: Blazing First Impressions

The moment he stepped closer, the air between us thickened like smoke after the flame had been put out. I wanted to say something snarky, something sharp to cut through the tension that clung to his movements. But my tongue felt heavy, an unfamiliar weight in my mouth. He wasn't the typical fireman I had imagined—loud, brash, maybe a little too quick to pat himself on the back after saving a kitten from a tree. No, this man was different. The way he held himself, the unspoken authority in the way he moved—he didn't need to speak, yet his presence screamed that he was a man who dealt in seriousness, in control.

His eyes were a strange shade of gray, too light to be considered blue but too dark to be anything close to silver. They looked at me as though they could strip me bare with just a glance. And it wasn't the first time I'd felt like I was under some kind of scrutinizing microscope. Hell, it was something I'd grown used to, having worked in the most high-stakes legal department in the city. But this was different. There was something unsettlingly calm about him, like he was trying to figure out exactly who I was—why I had the nerve to stand here and challenge the way things were unraveling.

"Shouldn't be hanging around here, ma'am," he said, his voice low and a bit gravelly, as though years of fire and smoke had somehow etched their way into his throat.

I felt a flicker of defiance stir within me. "I'm not the one starting the fires," I said, keeping my arms folded, my chin raised just a little bit higher, as if that would give me some semblance of stature against him. I wasn't going to let him intimidate me, not here, not now.

He raised an eyebrow, his lips curving into something that wasn't quite a smile but wasn't quite a frown either. "That's a fact. But you're still here. The question is why."

I could have easily brushed him off, but his words stuck with me, lingering in my thoughts like the acrid scent of smoke that stubbornly clung to my hair. Why was I still here? There were a thousand reasons I should have turned on my heel and walked away—my research had been clear, the area was too dangerous, and frankly, I had a lot of other things demanding my attention. But instead, my feet felt cemented to the spot, my curiosity pulling me closer to the mystery. There was something about the whole situation that gnawed at the back of my mind, an itch that needed to be scratched.

"You think I'm the one who's been starting these fires?" I asked, more to challenge him than to gain an answer.

He didn't immediately respond, his eyes flicking briefly to the half-empty canister in my hand. I hadn't even realized I was holding it, but I was. A small part of me hoped he wouldn't ask about it, that it would be left unexamined like a dirty secret under the rug. But he wasn't the kind of man who let things go easily. Firemen weren't, I supposed. "What's in the can, then?" he asked, his voice suddenly steely, but that edge still not quite leaving it.

It wasn't the sort of question I'd been expecting. Not after everything he'd already said. He wasn't accusing me outright, but I could feel the weight of his suspicion, that slow burn of uncertainty creeping into the air between us. I didn't want to answer him. Hell, I didn't even want to look at the can, but I found my hand moving like it had a mind of its own, giving him the kind of answer he was expecting without a word. The lid was bent slightly at the edge, evidence of my hurried departure earlier. But the contents—well, the contents weren't exactly legal.

"Don't worry about it," I said, my voice a little too sharp, a little too defensive. His gaze didn't leave me. It seemed to press against my skin, unraveling every layer of pretense until I was exposed for what I really was. I hated the feeling of vulnerability creeping in.

"Ma'am, I've seen things like this before," he said, his voice a mix of patience and some kind of grim understanding. "You should really rethink what you're doing."

I wanted to snap back at him. To tell him it wasn't his business, to remind him that he was just a fireman, and I was a legal researcher with my own things to worry about. But as I opened my mouth, no words came. My mind had frozen, unable to keep up with the sudden shift in the air between us. I could feel it now—the tension that had started with just a spark and was slowly escalating. This wasn't just about fires anymore. This was something else. Something deeper.

He tilted his head, as if to appraise me, to try to understand what made me tick. I couldn't quite place the emotion in his eyes, but it wasn't judgment. There was something else—something I couldn't name, but it made my pulse quicken just slightly. For a moment, I wondered if he saw something in me I wasn't even aware of. Maybe it was just the exhaustion of the past few weeks playing tricks on my mind, but I couldn't shake the feeling that there was more going on here. That his presence in this alley wasn't a coincidence.

Then, just like that, he turned and began walking away without another word.

I stood there for a long time, the night air thick with the scent of ash, my thoughts tangled in a web I couldn't yet untangle. I wasn't sure what had just happened. But one thing was clear: I wasn't finished with him. And somehow, I knew he wasn't finished with me either.

I didn't expect to see him again so soon, but fate had a funny way of insisting on things. The next morning, just as I was stepping into the cramped coffee shop on the corner—its doors creaking with a sound like a protest—I noticed him standing near the counter, his broad shoulders and tall frame unmistakable even in the dim lighting. His eyes flicked over to me with that same unsettling precision. It was as if he'd known I would be here, like he'd been waiting just for me.

I paused, hand still on the door handle, caught between my typical need to avoid confrontation and the growing sense that ignoring him wasn't an option. For all my reservations, my feet betrayed me, carrying me into the warm, cinnamon-scented interior like a moth to a flame. I had enough sense to keep my gaze down, pretending not to notice him, hoping the strange weight of the last encounter would fade into the background noise of the morning bustle.

But of course, it didn't.

"Fancy meeting you here," he said, his voice smooth, tinged with that same steady authority. I wondered if he was ever anything but composed, but I wasn't ready to find out.

I fought the urge to roll my eyes. "This is a public space," I shot back, taking my place in line as if I hadn't just made eye contact with the last person I ever wanted to see again.

His lips twitched, just the slightest curve. "Right. My mistake."

I wasn't going to look at him. I wasn't. The last thing I needed was to let him see how off balance he made me. But as I waited for my coffee, I couldn't help but glance up. His posture hadn't changed—still the same self-assured stance. Still the same unreadable expression.

"I didn't think you were the coffee shop type," I remarked, hoping it would come off as casual but bracing myself for whatever response came next. It was like poking a bear, I knew. But something in me didn't want him to have the satisfaction of thinking he had some kind of upper hand. Maybe that was it—he made me feel like I was walking on uneven ground, and I hated it.

"Well," he said, taking a step closer, "we all have our secrets." There was that wry smile again. This time, it didn't feel like an accusation. It felt like a warning.

I raised an eyebrow. "Is that your way of saying you're full of surprises?"

He grinned, and it wasn't as charming as he probably thought. "You could say that."

It wasn't until I saw the barista call my name that I was able to escape. I grabbed my cup, heat seeping through the cardboard sleeve, and turned to leave without another word. But of course, he wasn't finished.

"Don't forget," he said casually, his tone not quite masking the seriousness behind it. "I'm still keeping an eye on you."

The words struck harder than they should have. He wasn't being overtly threatening. Not in the obvious way. But there was something about the quiet certainty in his voice that unsettled me. It made me feel like I had become a puzzle he was intent on solving.

I didn't reply. I didn't need to. My feet carried me toward the door faster than I had intended, and just before I pushed it open, I stole one last look at him. He was watching me, but this time there was something different in his gaze. A flicker of recognition, maybe? A challenge? Or perhaps I was just imagining it, reading too much into a situation that didn't involve me as much as I liked to think.

It wasn't until I was halfway down the street, walking briskly to keep my mind from spiraling, that the thought hit me: I didn't really know what he was thinking. And worse, I didn't know what I was thinking. The last few weeks had been filled with enough distractions that I had forgotten what it was like to feel like I was in control. To feel like I could manage everything around me with just a little bit of finesse. But here, with him, all that was slipping away. It wasn't even about the fire anymore. It wasn't about the investigation. It was about something else. Something more dangerous.

I tried to push the thoughts away, focusing instead on the list of tasks I had to handle for the day. My job, the one that paid the bills and kept me occupied, had enough to keep my mind busy. But as I slipped into my office, I couldn't shake the feeling that my carefully organized life had just been thrown into chaos—and it had nothing to do with the fires in the neighborhood.

The day dragged on as usual. Meetings, emails, deadlines. My thoughts, however, drifted back to him far more often than I cared to admit. I couldn't explain why he bothered me so much. He wasn't my type—not that I had a specific "type" anymore, if I was being honest. My career had consumed most of my time, and dating was, at best, an afterthought. But he wasn't just anyone. He had a presence about him that made him impossible to ignore.

By the time the clock on my desk hit five, the tension in my shoulders had built to an unbearable level. I was sick of being on edge. I needed a drink. And I wasn't planning on going home just yet.

I slid my jacket on, grabbed my purse, and left the office without a second thought. The bar was just around the corner—a quiet place that knew how to make a good whiskey, and even better, knew how to keep a secret.

When I walked in, the usual hum of conversations and clinking glasses greeted me. But just as I was about to take a seat at the bar, I froze. There he was again. He didn't see me immediately, but I saw him—leaning against the far wall, a glass of something amber in his hand, and that familiar, unreadable expression on his face.

I wasn't sure whether to leave or face him head-on, but I wasn't about to let him think I was afraid. With a deep breath, I made my way over to the bar, choosing a seat far enough from him that I could enjoy my drink without being forced into another conversation. But of course, that wasn't how things worked out. As if he had sensed my arrival, he turned just as I sat down.

"Didn't expect to see you here," he said, his voice just low enough to carry over the music and laughter around us.

I looked up from the glass in front of me, surprised by how calm my voice sounded. "Funny. I was about to say the same thing."

The bar was starting to fill up now, the hum of chatter and clink of glassware rising around me. I could feel his presence across the room like a constant pull, as though he was some magnetic force I couldn't avoid even if I wanted to. I shouldn't be thinking about him—not here, not now—but I couldn't help it. The entire situation felt like something out of a film I'd rather not star in, one where the brooding hero kept showing up at all the wrong moments, leaving me unsure whether I should run or play along.

He hadn't moved since I sat down, still leaning casually against the wall, as though the entire bar existed solely for his observation. It made my skin itch, the way he seemed to be studying me from afar, as though he was waiting for some kind of sign that I was ready to have another round of this uncomfortable, silent standoff. It was like a game to him, or maybe it was just me that felt like the game. The kind of thing that made me want to finish my drink quickly and leave before the tension snapped.

"Not much for the crowd, huh?" he said, the words cutting through the noise in the bar and landing with unexpected sharpness. I glanced up, meeting his gaze for the first time since I'd walked in. He was standing just a few feet away now, his face illuminated by the neon glow from the sign overhead, his jawline sharper than I remembered. The fireman's uniform was gone, replaced by dark jeans and a faded leather jacket that looked as though it had seen its share of rough nights.

I couldn't quite figure him out. There was something magnetic about him, yes, but there was also a cold distance—a wariness that made me want to probe deeper, like he was holding something back. And something told me that wasn't an invitation. It was a warning.

"I like the quiet," I answered, leaning back in my seat, savoring the warmth of my drink as it slid down my throat. "Less... noise. Less opportunity for distraction."

He chuckled, but it wasn't the kind of laugh that invited camaraderie. It was almost cynical, as though he found something amusing in my attempt to play it cool. "I get that," he said, his voice low, almost like a growl. "But you can't hide from the world forever, you know."

I raised an eyebrow, the implication not lost on me. He was still trying to figure me out, still probing in that way he had of making everything feel personal. But for once, I wasn't giving him an inch.

"I'm not hiding," I replied, meeting his gaze with the same intensity he was throwing at me. "I'm just... taking a moment to breathe."

He tilted his head slightly, and for a second, I thought he was going to say something else. Something that might break through the brittle surface we had built between us. But instead, he just nodded. "Fair enough," he said, his voice quieter now, like the words had some weight to them that I wasn't quite catching.

I took another sip of my drink, the burn of the alcohol something I could almost focus on instead of the knot of tension still winding tighter in my chest. Why couldn't I let this go? I should've left an hour ago. But here we were, both stuck in some weird standoff, both pretending like this conversation wasn't absolutely maddening.

He moved then, stepping closer, but not enough to encroach on my space, just enough to make me aware that he wasn't finished with this yet.

"You know," he began, his voice a shade softer, almost as if he was telling me a secret, "you're not the only one who's tired of playing games. Not all of us like to go around pretending we're something we're not."

It hit me then—he wasn't talking about the fires, not directly. He was talking about something else, something deeper. And it wasn't just me he was questioning. He was questioning himself. I could see it now—the weight in his posture, the way his eyes darted away from mine as though he couldn't quite meet my gaze anymore.

"Right," I said, a little too quickly, my voice sounding sharper than I intended. "Because, clearly, you've been all about honesty so far."

His lips pressed into a thin line, and for a moment, I thought I might have finally cracked through that unshakable facade of his. But instead, he just let out a sigh, rubbing the back of his neck as if the gesture would make everything easier.

"I don't expect you to understand," he said, quieter this time, almost to himself. "Hell, I'm not sure I understand it myself. But when you're caught up in something, you just... start reacting. And you don't always get to pick how or why."

I couldn't help it; I laughed—a short, bitter sound that barely made it past my lips. "You're telling me this is about reacting?" I asked, incredulous. "That this is all just... a reflex for you?"

He looked at me again, his expression unreadable, the same way it had been that first night when he'd extinguished that fire with the same level of detached precision.

"You think I wanted any of this?" he asked, his voice barely above a whisper now. "You think I wanted to end up here, looking at you like this?"

The words settled between us like ash, and I didn't know what to say. Something about his tone felt too raw, too real for this strange game we had been playing. And just when I thought he might finally let me in, give me the truth I was so sure he was hiding, the door to the bar swung open with a loud bang.

I turned just in time to see the familiar figure of a cop step through, scanning the room with an almost predatory glance. He spotted me immediately, and his eyes narrowed.

"You," he said, his voice low and clipped. "You need to come with me. Now."

I froze, my drink halfway to my lips, as the weight of his words settled in. But before I could even process what was happening, I felt a hand on my shoulder, pulling me back.

"You really don't want to go with him," the fireman murmured, his grip firm as he leaned in close, his breath warm against my ear. "Trust me."

And for the first time, I wasn't sure who to trust.

Chapter 2: Sparks at Dawn

The apartment smells of burnt toast and half-finished coffee, the sort of smell that lingers like a bad memory, clawing its way into the corners of my kitchen. Leo is quiet, which, for him, is never a good sign. His little body is pressed up against my leg, like a stubborn shadow, as if the world outside had become too much. It's just after dawn, the soft light of morning peeking through the curtains, but there's no peace in it—no promise of a fresh start. The flames are closer today, licking at the edges of my world, just as the sun stretches its fingers over the horizon, casting long, uncertain shadows.

Connor's presence in my doorway isn't a surprise. I'd expected him to return, though I wish I didn't know that. His heavy boots tread across the worn wood floors with a slow, deliberate sound, almost like he's trying to make a point. The man's got a presence about him that commands attention, even when he's not speaking. His uniform is as crisp as it was last night, all pressed edges and fresh insignia, and yet there's something about him that looks like he hasn't slept in days. It's the way his eyes dart about, like he's searching for something he can't find, and his jaw is set in that hard line that tells me he's not in the mood for small talk.

"Morning," he says, his voice rough, like gravel underfoot. He doesn't smile, doesn't even make a move to offer a simple greeting. Instead, his gaze locks onto mine with an intensity that feels like it could burn through stone. "Got a minute?"

I nod, forcing my hand to steady as I cup the mug of coffee in front of me, trying to maintain some semblance of composure. Leo doesn't seem to notice, his focus entirely on the fireman standing in the doorway, eyes wide with a mix of fascination and fear.

"Is it really closer?" I ask, the words slipping out before I can stop them. It sounds almost ridiculous, like I'm hoping he'll say no, that everything will go back to normal, that this horrible feeling of dread will just dissipate.

Connor's eyes flicker with something, a hint of uncertainty, before he answers. "Yeah. A lot closer than last night. You might want to start thinking about—" He pauses, his voice tight, like he's weighing each word before he lets it out. "Evacuating. Just in case."

I swallow, my throat dry despite the coffee. Leo's small hand tightens around my leg, and for a moment, I wish I could promise him that everything's going to be okay. But the truth is, I can't even promise that to myself.

"Do you have any idea where it started this time?" I ask, my voice strained but trying to sound casual.

His gaze hardens, and I know immediately that he's not going to give me the details I'm hoping for. "We're still figuring that out. But it's not natural. Fires like this don't just happen. Someone's setting them."

The words hit me like a slap. I knew it was bad, but hearing it out loud makes it real in a way I wasn't ready for. My eyes lock onto Connor's, and for the briefest second, something flickers between us—something I can't quite place. It's not just the fire he's warning me about. It's something else, something I don't understand, but feel all the same.

"I'm not leaving yet," I say, the words coming out sharper than I intend. "I need to make sure Leo's okay."

His expression softens just a touch, but it's fleeting. "I understand. But you should at least get a plan together, just in case." He steps back, glancing once more at the smoky skyline visible through the window, the orange glow now unmistakable in the distance. "You won't have much time."

I watch him as he turns to leave, the heaviness in his gait betraying the weight of whatever thoughts are occupying his mind. He's not just a firefighter, not just a man doing his job. There's something else there, an undercurrent of doubt, of suspicion. I wonder if he's starting to believe what I already suspect—that this is no accident. But he's not about to share his thoughts with me, and that's fine. I don't need him to.

Leo clings tighter to my leg as the door closes behind Connor, and I bend down to ruffle his hair, trying to offer him some comfort I don't quite feel myself. "We're okay," I murmur, though I don't believe it. "We'll be okay."

But as the fire crackles in the distance, and the smell of smoke begins to curl into the apartment, I can't shake the feeling that this is just the beginning. And I have no idea what it's all leading to, but I know one thing for sure—our lives are about to change in ways I can't yet comprehend.

The day stretches before me, long and uncertain. The sky is too bright, too open, as if daring me to face whatever's coming. And I'm standing here, holding on to Leo, pretending that I have everything under control, when in reality, the world is slipping out from under me.

The moment Connor steps away, I feel a strange emptiness settle in. The door shuts behind him with a finality that rings too loud in the silence of the apartment. Leo is still clutching my leg, his small fingers pressing into the fabric of my jeans as if he's trying to draw strength from me. But I don't have any strength to give right now. I'm running on fumes, and I can already feel the sharp edge of panic starting to gnaw at me.

"Mom?" Leo's voice is small, but it carries a weight that I can't ignore. It's that same tone he uses when he senses something's wrong, when the world isn't quite right. I kneel down to his level, brushing the hair out of his face, trying to offer a semblance of calm that I don't feel.

"I'm here," I say, even though I'm not sure what "here" means anymore. "It's going to be okay."

But the lie feels bitter on my tongue. The smoke outside is already thick enough to taste, creeping through the cracks of the window, tangling with the air I breathe. The fire isn't just near anymore—it's on the doorstep. I can feel it, a growing presence that presses in on all sides.

I stand up and look out the window again. The streets are quieter than they should be for this time of day, the usual hum of traffic muted beneath the eerie silence that hangs in the air. It's as though the world knows, deep down, that something terrible is happening just beyond the horizon. The rising sun casts an orange glow over everything, but it's a sickly, unnatural hue, the kind that makes you want to close the blinds and pretend it's not real.

Leo's gaze follows mine, and I know he's thinking what I'm thinking. "Is it going to hurt us?" he asks, his voice a soft whisper.

I don't have an answer. I don't know how to tell him the truth without shattering whatever fragile sense of security he's holding on to. Instead, I pull him into my arms, clutching him close, inhaling the familiar scent of his hair, the warmth of his tiny body against mine. It's the only comfort I can give him right now.

The buzz of my phone breaks the moment, a sharp intrusion into our little world of fear and uncertainty. It's a message from my neighbor, Sarah, who's lived next door since I moved in, and I can already guess what it's about. She's one of those people who likes to keep tabs on things, especially when it involves the building we share.

"Have you heard? They're evacuating the building. The fire's worse than they're saying."

I stare at the message for a long moment, the words swimming before my eyes. Evacuating. I should be packing, gathering things, getting ready to leave. But where do I go? There's no place left for us to run to. I glance at Leo again, his face turned up to me with such trust, such dependence. How do I tell him that the world we know is burning away? How do I promise him that we're safe when everything feels so fragile?

Another knock at the door pulls me out of my thoughts, and this time I don't have to guess who it is. I'm already moving toward the door before I've even had a chance to think about it. My heart is hammering in my chest, and my palms feel sweaty. But there's no avoiding this.

When I open it, it's not Connor this time. Instead, it's a woman—tall, with dark hair that's been pulled into a loose ponytail, and the sort of face that makes you feel like you've known her forever, even if you haven't. She doesn't look like she's here for a friendly chat, though. There's an urgency in her eyes that immediately puts me on edge.

"Are you getting out?" she asks, her voice low but insistent.

I nod, unsure of what to say. "I'm thinking about it."

She glances at Leo, who's standing just behind me, clutching my leg again, his small face full of questions he doesn't have the words to ask. The woman's expression softens just slightly. "You need to move faster than that. It's not safe. The fire's close—closer than anyone's saying. You can't afford to wait."

I feel a sharp pang in my chest, the kind of instinctive fear that tells you something isn't right. But I can't get caught up in the panic. Not now. Not when Leo's looking up at me, trusting me to make the right call.

"I need to pack," I say, more to myself than to her. "I can't just—"

"You won't have time," she interrupts, her tone leaving no room for negotiation. "I've seen the maps. The winds are shifting. If you stay too long, you won't make it out."

I hesitate. The woman seems sure of herself, her urgency palpable. There's something almost reckless about her certainty. It's like she knows things that I don't, things that I'm not ready to hear. And that's the thing about the truth—it doesn't always come wrapped up in a neat package, especially when it comes to matters like this. The truth, in this case, is as hot and destructive as the flames that are coming.

Leo looks up at me again, his little face pale, and I know that this time, I don't have a choice. The fire is coming for us, and there's no more pretending it's not. The only question left is whether I can protect him long enough to get us to safety.

The woman is gone before I can even ask her name. Her footsteps echo down the hallway, fading away like the scent of something burning in the distance. I shut the door with more force than necessary, but the click of the lock does nothing to silence the chaos stirring in my chest. The fire, the evacuation orders, the warnings—it all feels too fast, too much, like the world's been yanked out from under me and I'm scrambling to keep my footing.

Leo is still standing there, his small hands wringing the hem of my shirt as if the fabric could somehow shield him from the terror unfolding outside. I kneel down, but instead of offering comfort, I feel myself pulling away, the gravity of the situation sinking in like a weight I can't carry.

"Mom?" His voice is barely a whisper, but it cuts through me. "Are we leaving?"

I open my mouth to speak, but the words get stuck somewhere between my throat and my heart. Leaving. It sounds so simple when you say it like that, but it's not. There's no map for this. No guide on how to pack up your life in a panic and keep your child safe while the world burns around you. I wish there were.

"I don't know," I say, the admission hanging in the air between us like a specter. I can't even promise him that we'll be okay.

Leo tugs on my arm again, more insistent this time. "Mom, I don't want to go alone. Can I stay with you?"

His words hit me hard. I'd always promised myself that I would protect him, keep him safe, no matter what. But this? This is beyond anything I ever prepared for. And there's something about Leo's pleading that makes me want to collapse into the ground. How do I do this? How do I protect him when I'm the one who feels like she's unraveling?

I try to stand up, but the room seems to tilt, just slightly, like the ground is shifting beneath my feet.

"Okay," I say finally, finding my breath again. "We'll leave. Just... just give me a minute to get our things." The words are out before I've even processed them, and I wonder if I'm saying them more to reassure myself than him.

I go to the bedroom, my feet dragging as I make my way toward the closet, but I stop before I open it. The weight of the decision hangs heavy on me. What should I grab? The usual list of things flashes through my mind—clothes, water, anything that might be useful—but it all feels so... insignificant. I can't shake the image of Leo's face, his innocent eyes wide with fear. What if we don't make it?

My hands tremble as I pull a duffel bag from the shelf, trying to fill it with whatever I can carry. But everything seems so trivial now. My phone. My charger. A jacket. The things that should matter feel absurdly unimportant in the face of all this destruction. But I keep packing, moving on autopilot, until Leo's soft voice breaks through the haze in my mind.

"Mom?" He's standing in the doorway now, his face drawn in a mixture of confusion and concern. "What if we can't go back?"

I pause, the question hitting harder than I expect. What if we can't? What if everything we have, everything we've known, is reduced to ash? The fire is more than just an emergency. It's a reminder of how fragile everything really is.

"We'll figure it out," I say, my voice sounding too calm for the storm raging inside me. I wish I could believe it. But the uncertainty gnaws at me, and I can't help but wonder if this is the end of something. Not just the fire, but the life we've known.

I finish packing the bag, throwing in a few of Leo's favorite toys, a blanket, and anything else I can think of in the short time I have. But as I move back toward the living room, I notice something odd—the silence is too thick. The kind of quiet that's not natural, not in the middle of a city. No sirens. No voices. No traffic.

I glance out the window, but it's worse than I thought. The orange haze from the fire is no longer just a glow on the horizon. It's closer now, creeping through the buildings like an unstoppable force. The wind must be shifting, because the smoke is coming toward us faster than I thought possible. It doesn't just fill the air—it chokes it. I can taste it now, sharp and acrid, coating the back of my throat.

"I think we need to leave now," I say, more to myself than to Leo, but he doesn't argue. He grabs my hand without a word, and for a moment, I let myself believe that maybe, just maybe, everything will be okay.

The door clicks open, and we step out into the hallway, the heavy scent of smoke thickening the air. The other apartments are eerily silent. No one is rushing. No one is packing. It's like they're waiting for something, waiting for someone else to make the first move. But I don't have the luxury of waiting. Not anymore.

"Where do we go?" Leo's voice is small, like he's afraid that the answer will be something terrible.

"I don't know yet," I say, but I'm already thinking about our options. There's a fire station nearby, but I'm not sure how safe it will be. There's a park, too, but it feels like it's too far. No matter where we go, the fire is moving too fast.

We make our way toward the stairs, my heart pounding in my chest with every step. But then, as I reach the landing, I hear something that stops me dead in my tracks. It's a sound, but it's not one I've heard before. A low rumble, like thunder, but there's no storm in sight.

It's the sound of something breaking. Something big.

And then, the building shakes. The walls tremble, and the floor beneath me seems to crack open. I hear Leo gasp, his grip tightening around my hand as the sound of destruction grows louder. It's too close. Too fast. We're not going to make it out in time.

The smoke fills the air, and all I can see is darkness. And then I hear it—the unmistakable sound of footsteps running toward us, fast, frantic, and far too close.

Chapter 3: The Smoke Screen

It was supposed to be just another Tuesday.

The morning air was sharp, bracing with a bite that had settled into my bones by the time I stepped outside. I had my usual cup of coffee—black, bitter, and just shy of burning the roof of my mouth—and tried to ignore the faint hum of anxiety that buzzed beneath my skin. The firehouse across the street loomed like a relic from another century, its brick walls coated in soot and the echoes of lives that had passed through it. I should've been focused on the mundane details of the day ahead, like filing the latest paperwork or checking the fire extinguisher tags, but there was something in the air today—something thick with the kind of tension that had a way of swallowing you whole if you weren't careful.

I'd only met Connor a handful of times since I arrived in town, but each interaction left an imprint—a tight knot that seemed to clench in my stomach the moment his name crossed my mind. It wasn't just the arrogance, though he had that in spades. No, it was the look in his eyes, like he was always a few steps ahead of me, playing some game I wasn't invited to. It made my skin itch, but that wasn't even the worst part. It was the little moments when I thought I saw something else in him—something not so certain, not so controlled.

The man had secrets. I could feel them, even if I couldn't prove them. And every time I tried to peel back the layers, he closed up like a shell, leaving me to wonder what was buried beneath the surface. He had the kind of face that could hide a thousand things. Sharp, angular features that looked like they'd been carved from stone, his jaw set like it could cut glass. The kind of face that made you want to believe he was as tough as he looked. But I wasn't convinced.

The first time I caught him off guard was almost an accident. It was after one of those endless meetings with the fire department brass, the kind where nothing ever gets solved but everyone leaves thinking they've done their part. I'd been walking out of the building, my heels clicking on the pavement like a clock counting down, when I caught sight of him leaning against the wall, his arms crossed, staring into the distance. He didn't notice me at first, and I don't know why I did it, but I lingered just a moment longer, watching him.

I've never been good at reading people—at least, not as well as I'd like to think I am. But I could see something flicker in Connor's expression, something that didn't fit the rigid shell he always wore. It was only there for a second, a brief chink in the armor, and then it was gone. I don't know what it was—guilt? Regret? It didn't make sense, but it gnawed at me. The whole thing unsettled me more than I cared to admit.

It wasn't long before I found myself doing what I always swore I wouldn't: digging into someone else's business. Connor's business. I didn't even know where to begin, but there was no denying it anymore. He wasn't just an arrogant investigator; there was something more, something tangled up in his past that was beginning to catch my attention in a way I couldn't shake.

My first stop was the fire department archives. It wasn't hard to get access, and I knew there would be whispers of past cases buried in the stacks of old files. The papers were thick with the scent of dust and age, a sharp, musty odor that clung to everything. I pulled up the records on Connor's career, hoping to find something—anything—that could explain why he'd become the man he was. The first few pages were standard enough. He'd joined the department straight out of high school, a golden boy with a reputation for solving the hardest cases. But the deeper I dug, the more the pieces seemed to fracture.

There were gaps, missing reports, incidents that didn't quite add up. And then there was the thing I couldn't shake: his name kept appearing in the context of strange, unexplained fires. The kinds that didn't fit the usual patterns, the kinds that left a trail of questions no one ever seemed to answer. It wasn't overt—nothing that would raise alarms on its own—but it was enough to make me pause.

I found myself at the local bar later that night, nursing a glass of wine and replaying every scrap of information I'd uncovered. The neon lights flickered overhead, casting a hazy glow over the rowdy patrons who filled the space with laughter and music. I wasn't in the mood for small talk, though. I just wanted to think, to piece together the fragments of a story that seemed to slip further from my grasp the harder I tried to make sense of it.

That's when he walked in.

Connor, of course. His broad shoulders filled the doorway, and just like that, the air in the room shifted. The noise seemed to dim around me as I stared at him, his eyes scanning the crowd before settling on me with that same unreadable look. There was something about the way he held himself, like he knew exactly how to command a room, even if he wasn't trying to. He made his way toward the bar without a word, his presence thick enough to almost feel like a physical force. But I wasn't about to let him intimidate me. Not tonight.

I took a deep breath and turned away, pretending to be absorbed in the swirl of my wine glass, but my mind was racing. This was ridiculous. I was here, poking around in places I shouldn't be, and there he was, standing at the bar like he belonged in every corner of this town. I couldn't decide if I was irritated or relieved, but the feeling in my gut was unmistakable. Something was coming—something big—and I wasn't sure I was ready for it.

Connor didn't speak to me for the rest of the evening, which only made the air between us heavier. I kept my eyes on the low amber lights of the bar, the hum of conversation around me filling the silence. Every time I glanced at him, he seemed to be more lost in the crowd, his gaze distant, focused on some invisible point far beyond the reach of anyone in the room. It was as if he had an entire world inside his head, one that didn't include any of the rest of us.

The longer I watched him, the more the familiar frustration began to rise in me. It was the same feeling I had whenever I tried to understand him—like trying to make sense of a puzzle where half the pieces were missing. He was an investigator, yes, but the more I learned about him, the more it became clear that he wasn't investigating just anything. There was something personal in the way he moved through the world. Something buried beneath that cool, implacable exterior that I had yet to decipher.

The door to the bar opened again, and the familiar clatter of boots and chatter spilled inside as a group of firemen from the station drifted in, laughing too loudly, their voices thick with camaraderie. I tried not to glance in their direction, but it was impossible not to catch snippets of their conversation. One of them, a burly man with a voice like gravel, was speaking to Connor, asking if he had "figured it out yet." I felt my heart skip. I couldn't catch all the words, but the ones I heard sounded too familiar.

"Still digging into that thing, huh?"

I could hear the smugness in the man's voice.

Connor's response, however, was more restrained, his tone clipped, almost mechanical. "No one's looking, so it's fine."

And there it was. That coldness again.

I didn't know what they were talking about, but I was certain it wasn't something trivial. The words bounced around in my head as I took another sip of wine, the taste suddenly bitter against my tongue. I could feel my pulse quicken, a familiar itch creeping under my skin as my mind started to race.

My eyes were trained on Connor now, watching him with a newfound intensity. He wasn't engaging in the banter with the rest of the guys, his face fixed in that unreadable mask, like he was trying to disappear into the background. But I wasn't letting him off that easily. I knew there was something here, something he was avoiding, and the more he shut down, the more I was convinced it wasn't just some personal grudge against me.

A few minutes passed, the chatter around me fading into the background as I tried to pick out any detail that might tell me more. His posture, the way his eyes narrowed when the conversation shifted toward an unrelated topic, the way he'd briefly looked at the door when another firefighter entered. There was something about it—something like a man waiting for something to happen. Or, worse, someone who was trying to run from it.

I couldn't take it anymore.

Without thinking, I stood up, my stool scraping against the floor in the quietest protest, and walked toward the bar. I had no plan, no idea what I was going to say, but my feet were already in motion, carrying me toward him. His back was still turned as I approached, but when I stopped beside him, he stiffened, ever so slightly.

"Connor," I said, my voice steady, even though my heart was now drumming in my ears. "What's going on?"

For a moment, he didn't respond, and I half-expected him to brush me off. But then he turned slightly, his eyes meeting mine. That mask was still there, but now I could see the slightest crack in it, just enough to make me wonder if I was getting closer to something.

"Nothing you need to worry about," he muttered, his voice tight, the words almost too quick to be genuine. But there was a glimmer of something else there, something that made me want to push harder.

"I'm not worried," I said, forcing the words out with more confidence than I felt. "I'm just curious. Everyone's talking like you're hiding something, and honestly, I think I deserve to know why."

His lips pressed into a thin line, and I could see the muscles in his jaw flex. He was holding back, and I wasn't about to let him control the conversation this time.

"What are you really investigating, Connor?" I asked, my voice quieter now, but still sharp. "I know it's more than just some fire. I can see it in the way you move, the way you talk. What is it? What aren't you telling me?"

There was a pause, and for a moment, I thought I saw something flicker in his eyes—something close to panic, but just as quickly, it disappeared. His gaze hardened, and he gave me a curt shake of the head, as if to dismiss the question entirely.

"You're imagining things," he said, his tone low, deliberately neutral. But I wasn't buying it. Not anymore.

I leaned in slightly, refusing to be dismissed so easily. "It's hard to imagine something that feels this real," I retorted, my eyes never leaving his.

For a long beat, neither of us moved. The noise of the bar around us seemed to fade, and in that moment, it was just him and me, standing on the precipice of something neither of us was willing to acknowledge. Then, as if snapping out of some trance, he gave me a tight smile, the kind of smile that didn't reach his eyes.

"You really want to know?" he asked, his voice quieter now, almost as if he were daring me.

I nodded, my heart in my throat.

"Get in the car," he said abruptly, nodding toward the exit.

It wasn't an invitation. It was a command. And against every instinct I had, I found myself stepping toward him, my curiosity outweighing every ounce of caution I'd been trained to follow. There was something dangerous in that look, something magnetic that pulled me in even as it warned me to stay away. But I wasn't walking away now. Not when the answers I was searching for were within reach.

The drive to the edge of town wasn't long, but the silence between us stretched like a taut wire, humming with unspoken words. The headlights of Connor's truck sliced through the dark, casting long shadows that danced across the winding road. The air inside the cab was thick with tension, each passing mile adding another layer to the heaviness hanging between us. I could feel the pulse of my own heartbeat echoing in the small space, a steady reminder of how far I was willing to push things—maybe too far.

"So," I ventured, breaking the silence that had hung like a fog. My voice was steady, but I could hear the quiver of curiosity sneaking through. "What exactly am I doing here?"

Connor's grip tightened on the wheel, his knuckles blanching in the dim light. He didn't look at me, but I could feel the shift in his posture, the subtle tension in his shoulders. "I told you. I've got something you need to see."

"You're really not going to give me any more than that?" I said, trying to keep the annoyance from creeping into my tone, but failing. "I'd like to think I'm not just a passenger in your little mystery car ride."

Connor's lips twitched at the edges, like he was amused by my persistence, but he didn't respond immediately. Instead, he kept his eyes on the road, his jaw working as though deciding whether or not to reveal anything more.

"I wouldn't get too comfortable," he finally muttered. "Things get... complicated."

I snorted, crossing my arms over my chest as the cool night air whipped through the cracked window. "Complicated. That's a classic. What, are you taking me to some dark, secret lair where you reveal your hidden agenda?"

He shot me a sideways glance, the corner of his mouth lifting slightly. "Something like that."

Great. I was following a man who could barely make eye contact without looking like he had something to hide, into God knew where, with nothing more than a cryptic promise of 'something to see.' Every instinct told me this was a terrible idea, but I wasn't about to back down now. Not when the threads of his story were dangling just beyond my reach.

The truck veered left onto a narrow gravel road, its tires crunching over the loose stones. The trees on either side crowded close, their branches thick and oppressive, the kind of wilderness that made you feel like you were being swallowed by the earth itself. I squinted out the window, trying to make sense of the dark shapes in the distance, but there was nothing to see but shadows.

"How much farther?" I asked, keeping my voice even despite the unease creeping along my spine.

"Not much," he replied, though the word had a finality to it. A tone that suggested this wasn't a casual stop, that whatever was coming next would be something I'd remember.

My pulse quickened.

After a few more minutes of silence, the truck stopped. The headlights illuminated a small, rundown building nestled in the woods. The paint was peeling, the windows dark, and the faintest scent of mildew clung to the air around it. It looked like the kind of place you only found when you weren't supposed to be there—isolated and forgotten. The hairs on the back of my neck stood up.

"This it?" I asked, half-expecting him to laugh and tell me I'd been punked, but his face was grim as he shifted the truck into park.

"Stay close," he said, his voice low and commanding. "And whatever you do, don't touch anything."

I almost laughed, thinking of the absurdity of it all. Here I was, trailing behind a man who could barely share a sentence without sounding like he was hiding something, walking into a decrepit building in the middle of nowhere because of a promise that "things get complicated." My better judgment had packed its bags and left long before I'd agreed to this, and now I was left to wonder if my curiosity was going to get me into something I might not be able to walk away from.

Connor was already out of the truck before I could process the thought, his boots hitting the gravel with a hard thud as he made his way toward the building's entrance. I hesitated only for a moment before following, my breath coming a little faster as the cold air wrapped around me.

The door to the building creaked open with a sound that echoed through the woods like a warning. Inside, the smell of decay was overwhelming, mingling with the sharp scent of old wood and rust. The single light bulb hanging from the ceiling swayed slightly, casting jagged shadows across the dusty floors. My eyes adjusted, taking in the space around me. It was an old workshop of some kind, its shelves lined with boxes and tools that hadn't been touched in years. But there, near the back of the room, a single metal table stood under a large tarp.

Connor didn't say anything as he walked toward the table, his footsteps slow, deliberate. The tension radiating from him was palpable, and for the first time, I saw him—really saw him—as something other than just an infuriatingly aloof investigator. He was haunted, his movements tight and controlled like a man who had been carrying a burden far too long.

"What is this?" I asked, my voice a whisper, like speaking too loudly would shatter whatever fragile peace this place held.

Without looking at me, Connor lifted the edge of the tarp, revealing what lay beneath. I took a step forward, my breath catching in my throat as my eyes landed on the object on the table.

It wasn't what I'd expected.

A photograph. Yellowed with age, crinkled at the edges, but unmistakably familiar. My heart skipped a beat as I recognized the faces. Two people. One of them was Connor, a younger version of him, standing next to someone else. Someone I didn't know. But the resemblance was too strong to ignore. It was the same, sharp jawline, the same piercing eyes. Only this person was dead. The photograph was taken at a funeral, the kind of solemn image you kept in a box at the back of a closet to remind yourself of the ghosts you couldn't outrun.

I looked up at Connor, searching his face, but it was unreadable, his eyes colder than I had ever seen them. He stood there, watching me, waiting for the reaction he knew was coming.

"Explain this," I said, my voice barely more than a breath, but the words felt like they were tearing through me, pulling at something I wasn't ready to face.

But instead of answering, Connor turned abruptly, his face now a mask of control again. He stepped back, his jaw tightening, eyes darting toward the door.

"We need to leave. Now."

Before I could ask another question, the sound of tires skidding on gravel reached my ears, and I froze.

Someone else was here. And we weren't alone anymore.

Chapter 4: Kindling in the Dark

The attic was suffocatingly warm, a strange humidity hanging in the air as I sifted through the forgotten boxes that had accumulated over the years. The dust settled like a cloud, catching in the faint light that trickled through the narrow window. It felt like I was invading someone else's memories, but they were mine—memories I didn't ask for and certainly didn't want to face.

I had never liked the attic. Even before everything happened, before the phone calls and the funerals and the endless paperwork that had taken all the brightness out of my days, I never could bring myself to go up here. The dark corners, the creaky floorboards, and the smell of old wood—it was as if the house was holding onto the past too tightly. And now, years later, I found myself here, crouched in front of a box that was sealed so securely it could've been a vault. Its contents were untouched, buried beneath layers of time, the weight of the past pressing down on my shoulders.

With a hesitant breath, I pried open the box, my fingers brushing over the brittle cardboard before pulling it apart. Inside, it was like I had opened a time capsule. Old letters, yellowed with age, a few tattered photographs, and a small collection of trinkets. For a moment, I thought I might find a relic of something softer—perhaps a keepsake from our honeymoon or one of the ridiculous souvenirs he'd picked up on our trips to nowhere special. But what I found instead froze me in place.

It was a business card, tucked carefully into the corner of the box, as if my husband had thought it important enough to keep but not quite enough to mention. I held it in my trembling fingers, the glossy surface catching the light, and for the first time in what felt like forever, I let myself wonder if I'd ever really known the man I'd married. The card was simple: just an address, a name, and a number. But the address? It was a place I'd never heard of, tucked away in a part of town I only passed through when I needed to get somewhere in a hurry. I'd always considered it a forgotten corner of the city, a place where people with lives far more complicated than mine went to disappear. Why had he been there?

I tried to push the thoughts from my mind, to rationalize it. Maybe it was business. Maybe it was a job he'd taken on that I didn't know about. After all, he'd been a private man, especially toward the end. But the feeling in my chest, that thick, constricting sensation, told me I was lying to myself. My breath hitched as I thought about the fires—the ones that had been set in various places around town, all of which had some link to me. My name had been whispered in the same breath as the destruction, but I hadn't made the connection until recently. And now, staring at this card, it felt like the world was unraveling all over again. I needed answers, but part of me was terrified of what I might find.

I barely noticed when the door creaked open behind me, the sound sharp in the silence. My heart skipped, and I turned, startled, to find Connor standing in the doorway. He had that same unreadable look in his eyes, the one that told me he was watching and waiting for something, though I had no idea what.

"Didn't mean to scare you," he said, his voice quiet, almost apologetic, though I knew he wasn't sorry at all. He never was.

I swallowed hard, the card still clutched in my hand. "You didn't. I didn't hear you come in."

His gaze flicked to the box at my feet, then back to me. He didn't ask about the contents, but I knew he saw it all—the same way he always saw everything, even when he tried not to. Connor had this way of looking at me, like he knew every crack in my armor, every corner of my mind, and it made me uncomfortable. I didn't want him to see me like this. It felt too raw, too exposed.

"What's that?" he asked after a long pause, his eyes narrowing ever so slightly as he stepped closer.

I hesitated, then held the business card out to him. "This. I found it in one of the boxes. It's... his." My voice faltered, but I didn't care. The name of the place on the card looked foreign in my hand, like a message from someone I used to know but couldn't quite remember anymore.

Connor didn't take it immediately, his gaze flickering between me and the card, like he was weighing the moment. Finally, he reached out, the tips of his fingers brushing mine as he took it. There was no judgment in his expression, but I could see the shift in his posture, the subtle tension in his shoulders.

"You don't think this is something we should talk about?" he asked, the question hanging in the air between us.

I shook my head, my throat tight. "I don't know what to think anymore."

He didn't push, but the look he gave me told me he understood that silence was all I could offer right now. The pile of clues on the floor, the fire that had taken so much from me, the card—none of it made sense, and I wasn't sure I was ready for it to.

The room felt colder, the shadows deepening as the light from the window flickered and dimmed, and I was left alone with my thoughts, my doubts, and a man who wasn't really mine, not in the way I needed him to be.

The silence in the attic felt oppressive, the kind of silence that only came when secrets were being carefully guarded. The air, thick with dust and old memories, clung to my skin like a shroud, heavy with the weight of things better left alone. I hadn't expected to uncover anything of consequence when I began sorting through the boxes, and yet, the discovery of that simple business card—small, unassuming, yet so inexplicably out of place—set something off inside me. My pulse quickened, and I felt a pull in my chest, like something had shifted just beyond my reach, pulling me toward something I wasn't ready to face.

FLICKER   33

Connor lingered at the door, the card still in his hand, his fingers unconsciously tracing the edges. He hadn't said anything, but I could tell the question was there, hanging between us, like a well-placed punch that hadn't yet landed.

"I don't suppose you have any idea what this is about?" I asked, my voice tight. I wasn't sure if I wanted the answer, but it escaped me before I could stop it. The words felt brittle in the air, like glass about to shatter.

Connor didn't answer right away, which only made my anxiety flare up. Instead, he took a step toward me, his gaze still flicking between the card and my face, as if he were weighing some unspoken truth. He was always so damn careful with his words, so deliberate in his silences. It made me want to scream.

"Maybe it's nothing," he said at last, though his tone didn't match his words. He sounded too detached, too calm for someone who was holding the key to a door I wasn't sure I even wanted to open.

I stared at him, the faintest thread of suspicion knotting in my stomach. "You really think that's true?" I asked, forcing the words through my teeth. "You think this means nothing? The man I married—he didn't talk about this place, didn't mention anything to me, but I'm supposed to believe it's just a random address, a coincidence?"

Connor met my gaze, his expression unreadable, and for a split second, I thought I saw something flash in his eyes. It was gone as quickly as it had appeared, but it was enough to make the hairs on the back of my neck stand on end.

"I didn't say it meant nothing," he corrected, finally breaking the tension in the room, though his voice was still steady, composed. "But I think you need to take a step back before you start jumping to conclusions. Your emotions are running high right now, and I get it. But whatever's going on here, it's not as simple as you think."

I couldn't tell if he was trying to protect me from the truth or if he was simply being cautious. Either way, I wasn't sure I could stomach much more of this. Every time I looked at him, I felt like he was standing just outside my reach, like he was holding onto something that wasn't his to keep, some part of the past that wasn't mine to uncover.

I took the card back from him, my fingers brushing against his in the process. The contact was brief, but it felt like a spark had flared to life between us, too brief to be intentional but enough to make the air feel suddenly charged. I folded the card in half and shoved it into my pocket, desperate to distance myself from it, from whatever it meant.

"We need to get some answers," I said, my voice firmer now, though the uncertainty still gnawed at the edges. I wasn't even sure where to begin, but something told me that the answers I was looking for weren't going to find me—they were going to have to be dragged out.

Connor watched me for a long moment, then sighed, rubbing the back of his neck in that familiar way he did when he was about to say something that made me regret asking. "Okay," he said, his voice low, like he was choosing his next words with care. "But I don't think you realize what you're getting into."

I met his gaze, the full force of his warning settling over me like a heavy cloak. It wasn't just about the fires anymore. It wasn't even just about the card. Something deeper, darker, was lurking beneath the surface, and I knew, with a sickening certainty, that it had something to do with me. With us.

"Then tell me," I said, my voice sharp, the rawness slipping out despite my best attempts at control. "Tell me what I'm getting into.

You're always so damn cryptic. You know more than you're letting on, and I'm tired of it. I want the truth, Connor."

His jaw clenched, his eyes narrowing, and for a moment, I thought he might say something—something that would finally make sense of all this. But instead, he remained silent, his gaze flickering to the dusty attic floor, then back to me. He opened his mouth to speak, but just as quickly, he closed it again, like he was holding something back, something he wasn't ready to share.

I could feel the air grow colder, the space between us stretching, becoming a chasm I wasn't sure how to cross.

Finally, after what felt like an eternity of staring at him, I took a step back, breaking the stalemate. "Fine," I said, my voice quieter now, the defiance still simmering beneath my words. "I'll find out myself."

I turned, making my way toward the stairs. My heart was thudding in my chest, but I wasn't going to let him see the crack in my armor. Not now. Not when I had already taken one step into the dark. The truth was out there, and I was going to find it, even if I had to do it alone.

Behind me, I heard Connor's footsteps follow, a steady reminder that he wasn't far behind. I didn't look back.

The night stretched on in that peculiar way it does when you can't sleep and your mind is relentlessly hunting for something you aren't sure you want to find. The house was quiet, too quiet. Every creak of the floorboards, every distant rustle of the wind outside, made my skin tighten with unease. My thoughts, tangled and sharp, kept bringing me back to that damn business card, to the address scrawled across it like a scar I couldn't quite touch. I could have easily let it go, tucked it away, convincing myself it was nothing, but it felt like I was standing at the edge of a cliff, and something—someone—was pushing me closer to the fall.

I had spent the last few hours pacing the house, trying to distract myself. But there was no escaping the pull of the unknown. Every inch of the room seemed to whisper something, a hundred small things that might be connected to this strange puzzle that was unraveling around me. There were no answers in the attic, no relief in the empty space where I had hoped the silence would drown out my thoughts. Connor was still here, lurking in the background like a shadow I couldn't escape, and it was starting to feel less like help and more like a noose tightening around my neck.

The clock on the wall ticked over to midnight, the soft chime cutting through the silence like a warning. I could feel his presence before I heard his footsteps—Connor, as always, appearing when I least expected it. His shoes, muted against the hardwood, stopped just behind me.

"You're still awake," he said, his voice soft but knowing. It wasn't a question, just a statement of fact. He could always tell when something was eating at me, even when I tried to bury it.

I didn't respond, though I felt him watching me, studying my every move. He'd been doing that a lot lately, as if he could read every crack in my facade, every flicker of doubt I tried to hide.

"You can't keep ignoring it," he added, his tone a mix of caution and something else—something I couldn't quite place. "Whatever it is you're trying to figure out, it's not going to go away. You're already in this too deep."

I didn't want to hear it. Not from him. Not now. But his words hit me like a punch in the stomach, something sharp and unavoidable. I had already started down this path, following the trail of clues, no matter how strange or out of place they seemed. I couldn't stop now, even if I wanted to. It wasn't just about the card or the fires anymore—it was about all the questions I had buried for years, the things I had let slide, the life I had tried to rebuild after my husband's death.

"You don't know anything," I snapped, turning to face him. My voice came out colder than I intended, but I couldn't stop it. "You're not the one who has to live with this. I don't need you here telling me what I can and can't do."

Connor held up his hands in mock surrender, his expression unreadable. "I'm not telling you what to do, I'm just pointing out that you've got a lot more to unpack than you're letting on."

I took a deep breath, trying to steady my pulse. I wanted to shove him out of the room, demand he leave me to sort through the mess on my own, but something in his eyes held me back. It wasn't pity or concern—it was something else, something darker. He knew more than he was letting on, and that knowledge, whatever it was, made the air between us feel thick, suffocating.

"I'm fine," I said, but it came out too quickly, too jagged, and even I could tell I didn't believe it.

Connor didn't answer right away. He just watched me with those unreadable eyes, and for a moment, I thought he might leave it at that. But he didn't. Instead, he moved closer, his presence filling the room in a way that felt more like a warning than anything else. "You're not fine," he said, his voice lower now, almost a whisper. "And I don't think you ever will be, not until you face this."

I wanted to scream at him, to tell him to stay out of it, but the words wouldn't come. I had never been good at standing my ground, especially not with him. There was something about Connor, something about the way he seemed to understand everything without ever saying it, that made me feel small. In a way, it felt like he was the one pulling the strings, keeping me off balance, and I hated it.

"I don't need saving," I said, my voice barely above a whisper, though I wasn't sure if I was trying to convince him or myself.

Connor raised an eyebrow, a slight smirk tugging at the corner of his mouth. "No one said anything about saving. But if you keep running from this, it's going to catch up with you."

I opened my mouth to argue, but the words died on my lips. Instead, I turned away from him, my back to the room, to the fire that seemed to burn just beneath the surface of everything now. I could hear him move, footsteps soft behind me, but he didn't touch me. Not this time.

"Where are you going?" he asked, his voice a little sharper now, though I couldn't quite place why.

"I need air," I said, my voice thin as I grabbed my coat from the back of the chair. "Just for a minute."

The door slammed shut behind me as I stepped out into the night, the cool air rushing to meet me like an old friend. I didn't know where I was headed, just that I couldn't stay there, couldn't stay in that house with all its ghosts, all its secrets. I needed distance, space, but most of all, I needed answers.

I wasn't sure how long I had been walking, but by the time I reached the corner of my street, the city stretched out before me, dark and quiet. The only sound was the soft rhythm of my footsteps echoing in the empty streets. And then I heard it—a sound so faint, so distant, I might have imagined it.

A voice. My name, whispered from behind me.

I froze.

Chapter 5: Wildfire Warnings

The doorbell rings, a sharp, insistent sound that cuts through the otherwise quiet house like a knife. I don't even need to check the peephole; I can feel it—the pulse of tension at the door, thick and undeniable, like a storm pressing against glass.

Connor.

The man's presence has a way of making everything else shrink into the background. I know what's coming before it even starts. But the door slides open anyway, and there he stands, a shadow framed by the porch light. His eyes, those endless eyes that seem to see right through me, flicker as he takes in the sight of my disheveled hair and the too-tightly clenched fists at my sides.

"You've been avoiding me," he says, his voice low and controlled, but there's an edge there. One that cuts through the air between us. "I thought we had an understanding."

I stare back, too tired for this, my thoughts still tangled from the last argument we had—weeks ago, but it feels like just yesterday. "I don't remember making any agreements with you, Connor," I answer, my tone sharp, like I'm pushing him away with each word. "You don't get to decide when I talk to you."

The storm in his eyes flickers, a pulse of frustration—or is it something else? I can't quite tell. He shifts his weight from one foot to the other, the silence stretching between us like an unspoken question. His jaw tightens, and for a second, I think he's going to say something—something that would cross a line I've been careful not to let him cross. But he doesn't. Instead, he steps forward, just slightly, and I instinctively take a step back.

"I'm here because there are things we need to talk about," he says, voice just low enough to make my stomach flip. "About your husband."

I freeze, my entire body locking into place, the muscles in my throat tightening as if his words have the power to strangle me. "What about him?" The words are out before I can stop them, too fast, too loud, too much.

He doesn't seem fazed by my reaction. In fact, he almost seems... satisfied? Damn him.

"You've been protecting him," Connor says, and his voice shifts, like a man peeling back layers of something long hidden. "I need to know what he's been involved in."

A cold chill sweeps through me, a breeze from nowhere that sends goosebumps prickling over my arms. My heart thunders in my chest. I want to slam the door in his face, lock myself behind it, but I can't. The words stick in my throat like shards of glass.

I exhale slowly, but the breath isn't steady. "You don't know what you're talking about," I manage to say, my voice coming out thicker than I want it to. "You've got it wrong."

But Connor doesn't look convinced. His gaze narrows, and I see the flicker of something darker behind his eyes—something that tells me he's not letting this go, not now, not ever. "I know you're hiding something, and it's not just about him. It's about you, too."

There it is. The accusation. The suspicion that's been hovering in the air every time he comes around, like a storm cloud threatening to burst open.

"Stop," I snap, the word sharp and final. But he doesn't stop. He leans in just a fraction, just enough that I can feel the heat of his body, the pressure of his presence.

"I need to know what's going on, and you're not fooling anyone anymore," he says, voice dropping lower, like he's about to whisper a secret I'm not supposed to hear.

I'm already shaking my head, even before the rest of his words can land. "You think I'm hiding something from you?" My laugh is brittle, the sound of it grating on my own ears. "You have no idea what you're asking."

But the longer he stands there, unwavering and intense, the more I feel the walls inside me begin to crumble. The thing is, I don't want him to know. I've spent years building this life, this façade, brick by brick, and now he's here, threatening to tear it all down with a single word.

Before I can say anything more, I hear it—a soft rustle behind me, faint, but unmistakable. My son, Leo, standing at the corner of the hallway, just out of sight, watching us with wide, innocent eyes.

My heart lurches, and the heat of Connor's gaze shifts from me to Leo, following the invisible thread of connection between us. I don't know how long he's been there, listening, but I can feel the weight of his silence pressing down on me.

The moment stretches, stretching like elastic, taut and fragile, about to snap. Connor doesn't break his gaze. His face softens just slightly, his posture relaxing, though the tension in the room is still palpable.

"You should be careful," he says, the edge of warning in his tone softer now. "I'm not the enemy here. But someone is, and they're much closer than you think."

His words linger in the air long after he leaves.

I don't know how long Connor's presence lingers in the air after he leaves—long enough for me to feel the knot in my stomach shift, tight and unwelcome, and yet, somehow, undeniable. It's as if his words have burrowed into the house itself, echoing through the floorboards and sticking to the corners, a constant reminder of things unsaid. The door clicks shut behind him with a finality that feels like the end of something, but my heart keeps racing, like it's still caught in the middle of a chase.

I can't shake the image of Leo, standing in the hallway, his small face framed in the dim light, eyes wide, unsure whether to run or stay. He didn't speak, didn't make a sound, but his presence filled the room, loud and unmissable. He knows more than I want him to. Of course, he does. He always does. But he's still so young, his innocence wrapped in layers of stubborn curiosity that sometimes makes me wish I could lock him away from the world for just a little longer.

I find him now, perched on the edge of the couch, legs swinging like a metronome as he flips through the pages of a book—one of the ones he'd claimed had "no pictures, just words," as though the absence of color would somehow make it more grown-up. I've watched him do this before, this way he swallows stories whole, savoring them in silence. But today, he's unusually still, his attention fixed on the pages but his thoughts clearly somewhere else.

"Leo?" I ask, even though I know he's already heard me.

He looks up, his eyes dark pools of quiet intelligence that remind me, painfully, of how much I've tried to keep from him.

"I heard," he says, his voice quiet, too quiet.

I sit beside him, unsure of how to bridge the gap. There's so much I should say—so much that I should have said before. But this isn't something you explain to a child. Not the mess I've made. Not the secrets that twist and tangle in the air between us, so thick they could choke a person if they weren't careful.

"I know," I say softly, my words almost an apology, though I'm not sure what for. "I'm sorry you had to overhear that."

He shrugs, unfazed, like he's used to me apologizing for things I can't fix. It's a small gesture, but it breaks something in me. Maybe it's the realization that no matter how many times I try to shield him, he's already been touched by things I can't control.

"Why was he asking about Dad?" Leo's voice trembles, just a fraction, but it's enough to make my heart skip.

I stare at him, the sharp edge of the question sinking in. He's too smart, my son. Too perceptive. But what else can I do but tell him the truth? It's the one thing I've always promised him: honesty. Even when it burns, even when it's a truth that feels like it could tear us apart.

I pull him into my lap, ruffling his hair with a hand that's more for comfort than anything else. "Your dad did some things in his past that are... complicated. Things that people might not understand."

"Is he a bad guy?" Leo asks, his gaze unwavering, steady in a way I can't quite grasp.

"No," I say, too quickly, my heart hammering. "No, he's not a bad guy. But sometimes people do things that... make things harder. For everyone."

Leo presses his lips together, a line of determination setting over his features. "Will we be okay?"

My throat tightens. What kind of answer can I give him? I wish I could promise him the world, but that's not how it works, not anymore. Instead, I lean in and kiss the top of his head, trying to make my voice sound certain. "We'll always be okay. You and me."

The words feel hollow the moment they leave my lips, but Leo doesn't seem to notice. He curls into me, his small frame pressing against mine like he's trying to soak in the comfort I can't quite provide. And for a moment, just a moment, everything is still. No questions. No secrets. Just the two of us, wrapped in the quiet.

But the peace doesn't last. It never does.

The next morning, I wake up to the shrill ring of my phone, an unfamiliar number flashing across the screen. I don't recognize it, but I pick it up anyway, my fingers betraying me as they press against the screen.

"Hello?" I answer, my voice a little too tight.

"Is this Mrs. Carter?" A woman's voice on the other end, cool and distant, like someone who has never once been caught off guard by the emotions of others.

"Yes," I say, swallowing. My pulse races again, a drumbeat that seems to echo in my chest. "Who's this?"

"This is Susan from the local sheriff's office. I need you to come down to the station as soon as possible. There's something we need to discuss regarding your husband's past."

The words hit me like a blow, a hammer against the ribs. I feel the air leave my lungs, the coldness of the room suddenly too much to bear. My hand shakes against the phone, and I have to steady it against my knee, trying to gather the pieces of myself before I crumble.

"I don't understand," I murmur, feeling the panic creep up my throat. "What are you talking about?"

"I'm afraid I can't give you details over the phone, ma'am. But it's urgent."

Urgent. The word alone is enough to freeze the blood in my veins. My husband's past, always lurking just beneath the surface, is finally coming back. The question is—what does it want now?

The drive to the sheriff's office is a blur of stoplights and indifferent road signs, the kind you pass every day but never notice until something disrupts the ordinary. I grip the wheel tighter than I should, my knuckles white, the pressure a small but constant reminder of the weight hanging over me. Leo sits quietly beside me, his gaze glued to the window, the corners of his mouth turned down in a way that makes my stomach churn. He hasn't said a word since I got off the phone. He doesn't need to. The silence between us is its own conversation, one we both wish we could avoid but can't.

The building that houses the sheriff's office is squat and grey, like the kind of place you'd expect to find only on a foggy morning or in a forgotten corner of town. I've been here once before, a lifetime ago, when we first moved into this area and the idea of the police felt both distant and oddly reassuring. Now, it feels like a trap.

I park and sit there for a moment, staring at the unmarked door, wondering what kind of mess I'm about to step into. The air feels heavy, weighted with anticipation, and I hate how familiar it is. It's the same feeling I had when I first found out about my husband's secrets—the realization that the life you thought you knew has cracks in it. So many cracks.

Leo doesn't move, his small hands clasped in his lap, his eyes unblinking. "You'll be okay, right, Mom?" The question is simple, but it hits like a freight train. I want to lie to him. I want to tell him everything's fine, that there's no reason to worry, that we'll walk out of here unscathed. But the truth is—what's happening right now? I don't know if I'll be okay.

"I'll be fine," I say, too quickly, my words sharp enough to slice through the silence between us. I smile, but it doesn't reach my eyes. "Don't worry about me, kiddo."

He nods, though I can see the doubt hanging in his expression. It's there, clear as day. He's too smart, my son. He sees things I can't hide.

I get out of the car and take a deep breath before walking toward the door, the heavy feeling in my chest growing with each step. The sheriff's office feels colder inside, the sterile smell of bleach and something else—something darker—hanging in the air. A man in a suit waits behind the front desk, his arms crossed over his chest. He looks like he's been standing there for a long time, just waiting for something to happen.

"Mrs. Carter," he says, his voice flat, emotionless. "Come on back. Sheriff's waiting for you."

I don't ask questions. There's no point. Not anymore. I follow him down a narrow hallway, my footsteps echoing too loudly in the silence. When we reach the door, he opens it without a word and gestures for me to enter.

Inside, the sheriff is sitting behind a desk, his chair tilted back just enough that I can see the smirk tugging at the corner of his lips. He's a middle-aged man, with sharp eyes and a hardened look that says he's seen it all. And then some. He doesn't stand when I enter. He doesn't need to.

"Have a seat, Mrs. Carter," he says, his tone casual, but there's something about it that sets my teeth on edge.

I sit, my knees suddenly feeling weak. Leo's shadow in the doorway behind me looms large, and I can feel him there, his presence like a quiet weight on my shoulders. I need to shield him from this. I need to keep him from hearing whatever they're about to say. But there's no getting out of it now. Not now that we're here.

"I'm afraid we've got some questions about your husband's past," the sheriff says, leaning forward slightly, his hands folding in front of him. His gaze sharpens, and the words come out like slow poison. "And it seems like it's catching up with him."

My stomach drops, and my pulse spikes. I try to keep my voice steady. "What do you mean? My husband's done nothing wrong. If this is about some old mistake, I—"

"It's not about mistakes," he interrupts, his voice cutting through me like a knife. "This is about something much bigger than that. And we need to figure out where you stand."

My mind whirls, but the words don't come fast enough. I feel trapped, pinned under the weight of their questions. My husband, Liam, has always been distant, enigmatic, the kind of man who wears his secrets like a second skin. But I never thought it would come to this. Never imagined that one day, those secrets would have a name—something tangible, something real.

"Liam's not here," I say, a hollow attempt at deflecting, but the sheriff isn't fooled.

"We know," he says, his voice cold. "He's been gone for a while now. But that doesn't mean he's not involved in something you might not be aware of."

I feel the walls close in on me, every inch of the room pressing against my chest. The questions start to tumble out, fast and relentless, their edges sharp. What do I know about Liam's associates? What do I know about the debts he left behind? What secrets was he hiding, even from me?

I try to hold it together, but the walls are closing in, and I can't breathe.

Then, just as quickly as it began, the sheriff stops. He leans back in his chair, studying me. "I'll be blunt, Mrs. Carter," he says, his voice oddly calm. "We think your husband might be involved in something much bigger than you realize. And I'm afraid you're more involved than you think. You might want to start thinking about where your loyalties lie."

The room goes silent. And that's when the door bursts open.

Chapter 6: Ashes and Echoes

I've never been one to back down from a challenge, but as I stood there, my boots crunching against the gravel outside the charred remains of the warehouse, I felt an unfamiliar knot tighten in my stomach. It wasn't the first time I'd found myself in a place like this—decay and neglect seemed to follow me around, especially since everything with Jackson went south. But this place, this abandoned shell of a building, felt different. It wasn't just an eyesore; it had a kind of haunting presence. The kind that sticks to your skin and won't let go.

Connor was already there when I arrived, standing in the shadows with his arms crossed, his jaw clenched as he stared into the blackened heart of the building. I didn't need to ask why he was so still. I felt it too—like the place had its own pulse, its own memory of the fire that had ravaged it. It wasn't just an old warehouse to us. It was a clue, a breadcrumb leading us toward something much darker.

When he noticed me approaching, his gaze flicked toward me, but it was fleeting—like I didn't even register on his radar, not really. It was a cold acknowledgment, the kind you give to someone you know you should be working with, but would rather be anywhere else than with them.

"You're late," he muttered, not even offering a smile.

I didn't even bother with a response. Let him think I cared about his judgment. I wasn't here to make friends, and certainly not to bond over burnt ruins with someone who still had an air of mystery clinging to him. He had his reasons for being here, I had mine. And it wasn't exactly a friendly collaboration we were building.

"What's our next step?" I asked, trying to cut through the tension that hung between us.

Connor ran a hand through his hair, the action more frustrated than anything. "We go in. We find out who he was talking to. Someone in that fire knew more than they should, and they're still hiding something. It's not just an accident."

His words made something inside me freeze, but I nodded, pushing the chill down. I was already in too deep. The fire, my husband's disappearance, the strange feeling of being followed—everything had led me to this place. And it wasn't going to get any easier from here.

Connor stepped forward, and I followed, feeling the temperature drop as we crossed the threshold of the warehouse. The air was thick with the scent of old smoke and dust. The walls were scarred, streaked with soot, as though the building itself still wore the marks of its violent past. But the silence was the worst part. It was like a grave, holding its secrets, daring us to disturb them.

The light inside was sparse, filtered through gaps in the broken windows. As our footsteps echoed through the empty space, the oppressive stillness settled over me. I scanned the surroundings, my eyes searching for anything that could give us a clue. The floor beneath us creaked and groaned, a far-too-living sound in such a desolate place. And then, I caught it—something glittering in the corner, half-hidden under a pile of debris.

"Over here," I called out, pointing toward it.

Connor was right behind me, his movements swift and precise, always calculating. He crouched down beside the pile, his fingers already brushing through the wreckage with practiced ease. His eyes were sharp, constantly alert, and I couldn't help but wonder what it was that drove him. He wasn't just here for me; there was something personal in his need to uncover the truth, something that tied him to the ashes just as much as it did to me.

He pulled out a shard of glass, thin and delicate, but sharp enough to cut through anything in its path. The reflection of the dim light caught in it, casting a brief flash of brightness on his face.

"This... this isn't right," he muttered. "These pieces don't belong here. This was staged."

I felt my heart quicken as he stood, studying the shard in his hand, his expression darkening. "What are you saying?" I pressed, though I already knew the answer.

He met my gaze, his eyes unreadable for a moment before he spoke. "This wasn't just a fire. Someone wanted this place to burn, and they made sure it did."

I felt a shiver crawl up my spine, but I forced myself to stand tall. There was no room for weakness here, not with Connor watching me like he was. His silence in the wake of his revelation wasn't comfortable—it was a challenge. A silent dare for me to keep up.

I had no choice but to take the bait. "And who do you think did this?" I asked, trying to keep my voice steady. I wanted to know the answer, but part of me was terrified to hear it.

Connor didn't answer right away, his eyes scanning the remains of the warehouse as though it would suddenly give him the answers. "Someone who knew what they were doing. Someone who had a reason to cover something up."

We stood there for a long moment, the tension building between us, a kind of electric charge that had nothing to do with the warehouse around us. Something about this place was making me reckless, and I couldn't decide whether it was the fear or the anticipation. The edge of something terrible was hanging in the air.

I was about to speak again when Connor's voice cut through the stillness. "We're not leaving until we know what really happened here. Whatever Jackson was involved in... it's not over."

His words were like a rope pulling me deeper into a place I wasn't sure I wanted to go. But, then again, what choice did I have? This was my life now, this mystery, this search for truth—whether I liked it or not.

"Fine," I said, my voice a little sharper than I intended, but there it was. "But we do it my way."

Connor turned to me, his lips twitching in the briefest of smirks. "Your way?"

"Yes," I replied, stepping closer, meeting his gaze head-on. "I have my methods."

He chuckled, low and dry. "I'm sure you do."

And just like that, the friction between us flared—a strange mixture of antagonism and something else, something heavier. I couldn't quite place it, but it was there, lurking beneath the surface, pushing us into uncomfortable proximity.

As we moved deeper into the ruins, the fire's echoes following us, I knew one thing for sure: things were about to get much worse before they got better. And whether Connor and I wanted to admit it or not, we were in this together, for better or for worse.

The deeper we ventured into the warehouse, the more the weight of the past seemed to press against us, the silence thick enough to smother any remaining hope of clarity. Each step I took seemed to disturb the ghosts of what had happened here—those lost whispers of fire, of betrayal, of secrets that had long since turned to ash. I couldn't shake the feeling that we weren't alone, that something was watching us from the shadows, waiting for the right moment to reveal itself.

Connor moved ahead of me, his steps fluid and measured, but I could see the edge in his posture. He was on high alert, as if expecting the walls to collapse around us at any moment. The man was either incredibly calm or absolutely terrifying. Either way, it was difficult to trust him, though I couldn't deny that I found myself more drawn to him than I cared to admit. There was something about the way he carried himself—so certain, so detached—that made my instincts both scream to run and scream to stay.

I caught up to him, careful not to make a sound as I crept closer. My eyes flicked over the ruined floor, past the jagged shards of metal and remnants of broken glass, until I saw what he was looking at. A series of blackened papers, crisped at the edges, scattered across the floor in a scattered pile like the remnants of a forgotten diary.

"Is that what I think it is?" I whispered, my voice quieter than I intended, as if the papers might hear me.

Connor didn't answer right away, but I could see his jaw tighten as he crouched down to gather the charred remnants in his hands. The papers didn't seem important at first—just another casualty of the fire—but the longer I watched, the more I realized how carefully he was handling them, like they were fragile pieces of evidence.

"Nothing is ever as simple as it seems," he muttered, his voice gravelly. He didn't look up, but I could sense the change in his energy. Something had clicked. "These weren't burned by accident. Someone was looking for something specific."

I frowned. "Looking for something? In a fire?"

He glanced up at me then, his expression unreadable. "When you want to erase something, you don't just let the fire do the job. You make sure it's gone. But whoever started this fire was sloppy. They missed this."

I bit my lip, the implications of his words sinking in. It wasn't just a fire. It was a deliberate attempt to hide something, to burn it out of existence. But why? And why leave behind pieces of evidence?

"You think my husband knew something about this?" I asked, though even as I said the words, a part of me wanted him to deny it, to say that Jackson had been caught in the wrong place at the wrong time. But Connor didn't indulge me with comfort. Instead, he took a long breath and shook his head.

"I don't know. But I'm betting whatever he got mixed up in, it's bigger than just you and me. And if we're not careful, it's going to pull us both down."

The coldness in his voice sent a shiver through me, but I swallowed it down. This was the game now. There was no turning back.

I took a step forward, determined to get some control back, even if it was just in the way I carried myself. "Then what do we do now?"

Connor stood slowly, scanning the room as if the answer was written somewhere on the walls themselves. "We find out who else was involved. If Jackson was digging around in this mess, then he wasn't the only one. People don't burn buildings down just for fun. Someone had a reason."

I nodded, though I didn't feel as confident as I wanted to. I had trusted Jackson, believed in him in ways that now seemed naïve. He had always been so careful, so meticulous. The thought that he could have gotten mixed up in something dangerous, something this ugly, made the world feel like it was slowly tilting beneath me.

The warehouse was growing darker as we moved deeper, the shadows pooling like ink in the corners. There was a sense of finality in the air, as though we were walking toward the edge of something we couldn't control. But I was past the point of turning back. I had to know the truth.

I glanced over at Connor, who was crouched again, his fingers brushing the scorched floor as if looking for something more—something I couldn't see. He was all tension now, his focus entirely on the wreckage, his mind somewhere far beyond this abandoned warehouse. I wondered if, like me, he'd been carrying something around, something dark that had driven him to this place.

"How did you get mixed up in this?" I asked, the question slipping out before I could stop it.

He looked up sharply, his gaze locking with mine. For a moment, I thought I saw something flicker behind his eyes—something almost human. But it was gone too quickly to be sure. "I don't get mixed up in things. I just follow the thread until it leads me somewhere useful. This just happens to be where the thread is."

It was the most vulnerable thing he'd said since we'd started this together, and for reasons I couldn't explain, it made me want to ask more questions, dig deeper into the parts of him that he was so carefully guarding. But I didn't. I wasn't here for him. I was here for the truth.

"Well, let's follow it, then," I said, forcing a note of steel into my voice. I had no intention of getting tangled up in whatever game he was playing. Not anymore. "We'll figure out what happened, and then we'll get out of here."

But as we moved through the wreckage, with nothing but our footsteps and the echoes of a fire long extinguished, I couldn't help but feel the weight of what was coming. We were standing on the edge of something much darker than I had ever imagined. And the worst part? I wasn't sure if I wanted to find the truth—or if I was afraid of what it might cost me.

The walls around us seemed to close in as we moved deeper into the warehouse, the air thick with the taste of something old, something ancient. I couldn't tell if it was the remnants of the fire still choking the life out of the space or the lingering tension between Connor and me, but there was a palpable sense of danger, like the place itself had been waiting for us to walk through the door.

I glanced at Connor, his profile sharp and rigid in the dim light. There was something so unnervingly calm about him, like he thrived on the chaos. Or maybe he was just good at pretending it didn't affect him. But I could see the way his fingers twitched at his side, like he was ready to strike at any second. It made me wonder how much of his cold demeanor was an act.

"What else are we looking for?" I asked, trying to sound braver than I felt.

He didn't look up at me, his eyes scanning the remnants of the place like he was seeing something I couldn't. "We're looking for a pattern. A connection. Whatever they didn't want us to find is still here."

I felt the hair on the back of my neck stand up at the thought. Jackson had always been the one to follow patterns, to connect the dots before anyone else could see them. Was this really about him? Or had I become a pawn in a game I didn't even understand?

"Do you ever get tired of the game?" I asked, mostly to myself, but I wasn't surprised when Connor's low laugh echoed back at me, dark and a little cynical.

"You think I'm playing a game?" His voice was smooth, but there was an edge to it now, one I hadn't heard before. "This is survival, sweetheart. No one wins a game when they're already losing."

I flinched, the words catching in my throat as I met his gaze for the first time in what felt like hours. It wasn't anger I saw in his eyes, but something darker, something almost predatory. I opened my mouth to say something, but the words died before they reached my lips. For the briefest second, I wondered if I was standing on the edge of a cliff, looking down into a void I wasn't ready to fall into.

I shook my head, trying to clear the thoughts that swirled like smoke. "I'm not afraid of you," I said, my voice steadier than I felt.

Connor just stared at me for a long moment, as if he could see right through me. Then he looked away, his eyes narrowing as they swept over the area again, his fingers twitching like they were itching to uncover something. "You should be."

That wasn't a threat, or at least, not in the way I expected. It was more of a warning, a quiet statement of fact. And in that moment, I realized that no matter how many times I tried to convince myself otherwise, I was just as tangled up in this as he was.

I turned away from him, trying to ignore the unsettling rush of adrenaline that was making my heart race. "Let's just find what we came for," I muttered, though I wasn't sure if I meant it or if I was just trying to convince myself that I could still walk away when all was said and done.

But as I stepped deeper into the wreckage, I felt it again—the pull of something else, something just beyond my reach. Something that didn't belong here, that was out of place in a space like this. My feet carried me toward the far corner, where a half-burned metal door stood ajar, leading into what looked like an old office space, its walls covered in soot.

Connor was beside me in a heartbeat, his hand on my arm, stopping me. "Don't," he said, his voice low but firm.

I met his gaze, ready to argue, but something in the way he looked at me silenced the words on my tongue. "This is it, isn't it?" I asked instead, my voice barely above a whisper.

He didn't respond at first. His eyes flicked to the door, then back to me, weighing the decision in his mind. Finally, he nodded once, sharply. "This is where it started. But we go in carefully. We don't know who might be waiting for us on the other side."

I was about to ask him what he meant by that when I saw it—a glint of light through the cracks in the door, a reflection of something metallic, something shiny, just barely visible. My instincts screamed at me to push forward, to see what was hidden behind that door, but the part of me that had learned to be cautious held me back.

"You're the one who said you weren't afraid," Connor reminded me, a dangerous grin flickering across his lips.

I opened my mouth to retort, but before I could, the sound of footsteps echoed through the silence. Footsteps that didn't belong to us.

Connor tensed, his body going rigid beside me, but instead of reacting immediately, he stepped back, his hand on my shoulder, guiding me into the shadows. "Stay quiet," he murmured, his voice barely audible.

I barely had time to steady my breath before the door creaked open, just enough for us to hear muffled voices on the other side. A man's voice. Too calm. Too familiar.

"Is it done?" the voice asked.

Another voice answered, low and gravelly. "Almost. But you'll want to clean up that mess. There's still too much heat around it."

The second voice paused, a short, sharp laugh echoing through the wall. "I'm not worried about the heat. You should be."

My heart stopped as I realized the implication. "They know we're here," I whispered.

Connor's grip on my shoulder tightened, and for a brief moment, everything felt too still, too quiet. Then, as if the universe had decided to stop holding its breath, the door opened further, and a figure stepped into the light.

But it wasn't the person I was expecting.

It was Jackson.

Chapter 7: Burned Bridges

The coffee shop smelled like overripe fruit and cheap cinnamon. The air was thick with the hum of idle chatter, the occasional clink of cups and saucers, and the soothing whir of the espresso machine. I nestled into my usual corner, the one with the cracked wooden table and chipped mug that made me feel more at home than I cared to admit. But today, even the comforting familiarity of this place couldn't settle the agitation that swarmed inside me like a hive of wasps.

Connor slid into the seat across from me, all sharp lines and brooding eyes, like he'd walked straight out of a storm cloud. I blinked at him, then quickly turned my gaze to the half-empty mug in front of me. The coffee had gone cold hours ago, but I hadn't been able to summon the energy to drink it.

"You're quiet," he said, his voice too soft for the setting, too full of intention. His eyes flickered over me, as though searching for something. His lips quirked into that knowing smile of his, the one that always made my pulse quicken before my better sense could catch up.

"Trying to figure out if I'm the problem here, or if it's just you," I shot back, my tone sharper than I'd meant. But the irritation inside me needed an outlet, and his proximity made it all the more impossible to ignore.

He leaned back, folding his arms, his gaze never leaving mine. "You think it's me?"

"No," I said, exhaling sharply. "I don't know. I just—" I trailed off, the words faltering on my tongue. It had been like this for weeks now, this unbearable back-and-forth, this tug-of-war between wanting to push him away and craving the pull of whatever strange, magnetic connection we seemed to share.

"You don't like being vulnerable, do you?" he asked, his voice laced with something unspoken, something almost predatory. He was teasing, but there was a bite to it, something that gnawed at me, that made me feel like he could see right through me.

I stiffened, my fingers curling around the handle of the mug, as if I could anchor myself to something real. "Not everyone enjoys wearing their heart on their sleeve."

He leaned forward just slightly, his gaze intense. "And yet, you wear it all over your face. Or have you forgotten?"

I shot him a look, but he was right. I had forgotten. Or maybe I had just refused to acknowledge it. It was too easy to pretend I wasn't falling for him when I was. It was too easy to mask it with sarcasm, with stubborn deflection, and with the excuse that we were just trying to solve a mystery.

But even then, the mystery wasn't about the answers. It was about him.

"I don't know what you want from me, Connor," I said, my voice quieter now. "We're not... whatever you think we are. This is about the case. Just the case." I didn't believe it, but I had to say it. I needed to believe it.

He smirked. That damn smirk. "Is it, though?"

I opened my mouth to retort, but the words didn't come. Instead, I was left staring at him, caught in the impossible tightrope between wanting to tear my eyes away and wanting to hold on for dear life. His presence had a way of filling the space, of wrapping around me like smoke, suffocating and intoxicating all at once. I couldn't tell if he was deliberately toying with me or if he genuinely didn't care enough to notice how he affected me.

"I thought you said you didn't want anything personal," he added, voice dripping with mock innocence. "No emotional entanglements, no messy feelings. Yet here we are, caught in the web we've both been so careful not to spin."

His words struck a chord, and it was almost too much to bear. I opened my mouth to snap back, but I stopped myself. I couldn't say what I was thinking. Not to him, not yet. Not when every word felt like a confession.

"You keep pushing me away," I muttered instead, half to myself, half to him. "And then you come back, and—" I broke off, unable to finish the sentence. I didn't know what to say. Didn't know how to make sense of whatever the hell this was between us.

He tilted his head, his gaze softening just enough for me to notice. "I'm not pushing you away. I'm trying to keep us from falling into something neither of us can handle. It's not... it's not what either of us need."

And there it was, the admission that shouldn't have felt like a blow, but did.

I nodded, a sharp, brittle movement that barely carried any weight. "Right," I whispered, as if saying it aloud would make it true. "Neither of us needs this."

His expression faltered for a moment, just a flicker of something I couldn't quite read before it was gone. "You're the one who can't stop looking for answers. The problem with you, you know," he said, leaning back once again, his eyes darkening with a new sort of intensity, "is that you always want to know the ending before you've even figured out the plot."

"And what's that supposed to mean?" I demanded, irritation creeping back into my tone.

He met my gaze, unflinching. "It means you're scared of the middle, the messy part. The part where things don't make sense and you can't control them."

I exhaled sharply, frustration mounting as I tried to force my thoughts into something coherent. "You're saying I'm scared of getting involved?"

"You're scared of being wrong," he countered. "Scared of trusting someone who might burn you."

And just like that, the air between us shifted, thickened with a tension that neither of us had the courage to break. I opened my mouth to protest, but the words were stuck. I was too scared to admit the truth—that he was right, that I had been running from the one thing I didn't know how to deal with.

We both knew the truth. But neither of us was ready to face it.

The next time Connor showed up unannounced, it was on a Thursday afternoon, the kind of gray day where the world feels like it's holding its breath, waiting for a storm that never quite arrives. I was sitting at my kitchen table, staring at a stack of paperwork that needed sorting, but my mind was elsewhere, spinning in circles around him. The clutter of unpaid bills and unsent emails seemed like the smallest of distractions compared to the knot in my stomach, the constant ache that lingered every time I thought about him.

The knock on the door was sharp, insistent, and immediately my pulse shot up like a bottle of champagne being opened too fast. I knew it was him before I even checked the peephole. I almost didn't answer it, but something inside me—the stubborn, reckless part I liked to ignore—had already reached for the handle.

When I swung the door open, Connor was standing there, his hands shoved into the pockets of his leather jacket, a faint, almost amused smirk on his lips. He wasn't asking for permission to come in. He never did.

"You've been avoiding me," he said, his voice a little too casual for my liking, like he didn't already know exactly why I'd been keeping my distance.

"Well, you're not exactly the most welcome guest," I shot back, my gaze flicking to the paper trail scattered across the table. I wanted to hide it from him, to pretend I wasn't drowning in work and trying desperately not to drown in him at the same time.

He arched an eyebrow, a hint of a smile curling at the corners of his mouth. "I'm not here to talk about the bills. Although, you should probably pay those before they start piling up." His tone was a little too knowing, a little too familiar, as if he'd been here long enough to have seen the mess before.

"Don't you have somewhere to be?" I countered, the irritation rising in my chest. Why did he always have to show up like this? Why did he always make me feel like I was on the verge of something I couldn't name, something that both terrified and excited me in equal measure?

"I might. But then again, I might not. I've got a few things I need to figure out," he said, stepping into the entryway, his eyes sweeping over the disarray of the room. "Looks like you're doing the same."

I didn't want to talk about the clutter. I didn't want to talk about how much I had left to do, how much I was avoiding. The last thing I needed was him turning this into some sort of existential interrogation.

Instead, I gritted my teeth and made a beeline for the kitchen, grabbing a couple of glasses. "Want something to drink?" I asked, even though I was certain the answer would be yes, and it would drag this conversation out longer than I could handle.

"Whiskey. Neat," he said, his voice dipping into something lower, something more serious than before. When he spoke like that, I almost forgot about the distance I'd built between us, the emotional barrier I'd tried so hard to fortify. I could feel the heat of his gaze on me, his presence in the room like an ember glowing just beneath the surface of my skin.

I poured the whiskey, the amber liquid sloshing a little more than I meant to. It took more than a little effort to focus on the task at hand. When I turned back to face him, he was standing by the window, his hands still tucked in his pockets, staring out at the street below. I almost didn't want to know what he was thinking, but I had the feeling that, just like always, he knew exactly what I was thinking.

"I thought you were supposed to be helping me with the case," I said, my voice a little too sharp, a little too desperate to move past whatever this was between us. I couldn't focus on anything else while he was here, while that damn smirk still lingered in the corners of his mouth.

"I am," he said, turning to face me. The easy smile was gone now, replaced with something darker, more intense. He stepped closer, until he was standing right in front of me, his eyes fixed on mine. "But I don't think that's the real reason you asked me to come over."

I stiffened, suddenly aware of the space between us—or rather, the lack of it. My breath caught, and I had to force myself to look away, to focus on the damn glass in my hand.

"I don't know what you mean," I lied, hating the way my pulse was hammering in my throat, hating the way my body seemed to betray me every time he was near.

"I think you do," he said quietly, his voice carrying a weight that left me breathless. He reached out, his fingers brushing lightly against the glass in my hand, sending a jolt through me that was almost painful in its intensity. "You're afraid of the answers. You're afraid of what's going to happen when you stop hiding behind all this work, all these walls you've built. And I—"

I cut him off, taking a step back, the glass slipping from my fingers and clinking softly against the counter. "I'm not afraid of anything."

He gave me a knowing look, one that made my stomach twist, the corners of his mouth lifting slightly, like he was savoring the moment. "Yes, you are."

I was about to say something else, something sharp and defiant, but then the phone rang, cutting through the tension like a knife. I stared at it for a moment, unsure whether to answer. But Connor's eyes never left me, the weight of his presence pressing down on me like a physical force, too much to bear.

"Answer it," he said, his voice low, urging me on. "You might just find your answers there."

I swallowed hard, my fingers trembling slightly as I picked up the phone. I didn't know what I expected to hear. But the voice on the other end—too familiar, too cold—made my blood run cold.

"I'm not done with you yet," came the voice. And just like that, whatever fragile balance I'd been clinging to shattered.

The voice on the other end of the phone sent a chill down my spine, and for a moment, I couldn't speak. My fingers tightened around the receiver as if somehow, I could crush the words before they fully settled into my brain.

"I'm not done with you yet."

It was him. The one I'd been trying to avoid. The one whose name I couldn't even dare to speak aloud because saying it made it too real, too dangerous. Too close.

"Who is this?" I demanded, my voice thin, shaky. I hated how much I was betraying myself in that one word—demanded. I wanted control, but all I had was the ringing in my ears and the cold sweat suddenly trickling down my spine.

There was a brief pause, as if he was savoring my discomfort. "You know who I am."

The line went dead before I could respond. I stared at the phone, the words echoing in my head like a drumbeat, my pulse quickening as I wondered how in the hell he'd managed to find me. How had he even gotten my number?

Behind me, I heard a movement, the rustle of clothing, and the sharp scent of cologne that was somehow too familiar, too close. Connor was still there.

I didn't need to turn around to know he was watching me, the weight of his presence making the air feel too thick, too oppressive. But I couldn't face him—not yet. Not with the storm swirling inside me, mixing confusion with anger, fear with frustration.

"You heard that, didn't you?" I asked, trying to keep my voice steady, but failing miserably. I cursed myself for it, for letting my emotions spill out like a cracked dam.

He didn't answer right away. There was only silence, thick and heavy, hanging between us. Then, his voice, low and deceptively calm, broke through. "Yeah. I heard."

I turned then, unable to stop myself. "What do you want me to do about it? Tell me, Connor. Tell me what I'm supposed to do now."

He stepped closer, his hands sliding out of his jacket pockets, his expression unreadable. "I don't know, but you're not the only one in danger, you know."

I flinched, the words landing like a slap across my face. "What are you talking about? What danger?"

He didn't answer immediately. Instead, his eyes flicked over my shoulder, to the phone still dangling in my hand, the weight of it somehow more significant now, like a beacon drawing attention to us. His gaze darkened, and a muscle in his jaw twitched.

"You've been digging too deep," he said, his voice growing colder. "The more you dig, the more people get hurt. Including you."

I couldn't decide if I wanted to throw the phone at him or run away. Maybe both. I took a step back, trying to create some space between us, even though there was no physical distance that could put out the fire he'd set inside me. "What's that supposed to mean? Who are you protecting? And from what?"

"I'm not protecting anyone. I'm trying to keep you alive," he replied, his words blunt, his eyes never leaving mine. "You're too close to something—too close to the truth. And that's the problem."

I shook my head, my thoughts a blur. The familiar buzz of adrenaline coursed through my veins, too much to make sense of in any meaningful way. "I'm just trying to figure out what happened. What's so dangerous about that?"

His gaze shifted briefly, flickering with something unreadable. "It's not what you're looking for. It's who you're looking at."

I blinked, the meaning of his words barely registering as something foreign in my mind. "What the hell does that mean?"

"Drop it," he said. His voice was low, almost pleading now, though I wasn't sure if I was just hearing what I wanted to hear. "Walk away from this while you still can."

But I couldn't. The pull of the mystery, the need to understand the chaos I was swimming in, had tangled itself too tightly around my heart. I was already in over my head, and I wasn't the type to give up when the stakes were high.

"I can't," I whispered, more to myself than to him. The admission tasted bitter on my tongue.

Connor's jaw clenched, and he took another step forward, closing the distance between us. His eyes locked with mine, the intensity of his gaze making my breath hitch in my throat. I could feel the heat of his body, his presence wrapping itself around me like a vice, making everything else fade away. "Then you're going to have to learn how to protect yourself. Because no one else is going to do it for you."

I wanted to respond, to argue, but his words struck too close to something I wasn't ready to confront. The truth that he'd been trying to warn me about wasn't just the danger outside—it was the danger I felt every time I saw him, every time he walked into a room.

I had been trying to ignore it, trying to push it down into some corner of my mind where it wouldn't have any power over me. But now, standing in front of him, it was impossible to deny.

"Why are you doing this?" I asked, my voice cracking, the vulnerability I had been fighting to hide slipping through. "Why are you still here?"

For a moment, his face softened, the hard lines of his expression smoothing out just a little, and for a fleeting second, I saw something—something human—before it vanished again, hidden beneath the layers of distance he kept so carefully intact.

"I told you," he said, his voice rough, "I'm not going anywhere."

The words settled heavily between us, and in that moment, I realized just how little control I had over this situation. The storm inside me was only growing, and I wasn't sure if I was more afraid of losing myself to it or losing him.

Before I could say anything else, the phone rang again. This time, it wasn't the cold, threatening voice from before.

It was someone else.

And they knew my name.

Chapter 8: Flammable Hearts

The night air carried the scent of smoke, thick and sharp, curling into my lungs like a warning. It was a familiar smell, but tonight, it was sharper. Nearer. I stood in the middle of the street, watching as flames crept closer, licking the edges of the old neighborhood. The fire engines had yet to arrive, and the heat seemed to shimmer in waves against the dark sky, orange light casting long shadows. In moments like these, everything becomes a blur—people shouting, the crackle of burning wood, the frantic scrambling of neighbors trying to get out. The world is caught in a slow-motion dance of panic and confusion, but then, a flash of movement, like an electric current, pulls my eyes.

Connor.

He was already there, at the edge of the blaze, his jacket unzipped, his face grim and focused. His hair was dark against the flames, tousled by the wind, but it was his hands that caught my attention—the steady, sure movements as he pulled an elderly woman from her porch. The woman's frail body had no chance of outrunning the fire, but Connor seemed to move in a different realm, one where time bent to his will. He didn't hesitate. Not even for a second.

"Come on, Mrs. Hawthorne," he grunted, his voice strong, but threaded with something softer, something that made my heart trip. "We're getting you out of here."

I didn't know where I found the breath to speak, but the words escaped before I could stop them. "Connor, wait!"

He didn't. Not even a flicker of acknowledgment that I existed. And in that moment, I understood. He wasn't a man who paused for anything or anyone. Certainly not for applause or thanks.

A small crowd had gathered now, eyes wide, mouths agape. Some were calling out to him, some were too stunned to do anything but watch. I should have been terrified. I should have felt something more than awe, more than admiration for the way he handled danger. But I didn't. The fear, the tension, the possibility of everything going wrong, they all seemed to melt away in the face of his courage. It wasn't just bravery. It was something else, something more human, more vulnerable. He wasn't doing this to be a hero; he was doing it because he couldn't do anything else.

He didn't look back when he finally got Mrs. Hawthorne to safety, just pushed her into the arms of two younger neighbors who'd started to organize a small evacuation line. The fire was roaring now, the heat pressing against my skin, but Connor didn't even flinch. His body was taut, every muscle pulled tight like a wire stretched just beyond its limit. And I realized then, not for the first time, how little I knew about him.

Connor had always been a mystery to me, wrapped in layers of cool indifference and sharp words. He was the kind of man who didn't let you in, didn't let you see the things that made him who he was. I always chalked it up to a well-guarded heart. But standing there, watching him move through the flames like he was made of something stronger, something more enduring than the rest of us, I realized how little I'd understood. He wasn't hiding. Not from me. He was hiding from everything.

The firemen arrived moments later, sirens blaring as they flooded the street, throwing hoses to the ground, positioning themselves with a practiced efficiency that had the flames contained within minutes. But for me, the fire had already burned something deeper. Something I wasn't ready to confront.

Connor was already pulling off his jacket, rolling up his sleeves, moving through the chaos as if it was all part of some routine. His face was streaked with ash, his eyes narrowed, but there was no mistaking the way his shoulders slumped once the action had subsided, how the weight of it all hit him the moment he stopped moving. He looked tired, every line on his face drawn deeper, his jaw clenched as if he could keep the exhaustion at bay by sheer force of will.

I took a step forward, then hesitated. What could I say? What could I possibly offer to a man who didn't seem to need anything, least of all my gratitude?

"Connor," I started, my voice cutting through the haze of smoke. He didn't turn at first, didn't acknowledge me. But I could see his body tense, could feel the shift in the air around him, as though my voice was the last thing he wanted to hear.

When he finally turned to me, his eyes were colder than I'd ever seen them. "Don't," he said, his voice sharp, the familiar edge there, like a shield he was raising higher. "I didn't do it for you."

I swallowed hard, a sudden lump in my throat. The words stung, more than they should have. More than I wanted them to. "I wasn't—"

"I know what you were doing," he interrupted, his eyes hard, focused on something in the distance. "You don't need to thank me."

His words were like a punch to the gut, and for a split second, the weight of the moment crushed me. I had been standing there, ready to offer the only thing I could give, and he didn't want it. Didn't want me.

"I wasn't," I tried again, but the words caught in my throat. How could I explain something he didn't want to hear? That I hadn't expected him to be a hero, but now that I saw him—really saw him—I didn't know how to process the feelings that were rising, unbidden, inside me.

But Connor didn't give me the chance. With a curt nod, he turned away, retreating into the throng of emergency responders, his figure swallowed by the crowd. I was left standing there, amidst the smoke and the fading sirens, wondering how someone so capable of saving lives could be so impossible to reach.

The morning after the fire, the air was still thick with the memory of it, as though the smoke had settled into the very fabric of the neighborhood. I could still taste the charred remnants of it, sharp and bitter, lingering in the back of my throat. But it was the quiet that unnerved me. Everything seemed too still, as if we were all collectively holding our breath, waiting for something—anything—to break the silence.

I woke up early, earlier than usual, my mind still racing with the night before. Connor's face kept flashing in my thoughts—those few seconds when I thought I saw something different in his eyes, something raw and unguarded. But that had been a fleeting illusion, hadn't it? The same Connor I'd known for months had turned away without a second glance, as if the moment we shared never happened.

I dressed quickly, knowing I'd have no peace until I could shake the memories loose. The smell of coffee beckoned me downstairs, where the house was as empty as the space between my thoughts. I poured myself a cup, the warmth of the mug grounding me, but it didn't take long for the guilt to creep in. The guilt of thinking too much, of wanting too much. Connor wasn't the kind of man who wanted to be seen, not like that. He wasn't my fantasy, and I wasn't his.

The realization stung, sharper than I'd expected. But at least now, I could accept it for what it was. I had always known Connor to be a man of few words, a man who preferred action over sentiment. The fire had shown me that—his raw, unyielding determination to save someone, to protect, had laid bare a side of him that was as compelling as it was unreachable. But it also reminded me that I wasn't in his world. I never would be.

By midday, I found myself walking down the familiar street, the one that led past Connor's place. I told myself it was a coincidence, that I was just taking a stroll to clear my head. But as I passed his house, I saw him out front, his hands tucked into the pockets of his jacket, his gaze aimed at the ground. He didn't see me at first, but I could feel the tension in the air, like an electric pulse ready to snap.

I paused, just for a moment, before deciding it was too late to back out. I could walk past him and pretend nothing had happened. I could do that. But instead, I found myself walking right toward him. My heart thudded in my chest, and I hated that it was so obvious. But then again, Connor probably knew everything without me having to say a word.

"Morning," I said, forcing a casual tone, as though we hadn't just survived a fire together and failed miserably to communicate about it.

He glanced up, his eyes narrowing when they met mine. His face was slightly soot-streaked from the previous night, though it was clear he'd washed away most of the remnants of his impromptu heroism. But the weariness was still there—heavy in his eyes, in the slump of his shoulders.

"Morning," he replied, his voice rough, as though the silence had been choking him.

We stood there for a moment, the space between us charged, but neither of us quite sure what to do with it. It wasn't a comfortable silence, not by any means. It was that strange kind of silence that only seems to grow more awkward the longer you leave it hanging.

"I, uh," I began, not knowing where I was going with it. "I wanted to say thank you again."

Connor shifted slightly, his lips pulling into a tight smile—one of those smiles that didn't reach his eyes. "I already told you. No need for thanks."

"I'm not sure you understand." I took a step closer, my pulse quickening. "You didn't have to do that. What you did... it was incredible. You saved her."

"I didn't save anyone," he muttered, his gaze drifting toward the street, away from me. "I just did what needed to be done."

There it was again, that cold detachment. I didn't know why it hurt so much, but it did. I couldn't seem to make sense of it—how could a man so willing to risk his life for someone be so unwilling to accept the simplest of acknowledgments?

I took a breath, steadying myself. "You're not just a guy who does what needs to be done. You're a hero, Connor."

He gave a short, humorless laugh, the sound bitter. "I'm no hero. Heroes don't do things for the wrong reasons."

The words hit me like a slap, and I felt something deep inside of me stir—something that had been hiding, just below the surface. "What do you mean by that?" I asked, my voice lower than I intended. "What reasons?"

Connor's jaw tightened, and for a split second, I thought he was going to walk away. But then, to my surprise, he took a step closer to me instead. His presence was overwhelming, his scent—the faint, smoky tang that clung to him from the fire—filling my senses.

"Look, you don't understand," he said, his voice dropping, rougher now. "I don't do these things for praise, for recognition. I do them because it's what I have to do. But it's not something you want to be around, believe me. People like me... we're built differently. We don't need people to thank us. We don't need anyone at all."

For a moment, I could only stare at him, the tension between us so thick it was almost tangible. It felt like he was pushing me away, and yet, the words were still pulling me in. There was something vulnerable hiding behind his mask, something fragile that he refused to let anyone see.

"I don't think you're built differently, Connor," I said quietly, stepping just a little closer. "I think you're scared. Scared that if you let anyone in, they'll see everything you're trying to hide."

He didn't say anything, his eyes now shadowed, his expression unreadable. But for the briefest of moments, I saw it—the crack in his armor. And that was all it took.

The following days passed in a haze, the fire a lingering presence I couldn't shake. Every time I closed my eyes, I saw the orange glow of the flames, felt the heat in my bones. But mostly, I saw Connor—his back to me as he turned away from my gratitude, his face unreadable in the smoke. I told myself it was nothing, that it didn't matter. That he was just doing his job, nothing more. But deep down, I knew I was lying to myself.

It wasn't just about the fire anymore. It wasn't about heroism or duty. It was about the way he'd looked at me—or rather, the way he hadn't. The distance between us had always been there, a cold barrier he'd erected between us, but now it felt almost suffocating. Like a door that had been slammed shut, leaving me on the outside.

I found myself walking past his house again, not on purpose, but because the streets felt too quiet without him in them. Every time I moved closer to his place, I could feel the weight of my own feet dragging me back, as if the very earth didn't want me to approach. But my legs carried me anyway, and soon enough, I was standing across from his house, half hidden by the overgrown bushes that lined the sidewalk.

I didn't know what I expected to see—maybe a sign of him, some clue that he wasn't as unreachable as he seemed. But the house was still, the curtains drawn, the front door shut tight. He wasn't there. I almost felt relieved, which in itself made me feel pathetic.

Turning to leave, I almost ran into someone.

"Well, look who's out and about," Sarah said, her voice breaking through the silence. "Taking a walk in the neighborhood or... just stalking the local hero?" Her grin was teasing, but there was a knowing gleam in her eyes, one that made me feel instantly uncomfortable.

"I'm not—" I started, but she was already cutting me off with a raised hand.

"Please. I've known you long enough to know when you're hiding behind some kind of excuse. Don't tell me you're just 'passing through' his street." She arched an eyebrow, leaning against the low stone wall that bordered the yard. "So? How's the 'hero' doing? Did you thank him properly for playing knight in shining armor?"

"Sarah, stop," I said, laughing a little too loudly, trying to deflect. "It's not like that."

She didn't buy it. "Come on, it's always like that. It's the way you talk about him when you think no one's listening." Her voice dropped to a whisper, and her eyes gleamed with mischief. "Don't even try to tell me there's no spark between you two. I know you. I've seen it."

I opened my mouth to deny it, but the truth hovered just behind my teeth, so close to escaping. Of course, there was a spark. Of course, there was something between us. Something I couldn't explain. But I wasn't about to admit it to Sarah—not yet. Not when I wasn't sure what it meant.

"Sarah, seriously," I said, half laughing, half exasperated. "We're friends, okay? That's all. And that's all it'll ever be."

She gave me a skeptical look, then shrugged. "Okay, fine. Keep lying to yourself if it makes you feel better. But don't come crying to me when your heart's in pieces."

I rolled my eyes, but inside, her words stuck to me, like a layer of grime I couldn't wash off. Could I really keep pretending it was nothing? Could I really ignore the way my heart raced whenever Connor came near, the way his presence left me feeling exposed and vulnerable? And why did that bother me so much?

I turned to leave, but before I could take another step, Sarah called after me. "Oh, and by the way, I saw him last night."

"Who?"

"Connor." Her voice was light, but her eyes were anything but.

"Sarah, you're making this—"

"No," she interrupted, voice low now. "I saw him leaving his place with... someone." She let the word hang in the air, unspoken but heavy. "They went inside, and they were there for a while."

The words hit me harder than I expected. A sudden, sharp twist in my chest made me feel like I'd swallowed something bitter. "What?" I asked, more sharply than I intended.

She raised her hands in mock surrender. "Hey, don't shoot the messenger. I just thought you might want to know."

I didn't say anything as I turned and walked away, my thoughts scattered like leaves in the wind. The image of Connor with someone else, someone who was there with him, in his space, pulled at something deep inside of me. I wasn't sure if it was jealousy or disappointment, or a mixture of both. All I knew was that it didn't sit right, and I didn't know why.

By the time I reached my front door, I could feel my heart beating faster. Not because of what Sarah had said—but because of the way it had made me feel. I had no claim over Connor. None. He didn't owe me anything, and I didn't owe him anything either. So why did it feel like the ground beneath me had shifted?

I walked inside, trying to shake off the tension building in my chest, but it wouldn't go away. My phone buzzed in my pocket. I pulled it out, half-expecting it to be another message from Sarah, but the screen flashed with a name I hadn't expected to see. Connor.

My fingers hovered over the screen, hesitation pooling in my gut. Should I answer? Or should I pretend like I didn't see it? I swiped the screen open before I could talk myself out of it.

It was a short message, just a few words, but they hit me like a freight train:

We need to talk.

And just like that, everything I thought I knew about Connor—and about myself—came crashing down around me.

Chapter 9: The Smoke and the Silence

The evening air carries a chill, the kind that settles deep into your bones. I pull my jacket tighter around me, though it's more for the feeling of control than any real warmth. The streets are quiet, too quiet, like the calm before a storm that's been too long in the making. My mind is still spinning from the note, from the unmistakable urgency of the warning. Someone doesn't want me digging into things, and they'll go to any lengths to stop me.

But I don't flinch. I never flinch. It's a family trait, this stubbornness. My mother used to tell me I was built for a storm, but I always thought she meant it figuratively, as a way to explain my reckless streak. Now, I'm starting to wonder if she saw something I didn't. A storm is coming, and I'm standing right in its path, refusing to move.

Connor's place is just up ahead, a small, unassuming townhouse that's too well-kept for my liking. Everything about him screams 'too good to be true,' from the way he keeps his space pristine, to the careful way he watches me without ever really seeing me. I knock on his door before I can second-guess myself, the sound sharp and final in the otherwise still night.

He opens it almost immediately, like he's been waiting for me. But there's a tension in his posture, a stiffness that wasn't there before, and it gnaws at me. The lines around his eyes seem a little deeper, the set of his jaw a little tighter. He's been under pressure. I can feel it.

"You look like you've got something to say." His voice is calm, too calm, like he's bracing for whatever is coming.

"Can we talk?" I ask, stepping inside without waiting for him to invite me. I'm already on edge, and I need to get this out before my thoughts spiral any further.

"Sure." His voice doesn't match the guarded look in his eyes, and it makes my skin crawl. Something's off. "What's going on?"

I pull the crumpled note from my pocket and hand it to him. His gaze flickers over the words, but his face doesn't change. He doesn't seem surprised, which sends a shockwave of anxiety straight through me.

"Who sent this?" I ask, crossing my arms. "And why didn't you tell me?"

"Because it doesn't change anything," he says, his voice low, measured. He hands the note back, his fingers brushing mine for the briefest moment, a spark of something dangerous passing between us. But I ignore it, focusing instead on the words that still echo in my mind.

"I don't think you understand. Whoever did this... they're not playing games. I'm not just some girl you can brush off." My voice cracks slightly on the last words, but I swallow the weakness. There's no time for that now.

He sighs, running a hand through his dark hair. "I know you think you're helping, but you're not. You don't know what you're up against. I do."

I can feel the heat rising in my chest, a mix of frustration and disbelief. "Then why don't you tell me what's really going on? Why the secrecy, Connor? You're not protecting me. You're just shutting me out."

He opens his mouth, closes it again. I see the battle in his eyes, the tension between wanting to tell me and knowing he can't. It's a weight he's been carrying for too long, and it shows. But it's too much for me to ignore anymore.

"I'm trying to keep you safe," he says, finally, the words heavy with something more than concern. But there's a defensiveness in his tone that doesn't sit right. It feels like a shield, not a reassurance.

"By lying to me?" I step forward, the space between us closing, my voice rising despite myself. "By pretending I don't have a right to know what's happening? You're not my knight in shining armor, Connor. You're just a man with secrets, and I've had enough of that."

For a moment, he doesn't say anything. His lips press into a thin line, his brow furrowing. I can tell he's debating something, weighing his options, but he's holding something back—something important.

"Please, just trust me," he finally says, his voice low, almost pleading.

I shake my head, my resolve hardening. Trust him? After everything? I don't think so. "No. I don't trust you, Connor. Not anymore."

His face darkens, and for a second, I see a flash of something in his eyes—anger, maybe, or hurt. I can't tell. But it's gone in an instant, replaced by the calm mask he's so good at wearing. He steps back, putting distance between us.

"I'm sorry you feel that way," he says, the words cold, final. "But this is bigger than you and me."

I stare at him, unable to process what I'm hearing. There's so much more to this, more than he's letting on, and it's becoming clear that the man I thought I knew is nothing like the one standing in front of me now.

"Fine," I say, turning on my heel. "But I'll find out, with or without your help." The words are harsh, but I can't stop them. I'm done playing by his rules. I don't need his permission to uncover the truth.

I leave before he can say another word, the door clicking shut behind me with a sound that feels like an ending. My breath is shallow, my hands trembling slightly, but I push the fear down. I've come this far, and I won't back down now. No matter what secrets Connor is hiding, I'm going to find the answers.

The city seems quieter than usual as I walk, the faint hum of traffic distant and muffled, as though the world itself is holding its breath. I'm far past needing comfort now, past anything that feels like safety. I have a goal, a hard, jagged thing lodged deep inside me, and nothing will stop me from pursuing it. Not Connor, not the faceless threat that's now shadowing me, and definitely not the creeping sense of doubt that gnaws at the edges of my resolve. I'm just about done with questions. From here on, it's answers or nothing.

The wind picks up as I head toward the café. The one where I met him first. The one I'd considered harmless—until now. Until everything had changed and the quiet familiarity of it all seemed suddenly suffocating. Still, there's a strange comfort in the routine. People always seem to forget how easy it is to lose yourself in something small, something constant, even when you know it's never been what you thought it was.

Inside, the familiar scent of freshly brewed coffee wraps around me, thick and warm, the hum of conversation filling the corners of the room. It's here, though, that I find myself hesitating. Because for all the reassurance the place offers, I know that not even the strongest latte can dull the sharp edge of betrayal curling in my chest.

I spot him before he sees me, a flash of that too-familiar green jacket tucked away in the far corner. Connor, with his perfectly styled hair and the too-cool-for-school expression that never quite meets his eyes. I know that look. I know it all too well—the one that tells me he's hiding something. That something has always been there, even if I didn't want to acknowledge it.

But I push it aside, because that's not what I came here for. No more distractions. The note, the message, the warning. It all circles back to one thing: I need to find out who's pulling the strings, and I'm running out of people I can trust.

He doesn't notice me at first, and for a moment, I almost turn around. I almost walk out. There's something about his stillness that unsettles me, the way he sits with his back to the room, as if he's waiting for me to find him, as if he expects me to walk right into whatever trap he's set.

I don't. Instead, I walk up to the counter, ordering a coffee with the kind of detachment I've been practicing for days. The barista is all smiles, unaware that everything I thought I knew is slipping away, leaving only sharp edges and unanswered questions. I take the drink when it's ready, but I can't bring myself to go over and sit with him—not just yet. Not until I know what I'm walking into.

So I pace, like a caged animal, as I wait for him to make the first move. The seconds drag on, and with each passing moment, I feel a little more exposed, a little less certain that this meeting is going to be anything close to the peaceful conversation I had envisioned when I first planned to confront him.

Finally, he turns his head, catches my eye. There's something there, something dangerous and unreadable, but I'm too far gone to turn away. Instead, I walk to the table, set my coffee down with deliberate calm, and take a seat across from him.

"Got your message," I say, staring straight at him. His eyes flicker, but only for an instant.

"I didn't send you a message," he replies, his tone even. Too even.

"Oh?" I let the word hang in the air, heavy with implication. "You don't think it's a bit odd that someone decided to slip an anonymous note under my door, warning me to stop asking questions? And it's got your name all over it?"

The silence between us thickens. He shifts in his seat, just slightly, enough that I notice, enough to confirm that my words have landed. "What do you want from me?" he asks, his voice low, barely above a whisper.

I lean forward, lowering my voice to match his. "I want the truth, Connor. I want to know why you're keeping secrets, and why you think I'm some kind of child who needs to be protected from the reality of the situation. If you're in over your head, then fine, but don't pull me into your mess and expect me to stay quiet."

His eyes narrow, the faintest twitch of frustration crossing his face. He opens his mouth to speak, then closes it again, as if he's measuring every word, weighing them in a way I'm not sure I trust. "It's not that simple," he finally says, his voice strained. "You wouldn't understand."

"Try me," I reply sharply. "You'd be surprised what I understand."

The words hang in the air, a challenge that seems to make him bristle. But it's not anger that crosses his features now. It's something darker, something more like resignation. As if he's been waiting for this moment, for me to finally drag whatever it is he's hiding out into the light.

"You really want to know?" he asks, voice barely audible. "You really want to understand how deep this goes?"

I nod, because there's no going back. No more pretending. "Yes. I do."

He stares at me for a long moment, his gaze hard and calculating, like he's trying to decide if I'm worth the trouble of telling. When he speaks again, his words are slow, deliberate. "You should have stayed away, but now it's too late. There's no turning back."

I'm not sure what I expected from him, but this? This feels like the beginning of something much worse than I had imagined. Something that might be far beyond my ability to control. But

I've already crossed that line, haven't I? And once you've crossed it, there's no going back.

The coffee in my hand has gone lukewarm, a forgotten vessel between my fingers as Connor's words hang like smoke in the air. "There's no turning back," he had said, his voice holding a sharpness I wasn't prepared for. He was serious. And for the first time, I wondered if I'd made a mistake by pushing this far.

But it was too late to turn back now, wasn't it? It was too late to act like everything was fine, to pretend I hadn't seen the signs—the little things that didn't add up. The hurried phone calls, the cryptic messages that never seemed to make it past his inbox, the guarded looks that spoke more than his words ever did. If I had any chance at understanding what was really going on, it had to be now.

"I don't understand, Connor," I finally said, my voice quiet but laced with an edge of frustration. "Why do you think I can't handle it? You think I'm just going to back off because someone slipped a note under my door?"

His eyes flicker, something akin to fear flashing behind them before he quickly masks it with an unreadable expression. He shifts in his chair, rubbing the back of his neck like he's trying to hide the fact that I've caught him off guard. But it's too late for that. The mask is slipping, and I can see the cracks beneath it.

"I never said you couldn't handle it," he murmurs, almost to himself. "I'm trying to protect you."

"Protect me?" I laugh, but it's not a pleasant sound. "From what, exactly? The truth?" The words feel bitter as they leave my mouth, but I can't stop them. "If you were really trying to protect me, you'd tell me what's going on instead of pushing me away."

His jaw tightens, and for a brief moment, I think he's going to say something, maybe even admit something—something important. But the moment passes as quickly as it came, and he settles into that cold silence that I've come to know too well. The silence that feels like an answer in itself.

I lean forward, unable to stop the words that spill out next. "What aren't you telling me, Connor? What's so dangerous that you can't let me in?"

For a moment, he just looks at me, and in that look, I see everything I've been afraid of. It's not just about keeping me safe—it's about something much darker. Something that involves more than just us, something that's been building long before I walked into his life.

"Get out of here," he finally says, his voice low, threatening. The words are a blow, a dismissal I hadn't expected but should have. He stands, his body blocking any chance of escape. "You need to walk away. Now."

I stand frozen, unsure if I'm hearing him right. "You think I'm just going to leave? After everything?"

He doesn't answer, just steps back and turns toward the door. The movement is sharp, deliberate. There's nothing gentle in the way he does it. He's done. And I can feel the door slamming shut behind me—not physically, but emotionally, the way he's shutting me out for good.

I want to shout, to demand answers, but something in me hesitates. Maybe it's because I can see the desperation in his eyes now. It's not the same look he had before—this one's full of something darker, something I've never seen from him.

I take a step back, my mind reeling. Was I wrong to push? Was I wrong to think I could get close enough to uncover the truth? But then again, what else could I do? Sit back and wait while the world spins around me, waiting for some miracle to make it all go away? No, I wasn't going to let it go. Not now. Not after everything that had happened.

My heart races as I back away from him, moving slowly as if trying not to disturb the fragile silence between us. I know I've lost something—something important—but I can't tell if it's trust, or maybe something even more vital.

The air between us is thick, oppressive, and I feel it pressing on my chest as I stand there, fighting the impulse to run. Every part of me wants to bolt, to get away from this, but I know that's not the answer. I can't run. Not now. Not when I'm this close to something.

I open my mouth to say something, anything, to break the tension, but before I can speak, the phone in my pocket buzzes—a sharp, insistent sound that cuts through the silence like a knife.

I reach for it, pulling it out before I even realize what I'm doing. It's an unknown number. My stomach tightens.

"I don't have time for games," I mutter under my breath, almost wishing I could throw the phone out the window. But curiosity, that damnable thing, pulls me in. I press the screen, bring the phone to my ear, and listen.

A voice I don't recognize—cold, distorted, almost mechanical—greets me. "Stop asking questions. We know what you're doing, and we're watching you. Don't push too far."

My heart skips a beat, and for the first time, I feel the cold fingers of fear crawl down my spine. "Who is this?" I demand, trying to steady my voice.

There's a pause, and then a laugh, soft and disconcerting. "You'll find out soon enough." The line goes dead.

I stand there, frozen, as the phone slips from my fingers. It's like everything—the world, the air, my breath—has stopped, and I'm standing at the edge of something I'm not sure I'm ready to face.

Connor watches me from the door, his expression unreadable. I don't know whether to run or stay, to confront him or keep pushing forward on my own. The walls are closing in, and everything I thought I knew is crumbling into dust.

"Tell me what's going on," I whisper, but the words hang between us, unanswered. The silence is deafening now, and I know that whatever happens next will change everything.

Chapter 10: Fanning the Flames

The doorbell rings at an hour where most sensible people are already tucked into their beds, dreaming of soft pillows and empty calendars. I glance at the clock. 11:42 p.m. That's just late enough for me to hesitate, wondering if I should ignore it, pretend I didn't hear the chime. But the urgency in the sound pricks something in me, a curiosity I can't ignore. My fingers grip the door handle, hesitant, as I wonder who it could possibly be at this hour. Then I swing it open, and there he stands.

Connor.

Of course it's him.

He's never looked more out of place. His usual sharp edges, his confident stride, the ever-present cocky smile—all gone. Instead, he's standing there, shifting uncomfortably from one foot to the other, a breath caught in his throat. The wind tousles his hair, and his shoulders, usually squared with ease, sag slightly under the weight of an unseen burden.

I raise an eyebrow. "You're... at my door. At this hour. It's not like you," I say, leaning against the doorframe, arms crossed, trying to mask the confusion and—let's be honest—mild concern bubbling inside me.

He shifts again, eyes flicking to the ground before meeting mine. "I know. I didn't think I'd be here either, but... I need to talk. If you have time."

A strange tension fills the space between us, the kind you feel just before the air cracks with a storm. I know I should say something, close the door, send him away. My instincts scream at me to protect myself from whatever this is—because I know, I know without a doubt, that the Connor I've come to know and the one standing before me are two different people. But I don't.

I step aside, motioning for him to come in.

"Yeah. Sure. Come in." I try to sound casual, but even I can hear the edge of hesitation in my voice.

He steps over the threshold like it's a decision he's spent far too long deliberating. The door closes softly behind him, and the quiet of the house seems to swallow us whole. The silence stretches between us for a long moment. It's awkward. Uncomfortable.

He runs a hand through his hair, a nervous gesture I've never seen from him before. The fact that it's happening now, here, in my living room, throws me off balance. Connor doesn't do nervous. But this? This is something else.

"I... uh, I don't even know where to start," he mutters, taking a step toward the couch and then quickly sitting down, but not quite settling. It's like his body can't decide if it's ready to relax or run.

I sit across from him, folding my legs beneath me, waiting. I keep my eyes on him, not saying a word, because I've learned by now that Connor won't speak unless the silence is unbearable enough for him to crack.

"Look, I'm not good at this. Talking about... things. But I can't keep pretending like I'm fine." He pauses, then lets out a bitter laugh. "I mean, I'm a mess. I don't know how to fix it, or if it can even be fixed. I don't even know why I came here."

I lean forward slightly, my curiosity piqued, my mind racing through a thousand possibilities. There's something in his tone that betrays his usual tough exterior. This is raw, real, a side of him I've never seen.

"Connor," I begin, my voice softer than I intend, "You don't have to do this. You know that, right?"

His eyes meet mine, and for the briefest second, there's a flicker of something that could almost be vulnerability. Almost.

"I don't," he agrees quietly, "but I need to."

The air grows thick with unsaid words, a weight that neither of us is ready to lift. I can feel it in the way he shifts uncomfortably in his seat, the way his fingers grip the edge of his jeans like they're his anchor.

And then he speaks.

"I never talked about my brother. Not to anyone. Not like this." He says it in a tone that's both matter-of-fact and broken.

I swallow, suddenly unsure if I'm ready for what's coming next. But I nod. "You don't have to. If you're not—"

"No, I want to," he interrupts, his voice quieter, more composed now, like he's making peace with whatever words are about to spill from his mouth. "It's just... my brother, he was everything to me. He was my best friend, my partner in crime, the one person who got me, you know? We were supposed to do all this stuff together. The big stuff. The important stuff."

His gaze drifts to the floor, and I can see the pain flicker behind his eyes, like a scar that never healed.

"I lost him," he says finally, his voice barely above a whisper.

The room feels too small all of a sudden, the silence heavy with his confession. I don't know what to say, because no words seem enough, no comfort adequate. Instead, I just nod, leaning forward as I search his face for something to anchor me to this moment, something to keep me tethered to the man who, for all his bravado, is now laid bare before me.

"Connor," I start, my voice shaky despite my best efforts, "I'm so sorry."

He shakes his head, but it's not in rejection. It's like he's rejecting the sympathy, the pity, because it's not what he wants. It's not what he's asking for.

"I don't want your sympathy," he murmurs. "I don't know what I want. I just... needed someone to hear me. To know I'm not as put together as I look."

I can feel the air between us crackling, a shift happening, something that pulls me in deeper, farther into a connection I'm not sure I'm ready for. But it's happening anyway.

His eyes meet mine once more, and for a moment, the world outside doesn't exist. The past doesn't matter. Only the weight of his words, the weight of the quiet understanding that seems to wrap around us, keeping us grounded in this shared space.

And I realize, with a jolt, that I'm playing with fire.

There's a strange stillness that settles around us, a quiet that stretches so thick I can feel it pressing against my chest, making it hard to breathe. Connor's sitting there, looking like a man who's just confessed the most important secret of his life and is now waiting for the world to come crashing down. I don't have anything profound to say to him—no neat phrases, no comforting words that will make this pain vanish. What I do have, though, is a quiet understanding, an awareness that sometimes the hardest thing to do is to just listen and let someone else exist in their truth for a while.

So, I sit. I don't rush him. I don't offer to fill the silence with my own stories, my own comforts. I just sit, letting the weight of the moment hang between us, giving him room to breathe, to think, to speak if he wants to.

Connor's fingers drum absently on the arm of the couch. The sound of it, steady and rhythmic, almost like a heartbeat, pulls me from my thoughts. When he looks up at me, there's something new in his eyes—something I wasn't expecting. It's not quite shame, not exactly regret, but something close. Something raw, something that says that, for once, he's not the one holding all the cards.

He shifts, drawing in a breath as if he's preparing himself to say something else. I can tell he's not done yet, that there's more beneath the surface, more layers to this story. And I can't lie—I'm dying to know what comes next.

"I used to think... I used to think I was invincible," he starts, his voice a little rougher now, like he's trying to choke back something more than words. "You know, I thought if I could just keep moving, keep pushing forward, I wouldn't have to deal with the things that came after."

He pauses, his gaze flicking to the window, as if the night outside could offer him some sort of solace. There's no solace to be found out there, not for either of us. The quiet of the night is just a mirror of the storm inside him. I'm not sure what to say, so I stay quiet, waiting for him to find his way through this storm of words he's trying to untangle.

"My brother," he continues, and the way he says it makes the name feel like a prayer, heavy with meaning. "He died in a stupid accident. Just like that. Gone. And there was nothing I could do. I wasn't there when he needed me."

I blink, the sudden shift in the air catching me off guard. This isn't what I was expecting. There's a crack in his voice now, just enough to make me realize how deep this pain runs.

"I wasn't there," he repeats, more quietly this time. "I was... too busy being a goddamn idiot. Too wrapped up in my own stupid world to see the things that really mattered."

It's hard to know how to respond to this, to this broken, fractured version of Connor, the one who's used to keeping his cards close to his chest, only showing what's necessary. I can't help but wonder just how long he's been holding all of this in, how many nights he's spent alone, pretending like everything's fine when it clearly hasn't been.

I don't know how to offer comfort without making it worse, so instead, I simply nod. "It's not your fault," I say, my voice quieter now, softer than I usually speak to him.

Connor looks at me then, really looks at me, as if trying to gauge whether or not I actually believe what I'm saying. I don't have all the answers. I don't even know if I believe it myself. But in that moment, I mean it. I mean that none of us are perfect, and sometimes the world throws curveballs we're not ready for. And it's not our fault when we can't catch them.

"I wasn't there for him," he says again, the words coming slower now, like he's trying to accept something that won't let go. "I didn't even go to the funeral. I couldn't face it. Couldn't face the idea that he was really gone. And then, I just... kept running. I kept doing everything I could to distract myself, to keep from thinking about how I failed him. How I let him down."

There's a tightness in my chest, a part of me that wants to reach out to him, tell him that I understand, that I'm here if he needs me. But I know he's not ready for that. Not yet.

Instead, I simply sit, letting his words hang in the air like smoke, heavy and curling around us. And then, something unexpected happens. He lets out a breath, a long, weary exhale that seems to release some of the weight from his shoulders.

"Anyway, I'm not really good at this talking thing," he says, managing a faint smile, though it's tinged with sadness. "I don't know what I thought would happen by showing up here. But I guess I just needed to say it out loud, to admit it to someone."

His gaze lingers on me for a moment, searching my face like he's waiting for something—some sign that I won't judge him, that I won't see him differently for it. And I realize, with a sharp jolt, that this is the part where he lets himself be vulnerable, where he risks falling apart in front of someone else. He's afraid of that. Afraid of what will happen if I see the cracks in his carefully constructed armor.

I don't say anything at first. I don't have the right words to make it all better, to fix the unfixable. Instead, I offer him a soft smile, the kind of smile that says, "I'm not going anywhere." And for a moment, just a moment, it's enough.

"You're not alone in this," I say, my voice steady now, more certain. "I don't have all the answers, but you don't have to carry it by yourself."

His eyes soften, and for a brief, fleeting second, I see something in him that I didn't expect—something fragile, something that needs saving. The thought makes my chest tighten, makes me realize just how much I've let him in without even trying.

But just as quickly as it appears, that moment fades. Connor stands up, pulling himself together with the ease of someone who's spent years hiding his vulnerability from the world. He's not ready for more than this. And I understand that. But I also know that something has shifted between us, something deeper, something undeniable.

"Thanks," he says, his voice quieter now, almost like a whisper. And with that, he walks out of the room, leaving me alone with the weight of everything he's shared.

And I'm left there, standing in the quiet, knowing that I'm in deeper than I thought. But I'm also not sure I want to get out.

The door clicks shut behind him with a finality that resonates in the quiet of my living room. The weight of what's just transpired hovers like a thick fog, settling in the corners, making it hard to breathe, hard to think. I stand there, watching him slip back into his usual armor, the one he's so practiced at wearing, as though nothing had changed. As though, just a moment ago, he hadn't let me see the cracks in his perfect façade.

It's disorienting, to see him like this. Vulnerable, for a split second, a person, not the walls he's spent years building around himself.

I'm not sure how long I stand there, frozen in place, watching him. His fingers are still flexing as if trying to shake off the memory of everything he's just said, every unguarded word he's let slip between us. He takes a step back, a few inches of space like he's suddenly realizing he's too close. To me. To the truth. To everything.

"Look, uh, thanks for listening," he says, his voice low and strangely tight. I wonder, for just a second, if he regrets saying any of it. But then again, this is Connor—he doesn't regret anything. He just moves on. Always moves on.

I force myself to speak, to fill the silence that has grown unbearably thick between us. "You don't have to thank me," I say, my voice steady, though I can feel my heart drumming in my chest, each beat loud and relentless. "It's not like I'm going anywhere. You've got nothing to hide here."

But as I say the words, I'm not so sure if I believe them.

Because for a fleeting second, I think maybe I need to hide. Maybe the truth—his truth—has opened something I'm not sure I can close again. The connection between us is sharper now, more electric, like a wire waiting to snap under too much pressure. I'm not sure how I'll navigate it, but I know, with unsettling clarity, that it's already tangled between us in ways neither of us can undo.

Connor hesitates, a momentary flicker of uncertainty crossing his face before he masks it again with that cool indifference. "I'll see you around," he says, his words clipped, almost too quick. And with that, he walks toward the door, each step deliberate and detached.

I don't want him to leave. Not yet. I don't know why, but I can't shake the feeling that there's something more here, something unspoken, something that's been building between us long before tonight. But I also know better than to reach out, to try and stop him. Because once I do, there's no turning back.

He opens the door, just a crack, then pauses, his hand lingering on the doorknob. It's like he's waiting for something—waiting for me to say something, anything, to break the silence between us.

I open my mouth, not sure what I'm going to say, but it's already too late. He's already gone, the door clicking shut with a finality that makes my chest tighten.

For the next few minutes, I stand there in the aftermath, feeling the weight of his words, the rawness of everything he just shared, pressing down on me like a thousand invisible hands. My mind races, trying to piece together the fragments of what just happened. It wasn't supposed to go like this. But then again, nothing ever does when Connor's involved.

I shake my head, pacing the length of the room. This wasn't supposed to happen. I wasn't supposed to get tangled up in his mess, in his history. And yet, here I am, standing in the middle of it, drowning in the weight of his confession. He's left, but his presence lingers, like smoke that won't clear, no matter how many windows I open to let the air in.

I move toward the window, pressing my palms against the cool glass, trying to focus on anything other than the storm inside my head. I can't stop thinking about what he said, about how he needed to say it out loud. But the more I think about it, the more I realize—he needs more than words. He needs someone who can carry the weight of that story with him. Someone who can understand what it means to live with the guilt, the regret. And I know, deep down, that I can't be that person. I can't carry that burden, not when my own heart is already full of things I can't sort through.

But as I stand there, staring out into the night, I realize something else. Something that makes my heart race in a way I don't fully understand.

Maybe I want to carry it. Maybe, just maybe, I'm already too far in.

My phone buzzes in my pocket, snapping me out of my spiraling thoughts. I glance down at the screen, half-expecting it to be a message from someone else—maybe my sister, maybe a work email, maybe anything to break the tense silence that's settled over me. But instead, it's a single, simple text from Connor.

We need to talk.

I feel the words hit me like a shockwave, the message loaded with something I can't quite decipher. My pulse quickens, the uncertainty swirling around me, knotting itself tighter and tighter. I stare at the screen, unsure of what to do next, unsure of what this even means. But as my fingers hover over the screen, ready to reply, I hear a knock on the door.

Sharp. Urgent.

I freeze, my breath catching in my throat. I don't need to check the peephole. I already know who it is.

And for the first time, I don't know if I'm ready for whatever comes next.

Chapter 11: The Heat of Confession

The smell of smoke lingered in my nose long after I stepped out of the fire station's dimly lit archives. The heavy scent of charred paper clung to me, a ghost of something once vital now reduced to ash. I should have never gone digging through those old files—should have left well enough alone. But curiosity has a nasty way of sneaking up on you, doesn't it? I had been there, of course, to search for something else entirely. Something less complicated. A box of fire reports that needed to be filed and sorted. But there it was, shoved in between stacks of reports that had yellowed with age, a small, charred notebook, its leather cover cracked from heat, yet still stubbornly holding together, like it had been waiting for me.

My fingers shook as I flipped it open, my heart thudding in my chest. The handwriting was unmistakable—Connor's. I recognized the loops and slashes of his cursive as if they were etched into my skin. The words inside were a mixture of a language only the fire could have understood and the sharp, honest pain of someone trying to make sense of things that didn't make sense. It was a piece of him I didn't know existed, a shadow I didn't know had been lurking in the corners of his mind.

I didn't want to read it. But I did.

Page after page, I found fragments of thoughts—grief, guilt, frustration. The kind of emotions that left no room for sleep. I could almost hear his voice in the words, as if he had been muttering them under his breath late at night, when the world around him was quiet enough for him to think. To confess. Each sentence was a cut to my chest. A reminder that, no matter how many years we had spent building a life together, there were pieces of him I would never fully understand.

I knew what I had to do. And I hated myself for it.

Connor was in the living room when I walked through the door. The soft glow of the setting sun filtered through the blinds, casting long shadows across his broad shoulders. He was sitting on the couch, his legs stretched out in front of him, a book balanced on his knee. But his eyes weren't on the pages. They were on me.

I could feel the tension crackling in the air before I even opened my mouth. He could tell something was wrong. Of course he could. He was my husband. He knew the rhythm of my heartbeat like no one else.

I didn't sit down. I didn't even bother to hide the journal in my hand. I just stood there, watching him, waiting for him to say something. Anything.

His gaze flicked to the notebook, and then back to me. "What is it?" His voice was low, steady, but the way his jaw tightened told me that something was happening beneath the surface. Something he wasn't ready to face.

I tossed the journal onto the coffee table, the thud of it landing between us sharp and final. "You tell me," I said, my voice barely steady, thick with the mix of disbelief and betrayal.

Connor's eyes darted to the journal, his expression unreadable, before he slowly reached for it. His fingers brushed the cover, and I could see the way he hesitated, as if trying to decide how to approach a landmine. The old leather creaked beneath his touch, and for a moment, the room fell into an unsettling silence.

"You found it," he murmured, his voice almost a whisper.

I nodded, my throat tight. "How long has this been here? How long have you been keeping it from me?"

His eyes met mine, and there it was again—something unspoken, a flicker of something behind his gaze that I couldn't quite place. But it wasn't guilt, not exactly. More like... regret. And maybe even fear.

"It's not what you think," he said, his voice low, but it wasn't reassuring.

The words stung, but I couldn't stop myself from pushing. "Then what is it, Connor? What's in it? What the hell have you been hiding from me all these years?"

I wanted answers. I needed them. The ache that had settled in my chest from the moment I opened that journal had grown into something almost unbearable. I wasn't prepared for what I might find, but I needed to hear it from him. I needed him to explain the parts of his life that had been closed off from me, the things he had carried silently, like a burden too heavy for just one person to bear.

Connor closed his eyes, inhaling deeply, as if he was trying to steady himself before facing whatever came next. "You deserve the truth," he said, his words deliberate, as if he were testing them in his mind before releasing them into the world.

And that was the moment. The moment when I realized that whatever he said next would change everything. Because there was something in the air—something crackling like an electrical storm, as though we were on the edge of something we couldn't take back.

He placed the journal in my hands, his fingers lingering over mine for just a second too long. "It's all in there," he said quietly, and I could hear the weight of the confession in his voice. "Everything."

I opened the journal again, flipping through the pages, each word a raw confession, a piece of a puzzle I hadn't known was missing. I could feel the heat of Connor's gaze on me as I read, the tension rising between us like the heat before a storm. I didn't know how much I was willing to hear, or how much of it I would be able to believe, but in that moment, I knew I couldn't stop. I needed to know everything. Every last secret. Every last lie.

I didn't know what I was expecting when I opened the journal again—maybe a confession, some kind of admission that would bring everything crashing down in one swift, inevitable moment. Instead, I found a jumble of thoughts that were as fragmented as the man sitting across from me. Connor's words poured out like a drip from a leaky faucet—nothing whole, nothing clear. But each sentence weighed more than the last, as if the pages themselves had absorbed years of regret and silent burdens.

"You were always the strongest person I knew," I read aloud. "But sometimes, that strength was the thing that kept us apart."

The words twisted inside my chest. I could feel his presence behind them, the way he had always held everything together, like some unsung hero who thought he could carry the weight of the world and never ask for help. He'd spent so much time trying to save everyone else, he'd never given himself the permission to be saved. Not even by me.

Connor shifted uneasily on the couch, the leather creaking beneath him, but he didn't interrupt. I could feel him watching me, his gaze heavy, desperate, and yet, strangely tender. Almost like he didn't want to be caught staring but couldn't tear himself away from whatever this was—the final unraveling of the threads that had tied us together for so long.

The next entry was less polished, more raw. I could practically hear the desperation in his words.

I keep thinking about the fire. The one that could've been avoided. What if I'd made a different choice? What if I hadn't been the one to respond? What if I hadn't tried to be the hero, the one who always gets there first?

I swallowed hard. The fire. The one that had nearly cost him his life. The one that I'd never fully understood, the one I had tried so hard to push to the back of my mind, along with the nightmares that had followed him for months. I didn't know how to help him then. I didn't know how to get through to him, how to get him to stop pushing me away when all I wanted to do was pull him close. But I wasn't the one who needed saving. He was.

I looked up at Connor, my throat tightening. "Why didn't you tell me? Why didn't you let me in?" My voice cracked, and I hated how fragile I sounded, how desperate.

He closed his eyes, the weight of my question clearly sinking in. His hand ran through his hair, the action slow, deliberate. I could see the weariness in his posture, the way his shoulders slumped with the weight of the years that had passed. Years where he had kept this side of himself hidden from me. From everyone.

"I thought I was protecting you," he said quietly, the words slipping out like an apology that wasn't quite enough to mend the gap between us. "I thought if I kept it to myself, kept it buried deep enough, it wouldn't destroy us. That it wouldn't destroy you."

I let out a bitter laugh, a sound that didn't feel like mine. "You think hiding things from me was protecting me?" I shook my head, my hands trembling with a mix of frustration and something deeper—something I couldn't quite name. "You think that after all these years, I wouldn't have been able to handle whatever you were carrying? You don't get to make that decision for me, Connor."

His lips pressed together in a thin line, and I saw the guilt in his eyes—raw, exposed. He was realizing, finally, what I had known for so long. That the walls he had built around himself were never going to keep me out. Not forever.

"You're right," he admitted, his voice thick with emotion. "I was selfish. I thought I could do it on my own, but I was wrong." His gaze softened, the flicker of something deep inside him—regret or maybe relief—sparking in his eyes. "I should've let you in. But I didn't know how."

I sat down beside him, the space between us now smaller, though still far too wide. I didn't know how to fix this. I didn't even know if it could be fixed. The truth, once revealed, has a way of altering things, shifting them into something unrecognizable. But there was something about his voice, the sincerity behind his confession, that made me believe—at least for a moment—that we weren't beyond repair.

I reached out, my hand tentative at first, but he caught it, his fingers warm against mine. And there it was. The familiarity. The connection that had always been there, even when we didn't want to acknowledge it. We had both been broken in different ways. But we had both carried the scars in silence, afraid to speak them aloud, afraid of what they might do to us.

But now, they were out in the open. The journal, the confession, the unspoken truths. We couldn't undo any of it, but maybe that was the point. Maybe it was only by facing it together that we could begin to understand how to move forward.

"I don't know what's next," I said, my voice quieter now. "But I can't keep pretending that everything's fine when it's not."

Connor nodded slowly, his thumb brushing over the back of my hand in a gesture that felt both fragile and comforting. "I never wanted to hurt you," he whispered, his voice cracking with the weight of it. "But I did. I can't take that back."

I squeezed his hand, leaning my head against his shoulder, not knowing what tomorrow would bring, but knowing that, for the first time in a long time, we weren't standing alone anymore. And maybe that was enough. For now.

The silence between us stretched out like a canyon, the distance between us unspoken and vast. I could hear the soft, rhythmic ticking of the clock on the wall, each second stretching into infinity. And then, as if the air itself had been holding its breath, Connor broke the stillness. His voice was low, gravelly, like it hadn't been used in far too long.

"I never meant for you to find it like this."

His words were simple, but they carried a weight that made my stomach twist. I wanted to throw the journal at him, to demand the truth in one big, explosive rush, but I knew better than that. If there was one thing I'd learned about Connor, it was that you couldn't rush him. Not in this. Not with something this big.

Instead, I watched him, his eyes flicking nervously between the journal and my face. His fingers fidgeted at the edges of the table, toying with the corner of a napkin. I knew this game too well—he was stalling.

I folded my arms across my chest and leaned back against the couch, not breaking eye contact. "So, what is it then, Connor? What is all of this? Because, from where I'm sitting, it looks like you've been keeping secrets from me. And not just any secrets. These are the kind of secrets that make people change. The kind that leave scars you can't see, but you sure as hell feel."

He opened his mouth to say something, but the words caught in his throat. I could see the struggle in his eyes—the fight between the man who wanted to tell me everything and the one who didn't know how to let go. I wondered, for a fleeting second, if the man I'd married had ever really known how to speak about his feelings. Maybe that was the problem all along.

"I didn't want you to see me like that," he said after a long pause, his voice quieter now. "I didn't want you to know the things I've seen. The things I've done."

The words hit me harder than I expected, like a punch to the gut. "What do you mean, 'the things you've done'?" My voice trembled, and for a moment, I hated myself for it. This wasn't about me, wasn't about my feelings. It was about him—about his truth and the darkness that seemed to have swallowed him whole.

Connor shifted uncomfortably in his seat, leaning forward with his elbows on his knees, his hands pressed together in a prayer-like pose. "You're not ready for that," he murmured, almost to himself.

My heart slammed against my ribcage, and the hurt rose up in me like a wave, fierce and overwhelming. "So, what? You get to decide when I'm ready? You get to keep things from me because you think I can't handle it? Is that it, Connor?"

He flinched, the edge of his jaw tightening. But I wasn't done. The words were tumbling out of me now, and I couldn't stop them if I tried.

"You think I haven't seen the way you've been pulling away? You think I haven't noticed the long nights, the late phone calls, the way you're never really here? You think I'm blind, Connor? Do you think I wouldn't notice the cracks forming, slowly at first, and then—"

His hand shot out, grabbing my wrist, silencing me in a split second. The contact was electric, jarring in its intensity. I hadn't expected him to touch me like that, and for a moment, I couldn't breathe.

"Don't," he said, his voice barely above a whisper, but there was something in it that made me freeze. "Just don't. Not like this. You don't know what you're asking for."

I stared at him, my pulse hammering in my neck. "Then tell me, Connor. Tell me what I'm asking for."

His grip loosened, and he pulled his hand back as though the contact had burned him. The tension in the room thickened, the words hanging in the air like a storm about to break.

"I don't know how to explain this," he said, the admission raw, vulnerable. "It's not just the fire. It's... everything after. The guilt. The things I've done, the things I've been part of. I never wanted you to see me like this."

I swallowed hard, every word that had come from him sinking deep into my bones. "And what do you want me to do with that,

Connor? Sit here, and pretend I don't know you're falling apart? Pretend I'm okay with you pushing me away every time you have a bad memory or a nightmare? You don't get to shut me out. Not anymore."

The look in his eyes shifted then. There was something deeper there, something I hadn't seen before. It was as though the walls he'd built around himself were crumbling, piece by piece, until only the raw truth remained.

"I never meant to hurt you," he murmured, his voice breaking as the weight of his confession seemed to crush him. "But I've been carrying this for so long, I don't know how to put it down. I don't know how to ask for help without making everything worse."

I didn't know what to say. What could I say? How could I fix something that felt so broken?

But before I could gather my thoughts, before I could make sense of the swirling mess inside me, there was a sound—sharp and sudden. A knock at the door.

It wasn't just any knock. It was quick, frantic, urgent. The kind of knock that makes your blood run cold.

Connor shot to his feet, his face draining of color. The air between us shifted again, this time with a sense of dread that coiled around my chest. He looked at me, his face tight with fear.

"I need you to stay here," he said, his voice tight, almost desperate. "Don't—don't open that door."

Before I could respond, he was already moving toward the hallway, his steps heavy, deliberate. The knock came again, louder this time, echoing through the house.

And just like that, everything changed.

Chapter 12: Scorched Secrets

I couldn't tell you the last time I had a moment of quiet. It seemed that in the days that followed the discovery of that journal, the world had become a blur of pressing deadlines and dangerous whispers. The pages of the journal sat on the kitchen table, open, as though daring me to keep reading, daring me to dig deeper into secrets I wasn't sure I was ready to face.

The soft hum of the refrigerator filled the silence as I wiped down the countertops for what felt like the tenth time. My hands, restless, moved in practiced circles, the rag gliding over the surface, but my mind was a million miles away. The journal was a constant presence, even when I wasn't looking at it. I could still smell the faint musty scent of the pages, like forgotten corners of some old attic I didn't want to visit. I hadn't told anyone about the discovery—well, not until Connor showed up on my doorstep in the dead of night.

His knock had been sharp, urgent. I knew it was him before I even glanced through the peephole. The tension in the air shifted when I opened the door to find him standing there, eyes narrowed, his hand gripping a black leather bag that I knew all too well. There was a fire in his gaze, something darker than the typical weariness of his late-night visits. He wasn't here to share a drink or swap stories like we usually did when the world felt like it was spinning too fast for either of us to keep up. No, tonight, there was something more.

"You're still up," Connor said, his voice rough with more than just tiredness.

I stepped aside to let him in, watching as he entered with that same, steady stride. He seemed to occupy more space than he really should, like a storm trapped in a man's body.

"I can't sleep," I said, even though the truth of it was that I hadn't wanted to sleep. Not after the things I'd read in the journal.

His eyes flicked to the table, where the pages lay scattered, betraying what I had kept hidden from everyone.

"Did you go through it?" he asked, his voice low, guarded.

I nodded. "I didn't have a choice, Connor. It was like... like it was begging me to open it. There's a group, something my husband was involved in. Dangerous people. People I don't recognize."

Connor's jaw tightened. He set his bag down with a soft thud, the tension in his shoulders palpable. "How much do you know?" he asked, already pulling out a few tools from the bag—keys, files, a small flashlight. All the things I had come to associate with him over the years.

"I know enough to be terrified." My voice cracked despite myself. "And I know I can't go back to pretending none of this exists." I swept a hand over the journal, the papers spread in all their chaotic mess, as if they were meant to be read, like a map of some dangerous path.

Connor's eyes softened for a fraction of a second, and I could see the weight of his own history pressing against the surface of his calm exterior. But he quickly masked it, leaning over the table and flipping through the journal with quick, efficient movements.

"This is bigger than we thought, isn't it?" His voice was barely above a whisper, as if he were trying not to wake the dangerous thing that lurked between the lines of those pages.

The world outside was dark, the night thick with shadows, but in that moment, the space between Connor and me seemed to stretch. Neither of us moved as we sat there in the heavy silence, the air thick with things unsaid.

I felt the heat of his proximity, the tension between us almost tangible. It wasn't just the journal that crackled in the room—it was something else entirely. A strange sort of electricity that surged with every accidental brush of his arm against mine, each time his fingers brushed the pages, as if we were both navigating a path that we couldn't turn away from.

"I don't know what to do with this," I confessed, my voice quieter now. The admission seemed to hang in the air between us, fragile, raw. "I'm not sure I want to know what it all means."

Connor's gaze softened, but his hands never stopped flipping through the pages. He was resolute, determined. I could see that in the way he held himself, in the way he worked through the mess of it all. I almost envied him.

"You don't have to do anything, not alone." His words were firm, and his eyes—those stormy eyes that never seemed to give anything away—met mine with a depth I wasn't prepared for. "We'll figure this out, okay? Together."

I blinked, my heart skipping a beat at the way he said it, as though he had already made up his mind about everything. About us. About what was coming next.

But I wasn't ready for that. Not yet. I couldn't afford to lose myself in the slipstream of whatever we were starting to build, whatever this unspoken understanding between us was becoming.

"I'm not sure I can trust anyone," I muttered under my breath, trying to pull myself back from the edge. "Not even you."

He didn't flinch. He just kept working, his hands moving methodically over the pages, his concentration unwavering.

"You don't have to trust me," he said with a soft, dry chuckle. "But you'll need me. And that, I can guarantee."

His voice, low and steady, wrapped around me like a rope, pulling me deeper into this strange partnership we were forming. Something told me I wouldn't be able to pull away—no matter how hard I tried.

I met his gaze again, this time with something less than uncertainty. But it wasn't trust. Not yet.

"It's getting late," I said, the words tasting strange on my tongue.

Connor gave a slow nod, the flicker of something between us smoldering. "We're not done yet," he said, his voice suddenly quieter, as though he, too, could feel the weight of what we were skirting around. But we kept going anyway.

In the quiet aftermath, the journal between us no longer seemed like an object of fear. It was a lifeline. A way forward. Together, we had no choice but to follow it wherever it might lead.

The clock on the wall ticked louder than I'd ever noticed before, each second dragging on, as though it knew exactly how tense the room had become. It had been hours since Connor first arrived, and though I'd barely touched the remnants of the bottle of wine I'd opened to try to loosen the tension between us, we hadn't spoken much. There was a quiet understanding that words wouldn't help anymore. We both had a habit of filling silence with noise, but tonight, we were letting the quiet speak for itself.

Connor had his head bent low over the journal, eyes scanning the pages with an intensity that made the air between us feel almost suffocating. The little lamp on the table cast long shadows across his face, softening the sharp lines of his jaw but only intensifying the fire in his eyes. I couldn't decide whether I wanted to keep watching him or look away entirely, because every time my gaze met his, something in me stirred—a familiar, unwelcome pull.

I shifted in my seat, trying to avoid the sting of awareness that was prickling down my spine. It had been like this for months now—this strange, invisible thing between us that had started so slowly, almost imperceptibly, like the first tremor before an earthquake. But now, every time I was near him, it felt like the ground beneath me was shifting, like I was walking on the edge of something far too dangerous to ignore.

Finally, Connor let out a frustrated sigh, tossing the journal onto the table with a sound that echoed in the otherwise still room.

"I'm not getting any closer to answers," he muttered, running a hand through his hair, his frustration evident.

I raised an eyebrow, leaning back in my chair, keeping my voice cool, even though I could feel the tension simmering between us. "You think this is supposed to make sense right away? This is the kind of mess that doesn't unravel in a single sitting." I crossed my arms, watching his movements. "And I'm still not convinced I want it to. It's... it's dangerous, Connor."

He shot me a look then, a look I could only describe as a challenge. "You don't get to say that. Not now, not after everything. You want to know what happened. We both do."

His words stung more than they should've, and my stomach twisted uncomfortably. He was right, of course. I didn't get to say that. Not anymore. The truth was, I couldn't keep pretending like this wasn't something I needed to face.

I turned away, breaking eye contact, as if it would stop the burn in my chest. But of course, it didn't. The truth always had a way of catching up with you, no matter how hard you tried to outrun it.

"Well, if we're doing this, we might as well get comfortable," I muttered. "It's going to be a long night."

Connor didn't respond right away, but I could feel him studying me, as though he were piecing together a puzzle he didn't quite understand. I couldn't blame him. After everything that had happened between us, after the close calls and half-spoken words, I wasn't an easy person to read. Not anymore.

He finally broke the silence, his voice softer, less sharp than before. "You know, you're right. This will take time. But there's no point in dragging it out longer than necessary." He pushed back his chair and stood, moving to the kitchen. "I'm making coffee. You might need it."

I watched him, my thoughts scattering like leaves in the wind. I hadn't realized how much I'd missed this—how much I missed the strange rhythm of being around him. The small, comforting moments of familiarity that made everything feel, for just a second, like it wasn't all falling apart.

I swallowed hard, brushing away the sudden wave of emotion. I didn't need this. Not now, not when everything was so tangled. But as I looked at Connor, a strange urge rose within me to reach across the distance, to undo the knot we had wound ourselves into.

But I couldn't. I wouldn't.

He returned with two steaming cups of coffee, setting one in front of me without a word. For a long moment, neither of us moved. The heat from the mugs curled up into the cool air between us, mingling with the tension that clung to the space like smoke.

Finally, Connor broke the silence again. His voice was quieter this time, though no less intense. "You know, you don't have to go through this alone. You're not the only one who's been hurt by this."

I felt a flicker of surprise at his words, but I didn't let it show. "What's that supposed to mean?" I asked, not quite able to hide the edge in my voice.

He looked at me then, a look I couldn't quite place, but something about it made my pulse race. "I'm not in this just for you. I've got my own reasons, too."

His honesty stunned me. We'd danced around our shared history for so long that the idea of Connor admitting that he had personal stakes in this—stakes beyond the work, beyond the journal—hit me harder than I expected.

"I didn't ask for your help," I said, my voice more brittle than I intended. "I didn't want any of this."

His eyes softened, but there was something else in his gaze now, something almost like understanding. "Neither of us did," he said quietly, "but it's here. And now we get to decide what to do with it."

I took a long, steadying breath, trying to ignore how his words seemed to sink into me, like I was letting him carry some of the weight I hadn't been able to let go of.

"Fine," I said after a beat, setting my coffee cup down with deliberate slowness. "We do this together. But on my terms."

Connor's lips quirked at the corners, a half-smile that didn't reach his eyes. "You don't get to make all the rules," he teased, but there was a soft, almost affectionate edge to his tone. "But I'll go along with whatever you want. For now."

For a moment, the world felt like it had narrowed down to just the two of us, the quiet hum of the apartment, the darkened streets outside, and the weight of a past that we were both trying to outrun. But the longer we sat there, the more I realized I wasn't sure I wanted to outrun it.

The night stretched on, slipping further into the early hours, but neither of us moved to end it. There was a quiet sort of truce between us now, a mutual understanding that the journal could only reveal so much, and the rest—well, the rest was something neither of us could fully prepare for. Every time I thought I understood what was at play, a new page would turn, another name would surface, and the web my husband had woven would grow even more tangled.

I could feel Connor's gaze on me as I skimmed the last page for the third time, looking for some shred of clarity, some piece of information that would make sense of the rest. The names were all so familiar, but the connections between them didn't fit in with what I knew about the quiet little town I'd once thought I understood. Dangerous figures. Hidden allegiances. This was far beyond any of the lies I had been told about my husband's past.

It wasn't until the sound of my breathing slowed and the pulse in my temples quieted that I realized Connor hadn't been speaking at all. I glanced up, only to find him leaning back in his chair, staring at me intently, as if he were trying to decide something in the silence.

"Something on your mind?" I asked, not sure if I wanted to hear the answer. It was a question more for myself than for him, the weight of the moment pressing between us.

Connor's lips pressed together, as if he were searching for the right words. "It's just..." He trailed off and ran a hand through his hair. "This is a mess. I don't think we can pretend it's anything else anymore."

I nodded, but the words didn't bring any relief. We both knew the mess wasn't just about the journal, and it wasn't just about the people connected to it. It was about what we were starting to uncover, and how easily it was pulling us both in. My heart skipped a beat as the tension between us thickened, an invisible thread tugging tighter and tighter.

"We're too deep now," I said, my voice barely above a whisper. "Even if I wanted to stop, it's not like I could."

Connor didn't respond right away. Instead, he pushed himself up from the table and walked to the window, peering out into the darkness. I knew the words had landed, but it didn't feel like a victory. It felt like a surrender.

"You're right," he said, his voice carrying a weight I hadn't expected. "We're already in the thick of it. The only choice we have now is to keep going."

I watched him for a moment, his silhouette framed by the dim light from the street. For a fleeting second, I thought about walking away from it all—leaving the journal behind, erasing the past, even if it meant losing myself in the process. But it was too late for that, and I knew it. I couldn't forget. Not after what I had already seen.

When he turned back toward me, the expression on his face was unreadable. But there was something in the air between us, an unsaid thing that buzzed like electricity, making the room feel smaller.

"Let me help you," he said softly, as if the words were as much a promise as a question.

I swallowed, unsure of how to respond. He had already helped in ways I hadn't expected, becoming someone I depended on without even realizing it. But there were lines I wasn't ready to cross, lines that I feared would change everything if I let him cross them with me.

"You don't know what you're asking for," I said, my voice unsteady. "This is dangerous. And I don't—"

But Connor interrupted, his tone firm and sure. "I know exactly what I'm asking for." His gaze didn't waver, locking onto mine with a clarity that unsettled me. "I'm asking to help you fix this. To make it right."

A nervous laugh bubbled up in my throat, but it quickly died, swallowed by the tension that hung thick between us. "There's no making this right. Not anymore."

Connor's eyes narrowed, his jaw tightening as if he were already planning the next move, the next step in whatever this was between us. "We can't change what's happened, but we can decide what happens next."

His words felt too heavy for the moment, too loaded with implications that neither of us was ready to unpack. I could feel myself unraveling, piece by piece, and the worst part was, I didn't know if I wanted to stop it.

The air seemed to thicken as the silence stretched on, wrapping around us like a blanket. Neither of us moved, and yet the world outside seemed to pulse with a life of its own, full of possibilities I hadn't dared to consider before.

Finally, I stood, breaking the stillness between us. I needed to move, to shake off the feeling that I was trapped in a room that was growing smaller with each passing second.

"I need air," I said, and Connor didn't argue, though I could see the hesitation in his eyes. He didn't want to leave things unsaid either. But he let me walk past him, the heat of his presence lingering behind me like a shadow.

The cool night air hit my skin as I stepped outside, the scent of rain in the distance mingling with the sharp tang of the city. I breathed deeply, feeling the tension ease slightly in my chest. But the relief didn't last long. The world was still spinning, and nothing felt stable.

Behind me, I could hear the sound of Connor following me out onto the porch, his footsteps steady but quiet.

"You shouldn't be doing this alone," he said again, his voice almost a whisper against the hum of the night.

I turned to face him, the weight of the past hours pressing against me. "I didn't choose this, Connor. You didn't choose this either."

His eyes met mine in the darkness, and for a moment, the distance between us closed. I could almost feel his breath on my skin, the heat of his gaze making my heart race.

"What if I told you I'm already in this? In more ways than you think?"

My breath caught, the question hanging in the air like a dare. The world around us seemed to hold its breath, waiting for my answer. But before I could speak, I saw something flash in the shadows behind him—movement. Too quick, too sudden.

I froze. My pulse spiked. Something—or someone—was watching us.

Chapter 13: Inferno of Betrayal

The night air clung to my skin, thick with the weight of tension that had only gotten worse with each passing minute. I stood on the edge of the fire escape, staring down at the city below, where the lights flickered like so many half-formed promises. A siren wailed in the distance, cutting through the quiet hum of traffic, but I barely noticed it anymore. Nothing seemed to matter except the raw, suffocating silence that had settled between Connor and me.

The conversation in the precinct had been brief, but it was still echoing in my head, like the ringing after a sharp slap. His supervisor, a man who wore his suspicion like an armor of steel, had made it clear that Connor's involvement in the case was now under scrutiny. His loyalty to me, his willingness to listen when the rest of them turned away, was a liability. The weight of it had cracked something deep inside me, something I hadn't even known was fragile until it shattered.

I could still hear the sharpness in Connor's voice as he tried to explain. Tried to justify his actions. But his words felt hollow now, like they were just echoes of something he'd promised to be for me, but could never fully deliver. He'd said he would protect me. He'd said we'd figure this out together. But it was always going to be a game of balance, wasn't it? His duty to the law, his loyalty to his team, pulling him away from me like the tides dragging at the shore. And all I could do was watch him drown in it.

I took a deep breath and felt the sharp bite of cold air fill my lungs. The city sprawled beneath me, indifferent to my heartbreak. But I wasn't sure how long I could pretend that I didn't care. I didn't know if it was pride or fear that kept me from going back inside and seeking him out, but I couldn't bring myself to do it. Not yet. Not after everything he'd said.

I was still stewing over it when I heard the soft crunch of footsteps behind me. I didn't have to turn around to know who it was. No one else moved like that. The slow, deliberate pace. The scent of his cologne wafted to me, familiar and oddly comforting, even now. Even with everything swirling between us, I couldn't deny that he had a way of making everything feel slightly less unbearable.

"Don't do this, Callie," Connor's voice was low, almost too quiet, but it was impossible to ignore. "You know it's not like that."

I turned, taking in his figure outlined by the dim light from the apartment, his face still shadowed but no less defined. He looked tired, worn in ways that made my chest tighten. It was a tiredness that was both physical and emotional, a weight I couldn't help but recognize. It was a weight I'd never wished on him. I wanted to reach out, to touch him, but I wasn't sure I even knew how to anymore. The space between us felt miles wide.

"It's always like that with you, Connor," I replied, my voice sharper than I intended. "You put your job above everything. Above what we had. Above the truth."

He flinched, the slightest twitch in his jaw, and I could see the immediate regret in his eyes. But then the hardness returned, the familiar stubbornness. He was the type who believed he could solve everything with brute force, with the unshakable certainty that if he just followed the rules, everything would be okay. But that wasn't how this worked. Not this time.

"You think I don't care about finding the truth?" His voice cracked, a rare break in his usually steady tone. "I'm doing everything I can, Callie. But I can't do it alone."

"You were supposed to do it with me," I shot back, crossing my arms tightly over my chest. "But now it's clear where your priorities are. And it's not with me. Not with anyone who's got a connection to this fire."

His eyes narrowed, and I saw the flicker of something—something hard and cold—that I hadn't noticed before. It was as though a wall had gone up between us, taller and thicker than I ever thought possible.

"I can't afford to have my judgment clouded by personal feelings," he said, the words coming out in a clipped, emotionless tone that didn't belong to him. "I'm trying to figure this out, Callie. But I need you to stay out of it. For your own good."

I couldn't help the bitter laugh that escaped my lips. It was sharp, a little too bitter, a little too full of disbelief. "For my own good?" I echoed. "You think I'm the one who doesn't see the danger in this? You think I haven't been living with it every single day since that fire? Don't talk to me about what's for my own good, Connor. I've had enough of that from everyone else. I don't need it from you."

"I'm trying to protect you." His voice cracked again, quieter this time, like it was a secret he wasn't sure he wanted to reveal.

"Protect me?" I stepped toward him, a pulse of heat sparking in my chest. "By pushing me away? By telling me I'm too close to the fire?" My hands were trembling, but I didn't care. I was done holding back. "I don't need your protection. I need the truth."

The silence that followed was thick, heavy with everything we weren't saying. I could feel the distance growing between us, could almost see it in the way his shoulders slumped, the way his lips tightened into a hard line. His gaze never left mine, but there was something about it—something final—that made me take a step back, my chest tightening painfully.

"I'll see you around, Callie," he said, his voice low, almost resigned.

And just like that, he turned away, his silhouette disappearing into the darkness of the hallway.

I didn't want to sit in the dimly lit bar, nursing a glass of wine I hadn't touched, but it seemed the only place where I could keep my thoughts from shattering into a million pieces. The low hum of conversations surrounded me, and the clink of glasses offered a rhythm I couldn't quite match. My reflection in the polished wood of the bar was distorted, as if the world around me couldn't quite catch up with the way I felt. Fractured, like the thin stem of a wine glass dropped just a second too soon.

The bartender leaned against the counter, eyeing me with practiced indifference. He'd learned the art of not asking questions long ago, and I was grateful for that. He'd probably seen a hundred people come in, a hundred different stories playing out in their heads while their faces stayed blank, as though they could keep their wounds to themselves. He wasn't wrong to think I had one, too. Everyone did.

I thought about the conversation with Connor—what I had said, what he had said, the finality in the way he walked away. That final glance over his shoulder, like he was trying to read me before I could disappear. That brief moment felt like a betrayal of its own, a quiet acknowledgment that we had reached the point of no return. But what could I have expected? He wasn't mine to keep, not truly. I had known that from the beginning. Still, watching him turn his back on me—it left a sour taste in my mouth, one I couldn't wash away with wine or words.

"You're still here?" The voice was familiar, but not quite welcome. My spine straightened instinctively, and I didn't have to turn around to know it was him. His tone was too casual, too disinterested, and yet there was something in it that made my stomach knot. There he was, standing a little too close, the faint scent of his cologne mingling with the stale air.

I didn't acknowledge him immediately, pretending to study the label on my untouched glass. I wasn't ready to face him. Not yet. Maybe not ever.

"You really are stubborn, aren't you?" Connor added, his voice a little sharper than before. "I thought you'd take the hint by now."

I set the glass down, fingers tracing the rim absently. "Hints don't work on me," I replied, my voice steady even if my heart wasn't. "Not when they come from you."

"You should've listened to me," he said, his words softer now, but still edged with frustration. He leaned in closer, and I could see the tension in his shoulders, the way his jaw clenched like he was holding back something he didn't want to say. "You've got a right to be pissed, but you're not helping anything by running from the truth."

"Running?" I scoffed, turning to meet his eyes finally. There was something in his gaze—a mix of regret and something darker—that I didn't know how to process. "Is that what you think? That I'm running? Because last time I checked, you were the one who pushed me away, not the other way around."

The heat in his eyes dimmed, just for a second, before it flared again. He didn't like being called out, especially not when it was about something he couldn't control. "I'm trying to do the right thing," he said, a sharpness creeping into his voice. "I thought I could keep both sides of this—protecting you, protecting the case—but I can't. It's too much."

I watched his hands as they balled into fists at his sides, the muscle in his jaw ticking with every breath. I felt a strange tug in my chest, the impulse to walk away, to leave this behind and never look back. But there was something in his face, something too raw for me to ignore. He was just as lost in this mess as I was.

"And what about me?" I asked, my voice low, dangerous even to me. "What am I supposed to do, Connor? Sit in the background while you play your part? Let you run off and chase your damn investigation while I wait for you to have time for me?"

He hesitated, his eyes softening for just a beat. "That's not what this is about. This isn't about you being sidelined. It's about what's best for everyone."

"I don't need you to tell me what's best for me," I snapped, the words escaping before I could stop them. "I've been taking care of myself long before you came into this."

He recoiled slightly, like I had slapped him. Maybe I had. Maybe he deserved it. But the look on his face—more disappointed than angry—hit me harder than I'd expected.

"Then why does it feel like you're pushing me away?" His voice was quieter now, softer in a way that disarmed me. I didn't know how to respond to that. Pushing him away felt like survival, but it didn't make it any easier.

"I'm not pushing you away," I said finally, but it sounded hollow, even to me. "I'm just trying to figure out what's left of us after all this. After the lies and the games and the things we'll never understand. Maybe I should've known better than to trust anyone who had to walk this tightrope."

His eyes hardened again, the softness slipping away as quickly as it had come. "I'm not the bad guy here," he said, a quiet fire in his words. "I'm just doing what I was trained to do. I never asked for any of this."

"Well, neither did I," I shot back, my voice tinged with bitterness. "But here we are. And I'm not going to apologize for it."

There was a long pause between us, thick with unspoken words, with things we were both too stubborn to admit. Finally, Connor stood up straighter, brushing off the discomfort with a shake of his head.

"Then I guess we're both just stuck, aren't we?" His voice was resigned, like he had already moved on. Like he had already accepted the fate of whatever this was between us.

I watched him walk away, his figure disappearing into the crowd like all the others. But this time, I didn't feel the relief I expected. I just felt empty. A quiet, hollow kind of emptiness that lingered long after he was gone.

The walk home was longer than it should have been. Every step felt weighted down with things unsaid, with the kind of tension that twists your spine until it's too late to fix. My apartment loomed ahead, a small, sterile space that had once felt like a sanctuary but now felt more like a prison. The silence inside was deafening, the hum of the refrigerator the only sound that dared disturb it.

I kicked off my shoes, too tired to care about the scuff marks I was sure I was leaving on the floor. The faint smell of old takeout containers and stale air hit me as I made my way toward the window, pulling back the curtain to let the moonlight spill inside. It cast a silvery glow across the room, a reminder that the night had a way of making things more complicated than they ever needed to be.

I leaned my forehead against the cool glass, watching the city below. Lights flickered, cars passed, people moved through their routines, oblivious to the storm brewing inside me. Connor's words played on a loop in my head, the sting of his last comment still fresh. *I'm trying to protect you.*

The irony wasn't lost on me. It was always about protection with him, wasn't it? Always about doing what was best for the people around him—except, of course, when it came to me. Then, it was just about control, about making sure I didn't get too close, didn't start asking the wrong questions. And for what? To keep his job intact? To save face in a world that didn't care about him or anyone else who wasn't a part of the machinery?

A knock at the door jolted me from my thoughts, and I spun around, heart pounding. I hadn't expected company. The suddenness of it sent a shiver down my spine.

I hesitated for a moment, then moved toward the door. Who could it be? The last time I checked, I didn't have many friends, and those I did have didn't come knocking at this hour. Not unless they had something important to say.

I opened the door, not entirely prepared for what I found. It wasn't Connor. But the man standing in front of me was just as unsettling.

"Detective Kessler," I said, trying to keep the surprise out of my voice. He was tall, wearing a crisp black suit that still managed to look rumpled around the edges, like he hadn't bothered to smooth out the mess of his day. His dark hair was combed back, but a few strands had escaped, falling across his forehead in a careless, almost defiant way. He looked like trouble, and I had a bad feeling that he was about to bring more of it into my life.

"Callie," he greeted me, his voice smooth and almost too polished for someone who had probably seen things in his line of work that would have made most people sick to their stomachs. "We need to talk."

I raised an eyebrow. "Do we?"

"I wouldn't be here if we didn't," he said, stepping past me before I could protest. He didn't wait for an invitation, didn't ask if I was even remotely interested in whatever it was he had to say. He just moved into the apartment like he owned the place. "You should sit down."

"Excuse me?" I blinked, disoriented by his sudden appearance and audacity. "Who do you think you are?"

"I think I'm the person who knows you've been digging into things that you shouldn't," he replied, his gaze sharp and calculating, as if he could see through every lie I told myself. His eyes flickered toward the small stack of papers on the coffee table—evidence I'd gathered about the fires, about the patterns, the anomalies no one else seemed to notice. I hadn't shared them with anyone. Not even Connor.

I moved quickly, blocking the papers with my body, a reflexive gesture that felt more like desperation than protection. "I'm not sure what you think you know," I said, forcing my voice to stay calm, even as my pulse quickened. "But I suggest you leave."

Kessler's lip curled into a smirk. "You're not in a position to be making demands, Callie. You've stepped into something that's way above your pay grade. You've been digging too deep, and it's only a matter of time before someone starts asking questions."

The weight of his words hit me like a physical blow. Too deep. It was what I had feared all along, but hearing it from him made it real in a way I hadn't been ready for. What had I done? What had I gotten myself into?

"I'm not the one who started this," I shot back, trying to stand my ground, even as my mind raced to catch up with the situation. "You can't intimidate me into backing off."

He took a slow step forward, his presence imposing in a way that made my skin crawl. "I don't need to intimidate you. You're already in too deep to back out now. The question is—how much further are you willing to go?"

I swallowed hard, my throat dry. He wasn't threatening me with words, but with knowledge. And that was more dangerous than any empty threat he could have made. My thoughts circled, trying to grasp at something solid, something that would help me understand what was happening, but there was nothing. No answers, just questions that seemed to multiply by the second.

"I'm not afraid of you," I said, my voice finally steady despite the dread creeping in.

"Oh, I don't think it's me you should be worried about," Kessler replied, the smile slipping from his lips. He took another step closer, so close now that I could feel the heat radiating off of him. "You should be worried about what happens when people like me start paying attention. And trust me, they're already watching."

The silence between us grew thick, oppressive, and then—just as the words began to settle in—the door slammed open behind me with a force that nearly knocked me off my feet.

I spun around, only to find myself face-to-face with Connor. His expression was unreadable, but the tension in his stance was unmistakable.

"I don't think she's the one you need to worry about," he said, his voice a low growl, and everything inside me froze.

Chapter 14: Embers of Doubt

The house smelled of coffee and old books, a faint perfume of something sweeter lingering just under the surface, like a memory I couldn't quite place. The kind that teased at the edges of your mind, elusive and fleeting, like the scent of a person's cologne you used to love but hadn't smelled in years. I leaned against the kitchen counter, staring out the window, watching the rain tap against the glass in delicate patterns. Each droplet made its own journey before sliding down, helpless against gravity, just like me.

Connor was out again, doing "firefighter things" as he called them, but I had begun to wonder whether there was something more to those things than he let on. It wasn't the job itself—no, I understood that part. It was the things he left unsaid, the pauses in his voice when he talked about his past, and how, every so often, his eyes would cloud over as though he were remembering a life he'd rather forget. He'd always been tight-lipped about it, offering only the barest of details, but lately, I couldn't shake the feeling that something wasn't right. Something just beneath the surface was beginning to unravel, and it had nothing to do with the fires he fought or the buildings he saved. It was something much closer to home.

I shook my head, as though trying to will away the questions that kept rising like the thick, acrid smoke from one of his firetraps. I couldn't think that way—not yet, not with everything else going on. And yet, I found myself slipping down that path more often than I cared to admit. It wasn't just Connor's guarded nature that was bothering me; it was the new presence in our lives—the stranger at the door that I hadn't seen coming.

I glanced down at the invitation on the counter, its corners slightly curled. A firefighter by the name of Ryan Dodd had arrived at the station two days ago, a childhood friend of Connor's who had apparently spent years trying to reconnect with him. At first, I'd chalked it up to an old bond, the kind that formed between those who faced danger together, the kind that held them when the flames died down. But then Ryan had come to our door. And something about him didn't sit right.

He wasn't much older than Connor, but there was a hard edge to him that spoke of battles fought not just on the job but within himself. He was all broad shoulders and rough hands, a man accustomed to lifting heavy things—both literally and figuratively. His presence in the house felt like a sudden shift, like a shift in the air that made the room feel smaller. And when he spoke of Connor's past, there was a weight in his voice that made my skin crawl, a darkness that I hadn't expected to find.

I remembered his words clearly, spoken with such casual certainty that they haunted me. "Connor doesn't talk about it much, but he lost someone in that fire. Someone who meant a hell of a lot to him. And when that happens, you don't just walk away. You carry that, whether you like it or not."

I had tried to brush it off, tried to convince myself that Ryan was just a man living in the shadow of his own experiences. But that night, I lay in bed next to Connor, his breathing steady beside me, and I couldn't shake the thought of it. What happened in that fire? Who had Connor lost? And why was he so determined to keep it hidden from me?

The door creaked behind me, and I turned, startled, to find Connor standing in the doorway. His uniform was damp from the rain, his hair falling over his forehead in that way that made my heart skip a beat every time. He flashed me a smile that didn't quite reach his eyes, and for a brief, cruel moment, I wondered if he could feel the distance between us, if he could sense the questions I was too afraid to ask.

"Hey," he said, his voice low. "You okay?"

I nodded, but the words caught in my throat. I could tell he was tired—he always was, after a shift—but there was something else, something more subtle that I couldn't quite place. Maybe it was just the weight of the day pressing on him, or maybe it was the way his eyes flicked toward the kitchen counter where Ryan's invitation still lay, a silent accusation.

I opened my mouth to speak, but before I could, the doorbell rang, its shrill sound cutting through the tension like a knife. Connor looked at me, and for the first time in what felt like forever, I saw something flicker in his expression—something I couldn't read. A hesitation, maybe. It was gone so quickly, I almost convinced myself I'd imagined it.

"I'll get it," he said, his voice steady, but there was an edge to it now, like he was bracing himself for something he didn't want to face.

I stood still, the weight of what Ryan had said pressing down on me. Something was wrong. Something was off about all of this, and I couldn't ignore it any longer. As Connor opened the door, I followed him into the hall, my heart thudding in my chest. I wasn't ready for what I might hear next. But somehow, I knew that whatever came through that door was going to change everything.

Connor's eyes lingered on the doorway, but his face remained unreadable, the mask he wore slipping back into place as if it had been there all along. I could hear the muted sound of footsteps, slow and deliberate, growing louder with each passing second. I wasn't sure if I wanted to face whoever stood on the other side of the door, but the fact that I was standing there, heart pounding like I was about to do something terribly wrong, told me I had no choice.

The door opened just enough for a figure to step into the dimly lit hallway, blocking out the cold rain that still battered against the house. It was Ryan, of course—who else would it be? He had a way of walking into rooms like he was entitled to be there, as though he'd known every creaking floorboard and cracked window pane long before. And then he turned, his gaze landing on me with an almost too-pleasant smile. That smile didn't quite reach his eyes either, and for some reason, that unsettled me more than anything.

"Hey there," Ryan said, stepping in with a confidence that bordered on arrogance. "Connor, good to see you still kicking."

There was no warmth in Connor's response. He nodded stiffly and stepped back to let Ryan in, his posture rigid, like he was bracing for an impact that hadn't quite arrived. I couldn't help but notice how they stood on opposite sides of the doorway—like two men with far too much unsaid between them. As Ryan brushed past me, the scent of his cologne hit me—a mix of musk and something sharper, like burnt cedar. It reminded me of an old firepit, where the smoke always lingered in the air long after the flames had died.

"Nice place you've got here," Ryan remarked, his voice carrying an edge of practiced charm. "Doesn't seem like the kind of place you'd expect a couple of firefighters to call home."

I forced a smile, but there was something about the way he said it, the unspoken judgment in his tone, that made my skin prickle. Was he testing me? Or was it just his way of making everything feel too casual, too easy? Either way, it felt like a game I didn't want to play. Not now, not with everything else weighing on me.

"We've tried to make it comfortable," I replied, my voice lighter than I felt. "You know, in between the fires and all the chaos."

Ryan chuckled, though there was something off in the sound—an odd note of recognition, maybe, or something darker. His eyes flicked back toward Connor, and for the briefest of moments, I saw it. That flicker of something. Not quite fear, but something close to it. He wasn't just visiting; he was here for something else.

I didn't know what, but I was certain of one thing—whatever it was, I wasn't going to like it.

"So, what brings you to town, Ryan?" I asked, trying to keep my voice steady, trying to keep the layers of suspicion from curling into the air like smoke.

Ryan's gaze lingered on Connor for a beat too long before he answered. "Just wanted to check in on my old buddy. See how he's doing, you know? Things have been rough for him since..." He trailed off, the unspoken word hanging between us like an iron weight. Since the fire. Since whatever it was that had happened to Connor all those years ago.

I could see Connor's jaw tighten at the mention, but he didn't say a word. Instead, he moved toward the kitchen, muttering something about needing to grab a drink. Ryan's eyes followed him, a silent understanding passing between them that I didn't quite grasp.

"Don't mind him," I said, offering a strained smile. "He's been...a little off lately."

Ryan raised an eyebrow, as though this was news to him, but he said nothing. Instead, he dropped into one of the chairs by the table, propping his boots up as if he'd lived here for years. It irked me—how casual he was, like he had a stake in all of this, even though he didn't. Not really.

"Do you know what happened?" I asked, my voice quieter than I intended. "Connor never talks about it. About the fire. Not with me, not with anyone."

Ryan's eyes flicked to me then, and I saw a strange light in them, a flash of something almost like pity. His mouth tightened for a second, as though he were considering whether or not to answer. "Connor's a proud guy," he finally said, his tone softening just a little. "He doesn't like talking about the past. But that fire—it changed him, you know? Lost a lot of good people that day. And when you lose people like that, it doesn't just go away. It stays with you."

I felt the weight of his words settle over me, thick and heavy. I knew that loss—how it could drag you down into the darkest parts of yourself, how it could silence you. But there was something in the way Ryan spoke, something in his voice that made me wonder if he knew more than he was letting on. He wasn't just talking about a fire. He was talking about a man haunted. A man carrying something too heavy for one person to bear alone.

"I don't think he's ever told me what happened that day," I murmured, more to myself than to Ryan.

Ryan's smile flickered, almost too quickly. "Maybe he doesn't need to. Not everything needs to be spoken aloud."

I wanted to press him, to demand more answers, but the cold knot of unease that had been sitting in my stomach all evening twisted tighter. This wasn't about what Ryan was willing to say. This was about what he wasn't saying. And what was worse, I was starting to wonder if I even wanted to hear it.

Ryan leaned back in his chair, stretching his legs out, as if he were trying to claim the space like a cat lounging in the sun. There was a casualness to him that made my teeth clench, a nonchalance that bordered on arrogance. He wasn't just here as an old friend, I realized. No, Ryan was here for something more, something I wasn't ready to face but couldn't ignore any longer.

I couldn't keep the unease out of my voice. "You said Connor lost people in that fire. What exactly happened?"

The words hung in the air like smoke, thick and suffocating. Ryan's gaze flickered to me, his expression unreadable for a moment. Then, just as quickly, his face softened into an almost pitying smile.

"People like Connor, they don't talk about it much. It's… easier that way. And I'm not sure he'd want me getting into all the details."

His tone was smooth, too smooth, as if trying to reassure me without truly saying anything. But the way his eyes avoided mine told me that was a lie.

"I'm not asking about anyone else. I'm asking about Connor," I pressed, my voice sharper now, a slight tremor betraying my nerves. "What happened to him?"

Ryan's lips pressed together, his jaw tightening as though he were trying to swallow something he didn't want to say. I could feel the tension building between us, thick as tar, and for a moment, I wondered if I should back off. Maybe this wasn't the time. But the knot in my stomach twisted tighter, gnawing at me like a hunger that refused to be satisfied.

He sighed, a deep, almost reluctant sound, before pushing himself upright. His eyes flicked to the kitchen, where Connor had disappeared, and I could feel the unsaid words building like pressure in the room.

"Let's just say... Connor's had his share of demons. And they're not the kind you just forget about." He said it so matter-of-factly, as if the weight of it all didn't crush him, too.

I crossed my arms, unable to sit still. "And you're here to remind him of that?"

Ryan's gaze sharpened, his smile faltering for just a second before it returned, colder this time. "I'm here because you need to understand. He's not the man you think he is. None of us are, really."

I didn't know whether to laugh or scream. "And you think you're some kind of expert on Connor? You haven't seen him in how many years?"

Ryan paused, and in that split second, something flickered behind his eyes—something old, something deep. He looked at me as though seeing right through me, his smile slowly fading.

"I knew him when he was different. Before all this. Before he became… this version of himself." Ryan's words were like ice against my skin. "I'm just here to make sure he doesn't drag you down with him."

The finality in his voice struck me like a slap, and for a moment, I couldn't breathe. What did he mean by that? Was this some kind of warning? And why did it sound like he was talking about someone else entirely, not the man I'd married? I knew Connor had a past—everyone did—but what was it really? What did Ryan know that I didn't?

I opened my mouth to respond, but before I could get a word out, Connor appeared in the doorway again, his expression unreadable. He didn't look at me, didn't even glance my way, his eyes instead fixed firmly on Ryan.

"Everything okay in here?" Connor's voice was low, almost flat, but I caught the edge of something that made the hairs on the back of my neck stand up. There was a tension in the air now, thick as the storm outside, as if the room itself was holding its breath.

Ryan straightened, his body shifting like a man readying himself for battle. "Yeah, just catching up on old times."

Connor's eyes darkened as he scanned Ryan's face, his jaw clenching. It was only for a second, but I saw it—the way he tensed, the way something behind his eyes shuttered. As if Ryan had opened a door to something that Connor wasn't ready to face.

"Well," Connor said, his voice steady but with an undercurrent of something I couldn't place, "I think we've had enough 'catching up.' Don't you?"

Ryan didn't flinch, didn't break eye contact. "Maybe. But I'm not done here yet."

The words hung in the air, unspoken, as if a secret was teetering on the edge of being revealed. I stood, frozen, the weight of everything suddenly crushing down on me. The storm outside, the storm inside—the two seemed to be one and the same.

"Connor," I began, my voice soft but firm, "what is he talking about? What happened? What aren't you telling me?"

Connor's gaze flicked toward me for the briefest moment, a flicker of something crossing his face before he masked it. His lips parted as if to speak, but no words came. For a long second, everything stood still. The tension between the three of us was palpable, suffocating.

Then, before anyone could speak, a loud crash sounded from the back of the house. I spun around, heart leaping into my throat, as I heard footsteps echoing through the hallway. My breath caught in my chest as I moved toward the noise, Connor and Ryan following closely behind. The air seemed charged with static, thick with the promise of something I wasn't prepared for.

The back door was ajar, the lock broken. I stepped into the backyard, and there, lying on the ground in the shadows, was a package—a small, nondescript box wrapped in brown paper, with a single word scrawled across it in black ink: For you.

My blood ran cold.

Chapter 15: Charred Promises

The ink had smudged in places, evidence of tears soaked into the thin pages of his journal. At first glance, the words were no more than scribbles, a jumble of half-formed thoughts and cryptic allusions. But as I sat there, the dim light from the overhead lamp casting its glow over the leather-bound book, the puzzle pieces began to fall into place. I wasn't just reading Connor's words—I was uncovering the parts of him he'd never been able to share, even with me. It felt like I was intruding on something sacred, something too raw for the world to witness.

His handwriting was usually neat, precise, the kind of cursive that left no room for doubt about its author. But here, the words were jagged, fragmented, as if they'd been written under duress, or perhaps in the frantic rush of someone who didn't have time to think through every sentence. I ran my fingers over the pages, each turn revealing more than I wanted to know.

"December 3rd," the first entry began. "I promised I'd protect her. But how can I protect her from the things she doesn't know about me?"

I froze. My breath caught in my throat as the weight of those words pressed down on me. Protect me? What did he mean? He'd always been the silent, steadfast type, but this was different. This was a crack in the armor, an admission of weakness that, frankly, I hadn't expected. I turned the page, my heart racing, desperate to make sense of it all.

Each new entry left me feeling more adrift, further removed from the man I thought I knew. There were mentions of an unnamed figure, someone he called "The Broker." The way Connor described him sent chills crawling up my spine—an enigmatic force, a puppet master pulling strings in the shadows, someone with enough influence to twist even the most iron-willed into submission.

"February 18th: The Broker demands more. I've done the things he asked, crossed lines I swore I never would. But I'm losing myself. How do I walk away from this?"

I turned the page faster now, the words blurring before my eyes. I wasn't sure if it was the weight of the confession or the rush of adrenaline, but I had to know everything. Every last secret.

Suddenly, the quiet in the room seemed to grow heavier, thickening around me like the air before a storm. That was when I heard it—a soft knock, tentative at first, then more insistent, like the steady beat of a pulse. My stomach lurched, a flutter of nerves spiraling inside me. I didn't have to guess who it was. My breath caught in my chest.

Connor.

I hadn't seen him in days, not since the argument that had driven us apart. The silence between us had stretched so long that I'd almost convinced myself I was better off without him. But as the knock echoed through the house, that sense of finality I'd tried to wrap myself in began to unravel.

I stood from the chair, my legs stiff, like they weren't sure if they should carry me to the door or let me sink into the floor. My fingers trembled as I reached for the knob, hesitating for only a moment before I swung the door open.

There he stood—Connor. The man I'd married, but more importantly, the man I barely recognized anymore. His face was drawn, the usual glint in his eyes replaced by something darker. Tired, maybe. Or maybe it was regret.

"I—" He paused, his voice hoarse, like he hadn't spoken in days. "I think we need to talk."

I said nothing at first. There were no words to say, no rehearsed speeches or angry retorts. There was only this strange, aching stillness between us. It stretched on for an eternity as I stared at him, wondering if the space between us was a wall or an invitation to something that had always been just out of reach.

"You've been reading my journal," he said, his voice a mix of accusation and something softer—guilt, maybe? I couldn't tell.

I nodded, the truth settling in the air between us like smoke, heavy and dense.

"I didn't mean for you to see that. I didn't—" He stopped, shaking his head as though he were trying to clear the thoughts clogging up his mind. "I didn't want you to know any of it, but it's not fair to keep you in the dark anymore."

The sincerity in his voice made my stomach twist. I wasn't sure if I was angry or relieved, or both at the same time. But one thing was for sure: this was the first time in days that I felt like we were speaking the same language, that we were on the same page.

"I'm listening," I said, my voice quieter than I expected. "Go on."

He stepped inside, his presence suddenly filling the room. The air felt heavier, charged with an intensity I hadn't felt in a long time. It was as though everything we had—everything we were—hung in the balance of the next few moments. He closed the door behind him and ran a hand through his hair, the weight of the world settling on his shoulders.

"I never wanted you to get involved in any of this," he began. "I thought I could keep it all from you—keep you safe. But I can't anymore."

The words hung in the air, fragile, like glass teetering on the edge of breaking. And for the first time in a long time, I realized something: we were no longer just partners in a marriage. We were two people, trapped by the secrets we kept from each other, now standing on the precipice of something neither of us knew how to navigate.

He took a step closer, his eyes never leaving mine. "I want to start over. To tell you everything. No more secrets. No more lies."

And just like that, the silence I'd buried myself in, the silence I'd grown accustomed to, felt like a distant memory, a ghost of something that once was. The door to understanding—real understanding—was open, and all I had to do was walk through it.

The weight of his words lingered in the room like smoke, thick and suffocating. I stood there, caught between the man I'd married and the stranger who had wandered into our life. His voice, rough around the edges, still held the familiar undertone of warmth, but it was strained—taut with the tension of unspoken truths. As if in slow motion, I watched him take another step forward, close enough now that I could feel the heat radiating from him, a silent invitation or a warning—I couldn't tell which.

"I'm not asking for forgiveness," Connor said, his gaze never faltering, "but I need to say everything. For us. For you."

There was something in the way he said it—like a man about to throw away everything he thought he knew in exchange for the possibility of something real. I wanted to tell him it was too late, to demand answers right here, right now, but something in his eyes held me in place. The vulnerability, the naked honesty. It was unlike anything I'd ever seen from him before, and maybe that's what stopped me. Maybe I was tired of all the walls—his, mine, ours. The ones that had stood between us, quiet and impenetrable, for too long.

"I never meant for it to get this far," he continued, his voice barely above a whisper, "but it has. And I can't keep pretending like it hasn't."

The truth hung between us, unraveling at a pace neither of us could control. I watched as his fingers flexed by his sides, as if he was holding himself back, fighting the urge to reach out, to touch something, anything to bridge the distance. His eyes flicked briefly toward the journal still clutched in my hand, the one that had torn away any semblance of calm I'd had before tonight.

"I never wanted you involved," Connor admitted, a tired laugh escaping him. "I thought I could protect you from it all. But when you read that, when you saw what I've been carrying... I don't know what I thought would happen. I've spent so many years in the shadows of things I've done—things I never wanted you to know. Things I'm not proud of."

I took a step back, my mind racing. The words on the page had been enough to make my pulse quicken, enough to make me question everything I thought I knew about Connor. But hearing him say it out loud—it twisted the knife. The man who had once been so open, so carefree, was now standing before me like a broken man, a man weighed down by ghosts I wasn't sure I wanted to meet.

"You're not the only one carrying baggage, Connor," I said before I could stop myself, my voice sharp, though it wavered with an edge I didn't recognize. "I have my own demons. But they weren't supposed to be yours. You promised me a future. A life."

His face softened at the words, and for a moment, I thought I saw regret—deep and real—in his eyes. But just as quickly, it was gone, replaced by the stoic expression I knew too well.

"I'm not asking you to understand everything, not right now. But I want you to know that I never stopped loving you," he said, each word deliberate, measured, as though he feared they might shatter if spoken too quickly.

I couldn't breathe. Not from the weight of his words, but from the way they made me feel—like I was standing on the edge of something I wasn't sure I could handle.

"You think love fixes everything?" I said, the bitterness creeping in despite myself. "Because it doesn't, Connor. Love doesn't make up for all the secrets. It doesn't make up for betrayal."

He took a step closer, and this time, there was no stopping him. His hand reached for mine, the contact warm, solid.

"No, it doesn't," he agreed quietly. "But it's the one thing that's kept me going all this time. And if you'll let me, I want to show you that I can be the man you thought I was."

I didn't pull away. Not immediately, at least. The feel of his skin against mine was enough to send a rush of memories flooding back—memories of us laughing together, of quiet mornings where everything seemed perfect. The weight of everything that had happened, the secrets, the lies, all of it settled around me, suffocating and unbearable. But still, his hand held mine, steady and certain. And I wasn't sure whether it was the touch I craved or the desire to believe in something, anything, that kept me there.

"I don't know if I can trust you again," I said softly, the words almost a confession. It was strange, how after everything, after all the distance that had grown between us, that was the hardest truth to admit.

He nodded, his eyes darkening. "I know. But I'm asking for the chance to prove it. I won't lie to you anymore. I won't keep things from you. What we have... what we could have, it's worth the fight."

A silence stretched between us, long and heavy. His fingers traced the back of my hand, the touch gentle, almost tentative, as though he was afraid I might pull away at any moment. And for the first time in what felt like forever, I realized that I didn't know what to do next. The air around us crackled with the kind of tension that could break hearts or heal them.

"I need to hear the truth," I said, my voice barely above a whisper. "Everything, Connor. I need to know."

His jaw clenched as if bracing himself for something that would break him. For a long time, he said nothing, his gaze dropping to our hands, entwined but fragile. When he finally spoke, his words were a quiet admission, not a confession, but something deeper.

"I'm not who you think I am. But I want to be. I want to be the man who deserves you." His voice cracked slightly, raw and unfamiliar.

And just like that, something shifted. The hardness in his posture softened, and for the first time in a long while, I saw him—truly saw him—as a man who was broken but willing to rebuild, not for the sake of himself, but for us. And I realized, in that moment, that maybe I wasn't ready to give up on him, not just yet. Not when there was a chance—however slim—that we could start over. Together.

I let the silence stretch between us, unsure whether I should pull him in or push him away. His eyes, those damn eyes that had once been so easy to read, now seemed like impenetrable mirrors. The way he stood there, so resolute, yet fragile in his stillness, made something tight and unfamiliar twist in my chest. I was both repelled and drawn in, a magnetic force pulling me closer while my instincts screamed to turn away.

"I can't just forget," I said, the words rough as though they had been waiting to spill out for too long. "It's not that simple. You've lied to me, Connor. And it's not just about the journal—it's about everything. You've kept me in the dark about things that could have destroyed us. And now, after everything, you want me to believe that I can trust you again?"

The room seemed to hold its breath, waiting for his response, but the seconds stretched long, too long, as if he were searching for the right thing to say. When he finally spoke, his voice was lower than usual, like he was feeling his way through a fog.

"I don't expect you to forgive me right away. Hell, I'm not sure I've forgiven myself," he said, looking away briefly before meeting my gaze again. "But I'm done with the lies. And I'm done hiding behind them."

The vulnerability in his words caught me off guard, slicing through the walls I'd carefully built. I'd always known that beneath the stoic exterior, beneath the man who held his secrets close, there was someone else—a man who feared losing everything. But hearing it, really hearing it, rattled me. He wasn't offering me a pretty story or some neatly wrapped apology. He was offering me the truth, as ugly and tangled as it might be.

"I need to know," I said, the urgency sharp in my tone. "I need to understand, Connor. Everything. The Broker, the deals, the lies. Why did you get involved in this in the first place? Why couldn't you tell me? Why didn't you trust me?"

His jaw clenched, the muscles in his neck taut, as though the questions were more than just questions—they were shrapnel, piercing through his defenses. His hand curled into a fist at his side before he ran it through his hair, pushing back the frustration that had begun to simmer on the surface.

"I didn't want you to know because I thought I could protect you from it. I thought that if I kept you in the dark, if you never knew about the things I was involved in, then you'd be safe. Safe from the consequences. Safe from the mess I'd made. And I didn't want you to see me as—" He stopped, his voice thick with something I couldn't quite name. Shame? Regret? Maybe both. "I didn't want you to see me as someone unworthy of you. Someone who—"

"Someone who made promises he couldn't keep," I finished for him, my words cutting through the air between us like a sharp knife.

He flinched at that, and it was enough to make me realize that he didn't need me to finish the sentence. He knew exactly how it ended. He knew the price of the lies. He knew the damage they had caused. And that was why he'd come back, standing in front of me like a man begging for a second chance—not because he deserved it, but because he was willing to try.

I stood there for a long time, staring at him, the weight of his confession sinking in. The room around us felt too small, too confining, as if the very air was holding its breath for what would come next. The hurt, the anger, they were all still there, lodged in the deepest parts of me. But so was something else. Something far more dangerous than I was willing to admit.

"I want to believe you," I said finally, the words coming out hoarse and raw. "I want to. But I can't just erase everything."

"I'm not asking you to," Connor replied quickly, stepping closer, his voice steady now, more certain. "I'm asking you for the chance to show you I can change. That I can be the man you need, the man you deserve."

His words hung in the air, the promise of them almost tangible. They offered hope, but they also carried the weight of the unknown. What would it look like to forgive him? What would it feel like to take that first step, to give him the chance he was begging for?

I took a deep breath, trying to steady myself, but it felt like standing on the edge of a cliff, the winds howling around me, urging me to jump. "You don't get to ask for that, Connor," I said, the words sharper now, though my heart was beating faster, the pulse thundering in my ears. "You don't get to ask for forgiveness without understanding what it costs. Do you know what it feels like to love someone who's kept this much from you? Do you know what it feels like to realize that you were just a pawn in someone else's game?"

He winced at the accusation, but I could see that it wasn't anger in his eyes. It was understanding. "I do now," he whispered. "I never wanted you to feel like that. I didn't want to hurt you. But I'm not the man I was when I made those promises. I'm not that person anymore. I swear to you, I'm not."

I searched his face, looking for any sign of doubt, any trace of the man who had deceived me so many times. But all I saw was desperation—the kind of desperation that only comes when someone knows they've lost everything they've ever cared about. And still, there was something about him that made me want to believe, something in the rawness of his admission that made the walls around my heart start to crack.

"I need time," I said, barely above a whisper, the words escaping before I could call them back.

Connor's eyes flickered with something unreadable, but he nodded, stepping back, giving me space. "I'll wait. However long it takes."

And just like that, he turned and walked away. I stood there, staring at the door long after it had closed behind him, the weight of his words and the silence that followed pressing down on me.

But as the hours stretched on, I couldn't shake the feeling that I was standing at the edge of something far darker than I had ever realized. And soon, the truth—whatever it might be—would come for me, whether I was ready or not.

Chapter 16: The Matchstick Man

The morning light sliced through the blinds in jagged patterns, a thin line of sunlight stretching across the kitchen table where I sat, cradling a cup of coffee that had long since lost its warmth. It wasn't the kind of morning I was used to—peaceful, soft, the sort where I could convince myself that everything in my life was perfectly fine. No, today felt different. There was a sharpness in the air, a kind of tension that I couldn't name, but that hung like an oppressive cloud.

I didn't have to wait long to find out why.

Leo came bounding down the stairs, his schoolbag bouncing against his back with each enthusiastic step. His face, always flushed with the excitement of starting a new day, faltered the moment he entered the kitchen. The smile he wore so often had slid off his face, replaced by something... uncertain.

"Mom," he said, voice tight, "someone asked about you today. At school."

I froze, the words hitting me like a bucket of ice water. My breath caught in my throat, and my grip on the coffee mug tightened until my knuckles turned white. I could feel my pulse quicken, the blood rushing in my ears as my mind raced through a dozen worst-case scenarios. Who could possibly be asking about me at Leo's school? No one from my past ever came knocking—at least, no one I wanted to see.

"Who?" I managed to choke out, my voice sounding thin, like I was trying to speak through water.

Leo shifted his weight from one foot to the other, looking awkward and uncomfortable, like he wasn't quite sure how to tell me what he had heard. "I didn't know his name. He didn't say it. He just... kept asking if you were my mom. And then, he kept saying how much he'd like to speak to you. He was tall, kind of thin, with glasses."

A shiver ran down my spine. Tall, thin, glasses. The description fit exactly what I had feared the moment I saw the man's silhouette in my thoughts, even before Leo had said the words aloud. He'd come.

The Matchstick Man.

I hadn't dared say the name out loud, even to Connor, though it had been creeping around in my mind ever since that strange encounter months ago. I had tried to brush it off, to convince myself it was nothing more than a fragment of a nightmare, a product of stress and sleepless nights. But now, hearing Leo speak about the man, it felt too real.

I stood up, the chair scraping loudly against the tile. Leo's eyes followed me as I crossed the room, my thoughts spinning out of control. A thousand possibilities flickered through my mind, each darker than the last. What did this man want? Why was he at Leo's school? Why had he asked about me?

"Mom? Are you okay?"

His voice, filled with a mix of concern and uncertainty, brought me back to the present. I forced a smile, though it felt tight and unnatural. "I'm fine, Leo. Just... just a little surprised, that's all."

He didn't look convinced, but thankfully, he didn't press. I ran a hand through my hair, trying to steady myself. As much as I wanted to protect him, to shield Leo from any threat, there was something else gnawing at me—a deeper, darker feeling that I couldn't ignore.

I turned toward the window, pretending the bright morning sun might somehow offer me clarity. It didn't. Instead, the memory of that night came rushing back, the night when I first encountered the Matchstick Man—a face in the crowd, a fleeting moment, a feeling of dread so sharp it cut through me like a blade.

I wasn't the only one who had noticed him. Connor had been there too, watching with the kind of suspicion that I had learned to trust.

"Connor," I said, my voice hoarse. "We need to talk."

He was already in the hallway, his boots scuffing against the floor as he entered the kitchen. His eyes locked onto mine, immediately sensing the shift in the air. He knew. He didn't need any more details. He could see it in the way my body was stiff, in the way I couldn't hold still.

"What's going on?" he asked, his voice low, almost guarded.

"Leo," I said, nodding toward our son, "he just told me about a man at school—someone asking questions about me. He said he was tall, thin, wearing glasses."

Connor's expression didn't change, but I saw the way his jaw clenched, the faint flicker of alarm in his eyes. It was a reaction I knew too well. He didn't need to say anything for me to understand. He was already thinking about the same thing I was: The Matchstick Man.

"This isn't good," he murmured under his breath. He ran a hand through his hair, pacing for a moment. "I'll take care of it. I'll find out who he is, what he wants."

His words should have been comforting, but they weren't. They couldn't be. The situation was spiraling, and I felt that familiar sense of helplessness I'd tried so hard to avoid.

I opened my mouth to say something—anything to push back against the unease gnawing at me—but before I could, Connor was already stepping out the door. He gave me one last look over his shoulder, his eyes filled with an unspoken promise.

"I'll keep you both safe," he said, his voice firm.

And just like that, he was gone.

I stood there in the kitchen, staring at the place where he had been, feeling more alone than ever.

FLICKER

I had always counted on Connor, always believed that somehow, he would protect us from whatever darkness loomed on the horizon. But now, as the door closed behind him, I realized how much I depended on that belief. For the first time, I wondered if even he could keep us safe from the Matchstick Man.

The air outside had the familiar bite of early fall, crisp and just cool enough to make you want to wrap up in something warm. I stood by the window, watching Connor's truck drive down the street, his brake lights flickering out of sight as he turned the corner. My mind wandered, the weight of the day pressing heavily against my chest. I had spent so many years convincing myself that I was capable of handling everything—that I didn't need anyone to step in and save the day. But here I was, staring at the empty street, wondering what the hell was coming next.

Leo had long since gone off to his friend's house, a welcome distraction, but his words still hung in the air like smoke. The stranger at school asking questions about me. About me. I didn't like it, didn't like it one bit. I had lived a quiet life for so long, and the sudden intrusion of someone poking around, especially someone connected to a name that I feared, felt like the ground was crumbling beneath my feet.

The Matchstick Man. It was the name I had given him when I first saw him months ago, an unsettling figure, a shadow more than a person, lurking on the fringes of my world. I had convinced myself it was nothing. An overactive imagination, maybe. Or a figment of some sleepless night. But now, hearing Leo speak of him in the flesh, the name felt all too real. Too dangerous.

I knew what was coming next. I could feel it in the pit of my stomach. It wasn't the first time Connor had been distant, but this was different. This time, his quiet determination was edged with something darker, something that tugged at the edges of my own dread. I didn't want to think about it, didn't want to let my mind wander to the possibilities of what this man could want, but I couldn't stop myself. I could almost feel him behind me, his presence pressing against my back like a cold breath.

The doorbell rang, cutting through the stillness of the house. I startled, my heart lurching in my chest. For a moment, I stood frozen, too afraid to move, too afraid to open the door. But then the bell rang again, a little more insistent this time. I took a deep breath and forced myself to walk across the room, my shoes tapping lightly against the hardwood floor.

I opened the door slowly, my eyes narrowing as I took in the figure standing on the porch. Tall, thin, wearing a pair of dark sunglasses, even though the sky had already begun to fade into evening. It was him. The Matchstick Man.

My heart hammered in my chest, my breath shallow as I stepped back instinctively. What the hell was he doing here?

"I'm sorry to bother you," he said, his voice soft but firm, like he had rehearsed the words. "I was hoping to speak with you. It's about your son."

His words froze me, each one sharp like a blade. My stomach turned, and I fought the urge to slam the door in his face. What did he want with Leo? Why was he asking about him? I opened my mouth to speak but found that no words came out. I was frozen, caught in the weight of the situation, and for a moment, I couldn't do anything but stare at him.

"Please," he said again, this time stepping closer, his face just a little too close for comfort. "It's important."

I shook my head, my voice finally returning, though it came out weaker than I'd wanted. "I don't know who you are, and I don't want to know. You need to leave."

He didn't budge, didn't flinch at my words. Instead, he simply stood there, his hands stuffed in the pockets of his long coat, his gaze unwavering. I could feel him sizing me up, studying me with a strange intensity. "I understand this is difficult," he said, his voice almost pitying. "But it's for your son's safety."

My pulse quickened, my mind racing with every possible scenario, none of them good. I thought of Leo, of how easily he could be caught in whatever this man was up to, and I felt a flash of panic.

"I don't care what it is," I said, my voice stronger now, fueled by the protective instinct that burned inside me. "I want you to leave. Now."

The Matchstick Man hesitated, as though my words had given him pause, but then he nodded slowly, almost as if he were conceding a point in a conversation. "I understand. But I will be back."

The cold, finality of his words lingered in the air long after the sound of his footsteps faded down the driveway. I slammed the door behind me, my body trembling, not from fear, but from the anger and helplessness that surged through me. What the hell was going on? Why was he targeting Leo? And why couldn't I shake the feeling that this was just the beginning?

I leaned against the door, my mind racing. Was this something I could handle on my own? Was this something I could keep Leo safe from? The moment Connor had walked out of the door earlier, a part of me had clung to the belief that he could fix this, that he could make everything okay again. But standing in the aftermath of the Matchstick Man's visit, I wasn't so sure anymore.

There was something more to this—something dangerous that neither of us could anticipate.

I glanced at my phone, the screen lighting up with a text message from Connor. I'm looking into it. Stay calm. Don't do anything reckless.

I didn't respond, couldn't bring myself to. The last thing I wanted was to stay calm. This wasn't the kind of problem that could be handled with calm. This was something bigger.

I turned toward the window, staring out at the world that felt so much smaller now. The house that had once felt like a fortress now seemed fragile, the walls closing in around me. Whatever was coming, I didn't think we could outrun it.

And then there was Leo. I didn't have the luxury of keeping him out of this, of sheltering him from the storm that was about to hit. If the Matchstick Man wanted him, then I had to face the truth—there was no place for hiding. Only surviving.

I wasn't sure if I was ready. But I had no choice.

It was late when Connor came home, long after the sky had turned black and the moon hung heavy, a silent witness to the tension that was thick in the air. I had heard his truck pull into the driveway, but I didn't move from the window where I had spent the last hour watching the street, hoping for something that would make sense of the chaos. The streetlights cast long shadows, and each time a car passed, my heart would race with the sickening hope that maybe, just maybe, it was the Matchstick Man retreating into the night.

When Connor stepped through the door, his face was hard, his jaw clenched tight in that way I had come to dread. He didn't speak right away. Instead, he pulled off his jacket, hanging it up with mechanical precision, as though everything in the world could be controlled except the storm brewing just beneath his skin. I stayed where I was, my hands wrapped around my mug, the coffee now cold and forgotten. I didn't know if I was waiting for him to say something or if I just couldn't bear the silence.

Finally, he turned to me, his eyes tired but sharp, the kind of tiredness that spoke of a long, dangerous day spent on the edges of something he couldn't quite grasp.

"I found him," Connor said, his voice low and unsteady, like he was measuring each word for weight.

My stomach dropped. I had expected the answer, but hearing it out loud made it real. Too real.

"And?" I asked, my voice tight, though I fought to keep it even.

He shook his head, running a hand through his hair, and I could see the frustration written in the lines of his face. "He's not just some random guy asking questions. The Matchstick Man is connected to something bigger. Someone's looking for something... and they're willing to do whatever it takes to get it."

I didn't need to ask him what "it" was. The air between us thickened, and I could feel the weight of the words settling on my shoulders, suffocating me. We were caught in a web I hadn't even realized was being spun, and the worst part was that it was already too late to escape.

"Do you think it's about Leo?" I asked, though the words felt like they scraped my throat on the way out.

Connor didn't respond right away, his eyes darkening with something I couldn't quite place. He didn't need to speak for me to understand that the answer was yes. My hands tightened around the mug, my grip shifting until my fingers started to ache.

"Who is he?" I asked again, my voice sharper this time. "Why is he here? What does he want?"

Connor finally met my gaze, his eyes searching mine, the tension between us heavier than I could ever remember. "I don't know," he admitted, the words coming out ragged, raw. "But it's dangerous, and it's tied to something from my past."

I felt a cold chill in the pit of my stomach. It wasn't the answer I had wanted, but it was the answer I feared most.

"Your past?" I repeated, confused. "What does that have to do with us? With Leo?"

Connor looked at me for a moment, his jaw tightening as if he were battling with himself over how much to reveal. Finally, he let out a long breath, dropping his shoulders in defeat. "Before we met... there were things. Things I should have left behind. But they're coming back, and they're coming after us. The Matchstick Man is only the beginning."

My mind raced, trying to piece together fragments that didn't fit. I had always known there were parts of Connor's life he kept locked away, but this... this was different. There was something much darker at play here, something far beyond what I could have imagined.

"I don't care about your past," I said, perhaps more harshly than I intended. "I care about keeping Leo safe."

Connor's eyes flashed, a spark of something unspoken passing between us. But before he could respond, there was a sound—soft, muffled—at the front door. The knock came again, almost tentative, like a warning.

Connor's face hardened, his muscles tensing as he shifted toward the door, his hand hovering just above his waistband. I didn't need to ask. I knew what he was thinking. He was already preparing for the worst.

The knock came again, louder this time, with an urgency that sent a chill running through me.

Connor took a step toward the door, his hand wrapping around the doorknob, but he hesitated just before opening it. I could see the indecision flicker in his eyes, the fear that even after all this, we might be stepping into something we couldn't control.

"What if it's him?" I asked, my voice barely a whisper.

"I don't know," Connor replied, his tone grim. "But we need to be ready. Whatever happens, don't open the door unless I say so."

I nodded, my stomach turning as I stepped back, my mind flashing to Leo—still at his friend's house, oblivious to the danger creeping ever closer. I could feel the weight of the minutes passing like a slow, crushing tide, the silence between the knocks stretching out like a taut wire, threatening to snap.

Then, with a suddenness that caught both of us off guard, the door opened.

There, standing in the threshold, was a face I hadn't expected. A face that sent a fresh wave of terror rushing through me.

It was Leo.

But something was off.

His eyes, wide and unblinking, were fixed on me with an intensity that felt... wrong. His hand was pressed firmly against the doorframe, his knuckles pale, almost as if he were holding on for dear life.

"Mom?" His voice was strained, almost frantic. "You need to come outside. Now."

Connor froze beside me, his eyes narrowing in disbelief.

I took a step forward, my heart pounding in my chest. "Leo, what's going on? Why are you—"

But before I could finish, Leo's head jerked to the side, his expression shifting, as though someone was standing just behind him.

"Mom, please," he repeated, but this time, his voice sounded different—cold, hollow.

And then I heard it. The unmistakable sound of someone else's footsteps, growing louder with each passing second.

Chapter 17: Burnt Offerings

I ran my finger along the faded pages of the journal, the ink slightly smudged from years of handling, but it still carried the weight of every secret it held. Each word seemed to burn into me, scorching the skin with its implications. Connor sat across the table, his brow furrowed in concentration, his lips tight as though even he knew what we were about to uncover would change everything.

The quiet hum of the overhead light buzzed like an insect in the corner, its presence a dull reminder of the world still spinning outside this room. But for me, time had stopped, each tick of the clock growing louder, more insistent, as if the universe itself was holding its breath, waiting for me to react.

"Did you see this?" Connor's voice was low, careful, as though testing the waters before diving too deep. He pointed to a section where the handwriting became more erratic, the letters larger, slanting to the right as if the writer had grown desperate.

I leaned closer, the scent of coffee and leather mixing with the stale air around us. The words blurred for a moment, my mind unwilling to fully comprehend what they meant.

"It says... 'The fire's not just about burning property anymore. It's about burning the past. A clean slate. Start over.'" My voice cracked halfway through the sentence. I could feel the weight of the words settle between us, heavy and oppressive.

I swallowed hard, my mouth dry. The world I thought I knew, the life I had carefully built, was crumbling under my feet. A clean slate. What had he done? Who was he, really? The man I had loved, the man who had kissed me goodnight every night before he left, the man who had promised to never hurt me... had he really been hiding this from me all along?

Connor shifted in his seat, running a hand through his hair. "This isn't just about the money. You see that, right? Whoever your husband's mixed up with—this is deeper. They're making a business out of destruction."

I wanted to scream. To throw the journal at the wall and demand that it all be a mistake, that this couldn't be real. But deep down, I knew it was. The evidence was piling up, too solid to ignore, too undeniable to wish away. The shock of it all left me breathless, dizzy, like I'd stepped off the edge of a cliff and the ground had been pulled from under me.

But as I sat there, staring at the pages, the words swirling in my head, one thought kept creeping in. I wasn't just angry with him—no, that would be too simple. I was angry with myself. How had I not seen it? How had I let him slip past the cracks in my awareness, wrapping his darkness in a pretty bow of charm and affection? How had I let him, and by extension, myself, fall so far?

"You don't have to do this alone," Connor said, breaking my spiraling thoughts. His voice was so soft, so caring, and for a brief, terrifying moment, I felt the overwhelming urge to collapse into him. To let him hold me, to let him take away the ache that gnawed at my chest. But I didn't. I couldn't. If I gave in, even for a second, I'd lose myself entirely.

"I'm fine," I said, perhaps too sharply, my words slicing through the silence. "I've always done fine. Alone."

Connor didn't press, but I saw the flicker of something in his eyes, an understanding that both comforted and unsettled me. He was trying to help, I knew that. But there was a part of me that recoiled at the idea of leaning on him. I had learned the hard way that dependence was a weakness, a vulnerability to be exploited. I couldn't afford to be weak now. Not with everything at stake.

The tension between us thickened, the space between us a chasm that neither of us could bridge. He cleared his throat, shifting in his seat again, and I noticed the way his gaze lingered on me, studying, assessing. But I refused to meet his eyes. I had no time for distractions, no time for whatever this... this thing between us was.

"We need to dig deeper," Connor said, breaking the silence, his tone matter-of-fact as if he hadn't just reminded me that I wasn't alone in this. His eyes didn't leave me as he spoke, but there was no judgment, no expectation. He was just... here. Offering what little he could, even as the world around us threatened to collapse.

I nodded, still avoiding his gaze. My hands were shaking now, and I clenched them into fists on the table, willing myself to stay in control. "Let's finish this," I whispered, but the words felt hollow, like I was speaking from a place far outside myself.

Connor's eyes softened, but he didn't argue. Instead, he reached for the journal, flipping through its pages with careful hands, each turn a reminder of how much had already been uncovered.

But there was one last entry that caught my eye. The ink was darker here, thicker, as if the writer had known what was coming. It was a name—my husband's—and beneath it, the words, "He'll be ready when we need him. He always has been."

I felt a chill run down my spine, the weight of that sentence crashing into me. Ready for what? Ready to burn more than just property? What had my husband really been doing all this time?

Connor looked up, his eyes meeting mine with a question. A silent one, but a question all the same. What was I going to do with this? What was I going to do now that the man I had known was slipping through my fingers, replaced by someone unrecognizable?

I didn't have an answer. Not yet.

I didn't want to think about it. The truth. The ramifications of it all, heavy and suffocating, curling around me like a noose I couldn't see. But no matter how I tried to shut it out, the words, the names, the half-hidden clues kept creeping into my mind. Every time I blinked, they were there, like shadows under my eyelids.

FLICKER

Connor wasn't leaving. He stayed seated, leaning back slightly in his chair, his eyes fixed on me. I didn't want to meet his gaze. If I looked, I might see the pity in them, and that was the one thing I didn't need.

"You know," Connor said, breaking the silence that had settled between us like dust in a forgotten room, "sometimes the worst part of discovering something like this isn't the revelation itself, but realizing that everything you thought you knew was a lie. The man you thought was one thing... is actually something else entirely."

The words felt like an echo of my own thoughts, but hearing them out loud made them more real. More irreversible. I knew he was right, of course. But somehow, knowing it didn't make it any easier to swallow.

"I'm not sure I can trust what's real anymore," I whispered. The words felt too vulnerable coming from my lips, too raw. But it was the truth, and sometimes the truth was all we had left.

Connor nodded, his jaw tightening slightly. "I get it. But we can't sit here letting the pieces fall apart without trying to put them back together."

I looked at him, feeling the weight of those words settle inside me. He had no idea. How could he? He wasn't the one who had married a man who now seemed to have been living a double life. He wasn't the one who had entrusted her heart, her future, to someone who was clearly a stranger.

"I don't know if I can fix this," I said, the bitterness of it turning the words sharp.

Connor's eyes softened, though I didn't want them to. I didn't want his sympathy. Didn't want the way he seemed to understand the depth of my turmoil. I wanted to be angry, to scream, to feel like I was in control of something, anything.

"You don't have to do it alone," he said again, his voice steady, like he was offering me an anchor in a storm.

But I couldn't take it. Not yet. Not from him. Not from anyone.

"I'm fine," I said, forcing the words out as if they could make it true. "I've been doing just fine for a long time. Alone."

The sharpness in my tone hung in the air between us, thick with unspoken things. Things I wasn't ready to admit, even to myself. There was a part of me that felt like I was losing control. A part of me that longed for the man I had married to suddenly appear in front of me, confessing that this whole mess was a misunderstanding, that everything would go back to normal. But that was a fantasy, and deep down, I knew it.

Connor didn't push. He never did. Instead, he just let the silence stretch between us, an unspoken agreement that we'd both been handed more than we could process in a single moment. He didn't need me to crumble. He didn't need me to need him. But there was an understanding there. A quiet recognition that we were both treading the same precarious ground, just on opposite sides of it.

The journal lay open between us, its pages now littered with scribbles, hastily written notes, and underlined phrases that had me squinting in disbelief. I traced the words with my finger again, as if that might somehow make them clearer. The name that had been written beneath my husband's—it stuck with me. Not because it was unfamiliar, but because it was one I should have known.

It was a name tied to a place. A place I had been avoiding for years. I hadn't realized how much I'd distanced myself from the darker corners of my life until now, but there it was, staring at me, daring me to face the truth.

I pushed the journal aside and stood up, my legs unsteady beneath me. The room felt too small, too stifling. I needed air, space to think, to breathe without the pressure of this new reality suffocating me. I walked over to the window, my hand resting lightly on the sill as I stared out at the street below, the headlights of passing cars blurring in the early evening haze.

"Do you think it's possible to ever really know someone?" I asked, the question hanging in the air like smoke.

Connor's voice was slow, careful, as if he was weighing his words. "I think people are capable of things we can't always predict. We like to think we know them, but... the truth is, we only know the parts they choose to show us."

I nodded, turning back to face him. His words were sharp, but there was no judgment. No condemnation in them. Just the cold truth, laid bare. And it was that truth that had me wondering what I had missed. What I had overlooked in my own marriage.

"I should have seen it," I muttered to myself. "I should have..."

But the thought trailed off, unanswered. There was no point in revisiting the past. The damage had been done.

Connor was still watching me, his eyes soft, but distant. I knew he wanted to offer comfort. Wanted to pull me out of this spiral of self-blame. But I wasn't ready for that. Not yet. Not when the pieces of the puzzle were still slipping through my fingers, always just out of reach.

"What now?" I asked, the words coming out like a dare.

Connor didn't flinch. He simply stood and walked toward me, his movements calm, assured. "We find the answers. We don't stop until we get them. And when we do... we deal with it. Together."

There was something in his tone that made me want to believe him, even as I resisted it. Even as the walls inside me thickened, pushing him further away.

But the one thing I knew for sure was that this wasn't over. Not by a long shot.

I hadn't meant to come here tonight. To this place where the world outside still seemed to function normally, where people went about their business without any inkling that beneath the calm surface, something dark and unyielding was about to spill over. But here I was, standing in front of the old warehouse that had once been nothing more than an abandoned building in my peripheral vision. Now it was the center of all my unraveling thoughts.

Connor hadn't followed me, but I knew he was still in the background, his presence hovering just at the edge of my awareness. His words about finding answers rang in my head, but they felt like a futile whisper against the noise in my mind. The man I had married, the man I had trusted, was not the person I had thought him to be. He was someone else entirely—a man whose ties to this network of arsonists had been carefully hidden behind a veil of normalcy. And all this time, I had been blind to it.

I let out a long breath, the cool night air biting at my skin. The city was quieter now, the traffic ebbing, the hum of life growing softer with every passing minute. There was something oddly peaceful about it, as if the world was waiting for me to make a choice.

I hadn't been back here in years. This warehouse had been a part of my past, part of a life I'd left behind long ago. A life I had buried under the weight of the present, under the illusion of a happy marriage, a clean slate. But now, standing here, it felt like all that had been fake. An illusion carefully constructed, and one that was about to come crashing down.

My hand brushed against the worn brick of the building, a touch that felt colder than I remembered. The soft scrape of my nails against the surface was the only sound in the stillness, a reminder that I was alone in this moment. Or, at least, I thought I was.

I heard the footsteps before I saw him. They were steady, deliberate, and when I turned, my breath caught in my throat.

"Thought you might be here," Connor said, his voice calm, but there was an edge to it. Something deeper that hinted at the turmoil he, too, was carrying. His gaze was locked onto mine, but there was something almost guarded in the way he stood now, his posture a little more rigid, like he was bracing for the storm I was about to unleash.

I didn't say anything at first. What was there to say? We both knew what I was here for. We both knew what was coming next.

"Why?" The question came out before I could stop it, the word sharp and raw. "Why didn't you tell me about this sooner?"

Connor's lips pressed together in a tight line, his eyes softening, but only slightly. "You were already carrying enough, and... I didn't know how to tell you. Didn't know if I could be the one to make you see it."

I scoffed, the sound sharp in the quiet air. "I don't need you to protect me. I need the truth."

He took a step forward, his hands tucked into the pockets of his jacket. "I didn't think you were ready for it. Still don't, actually."

I frowned, my pulse quickening with the realization of what he was saying. "And now?"

"Now?" He paused, his voice dropping an octave. "Now, I think you're already in it. Too far in to walk away."

The finality in his words hung between us, an invisible line that neither of us could cross, no matter how much we wanted to. I was in this, whether I liked it or not. There was no going back.

I turned my gaze away from him, staring back at the darkened building. My mind was swirling with thoughts I couldn't quite grasp, each one slipping away the moment I tried to focus. It was like standing in the middle of a whirlwind, everything moving so fast I couldn't tell which way was up.

"I don't know what I'm supposed to do anymore," I said, my voice quieter now, the weight of it sinking in. "I thought I had everything figured out, but now it's like I'm... living someone else's life."

Connor didn't respond right away. I could hear his breathing, steady and controlled, and I hated that it was so calm when everything inside me was fraying. "You're not the only one in the dark," he finally said. "None of us are. But we can still find the answers. You don't have to face it alone."

I closed my eyes for a moment, letting his words settle around me like a blanket, the warmth of them a stark contrast to the coldness gnawing at my insides.

"I don't need anyone," I said, even though it sounded hollow, even to me. The words tasted wrong, too bitter. I wasn't sure if I was lying to him or to myself. But it was the only defense I had left. "I can do this myself."

Connor didn't argue. He didn't try to pull me in, didn't push me to open up. He just stood there, letting the silence stretch between us.

But then, just as I thought the moment might pass, the faintest sound broke the stillness—the unmistakable sound of a door creaking open, followed by the echo of footsteps. Someone else was here.

My heart skipped a beat. I turned quickly, my eyes scanning the darkness.

And then I saw him.

A figure stepping out from the shadows, tall, broad-shouldered, his face hidden in the dim light. But even from a distance, I recognized him.

My husband.

Chapter 18: Rising Flames

The first crackle of the flames was barely audible, a soft pop that cut through the still night air like a dry twig snapping. But then, the fire surged. It licked at the house across the street with a hunger that made me freeze in place. I stood there, rooted to the spot, the heat on my face almost unbearable, even from a distance. The glow of it was blinding, turning the night into a grotesque shade of orange, the kind you only see in nightmares.

I couldn't breathe. The scent of burning wood, melting plastic, and something darker—something indefinable—stung my nostrils, choking me with its intensity. My mind raced, but it couldn't catch up with my heart, which was galloping wildly in my chest. I wanted to move, to run, to do something, anything—but my legs felt like they were made of stone.

There was a voice behind me. A low growl, actually, more like a command than anything, and my body jerked as if it had been shocked. "Get back. Now."

I spun around, barely registering the movement. Connor. His face was a mask of determination, a furrowed brow shadowed by the flickering light of the fire, and his hands were reaching for me, pulling me away, his grip firm on my arm as he guided me back from the street. He didn't wait for me to argue. He didn't need to. His urgency spoke volumes in the silence between us.

"I—" My voice was thin, strained, and utterly useless against the roar of the fire. "I can't just—"

"Yes, you can," he cut in, his words sharp as shards of ice. "You don't have to do this."

Do what? Stare helplessly at the destruction? Stand paralyzed as a neighbor's home went up in flames? My heart thudded in my chest, pounding so violently it made my thoughts dizzy.

But Connor wasn't waiting for me to understand. He yanked me further back, out of the range of the heat, until we were halfway down the block, far enough to make sure we wouldn't be caught in the blast of flames or the inevitable smoke that would choke the air. Still, the sight of it burned itself into my mind, and I couldn't shake the sense that it wasn't just some random accident. This was deliberate. It was meant to send a message.

I felt my legs tremble as we stopped near a streetlamp, its dim light flickering uncertainly as if it too were afraid of the inferno just beyond us. I glanced back. The fire was now fully engulfing the house, and the wind carried a sickly crackling sound with it, as if the flames were laughing at the helplessness of everyone watching.

My eyes welled up, but I refused to blink. Refused to let them fall. I wasn't going to cry. Not now. Not with everything hanging in the balance.

I felt Connor's hand at my back, steadying me as he kept me grounded. I was shaking now, unable to control it, but there was something about his presence—his steadiness—that somehow calmed the raw, frantic pulse of panic in my veins. He wasn't saying anything, but he didn't need to. He was here. He was with me. And that made all the difference.

"You can't stay out here," Connor finally muttered, the edge of frustration creeping into his voice. "You need to get inside. Away from this."

His words barely registered at first, my thoughts still tangled in the mess of fire and fear and... something else. The sudden, blaring realization hit me like a slap to the face: this wasn't just about the fire. This was about me. About us. I wasn't just shaken by the inferno across the street; I was shaken by the way my chest tightened when I looked at Connor. By the way his proximity seemed to both ground me and stir something beneath the surface that I couldn't quite understand. A longing. A connection. Something too deep and too terrifying to acknowledge.

I opened my mouth to speak, but the words stuck in my throat, tangled up with a hundred other things I couldn't put into the right order.

Connor's eyes found mine, and for a long beat, the world seemed to slow. The fire behind him pulsed like a living thing, casting strange shadows across his face, making him look both softer and more formidable all at once. He wasn't looking at me as if he saw a broken person. He was looking at me as if he understood the weight of what I was carrying—what we were both carrying—and in that moment, I could have sworn there was something more in his gaze. Something almost... tender.

But then he blinked, and it was gone, like a brief flicker of warmth snuffed out too soon. "We need to get away from here, now," he said again, his voice quieter, but still urgent.

My heart stumbled. "You think it's a warning, don't you?"

His jaw tightened. "Yeah. I do."

I wanted to argue, to tell him that he was reading too much into it, but the truth was, the fire felt like more than just an accident. It felt like the universe was screaming at me, reminding me of the fire that had nearly consumed me before. A fire I had barely escaped.

We had to get away. And yet, something in me couldn't bring myself to leave—not completely. I was too scared. Too rattled. Too aware of the danger creeping closer with every passing second.

I finally managed to nod, the simple gesture an admission I wasn't ready to voice out loud. "Yeah," I whispered. "Let's go."

And as Connor led me away, pulling me further into the safety of the night, I couldn't shake the feeling that the flames weren't the only thing closing in on me.

The air was thick, heavy with the bitter scent of smoke, as if the entire world had just caught fire. I could taste it on the back of my tongue, the acrid bite of something burning that had no business being in the air. Connor's hand was still at my back, a constant, solid presence against the frantic thrum of my heart. I glanced up at him, but his eyes were on the flames, his brow furrowed in that way he had when his mind was working overtime, piecing together a puzzle that had no easy solution.

"Should we—" I started, but the question died on my lips. Should we what? Go back? Risk getting caught in the chaos of it all? I couldn't think straight, not with the crackle of fire echoing in my skull and the thundering beat of my pulse in my ears.

Connor didn't answer. He didn't have to. He just shifted his grip on me, as if making sure I wouldn't run off or collapse or both. It was as though the fire wasn't the only thing threatening to consume me; it was the weight of everything that had happened. Of everything that was happening.

My chest tightened, and for a moment, the world felt too small, too confining, like the walls of this street were closing in on me. The lights from the fire danced across Connor's face, casting shadows that made him look impossibly far away and somehow, incredibly close. His eyes were unreadable, but there was a flicker in them, a knowing that made me uneasy. As if he'd just peeled away all the layers of my thoughts, leaving me bare in a way that didn't feel comforting. Not now. Not when I was still so raw.

"Are you sure it's just a fire?" I finally managed to ask, my voice trembling just slightly despite my best efforts to steady it.

Connor glanced at me, his eyes narrowing as if assessing whether I was brave enough to hear the truth. "If it's not... then it's a damn good warning." His jaw clenched, and he turned his attention back to the blaze, his hands tightening into fists at his sides.

I could feel the heat of the fire still, even though we were several houses away. It was as if the very air carried the weight of it, the intensity of the flames etched into my skin. The fear was bubbling up again, that insidious feeling I'd been trying to bury since the first fire. Since the moment I'd found myself standing at the edge of something I couldn't control.

"Do you think it's them?" I asked, barely above a whisper. The words felt heavy in my mouth, as though they didn't belong here, but they had to be said.

Connor's eyes flashed over to me again, and for the briefest second, something in his gaze flickered—something sharp, something unreadable. Then, just as quickly, it was gone. He exhaled slowly, like he was trying to find the words to say what neither of us wanted to hear.

"I don't know. But I'm not taking any chances," he muttered, more to himself than to me. His voice was low, steady, the kind of tone that made it clear he'd already made up his mind.

I swallowed hard, the words still sitting uncomfortably between us. I wanted to push him, to demand answers, but I could see it in the set of his shoulders—he was ready to face whatever came next, whether I was or not. And something in me—something deep and irrational—wanted to follow him. To let him take the lead, because for all the chaos swirling around us, Connor seemed to have a way of making things feel less dangerous. Or maybe I just wanted to believe that.

"I'm not going anywhere until I know it's safe," I said, my voice trembling despite the firmness I tried to inject into it. "Not again."

The words landed heavier than I expected. I wasn't just talking about the fire. I was talking about everything. The danger that seemed to lurk just beyond the corner of every quiet moment. The way I kept finding myself on the edge, teetering between fear and a strange, almost magnetic pull toward something I wasn't sure I could control.

Connor didn't say anything at first, just studied me in that quiet way he had, his gaze lingering for a fraction too long. It was almost like he was seeing something I hadn't said, some truth that hung between us unspoken, but all too obvious.

"You don't have to stay," he finally said, his voice quiet. "I'm not asking you to."

I wasn't sure why, but those words hit me harder than the fire ever could. I could see the way his jaw tightened again, like he was holding something back, something important. But for the first time in a long while, it didn't feel like he was holding back from me—it felt like he was giving me a choice. A way out, if I needed it.

I didn't need it. But I wasn't sure what I did need. And that terrified me more than anything else.

"I'm not leaving," I said, louder this time, forcing the words to make themselves heard, even if they didn't entirely match the panic inside me. "Not while there's still a chance to fix things."

Fix what? I didn't know. My life was a maze of half-finished plans and unresolved feelings, but for the first time, I wasn't willing to just run. Not from him. Not from this.

"Then we move," Connor said, his voice suddenly resolute, his tone shifting as if he'd made a decision for both of us. His hand brushed against mine, his fingers cold against my skin. "You follow my lead, and we keep moving until we figure out what comes next."

I wanted to ask what "figuring it out" meant, but the words got stuck in my throat. Instead, I just nodded. Because in that moment, I didn't need answers. I needed action. And for some inexplicable reason, I trusted him. Trusted that he wouldn't let anything happen to me.

We started walking, the weight of the world pressing down with every step. The fire behind us crackled like the ghost of something that couldn't be put out, but I didn't look back. I wasn't going to. Not when the future felt so uncertain, and yet, for once, the one thing I did know for sure was that I wasn't facing it alone.

The night air is thick with the smell of burning wood, a scent so pungent it seems to creep into every crack and crevice of my mind, refusing to be shaken off. I feel it pressing on me, squeezing the breath from my lungs, as if it's an invitation to panic, a reminder that the danger is only just beginning. The fire behind us rages, throwing shadows like demonic fingers across the street, and yet here I am, in this odd, tense stillness, walking beside Connor, as though we're just another pair of neighbors out for a midnight stroll.

I can feel the weight of his presence beside me, the heavy thud of his boots against the pavement, the warmth that lingers in the air around him, so close but not close enough to touch. We move through the empty streets, the world hushed except for the crackling behind us. Each step feels like it's leading us farther away from the chaos, but it also feels like we're walking directly into something worse.

"Where are we going?" I ask, the words a little too sharp in the silence, but I can't help it. The uncertainty is gnawing at me, my stomach twisting tighter with every passing moment.

Connor's gaze flickers to me, his lips pulling into a tight line. "Does it matter?"

I bite back a sharp retort, because it does matter. It always matters. If we're running, if we're trying to escape something we don't understand, then I need to know where we're going. I need to feel like we're heading somewhere with purpose. But I know him too well to push right now. Pushing him only makes him more determined to keep his thoughts locked away behind a wall I can't scale. So I settle for silence, my fingers brushing against the cool air as I walk beside him, feeling more alone than I ever have before.

We pass the old diner, its neon sign flickering like a heartbeat on the verge of failure. The place used to be full of life, full of stories told over greasy coffee cups and slices of pie. Now, it's just another casualty of time, fading away into the night like everything else in this town. I wonder how much longer it'll be before it's gone, too.

"I'm not going to let this happen again," I finally say, breaking the silence. My voice sounds small in the empty street, but it's more than I've said all night. I need him to hear this, to understand that I'm not just following him because I have no other choice. I'm following him because I'm terrified, yes, but also because I'm not ready to give up. Not yet. Not while there's still a chance.

Connor stops, and for a moment, I think he's going to say something. Maybe something reassuring. But instead, he turns, his eyes narrowing as if weighing my words. "It's already happening."

I feel a cold chill settle over me. His words are flat, devoid of the comfort I expected, and I'm not sure if he's trying to prepare me for something worse or if he's just stating the facts. But I don't like it. I don't like the way it sounds, as though everything I've been afraid of has already come to pass. I don't like the feeling that, no matter what I do, I'm just a spectator in a game I'm losing.

"Then what are we doing?" I push, the frustration I've been holding back breaking through. "If you think it's already happening, why are we running? Why aren't we—"

He cuts me off with a sharp motion, his hand slicing the air between us. "Because running is all we can do right now."

His tone is firm, and there's no room for argument in it. But there's something in his eyes—something that makes me question whether he believes that, or if he's just trying to convince himself.

"Connor," I start, but the rest of my sentence gets caught in my throat when I see it.

In the distance, just past the edge of the street, a figure stands in the shadows. I stop dead in my tracks, my pulse spiking as my mind races. There's no mistaking the silhouette of a person standing still, watching us. The figure is tall, too tall, and though I can't make out any distinct features, I can feel their gaze cutting through the darkness like a knife. My breath catches, and I take a step back, instinctively retreating toward Connor.

"Who is that?" I whisper, my voice barely audible.

Connor stiffens beside me, his posture going rigid, as if he's already calculating the distance, already preparing for a confrontation I don't understand. He doesn't answer right away, his gaze still locked on the figure, but I can feel the tension radiating from him like a heat wave. It's the same feeling I had when I first saw the fire across the street—like something is about to break, something is coming that I can't control.

"We need to keep moving," he finally says, his voice low, almost too quiet.

But I don't want to move. I don't want to look away from the figure in the distance. I need to know who it is, what they want, why they're just standing there like they have all the time in the world to watch us fall apart.

"I don't think we can outrun this one," I murmur, my throat tight with unease.

The figure doesn't move. Doesn't flinch, doesn't seem to care about us at all. It's almost as though we're invisible to them. And then, just as quickly as it appeared, the figure steps back into the shadows, disappearing from sight. The silence that follows is suffocating, the air suddenly too thick to breathe.

"I don't know what that was," I say, my voice shaky now.

Connor turns toward me, his eyes dark with something I can't name. "But I think we just found our answer."

Before I can ask what he means, the unmistakable sound of tires skidding on wet asphalt echoes from behind us. My heart lurches, and I spin around just in time to see headlights slicing through the darkness.

I don't have time to scream.

Chapter 19: Smoldering Glances

The coffee shop smells like cinnamon and wet earth, the kind of place where the warmth from the mugs seeps into your bones and settles there like an old friend. I don't usually linger, but today, with the autumn chill pressing against the windows, I'm content to curl into the corner booth, my fingers wrapped around a steaming cup as I watch Connor. He's leaning against the counter, his eyes fixed on a map of the town that's been spread out like a puzzle he's trying to solve.

I know better than to ask what's going through his mind. His silence speaks volumes, and I've come to recognize that look of concentration. It's not the first time I've seen it. But today, the tension in the air is heavier than usual, and for the first time, I wonder if it's because of me.

He glances up briefly, catching my gaze across the room. His eyes soften, just enough to make me feel the stir of something—something I've been trying so hard to ignore. He tilts his head slightly, that quiet smile pulling at the corners of his lips, but it doesn't reach his eyes. I try to tell myself it's because he's just focused on the problem at hand, but my gut tells me differently.

I set the mug down with a soft clink, unwilling to sit here and let the space between us grow. The hum of the coffee shop is a distant buzz as I walk over to him, my footsteps muffled by the worn wooden floors.

"What's the plan?" I ask, trying to keep my voice steady.

Connor straightens, running a hand through his hair before turning the map toward me. "We need to keep Leo safe, and we need to do it fast." His voice is low, the gravity of the situation coloring every word. But there's something more—something in the way his jaw tightens, the way his fingers tap against the paper as if he's working through something deeper.

"You're worried about him," I say, more a statement than a question.

He doesn't deny it. He just nods, his brow furrowing as he shifts closer to me, the air around us thickening.

"I'm worried about you too," he admits, his voice barely above a whisper.

I freeze, my heart stuttering in my chest. The words hit harder than I expect, and I blink, unable to mask the rush of heat spreading across my face. There's nothing casual about the way he says it, nothing dismissive. It's not the first time he's voiced a concern, but this feels different. More personal. And the way he looks at me, like he's searching for something in the depths of my eyes, makes me feel exposed in a way I can't quite handle.

"I'm fine," I say, the words coming out sharper than I mean. "I can take care of myself."

He doesn't respond immediately, and for a moment, there's a dangerous silence between us. He takes a step back, his eyes narrowing slightly. "I know you can. But I'm still worried."

The admission hangs in the air, heavy and unspoken, and I know that it's not just about Leo anymore. It's about us. The barrier between us, invisible yet impenetrable, is finally starting to crack, and I'm not sure if I'm ready for what comes next.

I open my mouth to say something, anything to deflect, but before I can, the bell above the door jingles, and the weight of the world shifts. A figure steps inside, cutting through the tension like a blade. I glance over my shoulder, relief flooding my veins when I recognize the newcomer. It's just a local reporter, someone I've dealt with before, eager to get the latest scoop on the town's drama.

I'm quick to pivot, plastering on the most neutral expression I can muster. "Hey, what can I get for you?" I ask, slipping into my professional mask without missing a beat.

The reporter grins, clearly unaware of the storm still brewing in the air between me and Connor. "Just a coffee. Black. Strong," they say with a wink.

"Right. Coming up." I move behind the counter, my hands steady but my mind spinning. I can feel Connor's gaze on me, the weight of it settling like a pressure I'm not quite sure how to escape. He doesn't speak, but I know that whatever we're both skirting around is going to surface sooner or later. I just hope, for the sake of whatever this is between us, that it doesn't come to a head too soon.

The rest of the exchange is mundane, a blur of motions and polite small talk. The reporter takes their coffee and leaves, and I feel Connor's presence beside me again, the silence between us all-consuming. I glance up, catching the flicker of something in his eyes, something like longing or maybe frustration.

He shifts closer, his voice quiet but insistent. "We can't keep pretending this isn't happening," he says, his words sending a shiver through me.

I open my mouth to respond, but my words are lost. For a moment, all I can hear is the rush of blood in my ears, and the world around us seems to blur. It's as if we're the only two people left in this small, crowded coffee shop, the weight of everything we've avoided crashing down on us at once.

"I know," I finally whisper, the admission falling from my lips before I can stop it.

And just like that, everything shifts.

The next few days slip by in a haze of half-sentences and shared glances, as if the world outside doesn't matter as much as the tightrope walk I'm trying not to fall off of with Connor. The more time I spend with him, the more the line between what's professional and what's personal becomes blurred—fuzzy, like the edges of a dream I can't quite remember but can feel deep in my chest.

I watch him now as he leans over the maps again, brows furrowed as he traces a line between roads and properties. The map is cluttered with red circles and notes, marking places of interest or danger zones where the fire could spread. His concentration is palpable, but his presence—the way he fills the room, the way he's always just a little too close—makes it hard to focus on anything else.

I try to break the silence, to say something that doesn't make me sound like I've been staring at him like a lovesick fool for the past half hour. "You think the fire will reach here?" I gesture at the map, hoping the question will distract him enough for me to regain control of the air around us.

His gaze flicks to the spot I pointed to, but instead of answering immediately, he tilts his head. "I've been thinking about us," he says quietly, as if the admission doesn't hang heavy in the air between us. "About how we're stuck. How we're not doing a damn thing about it."

I swallow, my heart leaping into my throat. "Stuck?" I echo, the word tasting foreign on my tongue. "I'm not stuck. We're just… careful."

He laughs, but it's not the easy sound I'm used to. There's a bitterness to it, a tension in the low pitch. "Careful," he repeats, shaking his head. "You know, sometimes I wonder how long we're both going to hide behind that word. Careful isn't going to save us, not from the fire, not from anything else."

I glance at him, trying to decipher what he means. What's he saying? That we're hiding? Hiding from what? My breath catches as I realize the implication—hiding from each other.

"I'm not hiding," I say, the words coming out more defensively than I intend. "I'm just trying to keep things professional, that's all."

He meets my eyes then, and for the briefest moment, I see something raw in them—something vulnerable, like he's laying himself bare just for me to see. But the moment passes as quickly as it comes, and he's the same calm, collected Connor I've known all along. He exhales slowly, like the weight of the world is on his shoulders. "You think I don't know that? You think I don't see the way you pull away every time things get too close?"

I look away, focusing on the flickering candle in the center of the table. "We have bigger things to worry about, Connor. The fire, Leo's safety—it's not the time for this."

"That's the problem," he says, his voice tight. "You keep making excuses. First, it's the fire. Then it's Leo. It's always something." He stands suddenly, pacing, frustration crackling in the air between us. "But it's never about us, is it?"

The words hit me harder than I expect, sending a rush of heat through my chest. He's right, of course. I've been dodging him—dodging whatever it is that's been building between us. The truth is, it scares me.

I glance up at him, my voice faltering. "What do you want me to say?"

He stops pacing, his body still but tense. "I want you to stop running from this. From me. From whatever this is that's hanging in the air every time we're in the same room."

I hold my breath, the words weighing on me like a hundred-pound anchor. I should say something, anything, but my tongue feels thick and heavy. The truth, the one I've been denying for weeks, sticks in my throat, and it's impossible to ignore it anymore.

He steps closer then, so close I can feel the heat of him. "You don't get to keep avoiding me forever," he murmurs, his voice barely a whisper. "Because you and I both know it's not just about the fire, or Leo, or anything else. It's us. It's always been us."

I don't know how much longer I can pretend that I don't feel the same. How long I can ignore the way my heart races whenever he's near, the way I ache for him when he's not. I want to say something, but the words don't come, don't seem big enough to express the chaos swirling inside me.

Instead, I reach for him, my hands trembling just enough to betray the calm front I've been trying to maintain. He doesn't pull away, and when I finally touch his arm, his skin feels like fire against mine. A breath passes between us, and I swear the world holds its breath with us.

"Connor..." I whisper his name, as though that alone can bridge the gap that's grown too wide between us.

His eyes are steady on mine, searching, but there's a flicker of something in them—something I've seen in my own reflection every time I try to make sense of what's happening here.

"Say it, then," he breathes. "Say what we both know is true."

But I can't. Not yet. Not while the weight of everything else—Leo, the fire, our worlds threatening to collide—is still so heavy. Instead, I press my forehead to his, letting the silence between us speak louder than any words could.

For a long moment, nothing exists but the two of us.

The morning air smells of smoke again. The breeze is thick with it, an acrid scent that clings to the back of my throat and makes my chest tight with each breath I take. It's as though the world is holding its breath, waiting for something to break—waiting for something to give way.

I'm standing on the porch, my fingers tracing the edge of the old railing, watching the clouds hang low in the sky, as if they, too, are carrying the weight of what's to come. The fire is getting closer, the smoke visible from here now, creeping up the hills like a beast in the night. It's hard to focus on anything when the very air feels like it's on fire, but my mind keeps returning to Connor. To us.

It's been days since that moment in the coffee shop, days since I almost told him everything. I think about what I would have said—what I should have said—if I hadn't frozen like I always do when it comes to matters of the heart. But the truth is, even then, when his lips were so close to mine, I wasn't ready. Not for him, not for me, not for whatever we could be.

A figure approaches from the driveway, a silhouette against the haze of the morning. I don't need to turn to know it's him—Connor, of course, always appearing just when I'm lost in my own thoughts. He walks toward me with that quiet confidence, that same intensity in his gaze, and my heart stutters in my chest. I want to say something, to greet him, but the words feel too small, too inadequate for the way he makes my pulse race.

"Morning," he says, his voice low, rough from the early hours of work.

I glance up at him, trying not to let the heat I feel in my cheeks show. "Morning," I reply, offering a half-hearted smile, more to myself than to him.

"Smoke's worse today," he says, his eyes scanning the horizon, his jaw tight as he takes in the smoke swirling in the sky. "Could be on us by midday."

I nod, the weight of his words sinking in. "We need to get the town ready. I've been thinking... we might need to evacuate sooner than we thought."

He shifts closer, his presence solid and warm, even though the air between us crackles with the same tension that's been building ever since that moment we almost crossed a line. "I'll handle it. I'll make sure everyone's prepared. You don't have to—"

"I know," I interrupt, turning to face him fully now, my hand still resting against the railing as if it might be the only thing keeping me grounded. "But I can't just sit here while people are in danger. I need to help. I need to do something."

He looks at me for a long moment, his expression unreadable, before he sighs and takes a step closer. "You're not in this alone," he says, his voice soft but firm. "I'm here. Whatever happens, we'll handle it together."

I want to believe him. I want to trust him. But the truth is, I'm not sure what "together" even means anymore. It's been so long since I let anyone in, since I let anyone matter this much.

"I know," I say quietly, though it sounds more like an apology than a statement. "It's just... everything's changing so fast. The fire, Leo's safety... and then there's this, between us." I gesture between us, though I don't even know if that makes sense.

His eyes darken slightly, the intensity of his gaze making the air around us feel thick. "You're not the only one who feels it. This thing between us. But right now... we can't. There's too much happening, too many people relying on us."

I want to argue. I want to tell him that it's exactly because of all that's happening that we should face this. That life is too short to keep pretending, to keep ignoring what's right in front of us. But instead, I keep quiet, nodding as though I agree, though part of me wants to scream that we're running out of time.

The silence between us stretches longer than I want it to. The crackling of the wind, the rustling of the trees, the distant sound of sirens—all of it swirls around us, a reminder that the world outside our little bubble of tension hasn't stopped. We still have a town to protect, a fire to stop, lives to save.

Finally, he speaks again, his voice quieter this time, almost hesitant. "We'll figure it out, you know. The fire, Leo, us... everything." He looks at me like he means it, like he believes it.

I wish I had the same certainty.

"I hope so," I say, my voice barely above a whisper.

And just as the words leave my mouth, a distant roar rumbles through the air, louder than I've ever heard it before. The ground seems to tremble beneath my feet, and the trees sway with a force I can't explain.

Connor turns sharply, his hand instinctively reaching for mine. "We don't have much time. We need to move. Now."

I don't argue. There's no time to argue. The fire is closer than we thought. The evacuation plans are no longer an option—they're a necessity.

We sprint toward the truck, my heart pounding in my chest, and for a moment, everything else—every word unspoken, every inch of space we've put between us—fades into the background. The fire is real. The danger is real. But the thing I've been avoiding—the thing between Connor and me—feels as real as anything else.

And as we drive toward the edge of town, the flames licking at the horizon, I realize that nothing will ever be the same again.

Chapter 20: The Flicker of Fear

I was used to darkness. In the quiet, you can hear everything—the whispers in the walls, the creaks of the floorboards, the way the air shifts. It was comforting in its own way. A thick blanket of silence, keeping everything at bay. I didn't mind it. Not until now.

Connor sat across from me, his eyes shadowed, even in the low light. He had always been the strong one, the one with the steady hands and the quiet resolve. He was always there, his presence a quiet anchor in the chaos of my life. But tonight, there was something different about him. The way he shifted in his seat, the tension in his shoulders, and the way his hand kept clenching the edge of the chair, all spoke of a struggle I hadn't known he was carrying.

I hadn't expected him to speak—certainly not about whatever demons haunted him. But then again, when you've spent enough time in someone's orbit, you begin to realize that even the strongest stars can burn out. I had seen the glimpses of it in his eyes before—the weariness, the flicker of something too heavy to carry. It was only now, in the dark, that he finally let it spill over.

"I'm not the man you think I am," he said, his voice barely more than a murmur, as though saying the words too loudly would shatter something fragile between us. He let out a breath, his gaze fixed on the floor as if he couldn't bear to meet my eyes.

I wanted to say something, to reassure him, but the words wouldn't come. What could I say to make it better? I wasn't sure what was wrong, but I could feel the weight of it in the way his chest rose and fell with each breath. Something in him was fraying, unraveling slowly at the seams.

There was a long stretch of silence, one that was neither comforting nor oppressive, but full of the promise of something unspoken. I shifted in my chair, leaning forward slightly, feeling the pull of his pain like an invisible thread tugging at me. But still, I said nothing. Some things can't be rushed, not when you're standing at the edge of someone's soul.

His hand tightened again, his knuckles turning white as he finally met my gaze. There was a flicker of something there—fear, maybe, or a quiet plea.

"I've been carrying this," he said, his voice rough. "For a long time. Longer than I care to admit. And I don't know if I can keep carrying it." He swallowed, and for the first time, I saw the faint tremor in his hands. "The things I've done—things I've had to do—they haunt me. I thought... I thought maybe if I buried it deep enough, I could forget. But I can't."

I felt my breath catch in my throat. The heaviness of his confession wrapped around me, and for the first time, I understood that the man I had come to trust wasn't the fortress I thought he was. There were cracks in his walls, jagged and wide, and through those cracks, I saw the fear that had been living inside him for so long.

"You don't have to carry it alone," I said softly, my voice trembling with a rawness I hadn't expected. The words felt like the first real thing I had said in hours, as though they were a bridge reaching across the gap between us. "Whatever it is, we'll face it. Together."

He looked at me then, his gaze intense and searching, as if he was trying to gauge whether I meant it. I meant it. Every word. It wasn't a promise I was offering lightly, but I had spent enough time with him to know that he was worth whatever it took.

Connor shook his head slightly, as though the weight of his own thoughts was pulling him back. "You don't know what you're saying," he muttered, more to himself than to me. "You don't know the kind of things I've done. The things I've had to live with."

But there was a flicker of something in his eyes, a flicker of trust. Just enough to make me press on.

"I know you," I said, my voice steadier now. "I know what you're capable of. But you're not defined by your past. You're not defined by mistakes. Not to me."

He let out a sharp breath, a sound like a soft release, and for a moment, I thought he might pull away. But instead, he seemed to fold inward, a tension melting from his frame, just slightly, as if the weight of his confession had been the only thing keeping him upright.

We sat there in the quiet, the world outside still and distant, and I felt a shift between us. A new understanding, perhaps, or the beginning of one. We didn't need words anymore. The connection between us was clear in the way our gazes locked, in the silent promise that stretched between us, unspoken but present, like an invisible thread tying our fates together.

I knew there was more to his story, but for now, this—this moment—was enough. Enough to give me hope, to let me believe that maybe, just maybe, we could heal. Whatever it was that had broken him before, I could help fix it. We could fix it. Together.

The air felt different after that. Lighter, somehow, despite the heaviness of what had just been revealed. Maybe it was the way he had finally let go of some of his burden, or maybe it was the simple act of standing beside him in his vulnerability. Either way, I knew that whatever came next, I wasn't walking away. Not now, not when I had already taken the first step into his world. And, as I glanced at him one more time, the flicker of fear still lingering in his eyes, I knew he wasn't walking away either.

Not from me. Not now.

The room felt smaller after he spoke, the silence somehow louder. The weight of his words lingered in the space between us, a presence I could almost touch. His confession had shattered something, but in the best way possible. It wasn't the kind of break that leaves you aching—it was a crack that let light through. And though I had no idea what kind of shape his pain had taken, or how deep the cracks ran, there was something in the way he looked at me now that made my chest tighten. Something raw and honest. A side of him I wasn't sure I'd ever get the privilege of seeing.

I had spent so long thinking of him as a fortress, this man who walked through life with an unshakable confidence. He was never rattled, never caught off guard, never showing the faintest crack in his armor. But now, in the dim light, I could see that armor wasn't made of stone. It was made of something softer, something that had been bent and twisted over time, until it was hard to even recognize anymore.

I couldn't help but wonder how many times he had put on this mask—how many times he had convinced himself that burying it all, keeping the darkness hidden behind that easy smile, was the only way to survive. There was a sadness in that thought, a truth that struck me harder than anything he had said aloud.

I was about to say something—anything—to fill the space, to reassure him that he wasn't alone. But before I could get the words out, he did something unexpected. He reached across the table, his hand warm and steady, and touched mine. Just a brief touch, his fingers grazing over mine in the kind of gesture that could easily be overlooked. But I didn't overlook it. I felt it down to my bones—the quiet tremor in his hand that betrayed the calm mask he was trying to wear.

I didn't pull away. I couldn't.

Instead, I let my fingers curl around his, just a little, the contact grounding me as much as it seemed to settle something inside him. He didn't say anything. We didn't need to. For once, words seemed unnecessary between us. I could feel the weight of everything he hadn't said, and for the first time, I wasn't afraid to shoulder it with him.

"You know," he said after a long pause, his voice thick with something I couldn't quite place, "I thought if I kept my distance… if I kept pushing people away, it would be easier. But it never is, is it?" His thumb traced the back of my hand slowly, the touch almost absent, but it carried so much meaning that I couldn't help but close my eyes for a second, letting it sink in.

I shook my head slightly, a small smile tugging at my lips. "No, it's never easier."

He exhaled, a soft laugh escaping his lips. "I think I always expected to be able to control everything. My life, my emotions—" He cut himself off with a wry shake of his head. "But it doesn't work like that. It's all messy. And the more you try to control it, the worse it gets."

There was something painfully honest in his admission, and I couldn't help but wonder how long he'd been grappling with that truth, trying to find a way to make the pieces fit when all they seemed to do was break apart.

"Yeah," I said quietly, "it does tend to get messy."

The words hung in the air, not awkward but heavy, like the calm before a storm. Neither of us knew exactly what the storm would look like, but there was an unspoken understanding that we were both about to ride it out. Together.

"Do you ever think," he started, his voice quiet, as though he was afraid to put the thought into the air, "that maybe we're just… doomed to repeat our mistakes?" His gaze was distant, but I could see the faint flicker of fear in his eyes again—the same one that had been there when he first spoke.

I squeezed his hand tighter, not out of urgency, but out of a need to anchor him. To keep him here. With me. "Maybe," I said softly, "but I think it's more about what you do after. The mistakes aren't what define us, Connor. It's how we choose to deal with them. Whether we keep running from them, or we stand up and face them."

He looked at me then, his expression unreadable for a moment, before something shifted in his eyes. A quiet understanding, or perhaps the beginning of one.

"You're right," he said after a beat, his voice steady now. There was no hesitation, no trace of doubt. "It's not about avoiding the mistakes. It's about learning from them. And I—" He stopped himself, eyes narrowing slightly as if he were grappling with the words.

"You what?" I asked, my voice low, encouraging.

He shook his head, a rueful smile tugging at the corner of his mouth. "I think for the first time in a long time, I'm starting to believe that maybe I don't have to do it all by myself."

The words hit me harder than I expected. There was a rawness to them, a vulnerability he had never shown before. I didn't know what it meant yet, but in that moment, I felt it—felt him, for the first time, trusting me with something deeper than the surface level, something raw and unfinished. It was a gift, and I wasn't about to let it slip through my fingers.

I squeezed his hand once more, a small but significant gesture, before I spoke again, my voice steady and clear. "You don't have to. I'm here, Connor. And I always will be."

He didn't respond immediately, and I wasn't sure if it was because he needed time to process or if he was simply searching for the right words. But I didn't need him to say anything. I already knew.

The air between us hummed with a quiet, undeniable shift, as if we'd crossed some invisible line. It was a feeling I couldn't quite define—something fragile, yet persistent, like a thread of electricity connecting us. He didn't pull away from me, though I could sense the battle raging inside him. There were things in him, things he'd buried too deep, that needed to come out. I wasn't sure if he was ready to dig them up, or if he ever would be. But the space between us had already been bridged, and I wasn't about to let him retreat into himself again.

"So," I said, breaking the quiet, my voice light, trying to pull him out of whatever thoughts had clouded his mind, "if we're being all vulnerable and honest, I should probably tell you something too."

He raised an eyebrow, a glimmer of curiosity sparking in his eyes, but I could see the hesitance there too. He didn't want to push, didn't want to pry, but there was a part of him that wanted to know—wanted to understand the person he had decided to trust.

"I'm listening," he said, his voice quiet, but his attention sharp.

I took a deep breath, then let it go, unsure whether this was a moment to reveal my own truths. It felt like it could be, but there was still that hesitation. The truth is, I wasn't sure how much of myself I wanted to let him see—how much of my own fears and insecurities I could expose without feeling like I'd lose some piece of myself.

"I'm scared," I said finally, the words leaving my mouth more easily than I expected. It wasn't just the fear of what lay ahead. It wasn't just the shadows of my own past creeping up on me, threatening to drag me back into a place I never wanted to revisit. No, this fear was something different.

He didn't say anything at first. He just watched me, his brow furrowed in that way he had when he was thinking hard. It wasn't judgment. It wasn't pity. It was a kind of quiet understanding, like he saw the battle within me and respected it.

"You're scared of what?" he asked, his voice soft. He didn't press. He just waited, letting the silence hang between us.

I swallowed, trying to steady myself. "Of not being enough." The admission came out in a rush, like a dam that had been holding back far too much. "Of not being able to carry the weight of everything you've put on me—"

His head snapped up at that, his eyes suddenly wide with disbelief. "I haven't—"

I cut him off with a shake of my head, holding up my hand. "No. It's not like that. It's not that you've asked me to carry anything. But there's a part of me that feels like I'm constantly teetering on the edge. That I'm not strong enough, not—" I faltered. "Not capable enough to handle everything, to be who you need me to be."

The words were raw, and they hung in the air like a thick fog. I could feel the weight of them, but I didn't regret saying them. If I was going to be here, if I was going to keep walking this path with him, then he needed to know me. All of me.

There was a long silence after that, one that stretched and stretched until it seemed like it might break. I watched him, my heart thumping in my chest, waiting for him to respond. But he didn't. Not immediately.

And then, finally, he reached out. His hand found mine again, warm and steady, as if he was offering me his strength in that simple touch.

"You don't have to be anything for me, you know that?" he said, his voice low but firm. "I don't need you to be perfect. I don't need you to be anything other than who you are. All this—" He gestured between us, as though it encapsulated everything we'd built, everything we'd shared. "I didn't ask for any of it. I just—" He paused, his eyes searching mine. "I just wanted to be with you. That's all."

I blinked, caught off guard by his words. It wasn't just the simplicity of them—it was the weight behind them, the way they cut through everything I thought I knew about what we had.

He was right. I had been carrying this idea, this expectation that I needed to somehow meet some standard, some unwritten rule. But that wasn't the truth. The truth was that we were here. Together. And that was enough.

I squeezed his hand, my pulse still racing, but for a different reason now. "I'm sorry," I murmured. "I didn't mean to make this harder than it is."

He shook his head, the faintest smile tugging at the corner of his mouth. "You didn't. But we've both been keeping our distance in our own ways, haven't we?"

I smiled, the edges of my lips lifting despite the weight of the conversation. "I suppose so."

"Well, no more distance," he said with a quiet determination. "We face this. Together."

I felt a surge of something within me—something warm and fierce, something that made me want to leap into this, headfirst. We had come so far, but now I could see the road ahead clearly, stretching out in front of us. It wasn't going to be easy. It wasn't going to be smooth. But for the first time, I wasn't scared anymore.

"Together," I agreed softly.

But as I said the words, a sound—a sharp, sudden sound—interrupted the moment. A knock at the door. A heavy, deliberate knock. My heart skipped a beat, and I felt my stomach tighten in an instant. The kind of knock that carries a warning, a foreboding that I couldn't quite place.

Connor's eyes narrowed, and for a split second, I saw something flash in them—something dark, something unreadable.

"Stay here," he said, his tone suddenly sharp, alert.

And before I could even process the change, he was up, moving toward the door with a fluidity that didn't belong in a quiet evening like this. He paused just before the door, his hand hovering over the handle.

"I'll handle this," he muttered, more to himself than to me.

But before I could respond, the door burst open.

Chapter 21: Shadows in the Firelight

The night had settled over the house like a heavy blanket, the kind that smothered rather than soothed. My fingers, stiff from gripping the phone, hovered above the screen as I stared at the shadow that danced just beyond the reach of the dim porch light. It wasn't an ordinary shape, one that could belong to a passing car or a drifting tree branch. No, this figure had weight. It had intent. I could feel it in the pit of my stomach, where something heavy and ancient curled into a knot, warning me with the same primal instinct that had once kept my ancestors safe from predators. I wasn't safe.

My voice trembled as I dialed Connor. "There's someone outside," I whispered, unsure of whether the words were meant for him or for myself. The silence on the other end was like a live wire, crackling with urgency.

"Stay inside, I'm on my way," he replied, the low rumble of his voice doing little to reassure me. The line went dead before I could say anything more, and the oppressive quiet of the house filled the space where his voice had been. My heart thudded in my chest, each beat a painful reminder that I was alone, even with the phone in my hand.

I had never liked the dark, but it wasn't until tonight that I realized how much I feared it. Fear wasn't something I had been familiar with before. In the past, I'd prided myself on my independence, my ability to handle anything life threw at me. But as I pressed my ear against the window, the shadows outside seemed to mock that sense of control. They didn't care about my strength, my confidence, or my well-practiced calm. The darkness outside knew things that I didn't, and it made me feel small, like a child afraid of monsters in the closet.

When Connor arrived, it was almost too quick. The sound of his car pulling into the driveway, tires crunching against the gravel, felt like a lifeline. I rushed to the door, my breath coming in shallow bursts as I threw it open to find him standing there, his broad frame illuminated by the soft glow of the porch light. His eyes scanned the perimeter, taking in the yard and the shadows that seemed to stretch and flicker with every gust of wind.

"Did you see them?" he asked, his voice a little more clipped than usual, a little more guarded. His hand rested on the doorframe, his fingers flexing like he was already bracing for something.

I nodded, stepping back to let him inside. "Just a shadow, but it was watching me. I'm sure of it." The words hung in the air between us, thick and suffocating, even though I couldn't fully bring myself to believe them. Who would watch me? Why?

Connor didn't speak at first, but his eyes were fixed on the window, narrowing as he took in the stillness of the night. He crossed the room with deliberate steps, his boots thudding softly against the hardwood floor as he moved toward the front door.

"I'll check the area," he said, not glancing back at me as he swung the door open. "Lock it behind me."

I hesitated, staring at his back as he disappeared into the night. The house felt even emptier without him in it, and the weight of the silence threatened to swallow me whole. For the first time since I moved in, I regretted not investing in more security. The idea of an alarm system had seemed like an unnecessary expense, something I could do without. Now, standing in the darkened living room, I wished I'd made that choice long ago.

I waited, my gaze fixed on the door, ears straining for the sound of Connor's voice or the crunch of gravel beneath his boots. The seconds stretched into minutes, each one heavier than the last. The unease that had settled deep inside me began to take root in the pit of my stomach, growing into a vine of doubt that threatened to choke me.

Then, the door opened again. But this time, it wasn't Connor.

My breath hitched as I saw the figure standing in the doorway. They were cloaked in the shadows, their features obscured, but the stillness of their posture sent a cold rush of terror through me. The figure didn't move, didn't speak. The air between us crackled with tension, thick enough to choke on. I couldn't make out their face, but I felt their eyes on me, burning through the darkness like twin coals.

And then, just as quickly as they had appeared, the figure was gone.

My mind raced, trying to make sense of what had just happened. I stumbled back, colliding with the wall behind me. A low, guttural scream clawed its way up my throat, but before I could make a sound, the figure was gone, vanishing into the night like it had never existed. I wasn't sure whether I should be relieved or terrified that they'd left so quickly.

But before I could gather my thoughts, I heard Connor's voice, sharp and urgent, calling from outside. "Get away from the door!"

I didn't think, didn't question. I just moved. The door slammed shut behind me as I hurried toward the back of the house, the blood in my veins turning to ice. Something was wrong. Something was very wrong.

Connor's footsteps echoed behind me, his voice growing louder, but I didn't dare look back. The sound of his breathing was heavy, his urgency unmistakable. "What happened? Are you okay?" he demanded, his hand landing on my shoulder, spinning me to face him.

I could barely form words, but I managed a fractured whisper. "They were here."

Connor's face softened for a moment, concern flooding his features. But then, something shifted. His eyes flicked to the door behind me, his jaw tightening as the gravity of what had just transpired seemed to settle over us. "We need to be careful," he muttered under his breath, his hand tightening on my arm. "This isn't over."

And just like that, the terror, the uncertainty, the fear… it all collided.

The night carried a heaviness that refused to lift, a weight that pressed down on my chest, making it hard to breathe, harder still to think. Connor hadn't let go of me since we stepped inside the house, his arms still wrapped around me, his warmth a comfort I didn't know how much I needed until it was there. His heart beat in a slow, steady rhythm against my back, but the world outside was anything but steady. It was relentless.

"Do you think they'll come back?" I finally managed to ask, my voice a ghost of what it usually was. The words trembled as they left my mouth, falling into the space between us like delicate snowflakes, each one carrying its own layer of fear.

"I don't know," Connor murmured, his hand gently stroking the back of my neck. His touch was meant to reassure me, to keep me grounded, but it only served to heighten the tension that coiled in the pit of my stomach. "But we'll be ready."

I swallowed hard, pulling away slightly to meet his gaze. His jaw was clenched, the muscles working beneath his skin as if he were trying to keep something contained. "Ready for what, Connor? What if we're not? What if we missed something?"

He didn't answer right away, his brow furrowing as he turned his gaze toward the window, scanning the darkness outside once more, his body taut and alert. The silence in the room seemed to pulse with a life of its own, stretching and thickening until it was nearly suffocating.

"You saw something," he said softly, turning back to me. "You didn't just imagine it."

The certainty in his voice cut through the fog of my confusion. He wasn't asking; he was stating a fact. The shadow outside, the way it had moved, the feeling of being watched—it had been real. It hadn't been a trick of the light or some paranoia brought on by stress. There was something out there. Someone.

"Do you think it's connected to... everything else?" I asked, my voice smaller now, barely above a whisper. The question hung in the air, unspoken but already known: the other things that had happened—the strange calls, the sense of being followed, the little clues that had started to pile up in the background, like dust settling on an old shelf.

Connor didn't look at me as he answered. Instead, his eyes were focused on something far beyond the window, something that only he could see. "I think it's the beginning of something bigger," he said, his tone grim. "We've been on the edge of this for a while now. You've felt it too, haven't you?"

I nodded. "I've been... waiting for it. But I didn't expect it to feel like this."

His gaze softened for a moment, and for the briefest second, I saw the man who had always been my protector, the one who would stand between me and anything that might harm me. But then the shadows outside seemed to deepen, pulling his attention back to the unknown. The unspoken fear between us lingered like a shadow of its own, the space between us growing heavier.

"I'll check around back," he said suddenly, breaking the silence. "You stay here. Lock all the doors."

I barely registered the words before he was out the door, his figure disappearing into the dark, his presence slipping away like a fading echo. And just like that, I was alone again, except for the house, the silence, and the feeling that something—someone—was still out there, waiting.

The seconds stretched into minutes, and the minutes into hours. The clock ticked away, each passing second adding to the unease that settled deeper into my bones. I paced the room, my footsteps too loud in the oppressive quiet. I glanced at the window every few seconds, watching the darkness outside like a hawk, waiting for any movement, any sign that it was more than just my imagination.

When Connor returned, he moved like a shadow himself, slipping through the door without a sound, his face set in a hard line. "No sign of anyone," he said, his voice low, but his eyes were scanning the room, alert, constantly on guard. "But that doesn't mean they're not here."

I was trying to focus, trying to keep myself steady, but the tension between us was palpable, like an electric current zipping through the air. It wasn't the kind of tension that came from a simple misunderstanding or a moment of heated words. This was something deeper. This was fear.

"We need to talk," I said, my voice trembling despite my best efforts to control it. I wasn't sure what I wanted to say, only that it had to be said. The weight of everything pressing on me felt like a mountain, and I couldn't carry it any longer, not in silence.

Connor turned toward me, his eyes meeting mine with a mixture of concern and something else—something I couldn't name. "About what?"

"About this," I gestured vaguely, helplessly, the words hanging in the air between us. "About all of it. You keep saying we'll be ready. But what if we're not? What if we don't even know what we're up against?"

He stepped closer, his hand brushing against mine, a simple gesture that sent a ripple of warmth through me, as though he could somehow calm the storm brewing inside. But I could see the worry in his eyes, the way his jaw tightened. He was fighting something, something he wasn't ready to share.

"Whatever's out there, whatever's coming," he said, his voice steady but low, "we face it together. That's all we can do."

The simplicity of his words should have been a comfort, but it only made the space between us feel wider, like a chasm was opening up that neither of us could fill. He was offering reassurance, but I knew, deep down, that neither of us truly believed it. Neither of us truly believed we were ready.

The night stretched on, filled with silence, filled with waiting.

The next few days passed in a blur of quiet unease. The kind of days where the air seems too thick to breathe, where even the simplest tasks become monumental. I kept the curtains drawn, the doors locked, and the windows closed tight. I wasn't sure if the world outside had changed or if I had. But something in me had shifted. It wasn't just the fear anymore. It was a gnawing, relentless sense of something—someone—just out of reach, a presence I could almost feel in the air, always watching, always waiting.

Connor stayed close, a fixture in my daily life, his constant presence both a comfort and a reminder of the dangers that loomed just beyond the edge of my perception. His vigilance was like a second skin, and though I appreciated it—no, needed it—I could see the toll it was taking on him. His easy smile, the one that used to come so naturally, was now rare. His eyes, once full of mischief and warmth, were shadowed, constantly scanning, always alert.

We'd taken to meeting in the kitchen each morning, an unspoken routine that felt oddly normal given the circumstances. It was our space, the place where we could pretend that everything was fine, even for a few minutes. I'd make coffee—too much coffee—and he'd stand by the window, his gaze drifting over the yard, past the boundary of the trees, as if something—someone—was hiding just behind the foliage, waiting to strike.

"You should get some sleep," I told him one morning, a hollow sympathy creeping into my voice. He hadn't slept much since that night, and it showed. The dark circles under his eyes were growing deeper, his movements slower, as if the weight of it all was slowly dragging him under.

He gave me a sharp look, his jaw set in that stubborn way I knew too well. "I'm fine."

I didn't push him further. Instead, I busied myself with stirring my coffee, watching the steam rise in delicate spirals. We both knew he wasn't fine. But it didn't seem to matter. Not with the looming presence of whatever—or whoever—was stalking us.

That afternoon, as the sun began its slow descent into the horizon, something changed. I wasn't sure what it was at first, a subtle shift in the atmosphere, like the world exhaled after holding its breath for too long. But when I saw Connor standing by the door, his body tense, his expression unreadable, I knew.

"Stay here," he said, his voice low but firm. It wasn't a suggestion. It was an order, one I wasn't about to argue with, even though the instinct to protest bubbled up within me. He was already halfway to the door when I called after him.

"What is it?" I asked, but he didn't answer. He didn't have to. The look in his eyes said it all. Danger.

I stood frozen in the center of the living room, my heart hammering in my chest, a mix of fear and anticipation rolling through me. He hadn't said much, but I could feel it in my bones—the danger had become something real, something tangible. And Connor, as much as he tried to shield me from it, couldn't protect me from the truth.

The hours seemed to stretch, each minute laden with weight. I paced the house, unable to sit still, the silence pressing down on me like a vise. I wanted to call him, ask if everything was okay, but I knew better. He didn't want me to hear the uncertainty in his voice. He didn't want to admit what we both knew: we were out of our depth.

And then the phone rang.

It was barely audible, the ring muffled by the walls, but it was enough to stop me in my tracks. I hesitated, my hand hovering above the receiver. What if it was him, telling me to stay inside, to lock everything up tight? What if it wasn't him? What if it was someone else? Someone who'd been watching me for longer than I'd realized, someone who knew I was alone, vulnerable.

I took a breath, steadying myself before lifting the phone to my ear.

"Hello?" My voice was a shaky whisper, a note of desperation slipping through.

There was a long pause on the other end. A slow, deliberate silence that stretched until I was nearly ready to hang up, convinced it was some sort of prank. And then, a voice, deep and unfamiliar.

"We know you're alone."

The words hit me like a slap to the face, their meaning sinking into my skin, settling like ice in my veins. I didn't speak. I couldn't. My mind raced, trying to make sense of the statement. We know you're alone. It wasn't just a threat; it was a message. A warning. Whoever this was had been watching me, knew exactly where I was, knew exactly what I feared.

The voice continued, smooth as velvet but with a chilling undercurrent. "It's only a matter of time now. You're not safe. Not with him."

The line went dead before I could even respond, the sudden silence deafening in its finality. I stared at the receiver in my hand, the cold sensation of dread spreading through my chest, my limbs frozen. I wasn't sure if I should cry or scream or run.

But before I could do anything, I heard it—soft at first, just a scrape of a sound against the front door. Then louder, a deliberate knock, followed by the sound of footsteps, slow and measured.

My breath caught in my throat. Connor?

I didn't wait to find out. I rushed to the window, my heart hammering in my chest, every muscle in my body tense with anticipation. But what I saw stopped me cold.

A figure stood in the yard, their back to me, silhouetted against the fading light. They didn't move. Didn't speak. They just stood there, as if waiting for something—or someone.

I pressed my hand to the window, my breath fogging the glass. And then, just as quickly as they had appeared, the figure turned, disappearing into the shadows of the trees, leaving me standing alone in the dark.

And in that moment, I knew: whoever it was, they were getting closer.

Chapter 22: Cracking the Code

The scent of cold coffee and the hum of my old desk lamp fill the dimly lit room, the only witnesses to my growing obsession. The journal lies open before me, its yellowed pages smudged and creased from years of handling, its ink faded yet stubbornly legible. Each word feels like a trap, luring me deeper into a labyrinth I wasn't prepared for. The silence stretches, thick and suffocating, broken only by the sound of Connor's steady breathing beside me. He's been here for hours, his brow furrowed in concentration, his fingers dancing across the pages with the precision of someone who has nothing to lose.

I can't look at him without the weight of everything between us pressing down on me, but I can't tear my eyes away either. There's a certain familiarity in the way he moves now—too comfortable, too easy. It's unsettling, how quickly he's become indispensable. The lines between ally and something more have blurred in ways I'm not sure I can navigate without crashing into the wreckage of my own desires.

"Do you think we're getting closer?" I ask, my voice barely rising above the rhythm of my thoughts.

Connor doesn't answer immediately. He just leans in closer, his shoulder brushing mine, sending an electric jolt through me. I stiffen, willing myself not to flinch, but the warmth of his proximity is undeniable. There's an odd comfort in it, a sense of solidarity that I never expected to find in this tangled mess. But the truth is, the more time we spend together, the more the line between caution and reckless longing blurs. His presence has become something I crave, even as I resist it.

"I don't know," he murmurs, eyes still glued to the journal. "But we have to be. We can't afford to stop now."

I nod, even though I'm not sure I believe him. Every word, every line I translate brings me closer to the realization that this—this mess, this dangerous game we're playing—is more than just about revenge or justice. It's about survival. My husband's journal, once a record of his mundane thoughts and the occasional cryptic musing, has turned into a map, leading us through a maze of corruption and conspiracy that reaches further than either of us ever expected.

The journal cracks open with a dry sound as I turn the page, the musty scent of old paper filling my nostrils. My fingers trace over the words, trying to decipher the code that seems to shift with every attempt. The symbols are becoming familiar now, patterns emerging where there was once only chaos. Connor's voice breaks the silence again, this time laced with a hint of frustration.

"This doesn't make sense," he says, his finger running along a string of symbols. "These names... why would they be connected like this?"

I glance at the page, my heart skipping a beat as I recognize a few of the names. Powerful names. Names I'd heard whispered in back rooms, names tied to people I'd never thought I'd be tangled with. A sense of dread crawls up my spine, like fingers brushing against the back of my neck. This isn't just a list of criminals—it's a list of people who control everything. The kind of people who can make or break lives with a single phone call.

Connor leans back in his chair, his hands raking through his hair in frustration. "These are the people who have been pulling the strings all along, aren't they?"

I swallow hard, my pulse quickening as the weight of the revelation sinks in. My fingers tremble as I reach for the page, my eyes scanning the list. There's a name there that chills me to the core, a name I never thought I'd see again. And yet, there it is—bold, unmistakable. My mind races, the implications of it all spiraling out of control. It's one thing to uncover a criminal conspiracy, but it's another thing entirely when it involves people you thought were untouchable.

"We're in deeper than I thought," I say quietly, my voice barely a whisper, as though speaking too loudly might make the whole thing real.

Connor doesn't answer at first. He's staring at the page, his face a mask of disbelief. Finally, he looks up at me, his eyes dark with something I can't place. "What are we going to do about it?"

I can feel the tension in his words, the unspoken question hanging between us. There's a part of me that wants to scream at him to leave it alone, to walk away and forget this ever happened. But the words get stuck in my throat. This isn't just about us anymore. It's about exposing the truth, even if it shatters everything I thought I knew. Even if it costs me more than I'm willing to pay.

"I don't know," I admit, my voice tight. "But we have to keep going. We can't stop now."

And just like that, the choice is made. There's no going back, not now that the walls have started to crumble, and the weight of what we know presses down on us like a collapsing sky. Every moment we spend here feels like it's drawing us closer to a point of no return, where the only way out might be through.

But then again, what's the alternative? Let them win? Let them get away with everything they've done?

No. That's not an option. Not for me. Not for anyone.

Connor's eyes meet mine, and I see the resolve there. It mirrors my own, sharp and unwavering, even as the ground beneath us shifts. We're in this together now—whether we like it or not.

The candlelight flickers as if caught in a moment of hesitation, uncertain whether it wants to illuminate or obscure the truth that lies scattered across the table between us. Connor's fingers drum softly on the edge of the journal, the delicate sound of his impatience only adding to the tension. His eyes are fixed on the page, but I know that his mind is far beyond it, dancing with thoughts that neither of us are ready to confront.

The revelation we uncovered earlier isn't something that can simply be processed in one sitting. The names alone seem to pulse on the page, each one a reminder that this—this nightmare we've inadvertently stepped into—is bigger than both of us.

I take a steadying breath, pushing away the feeling that the walls around me are closing in. The room feels smaller than it should, more suffocating with each passing minute. "You think they'll come after us?" I ask, though I already know the answer. We're not dealing with local thugs anymore. This is a game for bigger players. And they don't lose.

Connor doesn't look at me, his face tight with concentration. Instead, he picks up the stack of notes we've made, the ones where we've traced the connections between the names, the dates, and the locations. Each piece of information feels like a puzzle I'm just barely beginning to understand. It's all connected, all pointing to something so much darker than I ever imagined.

"I think it's more likely that we're already on their radar," he mutters, almost to himself, as he flips through the pages again. There's a quiet resolve in his voice, but the tension behind it is palpable. He's seen the kind of danger we're facing, and yet he's still here. I don't know if that's bravery or madness, but it feels like a fine line between the two.

A surge of frustration wells up in me, and I slam my palm down on the journal, the sound sharp and unexpected in the stillness of the room. Connor's eyes snap to mine, his expression unreadable, and for a moment, the air between us crackles with something else—something neither of us are willing to name.

"This is insane," I say, voice low but fierce. "We're chasing shadows, Connor. We're fighting ghosts. How do we even begin to take this on?"

He hesitates, the flicker of uncertainty in his eyes as he meets my gaze. There's a moment where I wonder if he's thinking about how much easier it would be to just walk away. But then he nods, his jaw tight. "We don't have a choice, do we?"

I want to argue. I want to tell him that we could still get out, that we could just turn our backs and walk away like the rest of the world does when things get too hard. But I can't. The weight of my husband's journal presses down on me, pulling me deeper into the web of deceit we've stumbled into. This isn't just about justice anymore—it's about survival.

I run a hand through my hair, trying to steady the storm brewing in my mind. "So, what's next? We just march into the lion's den and demand answers?"

Connor chuckles, though it lacks humor. "If only it were that simple."

His eyes gleam with something dangerous, something I haven't quite figured out yet. There's a fire in him, a need for something more than just closure, something deeper than justice. It's a dangerous kind of thirst, the kind that leads people to do things they never thought they were capable of.

"Is this how you usually operate?" I ask, leaning back in my chair, watching him with a mixture of amusement and disbelief. "Just dive headfirst into the chaos?"

He smirks, but there's a flicker of something vulnerable behind it. "If I told you, you'd think I was crazy."

I raise an eyebrow. "Try me."

The smirk fades slightly as he shifts in his seat. He seems to consider something, weighing his words carefully, before letting out a soft sigh. "When you've seen as much as I have, you stop waiting for permission to act. You just... do."

His words hang in the air, and for a moment, I wonder if he's speaking from experience, if he's done this before—gone up against forces far larger than any of us could hope to understand. But before I can ask, he's already back to the journal, scribbling notes in his meticulous, purposeful way.

"I don't think we have much time," he murmurs, his voice low and serious again. "If they've been watching us this long, they're going to make their move soon."

I lean forward, my heart thudding a little faster at the thought of what we're up against. "Then what do we do? Wait for them to come to us?"

Connor's gaze is sharp, calculating. "We take the fight to them."

I swallow hard, the weight of the decision pressing on me. This isn't just a choice. It's a point of no return. I can feel it in my bones, in the way my hands won't stop shaking. Once we make this move, there's no going back.

"I just need to know something," I say, my voice barely a whisper as I stare at the pages in front of me. "Are you sure you're ready for this? Because once we step into this world, there's no guarantee we'll make it out."

For a moment, he doesn't respond. Instead, he meets my eyes with a steadiness that cuts through the chaos in my mind. "I've been ready for this my whole life."

The words settle between us like a pact, and suddenly, I realize that there's no turning back. Whatever happens next, we're in it together. And that might be the most dangerous thing of all.

The clock ticks louder in the stillness, its hands moving like the relentless march of time itself, never waiting, never slowing. I can feel it now—the shift. The change in the air that tells me things will never be the same again. Every detail I've learned, every revelation that's come to light, seems to hang in the room like a dangerous melody. The silence between us is thick, suffocating, filled with too many unsaid words. But it's not the silence that grips me most—it's the knowledge that we've crossed a line. And I'm not sure we can ever uncross it.

Connor's gaze is unwavering as he stares down at the journal, his fingers resting lightly on the paper as if afraid that touching it too hard might break the fragile thread of our progress. I know he's thinking the same thing I am—this is bigger than us. It's bigger than the names we've uncovered, the faces that no longer seem like strangers, the connections that lead us deeper into a labyrinth of power and corruption.

"I never thought it would come to this," I say, my voice softer than I intended. The words come out as a confession, a weight lifted, yet it only adds to the heaviness in the air.

Connor shifts in his seat, his eyes darkened with something I can't quite read. It's not fear—I would know fear. It's something else, something older, more dangerous. "You think I didn't know what I was getting into?" he asks, his voice rough, as if he's been carrying this burden long before I ever found him.

"I don't know what you knew," I reply, my tone sharp, though it falters when I see the subtle strain in his features. "But you can't tell me this isn't starting to feel like we're playing with fire. Real fire."

He doesn't respond at first, just watches me for a long beat, his jaw tight, muscles working beneath his skin. Then, finally, he shrugs, the motion so casual that it almost feels like a lie. "It's always been fire. You just didn't see it yet."

I swallow, the words ringing in my ears, and I can't decide if I want to laugh or scream. He's right, of course. I didn't see it. I was too busy wrapping myself in the comfort of the life I thought I understood, too naive to think that the dangerous world

I'd married into could touch me. That the world my husband had left behind—its shadows, its lies—would come knocking at my door.

The journal lies there between us, the names like a whisper that won't stop. Each one feels like a betrayal, like an accusation. And yet, there's no escaping them. No running from them. We're too far in now.

I look at the page, my fingers trembling slightly as they hover over the ink. The list is a road map to everything I never wanted to know—about my husband, about the people he associated with, about the things he might have been a part of. It's a cold truth, one I can't unsee.

"There's no way out of this," I murmur, more to myself than to Connor. The weight of the truth presses down on me, and I can feel my thoughts spiral. "We're going to have to expose them. We have to. We're too far in, and they won't let us walk away now."

Connor's hand moves over the pages, as if he's reading something I can't see. "You're right," he says, his voice so calm that it sends a shiver down my spine. "We've already been exposed. There's no way to put the genie back in the bottle. Not now."

I can feel his gaze on me, and for the first time, it's not the heat of a shared secret or the spark of something I can't control. It's a cold, calculating focus—something hardened, something darker than the man I thought I knew. I don't know if it's the weight of the journal or the danger closing in, but there's a distance between us now. It's subtle, but it's there, like a thread pulled taut between two people who know they can't stay the same. Not after this.

The air seems to grow colder, and I shiver despite myself. The room feels too small, too confined, as if the walls are pressing in, making it harder to breathe. We're in it now. This isn't just a battle for answers or revenge anymore. It's survival. And I wonder, just for a moment, if I'm in over my head.

Connor's voice cuts through my thoughts. "We'll do what we have to do. We always do."

His words should reassure me, but they don't. Instead, they twist something inside me. He says them like he's been in situations like this before, like he's already made peace with whatever it takes. And I'm not sure that I have.

A sudden noise jolts me out of my reverie, sharp and unexpected—a faint scraping sound, almost imperceptible. But my heart jumps into my throat anyway, and I look up, my senses on high alert. The room is still. Too still. The soft hum of the city beyond our window, the murmur of traffic, the distant clink of glasses from the bar downstairs—all of it feels miles away now, as if I've been transported into another world entirely. One where secrets have weight, and danger is always close.

Connor stands abruptly, his chair scraping loudly against the floor. I freeze, my breath catching in my throat. "What is it?" I ask, my voice tight with sudden unease.

He doesn't answer at first, just moves toward the window, peering out into the darkened street below. The shadows of the alley shift like phantoms, the faintest trace of movement catching his eye.

"Someone's here," he says, his voice low, almost too calm.

I take a step back, my pulse quickening. "Who?"

But before he can answer, the door creaks open behind us, and the world I thought I understood shatters all over again.

Chapter 23: The Heat of Revelation

It hits me like a sudden storm, the kind that swirls up from the horizon with no warning, black clouds roiling in the sky and the scent of rain heavy in the air. One moment, everything is hazy and quiet—the soft hum of the refrigerator in the kitchen, the murmur of traffic beyond the windows—and the next, Connor's face goes pale, his eyes widening with disbelief. The piece of paper in his hand trembles, the printed name staring up at him like a brand, an accusation made manifest.

I don't even have to look at the words to know what it says. I've seen that name before, tucked away in a corner of my memory, hidden beneath the layers of time and mistrust. But now, it's a sharp edge of reality, its truth cutting through the thick fog of our lives like a knife through tissue. The betrayal stings, fresh and raw, because this is the kind of person you never expect to fall from grace. I'd met him once, shaking his hand in passing, and that simple moment of politeness felt like a lifetime ago.

"Not him," Connor mutters, the words thick in his throat as if saying them aloud will make the world stop spinning. I've seen that look before, the one where you realize the ground beneath you is cracked, and no matter how hard you cling to it, there's nothing left to hold onto.

I want to say something, anything, to ease the hurt that's so visible in the curve of his jaw, the slump of his shoulders. But what can you say in a moment like this? Words feel empty, like dry leaves blowing in the wind, no substance, no real weight. So, I do the only thing I can—I step forward and place my hand on his arm. A gesture so simple, but in this fragile moment, it feels like a lifeline.

For a beat, he doesn't react, lost in the shock of the revelation. His breath hitches, and the air around us seems to press in, heavy with unspoken grief. Then, slowly, almost reluctantly, he turns to me, his eyes desperate, searching for some sort of solace. I know I can't offer him answers. I can't undo the damage that's been done. But I can give him the one thing I have: my presence.

I don't know what drives me to do it, but before I can second-guess myself, I pull him into me. The hug is unexpected, awkward at first, like a dance between two strangers who don't quite know the steps. But then, he lets go, and I can feel the weight of his body sag against mine, the tension bleeding out of him.

"I trusted him," he whispers into my hair, and the words are a razor edge, sharp and deep. "I trusted him with everything."

I want to tell him that it's not his fault, that sometimes people disappoint us in ways we never imagined. But I can't find the words to explain how complicated it all is. Life isn't clean, or fair, or simple. Sometimes, the people we trust most are the ones who will betray us first, and no amount of reasoning or logic can change that.

So instead, I just hold him, my fingers curling around the back of his neck, grounding him in the here and now. The warmth of his skin beneath my fingertips burns, not with heat, but with a quiet intensity, a kind of urgency I can't explain. I don't want to let go. The walls we've both been so carefully erecting around ourselves—those impenetrable walls of self-protection, pride, and fear—begin to crumble in the face of something raw, something real.

And then, it's as if the universe sighs, and for a moment, everything fades away. The weight of his betrayal, the ever-present danger, the secrets we've been hiding from each other—all of it slips into the background. It's just the two of us, tangled in something neither of us fully understands but both of us can feel.

"I don't know what to do," Connor admits, his voice hoarse. "I can't fix this. I can't fix him."

"You don't have to fix anyone, Connor," I murmur, pulling back just enough to look up into his eyes. "Sometimes, the best thing we can do is let go of the people who aren't meant to be in our lives anymore."

He shakes his head, a soft chuckle escaping his lips. It's bitter, edged with frustration, but I see the flicker of something else there too—a hint of hope, as though my words have given him a lifeline in a stormy sea.

"Easier said than done," he says, his lips twitching in the faintest semblance of a smile.

I return the smile, but it's fragile, like a thin thread barely holding on. We both know it's not over, not by a long shot. The heat of the danger is still there, simmering beneath the surface, threatening to explode at any moment. But for now, in this moment, there's something else—something undeniable—that passes between us. Something that's been building from the very first time our paths crossed.

I can't explain it. I don't know how to put it into words. But when he reaches for me again, this time with purpose, the world seems to pause, holding its breath. The kiss is unexpected, a burst of heat and yearning that sets the room on fire, an overwhelming collision of need and desperation. It's not soft, not sweet. It's fierce, a declaration without words, a silent acknowledgment of the pull that's been there all along.

And when we pull apart, gasping for air, the silence between us is anything but awkward. It's full, brimming with unspoken understanding. The danger hasn't disappeared, the betrayals haven't been forgotten. But in this moment, I know one thing for certain—we are not alone.

We don't speak for a while. The room feels charged, as if the air itself is holding its breath, waiting for something to break. I can hear the clock ticking somewhere in the distance, a slow, deliberate sound that reminds me of how much time we've already lost. It's unsettling, the way everything in this world has a rhythm, a pace—and yet, for all the times we try to control it, time always slips away.

Connor doesn't pull away from me, not yet. It's like we're both unwilling to let go of the fragile connection that has finally taken root between us. His body is still warm against mine, but his mind, I can tell, is far away, tangled up in the mess of his feelings. I can almost hear the thoughts running in his head, fast and furious, like the nervous tap of a foot against the floor.

His grip tightens on my arms. "How do we fix this?" His voice is rough, desperate for an answer, as if somehow, if he can find the right words, he can undo the damage done.

I shift just enough to meet his gaze, my eyes searching his face, studying the lines of stress that have appeared there, the shadows under his eyes. This isn't just about the betrayal anymore; this is about the weight of everything he's carried with him—the trust that's been broken, the fear of what's coming next. He looks older, worn down, like a man who has fought one too many battles and hasn't seen the peace he's been promised.

"We don't," I say, the words slipping out before I can stop them. The truth, raw and unvarnished, lands between us like a heavy stone. There's a finality in the air now, a quiet certainty that this is the kind of thing you can't simply fix with enough effort or goodwill. Some things, once broken, are too far gone to ever be the same.

He exhales sharply, his breath catching as though he's been punched in the stomach. He doesn't look at me—he's staring straight ahead, his eyes lost in the distance, his mind still turning over the impossible task of finding a solution to an unsolvable problem. I reach up, my hand coming to rest on his cheek, and for the first time since I've known him, his skin feels like it's been carved from stone, cold and unyielding.

"You can't carry this alone," I say quietly, my voice a soft reminder. It's not a suggestion, not a plea—it's a truth. "You don't have to. Not anymore."

For a moment, I think he might pull away, retreat into himself the way he always does when the world gets too heavy. But he doesn't. His eyes meet mine then, and there's something in them that catches me off guard—a flicker of vulnerability, something raw and unguarded. It's a glimpse of the man he's been hiding from the world, the side of him that no one gets to see.

"I've always been alone," he says, the words coming out rough, like he's not entirely sure whether to believe them himself. "No one stays."

I wish I could give him the reassurance he's looking for, but the truth is, I'm not sure anyone really does. People leave, even the ones we trust the most. It's a bitter lesson I've learned in the quietest of moments, when the doors close behind them and you're left standing there, alone with the pieces of what's been broken.

But I don't say that. Instead, I press my forehead against his, letting the warmth of my breath mingle with his. "I'm not going anywhere," I tell him softly. And maybe it's a promise I can't keep, but in that moment, I need him to believe it, if only for a while.

The silence that follows isn't uncomfortable. It's full, as if everything that needs to be said has already been spoken, and now, we're just left with the quiet hum of something more—something unspoken but palpable between us.

His hands slide to my waist, pulling me in closer, and for a moment, I forget the world outside these four walls. I forget about the dangers lurking in the shadows, the threats we haven't even begun to confront. I forget about the lies we've been living with, the questions we haven't asked. All that matters is the heat between us, the way his lips move against mine with an intensity I can't name.

It's not the kind of kiss you plan for. It's desperate, almost frantic, as if we're both trying to convince ourselves that this—whatever this is—might be the one thing that keeps us grounded when everything else seems to be falling apart. There's no gentleness in it, no softness. Just a raw, unfiltered need that consumes us both.

When we finally pull apart, our breaths ragged and uneven, the room feels different, somehow. The air is heavier, charged with the weight of what just happened. But it's more than just the kiss. It's the way we've let down our walls, the way we've let each other in, even if only for a moment. And I know, deep down, that whatever happens next, this moment will stay with us. It's a thread that ties us together, fragile and delicate, but strong in its own way.

"You're not the only one who's been alone," I murmur, my fingers tracing the line of his jaw. The words feel like a confession, a weight I've carried for far too long. "I've been fighting this fight for a long time. And I don't want to fight it anymore."

His eyes search mine, as if trying to make sense of what I'm saying, and for the first time, I see something that resembles hope in them. It's small, barely there, but it's enough to make me believe that maybe—just maybe—we have a chance at something more than just surviving. Maybe we can find a way to make it through this mess together.

The silence between us is a heavy thing, thick with the unspoken weight of everything that's happened, everything that's still to come. The world outside doesn't seem to exist anymore, not with the way Connor's hands are pressed against the small of my back, steadying me as if the ground beneath us might give way at any moment. I don't know how long we stand like that, swaying together in the aftershock of something we're both too terrified to fully understand. But I can feel it—this slow unraveling of the tension that's kept us both at arm's length.

I should say something—anything—but my mind refuses to form words. Instead, I let the moment stretch out, lingering in the way his breath mingles with mine, the warmth of his skin a silent promise that for once, we aren't alone in this. The city hums quietly beyond the walls, its pulse a stark contrast to the chaos raging inside. But inside this room, with the door locked and the world outside kept at bay, there's a fragile sort of peace.

The moment doesn't last long, though. It can't. The air in the room shifts, sharp and electric, like the prelude to a storm. Connor pulls away first, his expression unreadable, eyes distant as they scan the room, like he's suddenly aware of all the things he should be doing, the problems that are waiting to be solved. I watch him as he steps back, the distance between us growing despite the pull I can feel between us, the attraction that neither of us seems able to ignore for much longer.

"Are you sure you're okay?" I ask, knowing how foolish it sounds as soon as the words leave my mouth. He's not okay. None of this is okay.

He meets my gaze, and for a moment, it's as if the layers of confusion, of anger and betrayal, fall away. There's a clarity in his eyes, a raw edge to his vulnerability that catches me off guard. "I'm as okay as I'm ever going to be," he replies, his voice flat, like he's trying to convince both of us that this mess can be cleaned up with a little effort. But I hear the cracks in his words, the fractures of a man who has been holding himself together by sheer will for far too long.

It's then that I realize we're not just in danger from the forces outside—there's a battle raging within him, a storm he's been fighting on his own. And I can't help him with that, not fully. There are things he has to face alone, things that have nothing to do with me, and yet, I'm here, unwilling to let go.

"I should be the one asking you that," I reply softly, reaching for him again, only this time, my touch is tentative, like I'm afraid he'll pull away completely if I reach too far.

Connor's eyes flick to my hand, then back to my face. His gaze softens, just a fraction, before his lips curl into a humorless smile. "You don't need to worry about me," he says, but I know it's a lie. It's always been a lie, this idea that we don't need anyone. It's the same lie that has kept both of us so damn good at hiding what we really need from the world.

But before I can respond, a sound—a sharp, sudden knock—breaks the fragile calm. It's quick, insistent, a staccato beat that rattles through the air like a warning. I freeze, my heart skipping a beat. Connor tenses beside me, his body immediately going stiff as he listens, the muscles in his jaw tightening. The knock comes again, louder this time, and this time, it's followed by a voice.

"Connor, we need to talk," the voice says, low and ominous. It's a voice I've heard before, but I can't place it, not through the haze of adrenaline and fear that rushes through me now.

Connor doesn't move at first, and I can feel the hesitation radiating off him like heat. He's trapped, I realize. The past is knocking at his door, demanding his attention, and there's no way he can ignore it any longer.

The voice continues, its tone dark with something I can't quite define. "You don't want to make this harder than it has to be."

Connor's hand clenches at his side, his fingers curling into fists. I can see the strain in his posture, the tension in his shoulders as if the weight of the world is pressing down on him all over again.

"Who is it?" I ask, my voice barely above a whisper, but he doesn't answer. Instead, he steps forward, moving to the door like he's been resigned to whatever comes next. The anger in his movements is unmistakable, a storm on the horizon.

"I'll deal with it," he mutters under his breath, and though his words are clipped, I hear the edge of something in them—a warning, maybe, or a promise he doesn't even realize he's making.

"Connor, don't," I say, reaching for him, but he's already moving, his hand on the doorknob, ready to face whatever—or whoever—is on the other side.

Before I can stop him, the door swings open. The man standing there is tall, his presence looming in the doorway like a shadow that refuses to be shaken. His face is familiar, but the sight of him sends a shiver down my spine. It's the kind of look a person gets when they're standing at the edge of something dangerous and they're not entirely sure if they want to take the step forward or retreat into the darkness.

The man smirks, an all-too-familiar glint in his eye. "You didn't think it would be that easy, did you?" he says, and before either of us can react, he steps forward, his hand gripping Connor's arm with a strength that seems to defy the air in the room.

I take a step back, my heart pounding in my chest as I realize that whatever is about to unfold, it's going to change everything.

Chapter 24: Fire Line

The house smells of charred wood and ash, a scent that clings to my skin like it's written into the very fibers of my being. Leo's small hands clutch at the sleeve of my jacket, his eyes wide with a thousand unspoken questions. His silence is the loudest sound in the room. He hasn't said a word since we left the clearing where the fire had danced with the sky, swallowing everything it could. We walk through the house, sidestepping the glass and debris that litter the floor. The walls, once so familiar, now seem foreign, as if they've turned their backs on us.

Connor's absence is a silent, looming shadow. Even though I know he's out there somewhere, chasing the echoes of destruction, it's his quiet withdrawal that hangs in the air, thick with unspoken words. I can feel it, a sort of crackling tension between us, like a live wire. He had been warm last night—too warm. And now, he's the fire, the flame I can't touch. I'm left standing here, surrounded by the remnants of a life I'm not sure how to rebuild.

I sit down on the old leather chair that faces the window, the one that used to be my sanctuary, where I'd sit for hours watching the sun dip behind the hills, feeling the weight of the world ease away with the fading light. Now, the hills are just a silhouette against a sky that feels too heavy, too full of unspoken truths. Leo climbs into my lap, his small body fitting against mine like it was meant to be there. I stroke his hair, running my fingers through the strands as his breathing slows, the quiet comfort of him anchoring me.

But even as I try to breathe, to center myself in this fleeting moment of peace, my mind drifts back to Connor. To the way he had looked at me this morning—eyes like steel, words sharp with something I couldn't name. Maybe I'm overthinking it. Maybe it's just that the weight of everything—the fire, the danger, the unknown—has made him pull back. But it doesn't stop the ache, the feeling of being left behind.

The door creaks open, and I glance up, expecting to see one of the men Connor has sent to watch over us. But it's not anyone from the team. It's someone I know well. Too well.

"Alice," I whisper, as if saying her name out loud might bring some semblance of normalcy to this mess.

Her eyes are bloodshot, her face drawn tight with worry. The sharp lines of her jaw betray the exhaustion that has settled deep into her bones. She's holding herself together, but only just. When she steps inside, she shuts the door behind her with a soft thud, as if trying not to disturb the delicate balance of this broken world we find ourselves in.

"Where is he?" she asks before I can even speak.

I sigh, not sure how to answer. It's like trying to explain the air—it's everywhere, and yet it's intangible. "Out there," I say, gesturing toward the landscape beyond the windows. "Hunting down the arsonists."

Alice narrows her eyes, her lips curling into something that's too close to a sneer. "And you're just supposed to sit here?"

The rawness in her voice stings, but it's not her fault. She's never been one to stay still when trouble is brewing, always the one to dive headfirst into the chaos, to fix things with her own two hands. I can see it in the way her fingers twitch, like she's waiting for an excuse to jump into action.

"I'm not supposed to sit here," I reply quietly, my gaze drifting to the floor. "But what choice do I have? He's made it clear that he's not letting us help. And... and I don't want to make it worse. Not now. Not with everything already falling apart."

Alice's eyes soften, just for a second, before she swallows whatever sympathy she might have felt. "You can't protect him from everything, you know."

I meet her gaze, the weight of her words sinking in like a stone. "I know."

There's a long pause as the two of us stand there, the silence filled with things left unsaid. Finally, Alice breaks the stillness.

"Come with me," she says, her voice hardening with resolve. "You need to get out of here. You and Leo both. If Connor's not going to let us help, then I will."

I hesitate, my mind racing as I try to figure out what to do. There's a part of me that wants to stay, to wait for Connor, to give him the space he seems to need. But then there's the other part, the part that knows we're already too deep in this. The flames have already come for us, and hiding here, alone in this house that feels like a tomb, won't keep us safe.

I stand, feeling the weight of my decision settle into place like a stone dropped in a pond. "Alright," I say softly, my voice barely a whisper. "Let's go."

Alice's lips quirk upward, the smallest hint of a smile. "Good. I was getting tired of waiting around for someone else to do it."

I grab Leo's hand, feeling the warmth of his little fingers in mine, and let Alice lead us out into the world that feels like it's falling apart.

The road is long, stretching out before us like a threadbare ribbon that's been trampled too many times to count. The car hums beneath us, the engine a steady, calming rhythm against the discomfort of silence. Alice drives with a practiced ease, her hands steady on the wheel, her gaze fixed forward, as though the world could end right now, and she'd still keep it all moving. I, on the other hand, keep my eyes on the rearview mirror, as though somehow I'll catch a glimpse of Connor driving after us, racing to stop us from leaving. As if there's any hope of that happening. He'd already made his decision.

Leo shifts in his seat next to me, kicking his feet impatiently against the floor, his head tilted to one side as he stares out the window. I reach over, absently brushing a strand of hair from his face, my fingers lingering for a moment longer than necessary. I don't know why, but I feel as though I'm trying to anchor myself to something that isn't about to vanish into thin air. I can't quite explain it, but the silence in the car feels like a threat, and I'm trying to fill the void before it swallows us whole.

"Where are we going?" Leo asks, his voice a little too bright, too hopeful. As if he's trying to convince himself that we're not just running away from something we can't outrun.

Alice glances at him in the rearview mirror, her lips twitching into a half-smile. "To a place where the fire can't reach us," she says, the words carrying more weight than they should.

I can't help but wince at the simplicity of her answer. The fire doesn't just come in flames, after all. It has a way of lingering in the air long after the embers have died out, leaving a smoke that clouds your vision and makes it impossible to see where you're going.

I turn my gaze to the side window, watching the passing landscape blur into a watercolor of browns and greens, the world moving too fast and too slow all at once. Everything feels off-kilter. Like we've somehow slipped into a world where nothing quite fits, and we're all just pretending it's fine.

"You should call him," Alice says suddenly, her voice cutting through the haze of my thoughts.

I look at her sharply, my pulse kicking up a notch. "What?"

"Connor," she says, her tone too casual for my liking. "You know, the one you're pretending you don't care about?"

"I don't know what you're talking about," I lie, even though I'm sure she's already caught on. I hate the way she can see right through me.

"You do." She grins, her eyes sparkling with mischief. "And it's okay, you know. I'm just saying, if you don't call him, I will. And you won't like how that goes."

I scoff, feeling the heat rise in my cheeks. "Please don't. He'll never let me hear the end of it."

"Exactly," she says, smiling like she's won some unspoken battle. "I'll do it for you, then. He's the kind of guy who'll never know how much you need him until you make him feel needed."

I bite my lip, my eyes flickering back to Leo, whose gaze is fixed on something outside the window, his mind clearly elsewhere. The last thing I want is to drag him into this mess, but Alice is right. If I don't do something, if I don't make a move to reach out, it'll be like I've given up on something that was never really mine to begin with.

"I'll call him," I say, the words coming out more defeated than I intended. I pull out my phone, but my fingers freeze over the screen.

Why am I hesitating?

My mind flashes back to that morning, to the coldness in Connor's eyes, to the way he'd walked away from me like it was easier than dealing with what had passed between us. I try to shake it off, but the feeling lingers, a heavy weight pressing on my chest.

"Hey," Alice says, breaking into my thoughts. "You know he's not going to come running just because you're scared of him pulling away. You have to give him a reason to fight for this."

I look at her, surprised by the sudden wisdom in her voice. Alice isn't exactly the poster child for heartfelt advice, but in this moment, she sounds like she knows exactly what she's talking about.

"I'm not scared," I mutter, even though I know it's a lie. "I just don't want to be a burden."

"You're not a burden," she says sharply, her voice softening just enough to show she actually means it. "But if you keep pretending you don't care, you're going to lose him before you even have a chance to figure out what this is."

I let out a shaky breath, my thumb finally swiping across the screen to dial his number. As it rings, my heart thuds against my ribs, each beat louder than the last. I wonder what I'll say, what I even want to say, as the phone continues to ring in my ear.

When his voice finally picks up, it's nothing like I expected. It's raw, laced with tension, as though the words are getting caught in his throat. "What do you need?" he asks, and there's a tightness in his tone, a sharp edge that hasn't been there before.

"I—" My voice falters. What am I even supposed to say to him? What can I say?

"I need you to be careful," I finally manage to get out, the words sounding too fragile for what's at stake. "You promised me. And... I don't know what I'd do if anything happened to you."

There's a long pause on the other end of the line, and for a moment, I think he's going to hang up. But then I hear the quiet sound of his breath, like he's fighting something. "I'll be careful," he says, and though the words are simple, they carry more weight than anything else he could have said. "Just... stay safe, okay?"

I nod, even though he can't see me. "I will."

And as the line goes dead, I feel something shift, a crack in the dam I didn't realize had been building between us.

The small house Alice leads us to is tucked away at the end of a gravel road that seems to belong to a forgotten part of the world. It's the kind of place that could exist in a postcard, the idyllic sort of home where the hustle and bustle of life seems a world away. The worn porch creaks underfoot as Alice pushes open the door, her shoulder brushing against mine as she steps aside to let me enter. I hesitate for a moment, the smell of wood smoke and pine seeping into my skin, but there's something about the place that's grounding. As if, for the first time in days, I can exhale fully without the weight of everything bearing down on me.

The moment Leo's feet hit the floor, he's off like a shot, racing through the house with the sort of enthusiasm that only children possess, as though he's been given the keys to an entire kingdom. I can hear him laughing from the next room, his voice an echo of innocence in a place that feels far removed from the chaos we've left behind. I turn to Alice, who's already hanging her coat by the door, looking more like someone who's about to settle in for a long stay than a temporary guest.

"You seem at ease," I murmur, trying to hide the bitterness in my own voice. It's not that I'm not grateful—this house, this moment of peace—it's just that everything feels so fragile, like it could shatter at any second.

She smirks, the corner of her mouth quirking up in that signature way of hers. "I've been in worse situations. A house full of chaos? A little too quiet for my taste." She glances over her shoulder, her gaze flickering toward the direction Leo's voice is coming from. "Besides, you're here now. And that's what matters."

But I can't help but feel the disconnect between us, the way she moves through the space with the confidence of someone who's already claimed it, while I stand on the edges, unsure of my place.

"I don't know what to do," I admit, the words spilling out before I can stop them. I run a hand through my hair, feeling the weight of it, all of it—Connor, the fire, the arsonists—bearing down on me like a storm I can't outrun.

"You're going to figure it out," Alice says with a sharpness that cuts through the fog of my thoughts. "One thing at a time. Start with breathing."

I shake my head, the tension in my shoulders palpable. "Breathing won't change anything."

"You'd be surprised," she retorts, an uncharacteristic softness threading through her words. "You don't have to fix it all at once. Just figure out the next step. You've done it before. You just don't realize it."

Before I can respond, Leo comes tearing back into the room, a wide grin on his face as he holds up a wooden toy car in each hand. "Mom, look!" he says, his eyes sparkling. "I made them race!"

I smile, my heart swelling just a little at the sight of him, but the heaviness still lingers, pressing against my chest like an invisible hand. I wish I could simply forget about the outside world for just a moment, but I can't. Not with everything happening. Not when Connor is out there, putting himself in danger, and I'm stuck here with no way to help.

"I'm glad you're having fun," I say, crouching down to meet his eyes. "But we need to settle in for now, okay?"

Leo nods, his attention already slipping back to his toys, and I stand, my legs a little stiff from the long drive. Alice steps up beside me, her hand briefly resting on my shoulder in a gesture of solidarity.

"You know," she says casually, "if you're really feeling lost, you could always help me with something. I've got a few leads on some of the arsonists Connor's been chasing. Could be worth looking into."

My heart skips a beat at the mention of Connor's name. "What do you mean? You've been tracking them?"

Alice shrugs nonchalantly, but there's something in her eyes—something guarded—that tells me there's more to this than she's letting on. "I've got my ways. Besides, you can't keep running forever. At some point, you have to fight back."

Her words hang in the air, heavy and unspoken. I can feel the pull of them, the temptation to step into the chaos, to go after the people who've set all this in motion. But I can't just leave Leo here, not when he's still adjusting to the shock of everything.

"What do you mean, fight back?" I ask, my voice sharper than I intend, but the unease in her expression only deepens.

She meets my gaze, her lips curling into a smile that doesn't quite reach her eyes. "You're more like him than you think."

I'm about to ask what she means by that, but before I can open my mouth, the sound of a car engine pulls both our attention toward the window. I don't need to look to know it's not Alice's car—it's the growl of something heavier, more purposeful. And it's pulling up to the house.

My pulse quickens, my mind racing as I wonder if I'm finally about to get the answer I've been waiting for, or if this is just another twist in a game that's playing me as much as I'm playing it.

The door slams open before I can even make a move, and I freeze.

"I need to talk to you," a voice calls out, one I recognize all too well. My heart leaps into my throat.

Chapter 25: Heart of the Blaze

The air was thick, heavy with the scent of burning wood and something more insidious, something that smelled of lost dreams. My fingers gripped the steering wheel until they ached, the grip tight enough to bruise, but it was the only thing that kept me tethered to the world outside the chaos. My son's quiet face flickered in the rearview mirror, as if some silent guardian was telling me that I was doing the right thing, that I could leave him for a while. But I wasn't convinced.

Connor. The name rang in my head like the warning of a storm—fierce, unpredictable, and carrying the kind of weight that threatened to collapse the world if you weren't careful. I couldn't seem to stop myself, though, the hunger to find him stronger than the fear gnawing at my insides. The news came through in broken whispers, fragmented voices straining against the urgency of the moment. Another fire. Another chance to lose him.

The car groaned under the strain of the road, its engine growling as I pushed it past its limits. The smoke from the blaze curled up into the sky, a dark, choking cloud that promised nothing good. It was the kind of smoke you didn't ignore, the kind that made your pulse race and your stomach twist. I pulled up at the edge of the scene, the flashing lights of emergency vehicles slicing through the haze like the sharp edge of a blade. I couldn't see much beyond the bright chaos, but I could hear it—the crackling roar of flames eating their way through everything in their path.

I was out of the car before it had fully stopped, my boots crunching against the gravel, my breath short and ragged. My heart had already begun to rise up in my throat, clawing for release, but I forced it down. I had to keep moving. There was no time to think, no time to breathe. The only thing I could focus on was the promise that Connor was somewhere in this disaster, that he hadn't disappeared, swallowed whole by the flames.

I walked into the scene like someone blind, only guided by instinct and fear. The firemen worked with a practiced rhythm, their faces smeared with soot, their eyes hard but distant, as if this was just another day at the office. But this was no ordinary day. This was a moment that would change everything.

I shoved past a paramedic, ignoring the protests, ignoring the hands reaching out to stop me. They weren't going to understand, they weren't going to get it. I was his mother, and that was all that mattered.

And then I saw him. Connor.

For a moment, time seemed to freeze, the chaos of the fire and the frantic rush of voices blurring into an indistinct hum. I took a step forward, but the heat from the blaze nearly knocked me back. Connor was standing near the edge of the fire, his face streaked with ash, his clothes torn and stained with what I could only assume was blood. But his eyes—they were still those familiar pools of green, still locked onto mine with the kind of intensity that made everything else fall away.

"Connor!" I cried out, my voice hoarse, thick with emotion.

His head snapped up, and for a fraction of a second, there was a flicker of recognition before his face tightened with something I couldn't quite read. His jaw clenched, and despite the surrounding chaos, he seemed almost serene, like a man who had already made peace with something far darker than fire.

"You shouldn't be here," he said, his voice a rasp, as if the flames had taken more from him than just his strength.

I didn't even register the words at first. I just moved, closing the distance between us until I was standing in front of him. His eyes shifted to the scarred skin on his arms, and I couldn't stop the wave of horror that washed over me. The fire had burned him. Not in the ways I feared, not in the places that would break him forever, but it had left its mark.

"I'm here," I said softly, my voice breaking against the rawness of the moment. "And I'm not leaving you again."

He didn't answer. Instead, he seemed to flinch at my words, stepping back as if he could outrun the pain I was feeling. His eyes flickered to the flames, his body tense, ready to move again.

"You can't keep doing this, Connor. Not with me, not with him." My words cut through the space between us, the air thick with the weight of unspoken things. "You can't keep walking away from us."

The look in his eyes was almost painful to see—like he was seeing something in me that I couldn't even comprehend. He opened his mouth to speak, but then he paused, a slight twitch in his lips as if fighting a smile, or perhaps the urge to tell me to stop being so damn stubborn.

"You think this is a choice?" His voice was quieter now, but the edge was still there, sharp as broken glass. "You think I get to decide what happens next? It's not that simple."

I shook my head, not sure what exactly he meant, but not needing to know. I took a step closer, my breath catching in my chest as I reached out, my fingers brushing the rough texture of his jacket.

"I don't care if it's simple or not," I said, my voice stronger now. "All I know is that I'm not walking away from you again. Not this time."

The smoke still clung to my skin like an unwelcome lover, the sharp, acrid scent seeping into my pores, refusing to be scrubbed away. The sky above was an angry smear of orange and red, the sun barely visible through the suffocating haze, casting everything in a disorienting glow. There were voices everywhere, each one straining to be heard over the roar of the fire, yet somehow, none of them reached me. I didn't want to hear anything. I didn't want to know why this fire had started, or how it was spreading so fast, or if they'd have enough resources to contain it.

What I needed, more than anything, was to know Connor was still here.

I pulled him closer, not sure if it was to shield him or to somehow make myself believe that I hadn't lost him. His breath was coming in ragged bursts, and though his body was still standing, I could feel the weight of the world pressing against him. Against both of us.

"I'm not letting you do this alone," I said, my voice steady, even as my heart drummed so loudly I could barely hear myself.

Connor's head turned toward me, the firelight flickering in his eyes, making them seem darker, more dangerous, like they were hiding something far deeper than the physical wounds he had yet to address. His lips parted, but he didn't speak right away. There was a tightness in his jaw, an expression that seemed to be fighting back a war of its own. I couldn't tell if he was angry, exhausted, or just overwhelmed. Maybe it was all three. He was a master at holding things in—too good at it, in fact, and I'd been the one who'd always had to pry the truth from him.

"I don't need you here," he said, the words clipped and strained, as if they were being dragged out against his will.

I barely held back a laugh. It wasn't because I thought what he said was funny—far from it. But the absurdity of it was almost too much. He was standing in front of a fire that had already burned through everything in its path, his shirt torn, his face cut, and his eyes empty, yet he was telling me I didn't need to be here? Of course I needed to be here. I needed to be with him, needed him to understand that there was no walking away from this. Not now, not after everything we'd already been through.

"That's not how this works, Connor," I said, my voice soft but resolute.

The wind kicked up, throwing ash and debris into my face, and for a moment, the world around us seemed to shudder, the fire roaring louder, as though it were responding to my defiance. It didn't matter. I had already made up my mind. I wasn't going anywhere.

His gaze softened, but only for a moment, before it became hard again, like a shell closing up around him. "You don't get it, do you?" he muttered. "This isn't just about you or me or us. This is bigger than that."

I tilted my head, my eyes narrowing as I took him in. The way he said it—like he knew something I didn't—struck a chord. I'd seen him in difficult situations before, had even seen him make decisions that shattered me in ways I couldn't explain. But this... this was different. There was a vulnerability underneath the anger and pain, something raw and exposed that he'd never allowed anyone to see before. Not even me.

"Tell me," I whispered. "Tell me what's going on. You can't just shut me out, not this time."

For a long beat, he didn't answer. I thought perhaps he wouldn't. But then his eyes flickered toward the fire again, the light dancing in his pupils, and he sighed—just a quiet exhale, like a man who had given up a piece of himself he never wanted to share.

"I'm not who you think I am," he said, the words so soft I almost didn't catch them.

My heart squeezed in my chest, a chill running down my spine. I had never heard him sound so defeated, so stripped of the strength I'd always relied on him to provide.

"Connor," I started, my voice laced with an edge of fear. "You're—"

"I'm not the hero, okay? Not this time." His words were sharper now, and he met my gaze with a look that could've burned a hole through steel. "I've made mistakes. Things I can't undo. Things that—"

"Stop," I said, my hand rising to his chest, just above the bloodstained fabric. "Don't you dare talk like that. You're not broken. You're not the sum of your mistakes. And you don't get to make me believe that."

He seemed to hesitate, his entire body shifting as if the weight of my words were pressing down on him, forcing him to confront something he'd buried deep. But then, like a man who had already made up his mind, he closed his eyes and pulled away, taking a step back.

"You don't understand," he muttered. "And I can't expect you to. Not after everything I've done."

I wasn't going to let him pull away—not physically, not emotionally. He was mine, in a way no one else could ever claim him. The thought of walking away, of leaving him to battle whatever war raged inside him, was unbearable.

"So tell me," I said, my voice low and steady. "Let me understand. I can't promise I'll like it, but I can't fight this if I don't know what we're fighting for."

His eyes locked onto mine then, and I saw something there, something fragile and uncertain, like he was finally considering that maybe he didn't have to carry it alone. The fire crackled behind him, but in that moment, it felt like we were in the eye of the storm. There was no noise, no distractions—just him and me, standing at the precipice of whatever truth he was too terrified to speak.

"You really want to know?" he asked, his voice trembling for the first time.

I nodded, my hand falling from his chest to his side. "I'm ready."

Connor's eyes flickered as if he were processing something too large for his mind to handle. His mouth opened and closed, but no words came out at first. The firelight cast strange shadows across his face, turning his skin an odd, ashen shade. His shoulders were tense, his back hunched as if he were bracing against an invisible weight. I could see the battle waging in his mind—the urge to pull away, to distance himself from me, was written all over his posture. But there was something else in him, something that seemed to unravel with every beat of silence between us. His fingers twitched at his side, like he was holding himself together, just barely.

"I'm not the man you think I am," he said, the words falling from his lips like stones, each one heavier than the last. "I never was. Not really."

I stared at him, the weight of his confession heavy enough to make the world around us seem to tilt. The fire roared in the distance, but for a moment, it felt like all sound had drowned out, like the only thing that mattered in that moment was him, here, with me, spilling pieces of himself he'd never shown before.

"You never were," I repeated, more to myself than to him, trying to piece together the puzzle of this man in front of me—the one I'd thought I knew, the one who had always been there, but now seemed to be slipping away, piece by piece.

His jaw tightened, his eyes narrowing in something akin to regret, or maybe guilt—it was hard to tell. He stepped back again, moving farther away from me.

"I didn't want you to know," he said, his voice strained as he glanced over his shoulder toward the flames. "Hell, I didn't want me to know, but it's too late now. It's all too late."

I felt my heart drop into my stomach, a heavy, sickening weight. "What do you mean by that?" I asked, my voice small, fragile, because the last thing I wanted was to hear what I was already fearing.

Connor ran a hand through his hair, the movement almost desperate, like he was trying to hold onto the last shreds of composure. "You don't know what it's like, to be at the center of something and realize you're not the hero you thought you were. You think you're doing everything for the right reasons, that you're saving people, doing the right thing... but what if you're just feeding into the same fire you're trying to put out? What if you're the reason it all burns?"

I felt a sharp sting in my chest as I watched him crumble before me, his armor of self-assurance and bravery cracking under the pressure of whatever confession was coming.

"Connor," I said softly, stepping forward, reaching for him again. "You're not the reason for this fire. You didn't start this. And you don't have to carry all of this alone."

But he didn't seem to hear me. His eyes were distant, focused on something beyond the blaze, something I couldn't see.

"I wasn't supposed to be here today," he murmured, almost to himself. "None of this was supposed to happen. But it did. And now I can't undo it."

A cold chill wrapped itself around my spine, prickling at the back of my neck. My instincts told me something was terribly wrong—wrong in a way that didn't just involve the fire. There was a deeper truth, something Connor was keeping hidden, something he was too scared to let me see.

"Tell me," I said, my voice firm, though the fear clawed at me like a wild animal. "Tell me what you're not saying."

He hesitated, the briefest flicker of hesitation crossing his face before he spoke. "There's something in the fire... something I didn't expect to find. And now that I've found it... I don't know if we can stop it."

I froze, a cold knot forming in my gut. "What do you mean? What's in the fire?"

Connor's eyes darkened, his face pulling tight. He seemed to be struggling with the weight of the words, his breath shallow as though the very air was suffocating him.

"I can't explain it all," he said, his voice tight, urgent. "But there's a reason this fire is spreading so fast, a reason it's burning so hot. And it's not just some random disaster. It's—"

But before he could finish, there was a sudden, deafening sound—like a crack of thunder mixed with the roar of an explosion. The ground beneath my feet shook violently, sending a rush of panic through me. I spun around, my heart racing. The fire had spread, much faster than I could have ever imagined. The roar of it was deafening now, the flames rising higher and higher into the sky, a monstrous beast that could swallow everything in its path.

"Connor!" I screamed, but he didn't answer. He was already moving, pushing past me, his face set in grim determination.

"You need to get out of here. Now!" he shouted over his shoulder, his voice urgent and thick with fear.

I didn't move. I couldn't. Not yet. Not with the mystery still hanging between us like a thick fog, and not without knowing what he was hiding.

"What's happening?" I called after him, my voice breaking as I stumbled toward him, my body unwilling to obey my mind.

He didn't look back.

"It's too late," he said, his voice barely audible over the roar of the fire. "You need to run, while you still can."

And then, as quickly as he had appeared, Connor vanished into the smoke, swallowed whole by the flames.

Chapter 26: Firestorm of Lies

The sun had barely begun to kiss the horizon when Connor and I stepped into the dimly lit coffee shop, the familiar scent of burnt beans and sugar-coated pastries clinging to the air. I wasn't sure what I was expecting, but the warmth of the place, with its worn wooden floors and mismatched furniture, was at odds with the tightness in my chest. The walls seemed to echo with the laughter of couples and the clinking of mugs, a mundane backdrop to the storm brewing inside me.

He was waiting for us, tucked in the far corner, his face shadowed beneath the brim of his cap. I recognized the slouch of his shoulders immediately, the kind that only came from a man who had been hiding too much for too long. I didn't need to ask if he knew we were coming—he was just as much a part of this mess as we were, tangled up in lies and secrets that had woven themselves into the fabric of our lives.

"Do you think he'll tell us the truth?" Connor's voice, rough with exhaustion, broke through the buzz of the coffee shop. He didn't need to elaborate. We both knew we were here for the same reason: to face the man who had been named in the journal—the journal that had been passed to me like a poisoned gift, a tangled map leading me down a rabbit hole of deception.

I shrugged, more for my own comfort than anything else. The truth, I realized, had become a commodity, something to be bartered for, fought over. And in the world I was stepping into, truth was as fickle as the wind. I thought about the years I had spent with my husband, how his eyes had always held a glimmer of something unreadable, something I now feared might have been lies. The secrets he'd hidden, the ones he said would always stay buried, had started to leak into the cracks of my life. Was it all a facade, a performance staged so perfectly that even I had believed it?

We approached him quietly, our footsteps muffled against the floor, but as we reached the table, his eyes flickered up, sharp and calculating. He didn't look surprised, but he didn't look relieved, either. His lips were tight, the lines etched deep in his face, as though he hadn't smiled in years.

"Well, if it isn't the curious pair," he said, his voice a low rasp. "What can I do for you today?"

I pulled out the journal, its worn leather cover too familiar in my hands, and set it down between us with a deliberate force. The creased pages seemed to pulse with a life of their own, each one a silent accusation. I didn't say anything at first, letting the journal speak for itself. Letting him feel the weight of it.

"How long were you planning to keep this from me?" I asked, my voice softer than I intended. It wasn't fear I felt, though—I'd left that behind somewhere along the way. This was something different, a sharp, guttural need to understand. To know how deep the lies ran. "How long did you think you could hide behind this veil?"

He let out a slow breath, his fingers tapping against the side of his coffee cup, a nervous tick I hadn't seen before. "You really want to go down that road?" he muttered, his gaze darting from the journal to Connor and back to me. "There's more at play here than you think."

"Then tell me," Connor said, his tone tight with a mixture of frustration and determination. "We're not leaving until you do. The journal doesn't lie, but I'm sure you've found ways to make your truths bend. So, go ahead. Show us how deep it goes."

The man's eyes narrowed, and for the first time, I saw a flicker of something like fear in them—fear, or was it guilt? The man had been a ghost in my life for so long, a figure who appeared only when necessary, a shadow lurking in the background. Now that he was fully exposed, he didn't seem so much like the man I remembered. He seemed like a man who had made too many deals with his conscience, a man who knew the weight of betrayal, and who was staring it squarely in the face.

"You want the truth?" he repeated, his voice lowering. "Alright. But you're not going to like it. You're not going to like anything that's been hidden. And that includes your husband."

I swallowed hard, the knot in my throat tightening. For a moment, the room seemed to close in around me, the sounds of the coffee shop fading into a muffled hum. Connor's hand, warm and steady, landed on my shoulder, the way it always did when the world started to tilt too far to one side.

"What do you mean?" I whispered, but even as I spoke, I felt a cold sense of dread creeping through me. What was he about to say? What was Connor involved in that he hadn't told me?

The man's lips curled into something that might have been a smile, but it didn't reach his eyes. "Your husband's a player in a game much bigger than you know. And this journal—" he glanced down at it, "—this is just the tip of the iceberg."

My heart hammered in my chest, but I forced myself to breathe. The man had played his part in keeping this secret for far too long. I wasn't going to let him have the last word.

"Tell us everything," Connor demanded, his voice a bit firmer, his grip on my shoulder tightening. "All of it."

The man hesitated, his gaze shifting between us, and for a moment, I thought he might just turn and walk away, leaving us with nothing but the mess we'd already uncovered. But then, as if something inside him cracked open, he leaned forward, his voice dropping to a whisper.

"You're not ready for the truth," he said, the words carrying more weight than I could bear. "But I'll tell you anyway."

And with that, he began to unravel everything.

The man's confession hung in the air like smoke, curling around me, choking out all the space that had once felt safe. I had known there was more, of course. Deep down, I had always known. But now that it was spilling from his lips, I couldn't grasp it all at once. I wanted to reach into the world he was describing, tear it apart, and find the truth hidden somewhere in the wreckage. But there was no wreckage here—just a carefully built lie, one layer on top of another until it was too dense to see through.

"Your husband," the man continued, his voice thick with something I couldn't quite identify, "wasn't just some passive observer in all this. He's... integral to the whole operation. I'm sure you've seen the way he's always one step ahead of you, the way he seems to know things before they happen. That's not coincidence. It's because he's been orchestrating a lot of what's been happening."

I could feel the air growing thick, the words sticking to my skin. Connor squeezed my shoulder tighter, a quiet anchor in the storm that was swirling through my thoughts. I didn't want to believe it. I couldn't. But somewhere inside, a part of me already did. This was the moment when the floor beneath me was starting to crumble. I hadn't been ready for it, but I had to stand firm.

"You're saying my husband is some kind of mastermind?" I managed to rasp out, my voice sounding alien even to me. It was strange, almost hollow. My chest felt tight, and I had to fight to keep from gasping for air.

The man leaned back, folding his arms, the weight of what he was about to say hanging between us. "Not in the way you think. It's not about control for him. It's about survival. Survival in a world where people like him—people with connections, with power—don't get to live normal lives. He's had to keep a lot of things from you. Keep you in the dark."

"Why?" Connor's voice was low, like a growl. "Why keep her in the dark? Why lie to her?"

The man's eyes flickered for a moment, something like regret—or was it guilt?—flashing before his features hardened again. "Because the truth would destroy her. And he knows that."

It was like a punch to the gut. Connor stiffened beside me, but I could barely feel him. My mind was already racing, spinning on a loop I couldn't stop. "Destroy me? How could the truth destroy me?"

The man's lips tightened, but he didn't say anything at first. It wasn't until I leaned forward, urging him with my gaze, that he spoke again, almost grudgingly.

"Your husband is more involved in this than you realize," he muttered, his eyes scanning the room as if he feared someone might overhear. "You think it's just a few bad deals, some things that went wrong in the past? No. This goes deeper than you can imagine. He's tangled up with people who aren't exactly... law-abiding."

I turned to Connor, my heart racing in my chest. "What does he mean? Who are these people? Why didn't you tell me?" The words spilled out in a breathless rush, the silence between us stretching too long.

Connor didn't move. He just stared at the man across the table, his jaw clenched tight, like he was holding something back. I wanted to shake him, to demand answers. But I couldn't. Not yet.

Finally, he spoke, his voice just above a whisper. "It's not what you think. I didn't tell you because I wanted to protect you."

"Protect me?" I laughed, but it was bitter, a sound that didn't belong in this room. "You think keeping secrets from me is protecting me?"

Connor's gaze softened as he turned to me, his eyes filled with something I couldn't quite decipher. "This isn't about you, Tess. It's about me. The people I got involved with... it wasn't supposed to go this far. I never wanted you to know."

The man cleared his throat, breaking the tension that had been building. "You've got to understand, this isn't a simple game. Your husband's not some villain in a story. He's just... trying to keep things from going completely off the rails. The people he's working with—they're dangerous."

I couldn't breathe. The walls of the coffee shop seemed to close in on me, pressing in from all sides. "Dangerous? How dangerous?" My voice shook despite my best efforts to keep it steady.

The man's lips twitched in something like a smile, but it didn't reach his eyes. "You really want to know what kind of danger we're talking about? How about murder? How about manipulating entire systems to their advantage? These people aren't playing by the same rules you and I are."

I recoiled, the world spinning around me. "What are you talking about? Why didn't you warn me? Why didn't you say something earlier?"

Connor didn't answer. He just stood there, his hands trembling slightly, his face pale. I reached for his hand, desperate for some kind of grounding in the storm that was threatening to engulf me.

But the man wasn't finished. He leaned forward, his voice dropping to a whisper. "Tess, you're tangled up in this now. You've been part of this story all along, whether you knew it or not. And the sooner you accept that, the sooner you'll understand what's at stake."

I felt a chill run through me, the weight of his words sinking in. What did he mean by that? What had I gotten involved in without even realizing it? And more importantly, how could I ever trust Connor again? How could I trust myself?

The man stood up suddenly, his chair scraping against the floor. "You've got no time to waste. If you're going to get out of this alive, you'll need to move fast. And you'll need to make decisions that aren't easy. Because in this world, the truth doesn't always set you free."

With that, he turned and walked away, leaving us alone in the quiet aftermath of his revelation.

The man's footsteps faded into the distance, leaving nothing but a raw silence in his wake. It wasn't the kind of silence that was soothing or calm—it was the kind that scraped against your skin, the kind that left your breath shallow and your thoughts scattered. I didn't know what to think, what to feel, or even if I could trust the knot that had formed in my stomach. The things he had said, the implications of them—they were like shards of glass, each piece cutting deeper than the last.

Connor's hand had never left my shoulder, a constant, grounding presence. But even with his touch, I felt the distance between us growing wider, like a gap that had always been there but had only just begun to show itself. I turned to him, the words forming on my lips, but they seemed too heavy to speak.

"What do we do now?" I asked, the question more an admission of helplessness than anything else. "Is everything... a lie? All of it? The life we've built?"

Connor didn't answer immediately. Instead, he stared at the spot where the man had been, his expression unreadable. I could feel the tension rolling off him in waves, a barely-contained storm waiting to break free.

"You think I don't want to know the answers to those questions?" His voice was a low rasp, worn thin by everything he had kept buried for far too long. "I want to understand just as much as you do. But the problem is, the more we dig, the more we uncover, the further down this rabbit hole we fall. And I don't know if we're going to be able to crawl back out."

His words landed with a thud in my chest. I had thought that the worst of it—the pain, the betrayal—was behind us. But now, I wasn't so sure. There were more pieces to the puzzle, pieces I hadn't even known existed. And every new revelation only made the picture more distorted.

"Then tell me the truth, Connor," I said, my voice breaking on the words. "What were you involved in? What did you do?"

He took a step back, his eyes flicking to the floor before meeting mine. "I didn't choose this, Tess. I didn't choose any of it. But somewhere along the way, I got pulled in. People started asking things of me, things I couldn't say no to. And I couldn't turn back, not once I realized what was at stake."

"What was at stake?" I whispered, even though I already had an inkling of the answer. But I needed to hear him say it. I needed him to confirm it. "Was it power? Money? Or was it something worse?"

He closed his eyes briefly, his face twisting in agony. "It was survival. It was always survival. These people... they don't care about right or wrong, Tess. They care about keeping themselves alive. And I was just another pawn in their game."

I wanted to believe him. I wanted to believe that there was more to the story, that he wasn't as lost in this mess as he seemed. But the words kept swirling in my mind, the man's voice echoing in my ears: "You're tangled up in this now." What did that even mean? How had I become part of whatever this was? And worse—how could I ever get out?

My hands trembled as I reached for my phone. My fingers hovered over the screen, but I couldn't bring myself to make the call. Every number I dialed felt like a decision I wasn't ready to make. Who could I trust anymore? Who was on our side?

"We need to find out who else is involved," Connor said, his tone decisive, but there was an edge to it, a hint of panic that he couldn't completely conceal. "If we can uncover the people pulling the strings, we might still have a chance to make this right."

"Make this right?" I echoed, the words foreign in my mouth. "How do we make this right, Connor? After everything we've uncovered, after what we've been through? How do we fix something that's broken beyond repair?"

"I don't know." He let out a harsh breath, rubbing a hand over his face. "But I do know this—we don't have a choice. If we don't find out who's behind all of this, it's not just our lives at risk anymore. It's everything we've built. Everything we've fought for."

I stared at him, a thousand thoughts running through my mind. The trust I had once placed in him—so unwavering, so absolute—was splintering. It was as if the foundation of everything we had was made of glass, and I was watching it shatter before my very eyes.

"I need you to be honest with me," I said, my voice low, pleading. "If there's more to this... if you're involved in things you haven't told me about... I need to know now. I need you to tell me everything, Connor. No more lies. No more half-truths. Just... the truth."

For a long moment, he didn't speak. The silence between us grew heavier with each passing second, the weight of it pressing down on me, suffocating me. And then, just as I was about to give up hope that he would ever speak the words I so desperately needed to hear, he looked at me, his eyes filled with something like regret.

"It's worse than you think," he said quietly. "There are people who will stop at nothing to make sure we don't get out of this alive. People who are watching us right now. People who know what we're trying to do."

My heart skipped a beat, the implications of his words landing like a blow to my chest. "What do you mean, watching us?"

Connor didn't answer immediately. Instead, he took a step toward me, his face hardening. "You're not safe, Tess. And neither am I."

A sharp sound, like the faintest creak of wood under pressure, broke the tension. I turned my head, my pulse racing, my breath catching in my throat. A figure stood in the doorway of the coffee shop—someone I hadn't seen before, but who I instinctively knew was not there by coincidence.

And then, without a word, they stepped forward, their eyes locking onto mine, and I felt the unmistakable chill of dread slide down my spine.

"Looks like you've been making some dangerous friends," the stranger said, their voice cold and measured, a hint of something dark lacing their words.

I froze. Connor stiffened beside me.

The game had just changed.

Chapter 27: Ashes of Betrayal

The room is still, too still. I can hear the hum of the refrigerator from the kitchen down the hall, a dull thrum that contrasts sharply with the silence hanging heavy in the air. The walls feel like they're closing in, and I clutch Connor's hand harder, as if his touch could tether me to something real, something solid, in the face of everything else collapsing around me. His hand is warm, but even that heat isn't enough to fight the chill creeping into my bones.

I glance at him—his profile half-illuminated by the soft glow of the lamp beside us—and there's a weariness in his eyes, a shadow that wasn't there before. He's always been a man of few words, but tonight, he's nearly silent, as if the weight of our shared discovery has stolen his breath. He hasn't let go of my hand since we pieced together the last of the puzzle, but there's something different in his grip now, something tighter. It feels like he's afraid I might slip away, and I can't decide if it's because of the past we're unraveling or the future we're about to face.

I pull my gaze away from him, letting it wander across the room. The space feels foreign now, like a house I've lived in for years but never truly known. The furniture is arranged the same way it always has been, but it all seems... off. The lamp flickers, casting a momentary shadow on the wall. I look away before it can make me see things that aren't there—things like ghosts of the people I used to trust, their faces warped by the truths we've uncovered.

"Do you ever think," I whisper, my voice barely a breath in the space between us, "that maybe it's easier to live in the dark?"

Connor shifts, the muscles in his arm moving under his shirt as he leans back against the edge of the kitchen counter. He doesn't answer immediately, and for a moment, I wonder if he even heard me. But then, with the weight of his usual gravity, he speaks, his words slow, deliberate, like he's carefully choosing them, as if he's afraid of where they might lead.

"The dark is only easier when you don't know what's waiting for you on the other side of it." His voice is low, rough around the edges, as though he's trying to swallow the emotions rising in his chest.

I can feel his eyes on me now, even without turning my head. The room is too small, too close, and yet we're standing on opposite sides of some vast, impossible divide. The truth we've uncovered—the truth that's been buried under layers of lies and half-truths—is still fresh, still raw between us. I should have known. I should have seen it sooner. How could I have been so blind? To think I had everything figured out when, in reality, I'd been stumbling in the dark, trusting the wrong people, believing in things that were never true.

"Do you ever wonder," I ask, my voice shaking slightly, "how we got here? How we got so lost?"

Connor exhales sharply, like the air is too thick for him to breathe properly. He rubs the back of his neck, his jaw tightening. "You don't have to carry all of this alone, you know," he says quietly, his words aimed directly at me but veiled with something softer—something tender. "We're in this together."

The words are supposed to comfort me, but instead, they sting, like salt in an open wound. Together. We're supposed to be a team, right? But what happens when the very foundation of that partnership is built on lies? How do you move forward when everything you thought you knew about the world, about the people you've trusted, has been torn away, piece by piece, until all you're left with is the rubble?

I close my eyes, willing myself to breathe, to clear the fog that's clouded my mind ever since the truth first came to light. It's hard to focus. It's hard to think about what happens next when the past is still so loud in my head, screaming at me, clawing at me from the shadows.

But there's something in Connor's voice—something steady, something unyielding—that cuts through the noise. He's right. We can't keep looking back, no matter how much it aches. The past is done. The lies, the betrayal—they're all in the past now.

I look at him, finally, and let the silence hang between us for a moment before speaking again. "What if we can't fix this? What if we've gone too far, and there's no way back?"

Connor steps forward, closing the distance between us in three strides, his expression fierce, determined. He reaches for my face, gently lifting my chin so I'm forced to meet his gaze. "You're not alone, remember? We'll figure this out. Together."

For a moment, his words are a lifeline, a promise. But in my heart, there's still a gnawing doubt, a fear that won't go away no matter how tightly he holds me. What if, despite everything, we can't find our way out of this mess? What if there's no path forward for us? The shadows of the past stretch long, and I can't help but wonder if they're too thick to ever escape.

But for now, I hold onto his words, letting them settle into me like a balm, soothing the edges of the jagged truth. There's a part of me—just a small part—that believes him. And maybe, just maybe, that's all we need to start moving again.

I try to breathe through the unease clawing at my chest, but the air feels too thick. It's one of those moments where I can't tell if the stillness is a relief or a trap, like a spider's web just waiting to tighten around me. Connor watches me closely, his eyes tracing the tightness of my jaw, the slight tremble of my hands. He doesn't say a word, but his silence speaks louder than any comforting words he could offer.

"I'm not sure I can do this," I admit, more to myself than to him. My voice is raw, laced with an exhaustion I hadn't realized had settled so deeply in my bones.

"You don't have to," he says simply, his voice low but steady, the kind of steady I wish I could borrow. "You don't have to do this alone. But if you want to do it, I'm here. Whatever comes next."

I wish I could feel the strength in his words the way I know he means me to. But instead, I just feel the weight of them, heavy and pressing, as if by agreeing, I'm committing myself to something I can't possibly undo. What if it's too much? What if I'm not who I thought I was anymore? What if everything I thought I could control is slipping away, and there's nothing I can do to stop it?

He leans closer, his thumb brushing against the back of my hand. I could pull away, but I don't. Instead, I let the warmth of his touch seep through the thin fabric of my shirt, a small reminder that not everything is fractured. I close my eyes for a moment, just long enough to gather myself. When I open them again, Connor is still there, still holding me. The raw edges of the night, of the revelations we've faced, feel a little less jagged.

I draw in a slow breath, gathering my courage like one might gather pieces of broken glass. "I don't know what's worse," I say, voice thick with frustration, "knowing I was lied to or knowing I allowed it to happen. That I let them all lie to me for so long."

Connor's lips quirk in a wry smile, though it's not one that reaches his eyes. "You don't get to beat yourself up for trusting people," he says, leaning in just enough that I feel the weight of his words settle into my bones. "Trust is a risk. And maybe you trusted the wrong people, but it doesn't mean you're weak. It means you're human. It means you're not jaded. Yet."

I want to argue with him, to insist that I should have known better, that I should have seen the cracks in the facade before they grew into something I couldn't ignore. But as he speaks, something inside me relaxes, just a little, in spite of everything. He's right. But then again, maybe he's wrong too. Maybe I should have known.

The silence stretches between us again, but this time, it's not suffocating. Instead, it's like a shared space where we're both waiting for something, for the next move, the next turn in this strange, twisted dance we're caught up in.

"I just don't know how to move forward," I admit, feeling the weight of my vulnerability crashing over me. "I don't know if I can ever trust again. Not after everything we've uncovered."

He steps closer, his presence a comfort as much as it's a challenge. "You don't have to trust anyone right now. Not me, not yourself, not anyone. But you can trust that we'll figure this out. Together."

I wish I could say those words to myself, repeat them like a mantra until I could feel them in my bones, until they were true. But the truth is, it's going to take more than words. It's going to take time, and patience, and maybe even a little bit of pain. And for some reason, I'm not sure if I'm ready for it.

I glance at Connor again, his face drawn with the same worry that clings to me. I want to pull away, to shield myself from the weight of it, but I can't. Not when it feels like everything I've been running from is finally catching up to me. Not when the truth of it all is so much darker than I ever could have imagined.

I pull my hand from his, the absence of his touch leaving an unexpected ache. It's almost like a shock to the system, and I can't tell if it's because I need the distance or because, somehow, I'm afraid of what might happen when I let go.

"We can't go back," I say softly, my voice unsteady, but firm. "We can't unlearn what we've uncovered."

Connor nods, but it's a somber movement, one that carries more weight than anything he could say. "No," he agrees. "But maybe we can make the rest of it mean something. Maybe we can still fight for something better."

The words don't quite settle into me. I want to believe him. I want to look at him and see the unwavering certainty he seems to have in spades. But the truth is, I'm not sure how we're supposed to pick up the pieces of a shattered world and somehow make it whole again.

"You make it sound so simple," I mutter, though there's a small, bitter edge to my voice that I can't hide.

"It's not simple," he says, moving toward the door. He pauses just long enough to look back at me, a half-smile tugging at the corner of his lips. "But you're worth fighting for, and that's something. You're not broken, even if you feel like you are."

I don't know if I believe him, but I nod anyway. As he walks out of the room, I sit back down, the empty space around me feeling colder, lonelier. But his words stick with me, like a thread woven through the fabric of my fear. Maybe it's not about fixing everything. Maybe it's just about finding something worth holding onto in the wreckage. And that, for the first time in days, feels like something I can work with.

The house feels quieter somehow, like the walls are holding their breath, waiting for something to break. The soft clink of my coffee cup against the saucer seems to echo, stretching into the heavy silence that presses against my chest. I try to concentrate on the feel of the mug, the warmth seeping into my hands, grounding me. But my mind keeps darting back to the mess we've uncovered, like an itch that refuses to go away, even when I scratch at it.

Connor is on the couch, sitting just a little too still, his broad shoulders hunched in a way that speaks to the weight of whatever thoughts he's trying to push down. It's not often I see him like this—he's usually the rock, the one with all the answers. But today, there's a crack in the armor, and I can't help but wonder how deep it goes.

"I can't believe it," I mutter, more to myself than to him, as I run my finger around the rim of my cup. "How did we miss all of this?"

Connor doesn't respond right away, and I wonder if he's still trying to process, trying to make sense of the mess. He's good at pretending things don't bother him, but I know better than to believe the silence means he's fine. It never does.

"I'm not sure I want to know," he finally says, his voice tight, like the words are scraped from the inside of his throat. "Maybe it's better to leave some things buried."

I glance at him, surprised by the sharpness in his tone. Usually, he's the one encouraging us to dig deeper, to confront the past no matter how ugly it is. But today, it feels like he's trying to outrun it, like the truth we've unearthed is something that might destroy us both if we stare at it too long.

"I'm not sure that's an option anymore," I reply, my voice soft but firm. "We're already in this. We can't just pretend it never happened."

Connor runs a hand through his hair, looking toward the window, as though the answer to everything might be hiding behind the glass. For a second, I think he might say something else, but then he's quiet again, his jaw working as he fights with whatever's going on inside his head.

"You're right," he says eventually, his voice taking on a defeated edge. "We can't undo it. But that doesn't mean we have to take the weight of it on our own."

There's a vulnerability in those words that makes me pause. I'm used to Connor being the steady one, the one who can handle everything without breaking a sweat. But this—this is different. This is personal. The lies we've uncovered aren't just about betrayal.

They're about trust, about who we've allowed into our lives, and who we've allowed to deceive us. And for him, I know this goes deeper than just the facts. It's about something I can't even name.

"I don't know what to do with it all," I admit, my words escaping before I can stop them. "I thought I had control over this. Over everything. But now, it feels like the rug's been pulled out from under me. Like I never knew anything at all."

Connor's gaze flicks back to me, and for a moment, I think he's going to tell me I'm overreacting, that I'm being melodramatic. But instead, he nods slowly, as if understanding exactly what I mean. "That's because you were never meant to know. None of this was your fault. You were playing by the rules they set, and they changed them when you weren't looking."

The words hit harder than I expect. They feel like a balm to a wound I didn't even realize was still bleeding. But there's no time to linger on the comfort they bring. There's still so much to untangle, so much left unsaid between us.

"You're right," I say after a moment, setting my coffee aside and standing up. The movement feels like a decision, like I'm finally ready to face whatever comes next, no matter how terrifying it might be. "We can't change what happened. But we can damn well make sure it doesn't happen again."

Connor watches me as I move across the room, the air between us still thick with tension. His eyes follow my every step, but there's something in them now—something deeper. It's not just worry. It's fear. Fear of what might come next, fear of what we'll uncover if we keep pushing, and fear of what will happen to us when it all unravels.

"We need to start making a plan," I continue, my voice hardening with determination. "We need to take control of this before it takes control of us."

I walk toward the bookshelf, pulling out a leather-bound journal that feels like an anchor, something I can hold onto when everything else feels uncertain. I flip it open, running my fingers over the pages like they might offer some clue, some thread to pull me out of the mess. But all they offer is empty space, a void waiting to be filled with answers.

Connor stands and approaches me, his footsteps heavy in the quiet room. He doesn't ask what I'm doing, doesn't question my decision to dive headfirst into a plan when we don't even know what we're dealing with yet. He just watches, waiting for me to make the first move.

"I'm in," he says quietly, his voice low but resolute. "But we need to be careful. Whoever did this... they're still out there. And I'm not sure they'll stop just because we've caught on."

I feel a chill crawl up my spine, the words settling into my gut like stones. The truth hangs in the air, thick and suffocating. He's right. Whoever is behind this isn't done. And that thought terrifies me more than anything else we've uncovered.

Suddenly, the sharp ring of my phone breaks through the silence, startling both of us. I hesitate, the weight of the moment pulling me in different directions. Should I answer? Should I let it go, pretend I didn't hear it, just for a moment longer?

I pick up the phone, my hand trembling slightly as I swipe to answer.

"Hello?"

The voice on the other end is unfamiliar, but it's the cold, familiar edge of danger that sends a shiver through me.

"I think you've uncovered more than you bargained for."

The line goes dead before I can respond.

Chapter 28: Smothered Sparks

The rain had been relentless all evening, a steady patter against the windows like a thousand tiny footsteps. It wasn't the kind of storm that shakes you awake in the night with flashes of lightning, but a long, steady drizzle that seemed to seep into everything — the air, the thoughts, the spaces between us. I found myself standing at the kitchen counter, staring at the untouched mug of coffee in front of me. The rich scent of it was still warm, but my mind was far from the comfort of its contents. It had been a week since Connor's unexpected confession, and the puzzle pieces were starting to form something that neither of us had expected, something bigger than I'd ever imagined.

There was a knock on the door. One that wasn't quite forceful enough to demand attention but loud enough to be heard. A rattle at the edges of my senses, a jolt of tension that had been building ever since Connor's last warning.

"Don't answer it," he had said earlier, his voice raw, like he had been fighting himself just to speak. But I couldn't ignore it. Curiosity, that old familiar companion, tugged at me in a way nothing else could.

I set the mug down, the ceramic scraping against the wood, and padded through the hallway, each step dragging like I was walking in a dream. The living room was silent, the kind of stillness that feels almost sacred. There was a flicker in my chest — a flutter of something I didn't want to name. Something dangerous.

When I opened the door, the figure standing on the porch didn't surprise me in the way I'd expected. It wasn't some dark silhouette of a stranger. No, this was a man I recognized, his eyes almost too sharp, his smile just a little too smooth.

Evan Hayes.

If there had been any doubt before, it was gone now. He didn't belong in our quiet little world. He had the air of someone who had spent too much time in places I didn't want to imagine. His dark coat hung loosely around him, the collar turned up against the cold, though it wasn't that cold anymore. But it wasn't the rain that made him look out of place. It was his presence. A man who had the ability to show up uninvited, yet make you feel like you were the one who had been waiting. And I hadn't been waiting for him, not in the least.

He looked over my shoulder, eyes scanning the empty hallway before resting back on me. There was a glimmer of something — amusement, perhaps — in the way he studied me. It wasn't exactly flattering. "I hope I'm not interrupting," he said, voice smooth like the curve of a blade, a hint of danger beneath the politeness.

I didn't answer immediately. Instead, I let the silence stretch, just long enough for him to feel the weight of my hesitation.

"You're Connor's wife," he said it like a statement, though there was a question mark hanging behind the words. He seemed to be measuring the space between us, deciding whether or not he could take a step forward. I could feel him trying to gauge the terrain, like a man plotting his next move.

"I am," I replied. "And you are?"

He smiled then, not the kind of smile that's friendly, but the kind that holds a secret. "A friend," he said. "From Connor's past. I think you've heard of me."

I swallowed, taking a step back, just enough to keep the door slightly ajar. "I don't believe I have."

"Oh, I'm sure you have," he said, his voice carrying a weight now, one that tugged at me, trying to reel me in. "Connor's never been good at keeping secrets, has he?"

The mention of Connor's name, his past, did something to the air around us, a shift that felt like static. Something was off, and I could feel the pull of it now, closer, pressing in on all sides.

I opened the door wider, just enough to let him in, though I wasn't sure why. The house felt smaller with him in it, the shadows hanging longer as if the walls themselves recognized the threat he posed.

"I think we need to talk," he said, stepping inside without waiting for an invitation.

I followed him into the living room, the soft thud of his shoes on the hardwood making the silence between us more pronounced.

"I'm not sure what you think we need to talk about," I said, my voice steady, though my heart was racing. He was everything I hadn't expected and yet nothing at all like I imagined. There was an ease to him, the kind of ease that had likely kept him out of trouble for a long time. It was disarming, like someone who knew how to get what they wanted without you even realizing it was happening.

He sat down without waiting for me to offer a seat. It was the first thing about him that made me uneasy, the way he simply took what he wanted without asking.

"You know more than you think," he said. "About Connor. About all of it."

"I'm not sure what you're implying," I said, my hands suddenly very busy, folding the sleeve of my cardigan over and over again. He was just a man, after all.

But there was something in his gaze that made me hesitate. Something that whispered of secrets buried deep, secrets Connor had spent a lifetime burying.

"You've been looking for answers, haven't you?" he asked, his voice low, almost conspiratorial. "Wondering why your husband can't let go of the past. Wondering if there's more to his story than what he's told you."

The words hit me with the force of a sudden gust of wind. He was too close to the truth. Too much of what he said resonated in a way that made my breath catch in my throat.

"You're lying," I said, more to myself than to him. "Connor wouldn't—"

"No," he interrupted softly, with the faintest trace of a smile. "He wouldn't. Not unless there was something at stake. Something worth protecting."

And in that moment, I realized how much more there was to this story, how much more Connor had left unsaid. The cracks in the facade I had been so careful to maintain were beginning to widen, and there was no going back from it now.

Evan leaned back in the chair, stretching his long legs out as if the room were his to command. His gaze flicked to the fireplace, where the flames were just beginning to settle into a steady burn, casting their glow in erratic patterns over his face. For a moment, I could almost hear the smile playing at the corners of his lips, like a man who knew the game better than anyone but wasn't ready to show his hand just yet.

I stayed standing, still unsure whether I should take the seat across from him or retreat to the kitchen, where I could pretend that this was all just some odd dream I'd wake up from. But there was something in his eyes that kept me tethered. Not just curiosity, though that certainly played its part. No, it was something deeper. An urgency, an unspoken warning. I could feel it in the way he looked at me—as if I were an unopened book, waiting for him to turn the pages at his own pace.

"You've always been a curious one, haven't you?" he said, his voice an easy melody, like someone who had spent years mastering the art of casual conversation. His eyes met mine, sharp and calculating, but with that same twisted kindness I had seen before.

The kind that makes you want to trust someone, but doesn't let you forget for a second that they might stab you in the back.

"I don't know what you mean," I said, though I felt the lie curling at the edge of my tongue. I wasn't entirely sure I wanted to know what he meant, but I couldn't turn back now. Not with the way he was looking at me, like I was the last piece of a puzzle he was desperate to solve.

"Oh, I think you do." He leaned forward slightly, eyes narrowing with something that almost resembled amusement. "Connor's never been very good at hiding his secrets. They're like open books to anyone who's paying attention."

My chest tightened, but I held my ground. "And you think you know everything about him?" I asked, willing myself not to sound defensive, even though I could feel the heat of my own words prickling my skin.

"I know more than most," Evan said, his voice low and smooth. "But don't worry. I'm not here to drag you into the past. I'm here to offer you a way out."

I raised an eyebrow, intrigued despite myself. "A way out of what?"

"A way out of the confusion," he said, his tone dropping into something almost conspiratorial. "A way out of all the tangled mess your husband has created." His gaze flickered again, this time lingering on me, as if he was searching for something I hadn't yet shown him.

I crossed my arms, the fabric of my sleeves catching on the movement. "You're being vague. I'm not sure I'm interested in any of this."

But I knew, even as I said it, that I wasn't entirely certain. I wasn't sure if I wanted to hear more, but I wasn't ready to dismiss him either. There was something in his words that hit too close to the mark. And Connor's guarded nature—his constant need to shield me from the past—had only made me more suspicious. The more Connor shut me out, the more I felt the need to dig into the darkness he had left behind.

Evan chuckled softly, his eyes gleaming with something I couldn't place. "I thought you might say that. But I think you're more curious than you're letting on."

He was right, of course. I was curious. But curiosity didn't always make you wise.

"I'm not sure how much more of your cryptic little game I'm willing to play," I said, my voice steady, but my stomach twisted with the knowledge that this conversation was far from over.

"You don't have to play the game. You're already in it, whether you like it or not." His words hung in the air, a quiet declaration that seemed to settle over the room like an unspoken truth. "Connor's past isn't as clean as he'd like to believe. And you—" He paused, his eyes narrowing as if assessing me once more. "You deserve the truth, don't you?"

I couldn't meet his gaze for a moment. The truth? The idea was intoxicating, but also terrifying. What if the truth wasn't something I could handle? What if the man I had married wasn't the man I thought I knew?

But then, the voice in my head reminded me of the undeniable truth I had already unearthed: my husband wasn't the saint I had believed him to be. No one was. Not even me. So why should I expect anything different from him?

I met his gaze again, this time with a steadier hand on the reins of my emotions. "I think I've already heard enough of your version of the truth. If I'm going to hear anything more, it'll be from Connor."

Evan's lips twitched, as though he found my defiance amusing. "You think he'll tell you? You think he'll ever be completely honest with you? He hasn't even told you everything about me, has he?"

I flinched, the words stinging more than I wanted to admit. "You're wrong," I said, a little too quickly. "He's told me everything that matters."

But Evan only smiled, a knowing smile that sent a chill up my spine. "And yet, there are still pieces missing. Pieces he doesn't even know are missing. He's protecting you, sure, but at what cost?"

I opened my mouth to respond, but the words didn't come. Instead, I found myself staring at him, the weight of his words pressing against my chest. I wanted to argue, to tell him that he was wrong, that Connor and I were fine, that I could trust him. But somewhere deep inside, I knew he wasn't entirely wrong.

"I don't want your pity, Evan," I said, finally breaking the silence. "And I don't want your game. I want my life back. The one I thought I had."

His smile didn't falter. Instead, it deepened, his eyes glinting like shards of glass. "You'll have it. Or at least, you'll have the chance to take it back. You just have to be willing to see things as they really are."

And with that, he stood, his movement swift and effortless, like a snake shedding its skin. "Don't worry. We'll see each other again soon."

He didn't wait for me to say anything else. He was gone before I could even blink, the door closing behind him with a soft click that sounded final. I was left standing in the same spot, my heart pounding, my thoughts scattered like leaves in the wind.

There were no answers. Only more questions.

The house felt colder after Evan left, as if his presence had somehow wrung the warmth out of the room. I stood in the center of the living room, my mind spinning, the silence around me only amplifying the questions racing through my thoughts. It wasn't the first time I'd felt the walls close in like this, but it was the first time I realized that I wasn't sure what was real anymore. How much of my life had been built on truths that weren't truths at all? How much of my marriage, my relationship with Connor, had been a carefully crafted illusion?

I should've called him. I should've reached for the phone right then, demanding answers, demanding to know what was happening. But there was a stubbornness in me, something that refused to give in to the panic, even though it clawed at me, trying to make itself known. I didn't want to hear him tell me that Evan was wrong—that he was just some relic from the past who had no place in our lives anymore. Because something in me knew that Evan wasn't lying. Not completely, at least. The things he said had struck too close to home, like fragments of a dream I'd been too afraid to acknowledge until now.

I needed to speak with Connor. I needed to hear it from him, needed to make sense of all of this, even if it tore apart everything I thought I understood.

I paced the length of the room, the sound of my footsteps the only thing filling the empty space. The storm outside had let up, but the air felt thick with unease, heavy with the sense that the storm had merely moved elsewhere, gathering strength for another round. My phone vibrated against the coffee table, an interruption that sent my heart skipping a beat. I glanced down at the screen, half-expecting it to be Connor. But it wasn't.

It was a message from an unknown number.

"You don't know everything about him. But you can. Meet me tomorrow, 7 pm, at the old pier. You'll find what you're looking for."

I stared at the message, my pulse quickening as I felt that old familiar sense of dread trickle down my spine. The pier. Of course. The place where Connor and I had spent our first summer together—sitting at the edge of the water, watching the boats come and go, talking about everything and nothing. It had been a place of peace once, a place where we'd shared secrets, our hopes for the future. Now, it felt like a symbol of everything we were losing, everything I wasn't sure I could hold on to.

I gripped my phone tighter, reading the message again, then again, as if the words might shift into something more concrete, something I could wrap my mind around. But they didn't. The implications were as heavy as they were cryptic. Whoever this was—someone who knew enough to send me to that exact spot—wasn't just a messenger. They were part of something bigger. And I had no idea if that was a warning or an invitation.

Without thinking, I hit 'send' on a text to Connor.

"I need to talk to you. It's important. Please come home."

I hit 'send' before I could talk myself out of it, as though hearing his voice would clear the fog in my mind, would somehow bring everything back into focus. The phone buzzed in my hand seconds later, but when I looked down, my heart dropped.

It wasn't Connor. It was Evan's name flashing across the screen, his number now saved in my contacts with a note beside it: dangerous.

I swallowed hard, the phone feeling suddenly heavier in my palm, as if it was a lifeline I wasn't sure I wanted to grasp. I stared at the screen, my thumb hovering over the call button. I should have ignored it. I should have gone to the pier alone, forced whatever information was buried in that place to surface. But something in me—the same stubbornness that refused to let me believe Connor was hiding something from me—had me answering the call.

"Hello?" My voice felt small, uncertain, in contrast to the rapid beating of my heart.

"Well, well, well. I was starting to wonder if you'd ever pick up." Evan's voice was light, almost too casual, like we were old friends catching up over coffee instead of two people trapped in a game neither of us fully understood. "I'm glad we're talking. Makes this a bit easier."

"What do you want?" My words were sharper than I intended, but I didn't care. The unease inside me was shifting toward something colder, something darker.

"I want you to know the truth," he said, and I could almost see the smirk in his voice, that same arrogance that had clung to him when he walked through my door. "But more importantly, I want you to understand that there's no going back from it. Once you know everything, you'll never look at Connor the same way again."

I gripped the phone tighter. "What do you mean?"

"You'll see," he said, his voice lowering, tinged with something I couldn't quite place. "You'll see tomorrow night. The pier. Seven o'clock. Don't be late."

Before I could respond, the line went dead. I stood there, staring at the phone in disbelief, the echo of his words still ringing in my ears. What could he possibly mean? How much more was there to uncover?

I didn't know. But I was about to find out.

The sound of a car pulling into the driveway snapped me out of my thoughts. My heart leapt into my throat as I rushed to the window, hoping—praying—it was Connor. But when I saw who was standing by the car, my stomach twisted with a new kind of dread.

Evan.

And he wasn't alone.

My breath caught in my throat. The last thing I had expected to see was him standing there, smiling like he was about to deliver some final, twisted truth. Something in me recoiled, desperate to avoid whatever new revelation was waiting at my doorstep. I took a step back, my heart pounding in my chest.

And then the doorbell rang.

Chapter 29: Silent Inferno

I never thought I would be here, on the edge of a secret so dark it sent shivers straight down to the marrow. But here I am, and here Connor is, sitting across from me in the dimly lit corner of the café, his presence like a steady pulse in the chaos of my mind. The weight of it all—my late husband's tangled mess of notes, Connor's crisp plans—settles heavy on the table between us, as palpable as the steam rising from our untouched coffee mugs. The smell of it, bitter and sharp, fills the room with an odd sort of comfort, grounding me to the moment, even as I feel the walls around us slowly closing in.

"You're sure this is the only way?" I ask, though I already know the answer. The question is for my own peace of mind, not for any real clarity. But there's no time for that anymore, no time to question the path that has already been carved out, sharp and unyielding, by hands I can't see.

Connor doesn't look up from the plans, the outline of his jaw tight, the lines around his mouth deepening as if the weight of our task has aged him in minutes. He taps the edge of the map, drawing a slow, deliberate circle. "It's the only way," he says, his voice low, like the rumble of thunder just before a storm. I want to argue, to throw myself into his arms and ask him to keep me safe, to tell me that we can go back to simpler times. But those times are gone, buried under secrets too deep to escape from.

His eyes flicker to mine, a rare softness momentarily passing through his usual mask of resolve. "I'll protect you, Emma," he adds, the words heavy and rich with meaning. But I'm not sure anyone can protect us now. The very ground we walk on feels fragile, as if it could crack open at any moment and swallow us whole.

I glance down at the yellowed, crinkled papers scattered in front of us—my husband's handwriting, erratic and frantic. His words still haunt me, even after all this time. What had he been trying to tell me? What had he uncovered that he thought would destroy him? The nights I spent listening to him mutter in his sleep, his hands trembling as he scrawled out cryptic notes, have come rushing back with the force of a tidal wave.

I never imagined that after his death, I would still be unraveling the mystery he left behind. But here we are. My husband, dead by his own hand—or was it? And me, caught in the web he wove, struggling to untangle it all. The sense of betrayal is sharp, a knife twist in my chest every time I look at Connor. He says he's here for me, that he's only trying to help. But the question still gnaws at me: What's in this for him? Why is he so determined to keep going, to keep digging into the heart of something so dangerous?

The door of the café creaks open, and I freeze. My pulse picks up, my hand instinctively reaching for the dagger I know I should never have taken with me, but I couldn't bring myself to leave it behind. It's a ridiculous precaution, one that will do little against a force I can't even name. I glance up, but it's only a man in a coat too large for his thin frame, stepping into the warmth with a cough. The tension inside me ebbs just as quickly as it arrived, but Connor doesn't miss the way I stiffen.

He gives me a small, reassuring nod, though the unease in his eyes doesn't go unnoticed. We've been here before, we've felt the weight of eyes on us more times than I care to count. The world outside, always bustling with its own noise and distractions, has turned into a maze of dangers we can't navigate without first looking over our shoulders.

"You should have seen the way they were looking at us last week," I say, the words slipping out before I can stop them. "The way they watched us leave that warehouse… It's like they knew."

Connor's gaze hardens. "They know more than we do. But we're not backing down. We can't."

I open my mouth to argue, to protest that there must be another way. But the words die on my tongue, swept away by the knowledge that there is no other choice. We've gone too far, uncovered too much. There's no turning back.

I shift the papers, pretending to study the details again, but the weight of what we're doing presses down on me with the suffocating force of a vice. The café has filled with people, the chatter and laughter of the evening crowd washing over me in an unfamiliar lull. The clinking of silverware and the hiss of the espresso machine sound distant, almost surreal, like a world I used to know but can no longer touch.

Connor's hand rests lightly on the edge of the table, inches from mine. I feel the warmth of his touch before it even reaches me, the electricity between us unmistakable. But there's no room for us in this moment, no room for anything other than the task ahead. I want to reach for him, to let him anchor me in the storm of uncertainty swirling around us. But I can't. I have to stay focused, I have to push forward, even if every step I take feels like it could be my last.

"We're not alone in this, Emma," he says, his voice soft but firm. "Whatever's coming, we face it together."

And for the first time in what feels like forever, I believe him.

The café begins to feel like a stage, the dim lighting casting long shadows against the brick walls, each flicker of the fluorescent bulbs overhead echoing the tension in my chest. The chatter around us rises and falls like waves crashing against the shore, but it's all background noise to the quiet storm gathering in the corner where we sit. Connor is right there, steady and unflinching, his eyes scanning the map with an intensity that could ignite a fire if he stared too long. Every once in a while, he looks up, as if measuring my reaction to his words, his moves, his plans. And every time, I try not to flinch under his scrutiny.

I wish I could focus entirely on the map, on the trail we've been following, the marks we've drawn in the hope that they might lead us out of this mess. But the truth is, I can't. My mind keeps drifting back to my husband's final days, to the fevered whispers I overheard, to the pages that smelled like him—of ink and desperation. Why did he have to hide so much? And why did he leave me to figure it out, alone? Did he know this was coming, or was he just as clueless as I am, caught in a web spun by hands far more powerful than his own?

The door swings open again, but this time, I don't even flinch. I'm getting used to the interruptions. I wish I could say that's a good thing, that it means I'm toughening up, becoming immune to the constant undercurrent of danger that pulses through every corner of this city. But instead, it just means I'm getting numb. A strange, hollow numbness settles in my chest, like I'm a passenger on a speeding train with no way to stop it.

I reach for the coffee in front of me, the warmth of the cup a small comfort against the cold air creeping through the room. Connor watches me, his gaze unwavering, but there's something more there now. A kind of frustration, like he's ready to move, but we're stuck. And he doesn't like being stuck.

"Emma," he says, and the sharpness in his voice makes my heart skip. "You're not listening."

I look up, forcing myself to focus. "I'm listening."

"No, you're not. Not really." He leans forward, his fingers tracing the edge of the map, his voice lowering. "We're running out of time."

The words hit me harder than I expect. Running out of time? Wasn't that the truth of it all? The clock has been ticking ever since my husband's death, and I'm starting to realize that no matter how much I want to slow it down, the inevitable is coming. But I can't let myself think like that—not now, not when we're this close.

"I know," I reply, my voice more brittle than I intended. "But if we're going to move, we have to be sure. We can't rush this."

Connor's eyes soften, but only just. "Emma, we don't have the luxury of being sure. We don't know how deep this goes, how many people are involved. But what we do know is that they're coming for us."

The words hang in the air, charged with the weight of their meaning. They're coming for us. And I don't know if it's fear or adrenaline or just the sheer fact that I'm finally facing the truth of it all, but something shifts inside me. I know he's right. There's no more time to tiptoe around this. The plans we've been poring over for weeks? They're not just maps anymore. They're lifelines. The only way out. And I'm not about to let anything—or anyone—stand in the way of that.

I take a breath, forcing my mind to focus, and reach across the table for the papers Connor's been working on. My fingers graze his, the brief touch sending a jolt of awareness through me. His gaze flicks to my hand, then back to my face, and for a moment, there's a silent understanding between us. The kind of understanding that doesn't need words. But words come anyway.

"We go tonight," I say, my voice firm, more confident than I feel. "We don't wait anymore. If we're going to do this, we do it now."

Connor doesn't answer immediately. He studies me, his jaw tightening, before he finally nods. "Alright. Tonight it is."

As the evening deepens, the café begins to empty out. The buzz of conversation dims, replaced by the steady clink of plates being cleared away. I'm aware of each movement, each sound, as if the world is getting smaller, shrinking down to just the two of us and the secrets we carry.

I stand, smoothing the wrinkles in my jacket, and glance toward the door. "We'll need to be quick. We can't afford any mistakes."

Connor rises too, his movements smooth, precise. His hand brushes against mine again, and this time, I don't pull away. "We won't make mistakes," he says, his voice steady. "I won't let that happen."

But there's something in his eyes—something I can't quite place—that makes the hairs on the back of my neck stand up. It's almost as if he knows something I don't, as if there's a part of this plan that I'm not seeing. And for a split second, I wonder if this whole thing has been a setup from the start.

I shake the thought away. Now is not the time for doubts.

As we step out into the cool night air, the city stretches out before us like a labyrinth, every shadow a potential threat, every unfamiliar face a stranger that could turn into an enemy. But for the first time in days, I don't feel afraid. I feel alive. And for whatever comes next, I'm ready to face it—whether it's with Connor by my side, or alone. Because in the end, this is my fight, too.

The streets outside the café are quieter now, the hum of city life growing faint in the distance, but the weight of the silence feels more like an omen than a reprieve. As we walk side by side, my boots click against the pavement with a steady rhythm, a sound I barely notice until it echoes too loudly in the empty night. We don't speak; there's nothing left to say that hasn't already been said in our eyes, in the tension between each of us, an unspoken agreement hanging in the air. There is no turning back now.

Connor moves with the precision of a man who knows exactly where he's headed, each step purposeful, and yet, there's an undercurrent to him tonight, something off-kilter that I can't quite put my finger on. It could be the weight of what we're about to do—or the fact that he's letting me take the lead now, in all of this. His trust in me is palpable, even if it's impossible to ignore the shadow of doubt that clouds his usually unshakable composure. He knows, just like I do, that we're skirting the edge of something dangerous, and this time, even he may not be able to save me.

The path to the old warehouse isn't far, but the closer we get, the heavier the air feels. There's something about the darkness here, about the way the streetlights flicker over the cracked concrete, that makes everything feel too sharp, too vivid. Every sound is too loud, every breath too shallow. The city has a way of swallowing you whole when it wants to, and I'm starting to wonder if that's what it's doing to us right now.

"I don't like this," I mutter under my breath, though I know Connor can hear me. I don't think I'm speaking to him as much as I'm speaking to the night itself, a futile attempt to make my fears go away.

"You think I do?" he replies, the words coming with a bite, though his voice is still low, controlled. "But we don't have a choice. We're already in too deep."

I want to say something sharp in response, to challenge him, but I can't. He's right. We've crossed a line, and now we're running on nothing but momentum, hoping that it carries us safely through the storm.

The warehouse looms ahead, its silhouette jagged against the night sky, a hulking mass of metal and concrete. I can feel my pulse quicken as we approach it, the place where this all began, where my husband's tangled web first started to unravel. It feels wrong, though, in a way I can't explain. Like we've missed something, like there's another layer to this that we haven't seen yet. But I don't have time to dwell on it now.

Connor steps ahead, his hand brushing the door, a practiced gesture as he swings it open. The creak of the hinges sounds deafening in the stillness. I freeze just inside the threshold, my senses on high alert. The place feels alive in a way that makes the hairs on the back of my neck stand up. There's something here, something waiting for us—though I have no idea what it is.

"Stay close," Connor mutters, his voice taut, more commanding than I'm used to. But I can't say I mind. It feels like the only safe thing to do.

We move deeper into the warehouse, the floor beneath our feet cold and unforgiving, the smell of rust and old wood heavy in the air. Our footsteps echo, bouncing off the walls and amplifying the stillness, turning it into a living, breathing thing that presses in around us.

"Do you ever think we're in over our heads?" I ask, my voice just above a whisper. It feels like the kind of question I should have asked days ago, but something about the dark, oppressive silence makes me vulnerable, makes me want to finally admit the doubts I've been burying under the weight of our mission.

Connor doesn't answer immediately, and for a moment, I wonder if he's going to brush me off. But then he stops and turns to face me, his gaze steady, almost regretful. "Yeah. I do. But if I didn't think we could do this, I wouldn't be here."

I look at him, really look at him, and I can see the cracks beneath the surface, the cracks he's been hiding from me. For all his strength, for all the walls he's built around himself, there's something in him that's unraveling too. I want to reach out, to tell him that we'll make it through, that somehow, we'll fix all of this. But I can't. There's nothing I can say to fix what's been broken.

And then, the sound. A footstep. Or maybe two.

I freeze. Connor doesn't even flinch, but his hand subtly moves to his side, where I know he keeps a gun—though he's never once mentioned it, never once even hinted at the need for something so drastic. I'm not sure if I should be comforted or terrified by that.

The footsteps grow louder, closer, until I can feel the presence behind me, feel the eyes of someone who's watching us with intent, with purpose. Someone who's been waiting for us.

I turn slowly, and then there's the figure—a tall man in a dark coat, standing just inside the shadows, his face hidden. I can't make out his features, but I don't need to. I know he's one of them.

"You should have stayed away," the man says, his voice smooth, almost cold.

I feel Connor tense beside me, his muscles coiled, ready to spring, but it's me who speaks first, my voice sharp and unwavering. "I don't think we're the ones who should be afraid."

The man laughs, a low, hollow sound. "You should be. Because this... ends tonight."

The air around us seems to freeze, the silence thick with the weight of his words. And then, before I can react, the sound of footsteps behind me. Another figure. Another threat.

But this time, it's not just him. It's them. And it's too late to run.

Chapter 30: Crossfire Confessions

It's strange, isn't it? How two people, both so stubborn, so fiercely wrapped up in their own stories, can crash into each other with the force of a tidal wave. I never saw it coming. Of course, I told myself I'd never fall for anyone again. The words slid off my tongue with practiced ease, a mantra I said so often I almost believed it. I told myself that after what happened with Adam, I'd never give another person the power to tear me apart. But, in the heat of the moment, when my defenses crumbled under Connor's penetrating gaze, I realized how foolish that belief was.

"Why didn't you tell me?" Connor's voice cracked through the air like a whip, cutting through the heavy silence between us. His face was tense, eyes sharp with an intensity that unnerved me, and yet, there was a vulnerability lurking behind them that begged to be noticed.

I swallowed, suddenly feeling the weight of the room pressing down on me, suffocating me with everything I'd kept locked inside. I didn't know what to say. My chest tightened, and for a moment, all I could hear was the sound of my heart pounding in my ears.

"I couldn't," I finally whispered. My words felt inadequate, like they could never truly capture the labyrinth of emotions tangled within me. "I couldn't bring myself to explain it. I couldn't let anyone see how broken I really was. How... how weak I felt." My voice wavered as I spoke, and I hated myself for it.

Connor's jaw clenched. "Weak? You're not weak. You're stronger than anyone I've ever known."

I looked up at him, not entirely convinced. "You think so? Because I've never felt weaker than I do right now."

He shook his head, the movement sharp, impatient. "You don't get it, do you? You're carrying a weight that isn't yours to bear, and you're still standing. You're still moving forward."

His words, though meant to comfort, did the opposite. They made my guilt sting sharper, like salt on an open wound. My husband was dead, and here I was, carrying on like nothing had happened. Like I wasn't the one who had let him go. My chest tightened, and I took a shaky breath, trying to keep the tears at bay.

"I failed him, Connor," I said, the words slipping from my mouth before I could stop them. "I wasn't enough. And now he's gone, and all I have left is this guilt. Every single day, it eats at me. What if I'd done things differently? What if I hadn't been so busy with everything else?"

Connor's eyes softened, and I saw something there that made my stomach twist—a mix of empathy and frustration. "You can't keep blaming yourself for things you couldn't control. You're carrying his memory, but you're also carrying your own life. And that matters too."

His words were like a balm, soothing the rawness of my thoughts, but I wasn't ready to let go of the pain just yet. Not after everything. I wasn't sure I'd ever be ready.

But then, as if in an unexpected turn of fate, he stepped closer. I barely registered the movement before he was right in front of me, close enough that I could feel the heat of his body, the weight of his presence pressing in on me like a gentle storm.

"Tell me everything," he said, his voice a low whisper that seemed to vibrate through my bones. "I don't care what it is. I need to know. You don't have to carry this alone."

For a long moment, I was frozen. His words lingered in the air, heavy with the promise of understanding, the kind of understanding I wasn't sure I deserved. But there was something in his eyes—something raw and unguarded—that made me want to believe him. To let him in.

I shook my head, my hand instinctively reaching up to wipe away the tear that had slipped down my cheek. "You don't want to know. You won't be able to look at me the same way if I tell you."

His expression darkened, a flicker of something like anger crossing his face. "Is that how you see me? Like I'm just going to turn away because of something you think might change how I see you?"

I flinched, the sharpness of his words cutting deeper than I expected. But instead of stepping back, instead of retreating into myself, I stood there, rooted to the spot. For the first time, I allowed myself to meet his gaze head-on, really look at him.

"No," I said quietly, my voice trembling, "I don't see you like that. But I see me like that. And I'm not sure you'll ever look at me the same way again once you know everything."

Connor's hand reached out then, his fingers brushing my cheek in a movement so gentle I nearly didn't believe it was happening. "Try me," he whispered. "Because, right now, the only thing I care about is you. And I'm not going anywhere."

In that moment, everything changed. The walls I'd spent so long building crumbled, and I found myself leaning into him, drawn to the warmth of his presence, the sincerity in his touch. It wasn't the grand gesture I'd imagined—no dramatic confessions, no sweeping promises. It was simpler than that. In the quiet of that moment, as the silence enveloped us, I realized the truth.

We weren't just surviving anymore. We were healing. Together. And that, in itself, was the most unexpected twist of all.

I wanted to say something—anything—that would dismiss the tender weight of his touch, his words. But the truth kept spinning in my chest, strangling my voice. All I could do was stand there, caught in the storm we had created, trying to make sense of what had shifted in the air between us.

Connor's gaze softened, but there was an edge there too, something I hadn't seen before. Not pity, never that. But a deep, steady resolve, the kind you find in people who've been through the fire and come out the other side. It was the kind of look that made me wonder what else lay behind his carefully constructed walls. The thought made something inside me tremble.

"You don't have to explain everything now," he said, his thumb brushing over my cheek again, as if memorizing the shape of me. "We'll get there. But I need you to know... you're not alone in this. Not anymore."

The vulnerability in his voice shocked me. I had seen so much of Connor's strength, his confidence, his near-obsessive need to protect. But in that moment, he wasn't trying to shield me. He was opening himself up, showing me a side of him I wasn't sure I was ready for. But I didn't look away.

"I'm trying," I whispered, half to myself, half to him. "But it's hard to let go of the things that have kept me together for so long."

The silence that followed felt heavier than it should have. We were standing so close, yet there was an unspoken distance, an invisible line drawn by the ghosts of our pasts, too tangled to unravel with a simple gesture. Still, I felt his presence like a lifeline. There was something about him—about us—that felt both impossibly broken and miraculously whole all at once.

He stepped back then, just enough to give me room to breathe, though the energy between us hadn't lessened. "I don't want to rush you," he said quietly. "But if we're going to keep doing this, whatever this is," he nodded between us, "we need to be honest. With each other. And with ourselves."

I could see it now—the way he'd been holding back, perhaps even before the beginning. This, whatever we were becoming, had been building under the surface for weeks. The moments we didn't acknowledge, the glances we pretended we hadn't caught, the way our conversations always seemed to stray closer to something deeper, more real. I was terrified of what it meant—what it could mean.

"You don't know what I've done," I said, the words spilling out before I could stop them. "I've hurt people. And worse, I've let people hurt me. I don't know how to fix that. I don't know if I even deserve to."

Connor looked at me for a long time before he responded, his brow furrowing slightly as though he was processing something more complicated than I had expected. "And yet, you're still here. Still fighting. That counts for something, doesn't it?"

It was the first time anyone had said something like that to me. Not a shallow compliment, not a vague reassurance. Just the recognition of the fight I hadn't realized I'd been putting up for so long. For a moment, I felt a strange warmth rise in my chest, an unfamiliar feeling that didn't sit well with my usual skepticism.

"Maybe," I muttered, taking a step back. "But what about you? What happens when all this—the things you're holding back—come crashing down?"

His expression hardened for a brief second, the mask slipping just enough for me to see the shadows he'd been concealing. It was only for a moment, but it was enough. I knew then that Connor wasn't as invulnerable as he made himself out to be. There was something raw, something dangerous lurking beneath his surface—a fire waiting to ignite if anyone dared to get close enough.

He ran a hand through his hair, a gesture that spoke of frustration. "I don't have answers for everything. But I've made mistakes, too. Big ones. I didn't protect you when I should've. I let you walk into this mess without offering you the help you needed. And now, I'm trying to fix it. Trying to fix me."

I was silent for a moment, absorbing his confession. His guilt was a mirror to my own, but for some reason, it wasn't as suffocating when it was him. Maybe because he was willing to face it, to admit it. I wasn't sure I could do the same.

"You don't owe me anything," I said, the words almost sounding foreign as they left my mouth. "I'm the one who's broken. The one who messed everything up. Not you."

Connor took a slow step toward me, his eyes steady and intent. "You're not broken," he said firmly, with the kind of certainty that felt like a promise. "You're just... lost. And I'm here, whether you want me to be or not."

The honesty in his voice stung, and I felt the old, familiar weight of resistance rising inside me. This wasn't supposed to be how it ended—me leaning on someone else, trusting someone else with the jagged pieces of my heart. I was supposed to be stronger than this. But the truth was, I didn't feel strong at all. I felt exposed, fragile, as if my entire life had been a string of half-finished attempts to keep moving forward without ever really dealing with what had happened.

"I don't need you to fix me," I said, the words coming out sharper than I intended. "I'm not some project for you to fix, Connor."

His gaze softened. "I don't want to fix you. I just want to be here. For whatever comes next. If you'll let me."

I hesitated. His offer was a dangerous one, one that could easily lead to heartache. But there was something in the way he was looking at me—something that felt honest and grounded. For once, I wanted to take a step toward something uncertain, something real.

I let out a shaky breath. "I don't know if I'm ready for this."

He nodded, and for the first time since I met him, I saw the trace of a smile tug at the corner of his lips. "I'm not going anywhere," he said, the words quiet but filled with quiet conviction. "We'll take it one day at a time."

And for the first time in a long time, I wasn't sure if that was a promise I could keep. But it was a promise I wanted to try.

I wasn't sure what hurt more—the raw truth of Connor's words or the sharp sting of my own confessions, the ones I never thought I'd utter aloud. He had opened the door, but I hadn't expected the flood of emotions that poured through it. I had thought I could guard the wreckage of my heart for a little longer, that I could keep it neatly tucked away, hidden under the guise of strength. But something in him—something in the way he saw me—made me drop the act.

I took a step back, needing space to breathe, to collect myself before I completely unraveled. The room felt smaller now, the air thicker. My skin prickled with the weight of everything we'd just shared, but underneath it all, there was a strange sense of relief, as if I had given him the keys to unlock a door I'd been trying to keep shut for far too long.

But of course, that wasn't the end of it. Nothing ever is, is it?

"I don't know what to do with any of this," I muttered, running a hand through my hair, trying to push the wave of emotions back down. "I don't know what comes next."

Connor didn't say anything right away. He just stood there, his eyes fixed on me with an intensity that made me want to squirm. But I didn't. Not this time.

"You don't have to have all the answers," he said finally, his voice calm but edged with something I couldn't quite place. "Not right now, anyway. We don't need a plan. We just need... to figure out what we're doing here. Together."

It should have been simple. The words should have been comforting, but instead, they left a bitter taste in my mouth. Together. It had always sounded so easy when I heard it in movies or read it in books. But in reality, together meant something entirely different. It meant risking everything. Trusting someone else with the jagged pieces of your soul. And frankly, that terrified me.

"You're right," I said, the words tasting foreign. I wasn't sure if I was convincing him or myself. "I don't have a plan. I don't even know what I'm supposed to feel anymore."

He took a step forward, closing the gap between us again, his hand reaching for mine. "I get that," he said softly, his voice almost a whisper. "But we're here now. And I don't want you to do this alone. Not if I can help it."

The quiet sincerity in his voice knocked the breath out of me, leaving me momentarily speechless. I wanted to say something—anything—but the truth was, I didn't know how to navigate this new territory we were stepping into. I wasn't ready to be vulnerable again. Not after everything I'd been through. Not after Adam.

But I also couldn't deny the pull I felt toward Connor. The way he made me feel like maybe I wasn't as broken as I thought I was. And the more I resisted, the more I realized I was only pushing him away, and with him, the only person who seemed to understand the weight I was carrying.

"I can't promise you anything," I said, finally, my voice low and shaky. "I can't pretend to know what this is, what we are. But I don't want to shut you out. Not completely."

His eyes softened then, the walls he'd built around himself slipping just enough for me to see the cracks in them. "That's all I'm asking for," he replied, his thumb brushing against my wrist in a slow, deliberate motion that sent a shiver down my spine. "Just don't shut me out. We'll take it one step at a time, okay?"

I nodded, even though I wasn't sure if I meant it. I wasn't sure of anything, except that every moment we spent together seemed to complicate everything I thought I knew about myself.

And then, just as I was about to breathe a sigh of relief, as if the storm had finally passed, the door swung open, and my world tilted once again.

"Am I interrupting something?" A voice, cold and sharp, cut through the air like a knife. I whipped around, my heart pounding in my chest as I saw the figure standing in the doorway.

It was a face I hadn't seen in weeks. But it wasn't a face I would ever forget.

Adam's brother, Ryan, stood in the threshold, his posture stiff, his eyes narrowed. His presence was a slap in the face, a reminder that I could never fully escape the tangled mess of my past. Not even here. Not even now.

I could feel Connor's tension immediately, his stance shifting as if instinctively ready for a confrontation. And I could practically feel the tension vibrating through the air as Ryan took a slow, deliberate step into the room, his gaze flicking between the two of us with that unsettling calm he always had.

"What are you doing here?" I asked, my voice coming out sharper than I intended. I wasn't sure if I wanted him to answer or if I just wanted him to leave.

Ryan didn't flinch at my tone. Instead, his lips curled into a tight smile, one that didn't reach his eyes. "I came to see how you're doing. Thought I'd check in on my dear sister-in-law." His gaze shifted to Connor, his expression unreadable. "Seems like you've made yourself comfortable."

Connor's jaw tightened, but he didn't take the bait. He stood his ground, his hand still holding mine, though his grip was firmer now, almost possessive.

"Didn't realize you were so concerned," I said, forcing a smile that didn't quite make it to my eyes. "I'm fine, Ryan. Really."

But Ryan wasn't looking at me anymore. His eyes were fixed on Connor now, assessing him with that cold, calculating look I remembered too well. The same look he'd worn the day he warned me away from getting too close to anyone else after Adam's death. The look that said he didn't trust anyone. Especially not men like Connor.

I held my breath as the tension in the room thickened, the air crackling with unsaid words and dangerous implications.

And just when I thought I might suffocate under the weight of it all, Ryan opened his mouth again, his words landing like a bomb.

"I hope you're ready for what's coming," he said, his voice low and dangerous. "Because it's not over. Not by a long shot."

Chapter 31: The Flame's Edge

The room felt different when I stepped inside. Maybe it was the subtle shift in the air, the way the shadows hugged the walls tighter, or the silence that now hung between us, thick and unnerving. I set my bag down on the counter with a soft thud, the sound echoing in the emptiness of our home. It had once been our sanctuary—his and mine, a place where the world outside didn't seem to matter. But now, each corner felt like it was taunting me, reminding me of how wrong I had been.

Connor, always the steady presence in my life, was standing at the window, his arms crossed as he stared out over the city. His silhouette, strong and protective, looked like it belonged to someone much older than the man who had stood beside me just weeks ago. The weight of our shared silence pressed down on us both.

"You're still awake," I said, my voice sounding too loud in the quiet room.

He turned slowly, his eyes tired but searching. "Couldn't sleep. I was thinking."

"About what?" I asked, my heart skipping a beat. I knew where this was headed, but I couldn't quite brace myself for it.

"The witness," he said, his gaze not quite meeting mine. "The one who saw him with the Matchstick Man. Do you believe it?"

My pulse raced, and I swallowed hard, trying to maintain my composure. "I don't know what to believe anymore."

Connor's brow furrowed, and his eyes softened with concern. "What do you mean?"

"I mean..." I hesitated, fighting the knot in my throat. "I've spent years looking at everything through one lens, trying to make sense of the world we built together. I thought I knew him. I thought I knew everything. But now, with this—this new piece of the puzzle—I'm not sure what's real anymore."

The fire of doubt flickered in my chest, and I couldn't suppress the wave of nausea that threatened to rise. If it was true—if my husband had been willingly involved with the Matchstick Man—then what did that mean for me? For everything I had believed about him? About us?

"You think he was involved, don't you?" Connor's voice was barely above a whisper, the question hanging heavy between us.

"I don't know," I replied, my voice cracking despite my best effort to sound strong. "But I have to consider it, don't I? I have to look at it all, no matter how much it hurts. It's the only way to understand this... this madness."

Connor took a step toward me, closing the gap between us, his gaze never leaving mine. "You don't have to do this alone. You never have to do this alone."

I nodded, but I wasn't sure if I believed him. Not anymore. The truth had a way of unraveling things, exposing secrets I wasn't ready to face.

"I keep thinking back to the last few weeks," I continued, my voice low and shaky. "The way he started acting differently. Like he was... hiding something. But I never thought it would be this. I never thought he would..." My breath caught, and I had to force myself to say it. "Betray me like this."

Connor's hand found mine, and he squeezed it, as if to remind me that I wasn't alone, even when the world felt like it was falling apart. "You don't know that for sure. We don't know anything for sure, except that this witness saw them together. That's all we've got."

"Then why does it feel like everything I thought I knew is slipping away?" I whispered, my voice thick with emotion.

He didn't answer right away. Instead, he led me over to the couch, where we sat side by side, his arm around me in the same protective way he always had been. But tonight, there was a distance between us, one that even his touch couldn't erase.

The silence stretched on, uncomfortable and tight, until I couldn't stand it anymore. "What if this is the end of the story, Connor?" I asked, my voice barely above a breath. "What if this witness is telling the truth, and my husband wasn't the man I thought he was? What does that make me? What does it make him?"

Connor exhaled slowly, his fingers running through his hair as he looked away, trying to collect his thoughts. "I don't know, but I do know this: You can't let someone else define who you are. You're not defined by him. Not by anyone."

I wanted to believe him. I really did. But the gnawing fear in my gut made it hard to hold on to those words.

"We need to find out more," I said, my mind already racing ahead. "The witness, the Matchstick Man—this is the key. If we can get to the bottom of it, we can make sense of everything else."

Connor nodded, his expression grim. "I'll make some calls. See what I can dig up."

"You'll do it carefully," I added, my voice steady despite the chaos inside me. "We can't let anyone know we're onto them. Not yet."

He agreed, but I saw the flicker of uncertainty in his eyes. This wasn't just about a case anymore. This was personal. And the more I thought about it, the more I realized—there were no easy answers. Only questions, and none of them seemed to lead anywhere I was prepared to go.

The next few days passed in a blur of restless sleep and waking moments that felt like slipping through fog. Every time I closed my eyes, the image of him—the man I thought I knew—haunted me. His face, once a symbol of comfort, now seemed distant, like a stranger's. The subtle shift in the lines of his smile, the way he had pulled away in those final weeks, it all started to make sense in a way I wasn't ready to accept. The more I pieced it together, the more the truth looked like a jagged puzzle, each fragment a new betrayal.

I kept myself busy, pushing aside the gnawing uncertainty by burying myself in work. The case demanded my attention, and for a while, it was the only thing that kept me tethered to reality. But the truth had a way of creeping in, worming its way into the corners of my mind no matter how much I tried to ignore it.

I was sitting in my office, staring at the files spread out before me like a trail of breadcrumbs leading to something I wasn't sure I was ready to face. A knock at the door pulled me from my thoughts, and before I could call out, Connor was stepping inside. He looked worn, like he hadn't slept in days, but his eyes were sharp, focused. There was something else there too—something I couldn't quite place. It wasn't just the case; it was something deeper, something heavier, weighing him down in a way I hadn't seen before.

"We need to talk," he said, his voice low, his usual calm demeanor tinged with an edge I hadn't expected.

I pushed my papers aside and gestured for him to sit, my heart beginning to race at the tone of his voice. "What's happened?"

Connor sat down slowly, running a hand through his hair as he exhaled sharply. "The witness. We've found more—more details, more names. People who were close to him. To your husband."

The knot in my stomach tightened, and I felt the room constrict around me, as if the walls themselves were closing in. "And?"

He hesitated for just a moment too long. It was enough to make me lean forward, my instincts flaring. "Connor?"

"There's a connection we didn't see before," he said, his words deliberate, his eyes never leaving mine. "The Matchstick Man—it's bigger than we thought. There's more to this than just one man starting fires for some twisted reason."

I swallowed hard, my throat dry. "What do you mean? What else is there?"

He sighed, a deep, frustrated sound that only made the tension between us grow thicker. "It's not just arson, it's... it's a cover-up. A diversion. A distraction from something more dangerous. We've uncovered financial records, shadow accounts. It's all connected to your husband. He was involved, not just by accident, not just a victim of circumstance."

The ground beneath me seemed to give way, and for a moment, I wasn't sure I could breathe. "No. No, that doesn't make sense. He was never like that. He never—he wouldn't—"

"Think about it, Paige," Connor cut in, his voice softer now, more measured. "The way he started pulling away, the way he changed. The signs were there, but we didn't want to see them. I didn't want to see them."

I stood abruptly, the chair scraping against the floor as I pushed myself to my feet. "So, you're saying he was part of this? That he knew? That he chose—" My voice broke, and I had to pause, the weight of the words catching in my chest. "That he chose to be part of this mess?"

Connor's gaze softened, his jaw tightening. "I'm not saying he chose it, but I am saying that he was involved. He made decisions. And now those decisions have led us to this."

I felt something crack inside me, a sudden fracture in the reality I had spent years building. The man I had loved, the man I had trusted with everything—was he capable of this? Of involvement in something so dark, so twisted? Or was he merely a pawn, manipulated by forces larger than him? I didn't know which option terrified me more.

"You're wrong," I said, but my voice lacked the conviction I wanted it to have. "He wasn't like that. He couldn't have been. I would have seen it. I would have known."

Connor didn't respond immediately, and for a moment, the room fell into an uneasy silence. He was giving me space to process, or maybe he was waiting for me to finally accept the truth. Either way, it felt suffocating.

I finally sat back down, burying my face in my hands as the weight of the situation pressed on me. "What now?" I asked, the question coming out like a gasp.

"We keep pushing," he said, his voice unwavering. "We follow the trail, no matter where it leads. It's the only way we'll get the answers we need. For you, for him, for all of this."

I looked up at him, my mind swirling with a thousand different thoughts, none of them making sense. "But what if the answers we find... break us?"

Connor didn't flinch. He leaned forward, his expression resolute. "Then we rebuild. Together."

I wanted to believe him. I wanted to believe that, after all of this, after all the lies and the betrayals, we could find a way to rebuild. But in the pit of my stomach, I knew that no matter what we uncovered, nothing would ever be the same. The truth was a flame, and it would burn everything to the ground. There was no escaping it now.

The city felt different the next morning, as though it had quietly shifted in the night without my notice. The air was heavier, pressing down on my chest like a secret too big to keep. I stood at the window of my office, watching the traffic below, the endless stream of lives moving in synchrony, unaware of the unraveling chaos just beneath the surface. If they only knew—if they only understood what was at stake—would they still carry on as they always had? Or would they, too, stop and wonder who was really pulling the strings? The thought made me sick.

Connor's presence beside me, as solid and constant as ever, didn't provide the comfort it once did. Not today. Today, I couldn't shake the feeling that we were both on the edge of something. The edge of a precipice, ready to fall, with nothing but the sharp claws of truth waiting to catch us.

"What's our next step?" I asked, turning to him, though I already knew the answer.

"We push forward," he said simply, his eyes dark with the same unease that had been gnawing at me. "We dig into those financial records, we track down more of the people connected to your husband's past. The deeper we go, the clearer it will all become."

I wanted to believe him. Hell, I needed to believe him. But something in the way he said it made my stomach twist. He wasn't just talking about a case anymore. We weren't talking about just names and numbers. We were talking about us—our lives, our choices, our beliefs.

"Do you think we can actually trust anyone involved in this anymore?" I asked, more to myself than to him. "Or are we just all part of a bigger game? Puppets with invisible strings tied around our necks?"

Connor didn't answer right away. His eyes flickered toward the papers on my desk, the ones that had started to blur together into something I wasn't sure I could untangle. He exhaled sharply, his jaw tight with frustration. "I don't know," he said at last. "But we're not giving up. Not yet."

We were both so caught up in the weight of it all that neither of us heard the knock at the door. It was only when the sound came again, louder this time, that I turned to find a figure standing in the doorway—someone I hadn't expected.

"You're still here," I said, my voice more accusatory than I intended.

Sarah stood in the doorway, her face pale, her eyes wide with something that looked like panic. She was holding a manila envelope in her hand, the kind that only carried information that was either vital or dangerous. She hadn't come here to chat, that much was clear.

"I—" She stopped herself, swallowing hard before continuing. "I thought you should have this. It's about your husband."

I reached for the envelope, my fingers trembling despite my best efforts to remain calm. "What is it?"

"Evidence," she replied, her voice shaky. "Something I found last night. I didn't know where else to go."

As I tore open the envelope, Connor leaned in beside me, his breath just behind my ear, making me shiver despite myself. Inside, there were a series of photographs—grainy, black-and-white, and clearly taken from a distance. At first glance, they seemed innocuous, but as I looked closer, my heart sank. They were taken on a rooftop, the light too harsh to make out the faces clearly, but there was no mistaking the man standing next to my husband. The Matchstick Man.

The photographs weren't enough to implicate anyone in anything, but they were damning all the same. They were proof that the two men had been together, that whatever they were involved in wasn't just an accident. This was intentional. This was planned.

I flipped through the stack of pictures, each one revealing more of the scene—more of the connection I wasn't ready to see. And yet, I couldn't tear my eyes away. The truth was sitting right there, laid bare in front of me, as clear as the daylight spilling in through the windows. And I hated it. I hated the way it made everything feel like a lie.

"Sarah," I said, my voice tight, barely above a whisper. "What else did you find?"

Her eyes darted nervously to the floor. "I—I didn't want to get involved, but there's something else. Something in his records. Something that might mean... might mean he knew more than he let on. Maybe even planned it."

I felt my pulse quicken. "What are you talking about?"

She stepped forward, lowering her voice as if she was afraid someone might be listening. "I found a note. A ledger, with dates, names, and a list of locations. All marked in code. It looks like a map, but it's more than that. It's a blueprint—of the fires. Where they were set. When."

My breath hitched, and I felt my knees go weak. "You're telling me that this—this wasn't just an accident? It was intentional, planned?"

She nodded, her expression one of guilt and fear. "Yes. But there's more. The ledger ends with a name—your husband's. It's the last entry."

I opened my mouth to speak, but no words came. My head spun, the room tilting as though everything was suddenly wrong. I could feel Connor beside me, his arm brushing mine, his presence a lifeline that threatened to snap under the weight of it all.

"Do you think we're too late?" I whispered, not sure if I meant to ask it or if the question had just slipped out in the chaos.

Before Connor could respond, the sound of footsteps echoed from the hallway, followed by a soft knock at the door. And just like that, the world around me shifted again, and I had a feeling that the truth we'd been chasing was about to catch up to us—whether we were ready or not.

Chapter 32: Embers of Truth

The rain never stopped, not for a single moment. It was the kind of drizzle that soaked you through without ever being heavy enough to warrant an umbrella. A persistent, sneaky kind of rain that made you forget it was even there until your hair was plastered to your neck and your shoes were squelching with every step. We were in the heart of the city now, the streets slick with reflection, the neon lights shimmering against the wet pavement as though trying to fight off the shadow of the night.

I wasn't sure how I'd gotten here, or if I even wanted to be. The pieces of the puzzle were scattered before me, some sharp and jagged, others worn smooth with time. But no matter how many corners I turned, how many doors I knocked on, the answers came at a price. A price I wasn't sure I was willing to pay, but somehow had no choice but to continue paying.

Connor was beside me, as steady as ever. His presence, quiet but unyielding, was like an anchor in a storm. I could see the tension in the set of his jaw, the way his eyes flicked from shadow to shadow, constantly scanning. I admired his ability to be calm when the world felt like it was on fire. But even Connor had limits. And I was testing them.

"We're getting close," he said, his voice low, but that quiet certainty always made me believe him. Even when I had no reason to.

"Close," I echoed, my words hollow in the space between us. It sounded so easy when he said it. So certain.

I turned my gaze to the darkened alley ahead, the faint sound of footsteps echoing through the damp air. The kind of sound that makes your heart race, makes you wonder if anyone else could hear it. Or if it was only the prelude to something worse, like the whisper of the storm that comes before the hurricane.

Connor squeezed my arm, his hand warm and solid. "I've got your back. We do this together."

I nodded, though the weight of the secrets we were unearthing gnawed at my insides. My husband, the man I thought I knew, the man I thought I could trust, had been tangled in a web so intricate and dangerous that I didn't even know where the lies began.

When I married him, I never imagined I would find myself standing in an alleyway at midnight, facing down the ghosts of his choices. Choices that had led us both into this mess. Every conversation, every decision he had made had been a carefully crafted lie. Or maybe not even a lie. Maybe he had been deceived, manipulated, trapped by forces far greater than either of us could ever have imagined.

But there was no turning back now.

We stopped in front of an unmarked door, the kind that could lead anywhere—or nowhere at all. The air around it was thick with a sense of foreboding, a warning that I hadn't asked for but couldn't ignore. My heart raced, but it wasn't fear. It was the sick, twisted thrill of knowing we were about to uncover the truth. The kind of truth that had the power to destroy everything I thought I knew about my life, my marriage, and maybe even myself.

Connor knocked three times, his hand firm but controlled. A beat passed before the door creaked open just a crack, a pair of eyes peering through the gap. They were too calculating, too sharp, too experienced for comfort.

"You're here," the voice said. It was gravelly, as if it had been weathered by years of holding secrets.

I didn't recognize the man who stood before us, but I could feel the weight of his gaze. He was someone important. Someone who knew things. Things I wasn't ready to hear but needed to.

"We need answers," I said, my voice surprising even myself. It wasn't a question. It was a demand.

The man's lips curled into a smile that didn't reach his eyes. "Answers come with a price."

I stepped forward, disregarding the warning in his tone. "I've already paid. And I'm not done yet."

Connor moved beside me, his eyes never leaving the man's face, his stance protective, but there was a tension in the air that even he couldn't entirely control. This wasn't just another lead. This was the final stretch, and we both knew it. No matter how much I wanted to turn away, the truth was already waiting for me, lying in wait like a predator.

The man took a long look at us, sizing us up, before stepping back and opening the door wide enough to let us inside. The dim light inside cast long shadows against the walls, making everything feel distant and ominous. We walked in, and I didn't have to look around to know this place had been the setting for too many deals, too many betrayals.

"Take a seat," the man said, his tone casual, almost too casual. I wanted to argue, to refuse, but the curiosity gnawing at me was unbearable. We sat.

"Your husband," the man began, tapping his fingers against the table, "wasn't in control of the situation. No one is ever really in control."

My heart skipped. The words felt like they were meant to tear me apart, and for a moment, I almost wanted to believe him. But something inside me, something sharp and defiant, kept me grounded.

"Then who was?" I asked, the question burning in my chest.

The man's gaze flicked to Connor, then back to me, as though trying to gauge whether I was ready for the truth.

And that's when I knew. The truth wasn't just something you learned. It was something you survived.

The man behind the desk let the silence stretch, like a rubber band pulled taut between us. The weight of his words hung in the air, thick and suffocating. I shifted in my seat, trying to ignore the uncomfortable sensation crawling under my skin. This place was too familiar, too sterile in its unspoken tension. Every inch of it screamed secrets, from the flickering overhead light to the way the shadows seemed to gather in the corners of the room like darkened memories waiting to be recalled.

I had no idea how we got here, but I knew we couldn't turn back now. This was it. The point of no return. I caught Connor's eye across the table, and for a brief moment, we shared something unspoken—mutual understanding, but also a shared dread that the answers we were about to get might unravel everything we had believed to be true.

The man in front of us tapped his fingers again, slower this time, dragging out the suspense for reasons that felt calculated. "You think you're looking for the truth," he finally said, his voice laced with something akin to amusement. "But truth is a slippery thing, darling. It twists itself into whatever shape it needs to take."

I resisted the urge to snap at him. It would only play into his hands, make him feel more in control than he already did. Instead, I leaned forward, my palms flat on the table. "I'm done with games. My husband's life is on the line, and I'm not here to play around with riddles."

Connor moved just slightly, a subtle signal to remind me to keep my temper in check. He was always the level-headed one. He'd been the calm in the storm all along, but now, even he looked like he was holding his breath, waiting for the next move. I could feel the same tension coiling in him, a taut wire just barely holding everything in place.

The man's lips curled into a smile, as if he found my frustration amusing. "You're right about one thing," he said, finally shifting in his seat. "Your husband was never in control. But you might be surprised to learn who really pulled the strings."

The words sent a cold shiver down my spine. I had expected this, of course—suspected as much. But hearing it spoken out loud was something entirely different. I swallowed hard, trying to steady myself before I asked the inevitable question. "Who?"

"Ah," he said, shaking his head as if the answer was far too obvious. "You'll get there. But not yet."

I didn't know whether to feel infuriated or relieved. There was a part of me, the exhausted part that had been fighting so long to put the pieces together, that just wanted the answers to come flooding out. To finally know who had been orchestrating the mess my life had become. But there was another, darker part of me that knew the moment those pieces clicked into place, there would be no unlearning them.

I glanced at Connor again. He was tense now, his eyes narrowing as he studied the man across from us. "We're done with games," Connor said, his voice low but firm. There was a quiet warning in his tone, something calculated. He wasn't going to let the man string us along for much longer.

But the man just chuckled, clearly not intimidated. He leaned back in his chair, folding his hands behind his head as though we were all waiting for a punchline. "You think you're in control, don't you? But in this world, no one is in control for long."

Something about his arrogance rubbed me the wrong way, the smug confidence that dripped from every word. It wasn't the bravado of someone who held all the power; it was the bravado of someone who was about to lose everything and wanted to make sure they took as many people down with them as possible.

I took a deep breath, feeling the rawness of my frustration clawing its way up. But I was so tired of being manipulated, so done with playing this game. "Who's behind this?" I demanded again, my voice louder now, desperate to break through whatever barrier he was hiding behind.

The man's smile faltered just the slightest bit, and for a split second, I saw something—something like fear, or maybe regret—in his eyes. But it was gone almost as soon as it had appeared, replaced by that same smug composure.

He leaned forward, his elbows resting on the table. "I told you, darling. You're not ready for the whole story."

But something about that made my stomach churn. Not ready? I wasn't sure what had convinced him I was still a naïve bystander in all this, but he was wrong. I was ready for whatever truth he was holding back. I had no choice but to be. The truth was the only thing that could free me from the weight of the lies.

"You're going to have to get ready," I said, my voice steady now, even though my heart was racing. "Because I'm not leaving here until you tell me everything."

Connor's hand found mine under the table, warm and solid. His fingers twined through mine, a quiet reassurance. I could feel his heartbeat, steady and strong, and for a moment, it calmed the wild thundering of my own. We were in this together, no matter what came next.

The man didn't respond at first. He just stared at me, studying me as if I had just said something profoundly stupid, something he was now going to relish tearing apart. But then, finally, the corners of his mouth twitched upwards, just the smallest hint of something like amusement in his expression.

"You want the truth?" he asked, his voice soft now, almost mocking. "You want to know who's pulling the strings? It's not someone you're going to like."

I leaned in, my eyes narrowing, unwilling to back down. "I don't care who it is. I just want to know."

The man smirked and let out a slow breath. "Fine," he said, his words coming out almost in a whisper. "Your husband wasn't the only one who was fooled. The truth is, the person behind this is someone you already know. Someone you'd never suspect."

My pulse quickened, a cold sweat breaking out across the back of my neck. No, I thought. No, that can't be right. It couldn't be. I looked at Connor, but his face had gone pale, his eyes wide with disbelief.

And just like that, the pieces I had worked so hard to fit together scattered once more, falling away into a new, darker shape I wasn't ready to see.

The words hung in the air like smoke from a dying fire, curling and twisting, almost too much for me to breathe in. Someone I already knew. The thought lodged itself in my chest, sharp and cold. I blinked, willing the words to make sense, willing the man across the table to backpedal, to retract the statement. But the look on his face told me everything I needed to know. He wasn't joking. He wasn't playing some cruel game.

My heart slammed against my ribcage as if trying to claw its way out. "Who?" The word slipped out in a breathless rasp, barely more than a whisper. It felt as though I was being suffocated by the weight of the unknown, the fear creeping through me like an unseen current. I didn't want to hear the answer, but it was already too late. There was no going back now.

The man before us seemed to take a twisted delight in my panic. He leaned back in his chair, fingers tapping lightly on the edge of the table, his expression unreadable. A smile tugged at the corner of his mouth. "Oh, I think you know her very well. In fact, you've probably trusted her more than anyone else in your life."

I felt the blood drain from my face. "No." The word slipped out in a sharp exhale. I shook my head, refusing to believe it, even as a cold certainty gripped my insides. The pieces were clicking together in a way I didn't want them to, like a puzzle I was better off leaving unsolved.

His eyes glittered with something dark and knowing. "Yes. It's her."

I wanted to deny it, to throw the man's words back in his face, but the truth had a way of finding its way into the cracks of the lie you told yourself, no matter how tightly you sealed them.

"I'm not—" I started, but my voice faltered, the words catching in my throat. This was too much. My mind scrambled for something, anything, to hold on to. But I knew—deep down—I already had the answer. The woman he was talking about, the one who had been pulling the strings all along, was closer to me than I could bear.

"Who is it?" Connor's voice was a low growl, cutting through the air like a blade. He, too, had heard the truth in the man's words. But unlike me, Connor's expression was a storm of unreadable emotion—anger, frustration, maybe even betrayal. I knew he was trying to shield me, to protect me from the pain of it all, but there was no protecting me from this.

The man didn't need to say another word. His silence was enough.

I stared at him, the room around me shrinking as my mind reeled. The woman I had trusted, the one who had been a fixture in my life for years, the one I had turned to for advice, for guidance, for everything—I had been blind. Blind to the lies, blind to the manipulation, blind to the fact that she had been playing me all along. She had been the one pulling the strings, feeding me half-truths and whispers, setting the stage for the disaster that had unfolded.

It was her.

The thought twisted in my chest, and a cold sweat broke out across my skin. I wanted to scream, to lash out, to run as far away from the truth as I could. But the world had already caught up with me, and there was no escape. The woman I had called a friend, a confidant, was the very reason everything had fallen apart.

I looked at Connor, my eyes wide with disbelief, but also a desperate need for reassurance. I needed him to tell me I was wrong. That it wasn't possible. That the world I had known was still intact, that the foundation I had built my life upon hadn't crumbled to dust at my feet.

But he was silent, his jaw clenched tightly, his eyes scanning the room as though he were trying to piece together the next step in this madness. I could feel the weight of his thoughts pressing down on me, as if he, too, were trying to make sense of the puzzle, but couldn't.

"Who is it?" I managed to ask again, my voice trembling.

The man just smiled again, but this time, it wasn't a cruel smile. It was something darker, something that made my skin crawl. "You know who it is," he said softly. "You've always known. Deep down."

It felt like the floor had been ripped out from under me, and I was falling, tumbling through a void of confusion and disbelief. The person I had trusted most in my life had been orchestrating everything behind my back. Had set this entire chain of events into motion, watching as I stumbled blindly through the darkness.

"I don't believe you." The words tasted like acid in my mouth, but they were all I had. "You're lying."

The man's smile didn't falter. "I'm not lying. You'll see for yourself soon enough."

I wanted to scream at him, to shake him until the truth spilled out of him like water from a broken dam, but I couldn't. The realization that I was already too deep in the web, too far gone to escape it, settled like a stone in my stomach.

Connor stood abruptly, his chair scraping against the floor with a harsh screech. "We're done here," he said, his voice cold.

I looked at him, his face tight with resolve, and for the first time, I wasn't sure if he was talking about the conversation or us. Was this the end of the line? Had I pushed him too far, or was he just as trapped as I was in this web of lies?

The man before us didn't move, didn't even flinch. "It's not over," he said, his voice almost a whisper. "Not by a long shot."

I didn't want to hear any more. I couldn't. And yet, I couldn't tear myself away from the tangled mess of this truth. A truth that felt like it was burning through me from the inside out.

As we turned to leave, the door behind us slammed shut with a finality that sent a shiver up my spine. And as we stepped out into the cold night, I felt the weight of what had just been revealed settling in.

Someone I had trusted. Someone I had called a friend.

And as the rain began to fall harder, I knew the storm was only just beginning.

Chapter 33: Unquenchable Flames

The night air tasted different, like it was holding its breath. A kind of anticipation sat on the edge of everything, thin and brittle, as though the world was waiting for something terrible to break through. Connor's hand in mine was the only thing that felt real, the only thing I could trust in that moment. His fingers curled around mine, warm and firm, a small comfort amid the frantic chaos that was overtaking our neighborhood.

It was always easier to pretend we were safe in the daylight, when the sun washed over the houses, painting everything in soft, golden hues. But now, under the cover of darkness, the shadows seemed to grow, creeping into every crack and corner of the streets, of our hearts. It was easy to forget, until now, how much the world could shift in the blink of an eye, how thin the line was between normal and disaster.

"Are you sure?" I asked, my voice barely above a whisper, the weight of my fear hanging heavily between us.

Connor didn't look at me, his eyes scanning the narrow alleyway, the only escape route in case the worst happened. He was always like this—quiet, intense, the kind of person who absorbed every detail, even the ones most of us missed. "We don't have much time," he murmured, squeezing my hand tighter, as if the simple action could steady both our hearts.

I knew what he meant. The Matchstick Man wasn't just a myth anymore. He was real, dangerous, and far too close for comfort. The rumors had started small—a fire here, a house burned down there—but now, after the third attack in as many months, the fire was creeping closer. And this time, he was coming for us. The whole neighborhood. It wasn't just about the destruction anymore. It was personal. He was targeting us, every single one of us, in some twisted game of power and fear.

"You really think they'll listen?" I asked, my voice a little more brittle than I intended. My thoughts kept tumbling over each other, the weight of what we were about to ask of everyone suffocating me.

Connor's jaw tightened. "They'll have to." He paused, his gaze catching mine, and in that brief moment, I saw the fear flicker in his eyes—quick, sharp, and gone before I could fully process it. "We're all they have left now."

I nodded, swallowing hard. He was right, of course. The whole neighborhood had relied on the promise of safety, on the idea that the world outside was something they could control. But that illusion was shattering. People didn't want to face it, didn't want to believe that the danger was real, that it could touch them just as easily as anyone else. The Matchstick Man wasn't some random arsonist. He was deliberate, methodical. And his next fire, the one he was planning now, would burn down everything.

Connor and I had been working together for months to try to understand him, to figure out why he did what he did. But even the best minds couldn't predict the unpredictable. All we had now were our instincts, and those had led us here, to the edge of the cliff. No going back.

I glanced down the street toward Leo's house. He was probably still holed up inside, wondering why I hadn't called him yet. I should've told him, should've warned him that this was coming. But I hadn't, because if I said the words out loud, they might become real. And maybe, just maybe, I wasn't ready to face that.

"Is he still out there?" I asked, my voice suddenly thin with worry, though I tried to keep it steady. "The Matchstick Man. Do you think he knows we're onto him?"

Connor didn't answer right away, his gaze darting to the shadows at the end of the street. He was still scanning the area, like he expected to see something—or someone—step out of the darkness. I followed his gaze, but the street was empty. Silent. The sound of our footsteps echoed in the quiet, and for a moment, it felt like the whole world was holding its breath along with us.

When he did speak, it was low, barely audible. "I don't know." He glanced over at me, his expression grim. "But we don't have time to find out."

I nodded, understanding. If the Matchstick Man was still out there, we didn't have the luxury of waiting for him to make the first move. We needed to act now, before he had the chance to burn everything to the ground.

"Let's go," I said, my voice firmer than I felt. "We need to rally everyone. Every last person. If we're going to make it through this, we need to be ready."

Connor didn't need any more prompting. He tugged me forward, and together, we started walking down the street, toward the community center where everyone would be gathering. There was no more pretending, no more hoping this was all just a bad dream. The fire was coming. It was only a matter of time before we had to face it head-on.

As we walked, the tension in the air grew thicker, almost suffocating. People were already starting to trickle out of their houses, drawn by the sense of urgency, their faces drawn with worry, their eyes flicking nervously toward every corner, every shadow. Some of them whispered to each other, their words too quiet for me to catch. But I didn't need to hear them to know what they were thinking. We were all thinking the same thing: How much longer could we keep pretending we were safe? How long could we keep running from the fire before it found us?

Connor's grip on my hand tightened again, his thumb brushing over my skin in a quiet rhythm. It was the only thing that grounded me, the only thing that reminded me we weren't alone in this. We were in this together.

The community center was a hive of frantic energy when we arrived, the air thick with tension, people murmuring in hushed voices as they gathered in small clusters. There were the usual faces—the ones who showed up for every event, every neighborhood meeting, the ones who made sure they knew exactly what was happening before anyone else. But tonight, even they seemed unsettled. The woman who usually spoke so confidently about budget issues was now pacing, her hands wringing together as if she could squeeze the worry out. A few of the men stood near the back, talking in low, clipped tones, glancing nervously out the windows.

Connor and I moved toward the front, where the makeshift podium had been set up. I could feel the eyes of the crowd on us, expectant, desperate for answers. I glanced over at him, the briefest flicker of uncertainty crossing his face before he squared his shoulders and stepped forward, the movement so confident, so commanding, that I couldn't help but admire him. This wasn't the first time he had taken charge in a crisis, but tonight felt different. Tonight, it wasn't just about organizing; it was about survival.

"Alright," he said, his voice carrying through the room with the kind of authority that made the room fall silent. "Listen up. We don't have much time."

I stepped up beside him, feeling the eyes of the entire room turn to me, their collective worry settling into my chest like a stone. "The Matchstick Man isn't just some arsonist," I added, my voice calm but firm. "This is personal. He's targeting us. He knows the layout of this neighborhood, the gaps in our defenses, and he's coming for us again."

I paused, watching the crowd react. Some nodded, their faces grim, while others exchanged wary glances, as if they weren't sure whether to believe me or not. Fear, I realized, had already taken root. And fear, when left unchecked, could spread faster than any fire.

"We've got a plan," Connor continued, pulling out a map of the neighborhood. It was dotted with little markers, showing the fire's likely paths and possible points of entry. I could see the effort he'd put into this, the careful thought, the strategy behind every line and every note. "We've marked out escape routes, set up firebreaks, and designated areas for us to regroup if things go south."

The map was large, taking up almost the entire length of the table. There were red Xs all over it, places where we would have to fortify, places where we'd need to evacuate. I leaned in, my finger tracing the path of each planned escape, my mind racing. Every detail mattered now, every decision. And yet, as much as we tried to plan for everything, the one thing we couldn't control was the fire itself.

A voice from the back interrupted my thoughts. "How do you know he's coming for us? How do we know this isn't just another rumor?"

I didn't look back as I answered. "We know because he's done this before. And we know because he's left a trail." My voice didn't falter, but my chest tightened. "We've seen the signs. The pattern. It's always the same—targeting the heart of the community, burning things down bit by bit, until nothing's left."

There was a collective intake of breath. Even the skeptics in the room were starting to lean in, the gravity of our situation settling over them. It was a strange thing, how quickly fear could shift into action once the truth was laid bare.

Connor's hand brushed mine again, a fleeting touch that grounded me, pulling me out of the spiraling thoughts that were threatening to consume me. His eyes met mine briefly, and I saw it again—the flicker of something unspoken, something heavier than the weight of the moment. We were in this together, yes, but the enormity of what lay ahead was beginning to sink in.

"Alright," Connor said again, his voice firm and commanding. "Now we need volunteers to help secure the perimeter. We're going to need everyone. No one can sit this out."

A murmur rippled through the crowd. People shuffled, exchanged looks, and slowly began to stand, making their way to the front to sign up. It was almost surreal, seeing the neighborhood shift from fear to action. The same people who had once stood in line for town meetings, discussing the merits of better lighting or the need for more green space, were now making plans to fight for their homes, their lives.

As the crowd began to disperse to take on their assigned tasks, I noticed a familiar face toward the back. It was Leo, standing in the doorway, his hands shoved deep into the pockets of his jacket. He looked out of place, the uncertainty on his face mirroring my own. I excused myself quickly, my feet carrying me toward him before I could second-guess it.

"Leo," I said, my voice low enough that only he could hear me. "What are you doing here?"

He looked up at me, his eyes tired but sharp. "You think I'd miss this? You've got no chance of stopping this guy without me."

I frowned. "You shouldn't be here. You've been through enough already. This is dangerous. You don't have to—"

"I know," he cut me off, his tone quieter now, more serious. "But I'm not just sitting back while everyone else fights. I owe you too much."

His words hit me harder than I expected, a sharp reminder of everything we'd been through, everything that had brought us to this point. I opened my mouth to argue, but he was already stepping forward, eyes fixed on the map where Connor was laying out the next set of instructions.

"Let's get to work," Leo said, a quiet determination settling in his voice. "I'm not going anywhere until we're done."

I didn't argue. Instead, I gave him a single nod, the smallest sign of solidarity, before turning back to the group. We weren't going to be able to stop the fire alone. But together, maybe, just maybe, we had a chance.

The sounds of the community center echoed with the shuffle of feet, the murmur of voices, and the rustle of papers as everyone worked to prepare. It was strange, the way things could turn from routine to urgent in the blink of an eye. A few hours ago, this place had been set up for a simple meeting about the park's new playground equipment. Now, it was a war room. I glanced over at Connor, who was deep in conversation with a small group of volunteers, pointing out various spots on the map where they'd need to secure firebreaks. He moved with purpose, his brow furrowed, the weight of responsibility heavy on his shoulders. I wanted to ask him if he was okay, but I knew he'd just brush it off. He had this way of shouldering everything himself—like he thought if he could just control it all, nothing would go wrong.

I exhaled, trying to push the anxiety that had started to build in my chest to the back of my mind. I couldn't afford to be distracted, not now. The plan was starting to take shape, but there was a gnawing feeling in my gut that refused to be ignored. Everyone was doing their part—people who had never picked up anything more dangerous than a rake were now preparing to fight fire with whatever they could get their hands on. There was something both comforting and terrifying about it. I had spent years watching these people, knowing them by name, by face, and yet tonight, they felt like strangers. I realized with a jolt that we were all strangers to each other now, united only by the shared threat looming just beyond the horizon.

"Hey," Leo said, pulling me out of my thoughts. His voice was calm, but there was a glint of something dangerous in his eyes. "You good?"

I gave him a weak smile. "Just a little... overwhelmed. But we'll manage, right?" My attempt at reassurance sounded as hollow as I felt. Leo didn't say anything, just watched me with those sharp, calculating eyes of his. He didn't need to say anything to make me feel like I was walking on the edge of something that could easily break beneath me.

"Yeah," he replied, almost too easily. "We'll manage. We have to."

His words hung in the air, heavy and loaded. I could feel the weight of what he wasn't saying—how we were all teetering on the edge of an impossible situation, and how, no matter how hard we tried to pretend otherwise, no one was coming to save us.

I was about to say something, to ask him if he had any idea what was going through his head right now, when Connor called over to us. "We need to head out. Check the perimeter one last time before dark."

We all filed out of the community center, the warm glow of the streetlights casting long shadows on the pavement. It was odd, this sense of normalcy hanging in the air, despite everything. Cars drove past, their headlights sweeping over the streets, but no one waved or acknowledged the other. It was as if the world outside had gone on, oblivious to what was unfolding in our little corner of it.

The volunteers had already started setting up, with buckets of sand, fire extinguishers, and large plastic sheets ready to be deployed at a moment's notice. The air was thick with the smell of gasoline, metal, and something more volatile—fear. It clung to everything, making the hairs on the back of my neck stand on end.

I tried to focus on the task at hand, on the people who were counting on us, but my mind kept drifting. I had known this neighborhood like the back of my hand for years, had taken comfort in the familiarity of every street, every house, every crumbling brick of the old walls. But now, everything felt unfamiliar. The old oak tree near the corner, once a quiet symbol of stability, now felt like an ominous sentinel. The narrow alleyway between the houses, usually a safe passage, now seemed to hold a hundred dark secrets. The Matchstick Man was among us, moving like smoke, unseen but felt in every step.

Leo was ahead, already walking toward the first block where we had set up a checkpoint. Connor followed closely behind him, his silhouette just a step too far from mine, like he knew I needed the space but also didn't want to be too far if things went sideways. I stood still for a moment, watching them, trying to shake off the feeling that something was wrong—something I hadn't figured out yet.

"All good?" Leo asked, glancing back at me as he slowed his pace.

I nodded, forcing a tight smile. "Just keeping an eye out. You know how it is."

Leo raised an eyebrow but said nothing. The three of us had always been like this—Connor, the quiet strategist; Leo, the unpredictable wildcard; and me, always trying to keep both from imploding. But tonight, I couldn't help but feel like I was the one who was going to break.

We reached the end of the block, where a cluster of houses had been marked as potential hotspots. I took a deep breath, trying to steady my nerves. The first few houses were quiet, too quiet, their windows dark. It was eerie how still everything seemed, how abandoned it felt, even though we knew people were inside, watching from behind their drawn curtains. I knew they were scared. Hell, I was scared. But we had no choice now. We had to stand our ground.

The three of us moved methodically, checking each house, securing doors, making sure windows were locked, and the areas surrounding the properties were clear. It wasn't until we reached the old hardware store at the far end of the block that something shifted, something I couldn't quite place. The air was heavier here, thicker, as though the fire had already begun to spread, curling its tendrils around us. My eyes flicked to the side, scanning the shadows, but there was nothing. No movement. No sound.

Then the wind shifted, bringing with it the faintest scent of smoke.

"Did you smell that?" I whispered, my heart picking up speed.

Leo's eyes darted toward the horizon, his jaw tightening. "Shit," he muttered under his breath. "That's not good."

Connor didn't wait for either of us to say anything more. His hand found mine again, his grip fierce as he tugged me forward. "We need to move. Now."

We turned to head back, but before we could take more than a few steps, a flash of light split the darkness, followed by the unmistakable crackling sound of flames.

And then, a voice—too close—suddenly broke through the silence.

"Running out of time, aren't you?"

We froze. The matchstick man was already here.

Chapter 34: Heat of the Moment

The moon was a silver sliver hanging too high, its glow barely cutting through the dense curtain of night. My fingers gripped the edge of the window sill, knuckles pale and aching from the tension that had begun to gnaw at me hours ago. Each breath felt heavier than the last, the kind that fills your chest with a pressure you can't escape, no matter how deep you try to inhale. I stared out into the blackened streets, seeing nothing but shadows, wondering if they could see me, if they could feel the uncertainty creeping in the same way I did. The world outside felt like a painting—beautifully still, but utterly unreal.

Inside the apartment, the silence was deafening. The hum of the fridge seemed too loud, the faint tick of the clock on the wall mocking me as it dragged the time forward with agonizing slowness. Each second was a small eternity, and each minute brought me one step closer to breaking. I couldn't shake the image of Connor, somewhere out there in the dark, on the other side of whatever plan we'd crafted, fighting a fight I could never fully understand.

The team had been preparing for weeks, narrowing down the arsonist's hideout, piecing together clues that didn't always fit, and meeting under the cover of night, plotting the assault that could end it all. The hours had bled into one another, each minute a silent countdown to a moment I had no control over, and it was driving me mad.

I hated feeling like this—like I was sitting in the sidelines of my own life, helpless and small. I hadn't asked to be part of this, not really. It had all started as a simple request from Connor—no, not a request, more like a plea. He'd needed someone on the inside, someone he could trust who wasn't wrapped up in the thick of it all. And foolishly, or maybe just out of some misguided sense of loyalty, I'd agreed. The problem was, that decision had come with a price I hadn't been prepared to pay.

The floorboards creaked behind me, and I didn't need to turn around to know who it was. Connor's presence always filled the room in a way that was impossible to ignore, like the weight of his decisions, his promises, his actions, always pressing in from every corner.

I took a breath, steadied myself, but didn't look at him. I couldn't look at him. Not until he told me what had happened. What was happening.

"I know you're awake," he said softly, his voice rough like gravel, but there was a steadiness there, a quiet strength that made me exhale without realizing I'd been holding my breath.

"Did you find him?" I asked, the words rushing out of me before I could stop them. My heart was a wild thing in my chest, and I could hear the pounding of it in my ears, louder now, as if it could drown out everything else.

He didn't answer immediately, and in that pause, I felt the air shift between us. There was a certain sharpness in his silence—a pressure I could almost feel, like an impending storm. And then, finally, he stepped forward, closer, until I could hear the faint rustling of his boots on the floor.

"He's not going anywhere," he said, each word deliberate and low, almost too calm.

I turned to face him, instinctively, but the sight of him stopped me cold. He was standing there, his eyes dark, like pools of ink, his clothes torn and smeared with something I couldn't immediately identify. His hair, usually so neat and controlled, was wild, sticking up at odd angles, and there was a bruise forming across his jaw. Blood—his blood, maybe—streaked across his forehead, and for a brief, terrifying moment, I thought I might faint.

"You're hurt," I whispered, stepping closer.

He shook his head, the movement stiff. "I'm fine," he said, though the words didn't match the pain that seemed to echo in his gaze.

I reached up without thinking, my fingers brushing against his cheek, feeling the heat of his skin beneath my touch. It was warm, too warm, and the shiver that ran through me wasn't entirely from concern. There was something else beneath the surface of it all—something raw and unspoken, something that seemed to pull us closer even as the weight of the moment pressed in on us.

"Connor," I whispered, and this time, my voice trembled, betraying the fear I hadn't wanted to admit.

He stepped back, just enough to meet my eyes fully, his lips curving in a faint, wry smile that didn't quite reach his eyes. "You worry too much."

I wanted to laugh, but the sound caught in my throat. It was easy for him to say that, easy for him to brush it off. But I'd seen him in action. I'd watched him make decisions that cost more than anyone could imagine, decisions that had left scars on him—scars I hadn't even known about until I'd seen them for myself.

"You're impossible," I said, almost smiling despite myself. "But I'm glad you're back. You always come back."

There was something about the way he looked at me then—intense and searching—that made my heart lurch. His gaze softened, just for a moment, before he drew in a breath and spoke again.

"We got him. The arsonist. He's done."

I blinked, surprised. "For real?" I couldn't help but ask.

"For real," Connor confirmed. His voice dropped, barely a whisper. "But it wasn't easy. And it won't ever be the same."

I took a step back, trying to process the weight of his words. But all I could think about was the space between us. The unsaid things that had always lingered in the air like smoke, curling around us and pulling us together, no matter how hard we tried to ignore them.

The tension in my chest began to loosen, and for the first time in what felt like forever, I dared to believe that maybe, just maybe, this was the end of it. The end of the chaos, the danger, the unrelenting fear that had shadowed us all this time.

And as Connor moved to close the distance between us, his hand brushing mine with an intimacy that made my heart leap, I knew that nothing would ever be the same again. Not with him. Not with us.

But for the first time, I didn't mind that at all.

It wasn't relief that washed over me when Connor stepped closer, bruised but standing tall. It wasn't even joy. It was something far simpler, more visceral. I didn't need words to know he was here—alive, whole enough to get us through this. He didn't speak right away, and neither did I, but his presence filled the silence like an unspoken promise.

For a moment, I let myself breathe in the scent of him: the familiar musk of leather and the faint hint of gunpowder that clung to his clothes like a second skin. He wasn't a man who left his mark easily, but when he did, it was something impossible to ignore.

"You're alive," I said, though it was more of a statement than a question.

He nodded, the movement slow, almost deliberate, like he was weighing something in his mind. Then, in one smooth motion, he stepped even closer, his hands settling at my sides, just below my ribs. His touch was a map of everything that had been left unsaid. His fingers grazed over my skin, barely a whisper, but enough to make my pulse stutter. The room suddenly felt too small, as if the world outside didn't matter anymore, not when the man who'd been in the center of it all was right in front of me.

"You're worried," he said, his voice quiet, steady. He didn't need to ask; he knew it already. "I can see it in your eyes."

I shook my head, trying to brush off the heaviness that had gathered there. "I'm not worried," I lied. "Not anymore."

He didn't laugh, didn't offer the typical banter that usually followed one of his near-death experiences. This was different. We both knew it.

"Good," he muttered, the roughness in his voice somehow more tender now, like the remnants of a storm that had passed. Then, without warning, he pulled me into him, the force of it both sudden and necessary. I could feel the heat of his chest against mine, the solid reality of his body pressing into mine like a reminder that we were still here.

It wasn't just the physical act of holding me—it was the simple fact that he had chosen to come back. Chosen me.

The weight of the night's events, the uncertainty that had loomed over every passing hour, started to crumble, piece by piece. It wasn't victory that we were sharing in this moment. It was survival. And with it, something far more delicate, something that neither of us had been brave enough to fully explore until now: trust.

When he finally pulled away, his eyes softened, but there was a flicker there, something that made my stomach twist in ways I couldn't quite name. "We've still got work to do," he said, his tone back to its usual clipped sharpness. "But we'll get there. We always do."

I wasn't sure if he was reassuring me or himself, but I couldn't bring myself to argue.

"And the arsonist?" I asked, my voice barely above a whisper.

Connor's gaze hardened for a fraction of a second, the familiar mask of determination slipping back into place. "Handled. He's not going to be setting any more fires."

But something about the way he said it—too final, too quick—left me with more questions than answers.

"Connor," I started, my voice carrying a hesitant edge, "what aren't you telling me?"

He met my eyes then, his jaw tightening as he considered me, as if weighing the cost of honesty. It was a look I'd seen too many times before: the guarded, protective expression he wore like armor, even now, even with all we'd been through.

"You don't need to know everything," he said, the words laced with something unreadable. "Not right now."

I wanted to push, wanted to demand the details that were gnawing at the back of my mind, but something about his presence in that moment stopped me. It was the way he stood, unshaken, and yet so... vulnerable. The cracks in the foundation were there, but they weren't for me to fix—not tonight.

I nodded, but it didn't stop the questions from swirling inside of me. "Fine," I said, swallowing the lump in my throat. "Just... be careful."

His lips curled into a smile that didn't quite reach his eyes. "I'm always careful."

And maybe he was. Maybe he had been in that dark alley, or when he'd cornered the arsonist, or when his plan had begun to take shape, despite every risk. But there was something in the set of his shoulders, in the weight of the decision that still hung between us, that told me he wasn't done yet.

"Connor, wait—"

Before I could finish, the sudden shrill ring of his phone sliced through the air, cutting off whatever else I had intended to say. He exhaled sharply, the briefest flash of frustration passing across his face. "Always when you don't need it," he muttered, reaching for his phone.

I didn't ask who it was; I already knew.

"Yeah?" Connor answered, his voice returning to its businesslike tone. His eyes never left mine, but something had changed. There was a tension there now, a quiet warning that tightened the space between us.

The words were quick, clipped, and though I couldn't make out all of them, I caught the dangerous undertone that was becoming all too familiar. "Got it," he said, then disconnected the call without another word.

"Plans changed," he said, his voice now low, serious.

"What does that mean?"

He didn't immediately answer, his eyes narrowing slightly. "It means you need to get out of here. Now."

I froze, disbelief spreading through me like ice. "What? Why?"

"Because this isn't over. Not yet."

I stood there for a moment, caught between him and the truth I wasn't sure I was ready to hear. Whatever had happened in the last few hours, it wasn't enough. Not by a long shot.

Connor's words hung in the air, sharp and unyielding. "You need to leave. Now."

The moment his voice cut through the tension, I felt it—something deeper, darker, that shifted in the very space between us. His gaze, though firm, was strained, as if he was holding back something, something he wasn't yet ready to share. But there was no mistaking it now: this wasn't over.

I took a half step back, my pulse spiking, my feet cemented to the floor. "What are you talking about?" The words slipped out before I could stop them, brittle with disbelief.

"Do you trust me?" He wasn't looking at me anymore, his focus elsewhere, as if he were mentally preparing for something that was yet to come.

"Of course I do," I said, though it felt like a question more than a certainty. "But—"

He held up a hand, cutting me off. "Then you need to go. I'm serious."

The force of his words—no, the weight—was undeniable. Something had shifted, something I wasn't seeing, but I could feel it in my bones, a low hum beneath the surface of his words. "I'm not leaving you," I said, my voice more stubborn than I felt.

Connor's eyes snapped back to me then, fire burning in his gaze. "This isn't a debate. There's something coming. Something bigger than we anticipated. I can't keep you safe if you're here. Do you understand?"

His words pierced through me like cold steel. I wanted to argue, wanted to protest, but there was a cold, hard truth in his tone that made the words freeze in my throat. I didn't know what was happening, not fully, but I could see it in his face—the fear he was trying to suppress. And that was enough.

I swallowed, my mouth dry. "You're asking me to walk away? Now? After everything we've been through?"

A muscle in his jaw clenched, and his expression tightened, but he didn't look away. "I'm not asking you to walk away. I'm telling you to walk away. The longer you stay, the more danger you're in."

I wanted to scream, wanted to shake him and make him see reason, but the hardness in his eyes, the way he held himself so rigidly, told me that this wasn't just him being protective. Something had happened. Something that had shattered whatever small sense of security we'd both been clinging to.

I opened my mouth to speak, but the sound of a car engine revving outside caught my attention. My heart lurched, and before I could process the noise, a shadow darted past the window. My stomach dropped, an icy chill running through my veins.

Connor's head snapped toward the window, his eyes narrowing as the sound of the engine grew louder, closer.

"Shit," he muttered under his breath, his voice thick with urgency.

"What is it?" I asked, fear creeping into my voice.

He didn't answer immediately, and that terrified me more than anything. He moved to the door, peeking through the blinds, his body stiffening as he scanned the street outside. "They're here," he said, barely above a whisper. "We don't have much time."

I felt the blood drain from my face. "Who? What's going on?"

"Those bastards didn't take the bait," he said, his eyes hardening. "They've got someone else. They know we're onto them."

The realization hit me like a brick, and I staggered back, my mind spinning with confusion and fear. I had no idea who "they" were, or what the hell was happening, but I knew enough to understand the gravity in his voice.

"You said it was over," I whispered, my voice shaking. "You said it was finished."

Connor's jaw tightened, and the air between us grew thick with tension. "I was wrong."

"Then what the hell is going on?" My words were louder than I intended, the panic rising in my chest.

He was moving again, his eyes scanning the room as if searching for something, but when his gaze landed on me, it softened—just for a second. "Get out of here," he said again, more forcefully this time. "Go."

I shook my head, my chest tightening. "I'm not going anywhere without you."

Connor stopped, his face unreadable for a split second before his expression darkened. "This isn't about you, damn it." His voice was rough, edged with something darker than I had ever heard before. "I'm not leaving you behind, but if you're not going, then you're in this with me. And there's no going back from that."

For a moment, I didn't know what to say. My mind was spinning, trying to latch onto some kind of logic, some way to make sense of the chaos that was unfolding around us. But there was none. All I had was the pounding of my heart, the cold sweat forming on the back of my neck.

"I'll stay," I said, my voice steady even though every inch of me was shaking. "But you're not doing this alone. Not again."

Connor didn't answer right away. He just stared at me, his eyes hard and distant, as though weighing the cost of every word that hung between us. Finally, he nodded, slow and deliberate. "Fine," he said, his voice low. "But you stay close."

Before I could respond, the door slammed open. I didn't even have time to react. A blur of movement filled the room—masked figures, dark shapes that flooded in from the hallway like shadows that had come to swallow us whole.

Connor was already moving, his hand reaching for the weapon tucked beneath his jacket, his body coiled like a spring. I didn't know how he could move so fast, how he could slip back into this mode as if it was second nature.

The air was thick with tension as the first figure lunged toward him, and then—

Gunfire.

The sharp crack of a bullet echoed through the apartment. The world went silent for a moment, and all I could hear was the ringing in my ears and the frantic thumping of my heart.

Then, everything exploded into chaos.

Chapter 35: Rekindling Trust

The air smelled different in the mornings now—fresher somehow, as if the world had taken a deep breath and decided it was time to start again. I hadn't realized how much the weight of the past had clung to me, how tightly the old wounds had shackled me, until they began to loosen. Until I saw the world through new eyes, through the eyes of someone who had learned to trust again, who had learned to let go of the suffocating grip of fear.

I woke up earlier than usual that day, the sunlight filtering through the curtains in soft, honeyed beams. The silence of the morning felt intimate, like the kind of moment you don't share with anyone, not even yourself. The house was still, but I knew the kitchen would be warm with the scent of coffee by now, and I could hear the faint sound of Connor moving around in the next room, probably making breakfast, maybe even whistling—something he did when he was trying to distract himself from whatever worry was trying to chase him. It was his own brand of armor, that whistling, and I had come to recognize it as a sign that things were, in fact, okay.

When I stood and stretched, I felt the familiar ache in my bones, the kind that came from living through storms, from surviving when everything around you was breaking apart. But I didn't feel alone anymore. Not like I used to. Not when I could hear the rustle of his footsteps, the soft clink of the mug on the countertop, the low hum of his voice as he spoke to no one in particular. The little things were becoming our things, shared without needing to be said.

I pulled on my robe and walked toward the kitchen, the cool floor beneath my feet grounding me, reminding me that even in a world that had always felt like it might slip away, I was still standing here, in this moment, on this floor, breathing, living.

Connor looked up from where he stood in front of the stove, a frying pan in hand, a smile already tugging at the corners of his lips. "I made pancakes," he said, like it was the most casual thing in the world. Like he hadn't just learned to navigate the delicate balance between us, like we hadn't spent days, weeks, untangling our lives from each other's—sometimes with more difficulty than I cared to admit.

"Pancakes," I repeated, a laugh escaping me before I could stop it. It felt so...normal. Like we were just two people, having breakfast on a lazy morning. It was the first time in ages I'd felt that simple, uncomplicated joy. "You've really outdone yourself."

He chuckled, turning to flip the pancakes with a practiced ease. "I'm telling you, I could make a career out of breakfast. You should see my omelets."

I leaned against the doorframe, crossing my arms, watching him with something that felt dangerously close to admiration. "That's impressive," I said, and for a moment, there was silence, just the quiet clatter of the kitchen, the gentle sizzling of pancakes cooking. The unspoken understanding between us hummed louder than anything else.

Connor turned back, meeting my gaze, his eyes softer now. "How's the leg?"

It wasn't the first time he'd asked, but somehow it felt different this time—less about the injury and more about the person behind it. Like he really cared. Really wanted to know. And I realized, then, that I was no longer the person who pushed people away, who deflected concern with a quick joke or a sharp word. I was no longer the person who feared needing anyone.

"It's fine," I said, shrugging a little. I had learned not to overthink things. "It hurts less now, mostly just when I try to run or dance." I smiled, an easy, carefree thing that slipped out before

I could stop it. "But I think I'm safe from any impromptu ballet performances for a while."

He grinned back, his eyes twinkling. "Well, that's a relief. Can't have you breaking out into pirouettes on me."

I snorted, shaking my head. "Not likely."

We fell into an easy rhythm then, talking about small things—anything and everything except the heavy stuff. The stuff that had broken us in the first place. It felt almost absurd, how simple it was to be here with him, to let go of everything we'd carried for so long. But I also knew that this was only part of the process. The healing had begun, yes, but it wasn't a linear thing. It never was. There would be days when we'd still stumble, when the weight of the past would come crashing in again, but for now? For now, I was content to let the morning wash over me, to let the mundane moments fill in the cracks we'd left behind.

He set the pancakes on the table, the syrup already poured in neat little pools beside them, and we sat down to eat, the soft sound of cutlery clinking against plates a kind of music to our ears. We were quiet for a few minutes, both of us savoring the simplicity of this moment. But I could feel the tension still, just under the surface, like an echo of the battles we'd fought to get here. I could feel it in the way we sometimes hesitated to speak, in the unspoken questions we didn't ask. How long would this last? Was this a new beginning, or just a temporary peace before the storm returned?

Connor broke the silence, his voice low but steady. "I don't want to rush this, you know. Us."

I looked up from my plate, surprised by the raw honesty in his tone. The vulnerability. It was like hearing a confession, but without the burden of guilt. Just a simple truth that hung in the air between us. And for once, I didn't want to run from it.

"Neither do I," I said, meeting his gaze. "But I'm willing to try."

He smiled, and this time it was different. Softer. Real.

We ate our pancakes in silence, but there was something unspoken between us now, something that felt more like a promise than anything else.

The weeks that followed were quiet in the most unsettling way. They weren't the kind of quiet that comes after a storm, with the promise of change or new growth, but the kind where everything seems to have stopped moving, waiting for something—anything—to break the stillness. I had learned, through trial and error, that time had a way of hiding its healing. It passed in long stretches, each day blending into the next, but nothing felt completely resolved. Not yet.

The way I saw Connor now was different. It wasn't just the way his eyes softened when he looked at me or how his hand always seemed to find mine when we were in a crowd, but something deeper, a knowing between us that was born from years of unspoken things. It was in the quiet moments, when we would sit side by side without the need for words, when the comfort of just being with someone felt like the most significant thing in the world.

Still, there was a distance—a space between us, though not one of bitterness or regret, but of caution. It was the kind of space that only time could fill, a space that was earned rather than expected. I knew I wasn't ready to give him all of me again, not yet. And Connor, with all of his quiet understanding, didn't push. But I could see the way he watched me sometimes, like he was waiting for something to shift, something to finally bring us back to where we had once been, only better, only stronger.

One afternoon, I found myself standing in the small garden out back, the late spring air thick with the scent of jasmine and the soft buzz of bees busy at their work. The garden had become my sanctuary in those early mornings when I needed to find space in my own head, a small patch of calm in the middle of everything.

The old bench near the back fence had become my thinking spot, a place where I could sit and let my mind wander to places I wasn't always sure I wanted to visit. But today was different. Today, the weight of the world felt lighter, the future felt closer, and as I stood there, brushing the stray strands of hair out of my face, I thought maybe it was time to take that first step forward.

But then, of course, Connor found me.

He always found me in those moments when I thought I was alone, when I thought I could hide from whatever it was I was avoiding. The sound of his boots on the grass came first, quiet at first but growing closer until I felt his presence just behind me, like a familiar shadow. I didn't turn to face him immediately. I didn't need to. I could feel the quiet expectation radiating off him, the way he always seemed to know when I was close to something, when I was on the verge of making some big decision, even if I hadn't said a word.

"You know," he said, his voice cutting through the stillness, "you're going to wear a hole in that bench if you keep coming out here to think."

I smiled without meaning to, the corner of my mouth curving up as I glanced over at him. He stood there, arms crossed, leaning casually against the wooden fence, his face unreadable, but there was something in his eyes—something that felt too intense for just a casual comment about benches.

"Maybe," I said, giving him a look. "But I think it's worth it."

He tilted his head, and for a second, I saw a flicker of something deeper in his gaze, something that told me he wasn't just talking about the bench anymore.

There was a pause, the kind that always hung between us when neither one of us knew how to bridge the distance we'd built. But then, just like that, the moment was gone. He pushed himself off the fence and walked toward me, his hand reaching out in that slow, careful way he had, like he was afraid I might pull away if he moved too quickly.

His fingers brushed against mine, and it was enough to send a shiver down my spine. It was a simple touch, but it was everything. There was no need for more words, no need for declarations. For once, all I had to do was let myself feel what was there, just as it was.

"I've been thinking about you," he said, his voice low, barely above a whisper, like the words were too heavy to be said too loudly.

I didn't say anything for a moment. What was there to say? What could I say when he'd already stripped away every defense I'd built? What could I say when I felt the truth of his words like a quiet pulse in my chest? I turned to face him, not completely, but enough to catch the steady gaze he held on me.

"I know," I said softly. "I've been thinking about you too."

The words hung in the air, unspoken but understood. And in that moment, I realized that we were both standing on the edge of something new. But neither of us knew how to take the first step, and that knowledge made everything feel fragile. We weren't running from the past anymore, but the future? The future still felt like an open question, and neither one of us had the answer.

We stood there, the space between us charged with that quiet electricity that had always existed, only now it was softer, gentler. A kind of calm before the storm, but not in the way I'd always feared. This wasn't an impending disaster. This was something different. Something that could be built slowly, piece by piece, until we had something we could hold onto, something that might just last.

Connor reached out again, this time taking my hand in his, his fingers warm against mine. His thumb stroked the back of my hand in slow, deliberate motions, like he was memorizing the feel of me, like he was trying to remind himself of what it felt like to be this close to someone.

"I know we're not there yet," he said, his voice rougher now, like he was finally letting himself be real. "But I want to be. I want to get there with you. If you'll let me."

I didn't know what the future held. I didn't know if I was ready to take that step. But standing there in the garden, with the scent of flowers filling the air and Connor's hand in mine, it didn't feel like such a scary thing anymore. It felt like something worth fighting for.

"Let's see where it takes us," I said, my voice steady, sure of nothing but this moment. And maybe, just maybe, that was enough for both of us.

The days seemed to stretch out like a series of small, deliberate choices—each one a new thread in the tapestry of this new life we were stitching together. But the quiet that settled between Connor and me was a double-edged sword. There was comfort in it, of course. The way we could just exist in the same space without needing to say much, the way our silences felt like an unspoken promise. But there was something else, something deeper, lurking beneath that quiet—something that neither of us could avoid forever.

I had learned to trust him again, or at least I thought I had. But the truth, as I was discovering, was that trust wasn't something you simply reassemble after it's been shattered. It wasn't like picking up the pieces of an old vase and gluing them back together, hoping no one would notice the cracks. It was a slow, cautious thing, a feeling you nurtured and fed until it grew strong enough to stand on its own. And sometimes, trust didn't come in grand, sweeping moments of revelation—it came in the small, seemingly insignificant choices you made every day. Choices that built upon each other, until, one day, you realized you were standing in a place you never thought you'd get to.

It was on one of those ordinary days that the ground finally shifted beneath us, though neither of us saw it coming.

I had been in the kitchen, lost in the hum of chopping vegetables for dinner, when I heard the unmistakable sound of Connor's boots on the floor behind me. He had a particular rhythm to his steps, a steady, purposeful kind of movement that never seemed rushed. There was a brief silence, and then I felt the familiar presence of his body just behind mine. His breath was warm on the back of my neck, and I could almost hear his thoughts in the quiet tension that seemed to fill the space between us.

"You've been quiet today," he said, his voice low, not accusing, but just... curious.

I didn't turn to face him immediately. Instead, I reached for the knife, slicing through a carrot with more force than necessary. "I'm fine," I said, too quickly. I wasn't sure why I felt the need to be defensive, but there it was. A small wall between us. The kind of wall that only appeared when I was afraid—afraid of being too open, afraid of being too vulnerable.

"Is that so?" he replied, his voice laced with a soft amusement that made the tension between us feel... misplaced. "Because it feels like you're holding something back."

I finally turned to face him, setting the knife down with a sharp clink that echoed in the quiet kitchen. He stood there, arms folded across his chest, an eyebrow quirked in that way of his—one that always made me feel like he could read my thoughts, if only he bothered to try.

"You know," I said, my words a little sharper than I intended, "sometimes it's just a matter of needing space. Is that so hard to believe?"

He didn't flinch, didn't react with defensiveness or irritation. Instead, he simply nodded, the smallest shift in his stance. "Not hard to believe," he said. "But that doesn't mean I'm not going to ask. You've never been one to hold things in."

I felt a knot form in my stomach, but I forced myself to stay calm. "Things change."

The words hung between us for a moment, and then, without another word, he stepped forward, close enough that I could feel the warmth of his body. "You know, you don't have to carry all of it by yourself," he said, his voice softer now, like he was trying to thread his way through the delicate fabric of my emotions. "Not anymore."

I swallowed, my throat suddenly dry. "I'm not carrying anything."

But I knew that wasn't true. Not entirely.

We stood there, the space between us filled with the unspoken weight of everything we hadn't said, of everything we still needed to navigate. And then, as if sensing the shift in the air, Connor reached out, his hand grazing my wrist, gentle but steady. "We've been doing this dance for a while now, haven't we?"

I nodded, my breath catching in my throat. It had been a dance, hadn't it? A series of steps we both knew, but neither of us had been brave enough to lead. Not fully.

And that's when the real question surfaced—the one we had both been avoiding. Was I ready to let him lead? Was I ready to trust him in a way I hadn't trusted anyone in years?

Before I could answer, before I could even fully formulate my thoughts, the sharp ring of my phone broke the tension, slicing through the moment like a knife. I reached for it instinctively, glancing at the screen. The name that flashed across it made my heart skip, then race.

It was my sister.

"Hey, I was just about to—" I started, but she cut me off, her voice frantic, urgent.

"You need to get here. Now."

I straightened, the world narrowing around me, the edges of the kitchen fading as her words sunk in. "What's going on?" I asked, my pulse quickening.

"It's Dad," she said, her voice trembling. "Something's happened. I don't know all the details, but it's bad. Please, just come."

I didn't hesitate.

The phone fell from my hand, landing with a soft thud on the counter. My mind was already racing, already picturing my father, imagining the worst-case scenarios.

Connor's gaze was fixed on me, unreadable, but his presence felt like a weight, anchoring me in place. "What is it?" he asked, his voice low, steady.

I met his eyes, my own wide with panic. "It's my dad. Something happened. I need to go."

Without another word, he grabbed his jacket, the gesture quick, instinctive. I barely registered the movement, but by the time I'd reached the door, he was right behind me. "You're not going alone," he said.

And then, before I could respond, the phone rang again. This time, it wasn't my sister. It was a number I didn't recognize.

I answered, my breath shallow, heart hammering in my chest. "Hello?"

The voice on the other end was a cold, unfamiliar tone, and the words that followed made everything inside me freeze.

"Your father's in trouble. And we're just getting started."

Chapter 36: Flames of Forgiveness

The air was thick with the smell of rain, a scent so sharp it could cut through the fog of my own thoughts. I stood at the edge of the cemetery, fingers clutching Connor's hand like it was the only thing keeping me tethered to this world. His skin was warm against mine, a stark contrast to the dampness that clung to the grass at our feet. We didn't speak at first. The silence between us wasn't heavy, though. It was more like a delicate pause, a quiet acknowledgment of the weight of what we were doing here, what I was doing here.

I had never imagined this moment. Not in the wildest reaches of my grief, not in the dreams where I'd come to terms with the loss of my husband. He had been my world, the center around which everything else had revolved. I thought that love, once given, would never fade. But life had a funny way of showing me how wrong I was. I had spent months buried under the layers of hurt, anger, and betrayal that came from the truth I'd discovered—truths about him, about myself.

And yet here I was, standing at the foot of his grave, trying to make peace with a man who could never ask for forgiveness.

Connor's thumb brushed over the back of my hand, a quiet reassurance that he was there, that I wasn't alone in this. I didn't need him to say anything. The softness in his touch spoke volumes. It was more than enough. It was everything.

I let out a breath, long and slow, as if releasing it from some far-off place deep within me, where I'd kept it locked for too long. My gaze shifted to the headstone, cold and unyielding, a cruel reminder of everything I had lost. And yet, there was a strange sense of peace in the finality of it. The past couldn't haunt me anymore. I had carried its weight for too long, letting it dictate the shape of my days. But that was over now. I was ready to let go.

Turning slightly to face Connor, I saw the softness in his eyes, the understanding, and the quiet strength that had pulled me through so many of my darkest days. I could have cried, could have fallen apart right there in the rain-soaked earth, but something told me I had already done enough of that. This wasn't about weakness. It wasn't about the cracks that had been carved into me over the years. It was about standing tall in the face of it all and saying, "I'm still here."

"I'm ready," I whispered, the words feeling like a release in themselves.

Connor's hand tightened around mine, a small squeeze, and we walked together toward the grave. With every step, it felt like I was shedding pieces of myself, the old versions of me that had been tethered to a man who was no longer here, to a past that no longer fit. The world around us was still, save for the soft murmur of the wind through the trees, the subtle rustling of the leaves, the gentle patter of rain on the ground. It was as if the world itself was holding its breath, waiting for me to make peace with my own soul.

When we reached the gravestone, I stopped. My fingers trembled for a moment, but then they steadied. I didn't need to speak his name. He had been a part of me once, a chapter in my life that I had read over and over again, but that book was finished. I wasn't turning back to it anymore.

"Goodbye," I said, the word barely more than a breath, but it held all the weight of years of love, loss, and longing. "Goodbye to the person you were, and to the person I thought I was."

Connor stepped closer, his presence warm beside me. It was strange how the sound of his voice, the quiet way he always seemed to know what I needed, made the world seem just a little less harsh. "You've done it," he said softly, his words wrapping around me like a blanket. "You've let him go. Now, it's your turn. It's time for you to live, truly live, without the burden of the past on your shoulders."

I nodded, though I didn't trust my voice just yet. I wasn't ready to speak again. Not yet. But the truth of his words echoed through me, settling into the spaces where doubt had once lived. He was right. It was my turn now.

The rain, which had been falling steadily, seemed to pause for a moment, as if the universe itself was taking a breath with me. I could feel the change in the air, the shift, the quiet promise of something new waiting just beyond the horizon. I wasn't sure what that something was yet—whether it would be easy or hard, whether it would be smooth or rocky—but I was ready for it. I was ready for whatever came next, because for the first time in so long, I knew I wasn't walking alone.

With one final glance at the grave, I turned away. Connor was at my side, always there, and we walked into the rain together. Each step felt lighter than the last, the weight of the past lifting slowly but surely, leaving behind only the possibility of a future untold, untried, and full of promise.

The rain had softened, its rhythmic patter now more of a gentle whisper against the earth. We walked side by side, the air fresh and alive, each drop a reminder of the transformation that was happening in me, in both of us. Connor's footsteps matched mine, steady, unhurried, as if the world was stretching its arms wide, inviting us to take our time, to breathe deeply before we dove into whatever waited on the other side.

I could feel the weight of the past still clinging to the edges of my thoughts, but it was fading, like fog lifting in the early morning light. I had spent so many months locked in a battle with myself, torn between love and betrayal, guilt and forgiveness. But the further we walked, the less it seemed to matter. The sun peeked through the clouds, casting the landscape in a soft, golden glow, and for the first time in a long time, I didn't feel like I was drowning. I felt like I was breathing again, the air richer, more vivid than it had ever been before.

Connor squeezed my hand, pulling me gently from my thoughts. His eyes were darker now, a mix of concern and something I couldn't quite read. But there was something comforting in it. Like he saw the shift in me, felt it too, and he was holding on just as tightly as I was, not out of fear, but out of trust.

"You're quiet," he said, his voice low, the edges of his words almost swallowed by the sounds of the world around us. "What's going on in that head of yours?"

I turned to him, my lips curving into a smile that wasn't quite a smile, but close enough. "Just thinking about how strange it is, you know? To feel like you've been carrying this weight, and then... suddenly, it's gone." I shook my head, still trying to wrap my mind around it all. "It's like I've been holding my breath for months, maybe years, and now I can finally exhale."

Connor chuckled softly, the sound a warm hum that vibrated through me. "Exhaling is overrated," he teased, nudging me with his shoulder. "It's the holding your breath part that's the real challenge. The exhale's the easy part. It's the in-between that gets you."

I laughed, the sound bubbling up like it had been trapped in my chest for too long. The sound felt foreign, but good. Alive.

"Yeah, well," I said, glancing over at him with a grin, "I'm getting pretty good at the exhale. Just don't ask me to hold my breath for any longer than necessary."

"You'll be fine." Connor gave me a sidelong look, the corners of his mouth turning up ever so slightly. "And if not, I'll be right here. Ready to catch you."

There was an easy confidence in his words, a sense of certainty that seemed to seep into my bones. The past had been full of questions, full of "what ifs" and "could haves," but now, standing next to him, I felt like I could face whatever came next without hesitation. And for the first time in a long time, I realized that maybe, just maybe, the future didn't have to be a terrifying unknown. It could be something... else.

"Thank you," I said, my voice quieter now, the words slipping out before I could stop them. "For being here. For not making this harder than it had to be."

Connor's expression softened, and for a moment, his gaze flickered to the horizon, as if searching for something out there in the distance. When he spoke, his voice was low, steady, like he was saying something he had known all along.

"I didn't do anything, really," he said, his eyes finding mine once more. "I'm just here. That's all you needed, right? Someone to be here with you. Not to fix anything, but just... to show up."

I nodded, the weight of his words settling over me in a way that felt grounding, like the very earth beneath my feet was offering its support. It wasn't the grand gestures or the sweeping declarations that made a difference. It was the quiet presence. The willingness to stand beside someone in their mess and not try to fix them, but simply to hold their hand until they could fix themselves.

We walked for a while longer, the world around us coming alive as the rain began to dwindle into nothing more than a light mist. The trees swayed gently in the breeze, their leaves rustling like whispers of a forgotten conversation. Everything felt... possible. Like the world had just cracked open and offered us something new, something fresh.

But even as we walked, there was a nagging feeling at the back of my mind, something I couldn't quite shake. It wasn't the past, or the mistakes, or the ghosts of old arguments. It was something else, something I hadn't expected.

I had thought that letting go would feel like freedom, and in many ways, it did. But there was a deeper ache, one I hadn't anticipated. It wasn't sadness, not exactly. It was a strange sort of emptiness, as though I had been wrapped up in something for so long that now, without it, I wasn't quite sure who I was anymore. The woman I had been with my husband—the woman I had been before all the pain—was gone, leaving behind someone new. Someone who was still figuring out how to stand on her own two feet, how to fill the space that had once been filled with love and betrayal and grief.

I stopped walking, suddenly aware of the weight of my own thoughts, and turned to Connor. "What if I don't know how to be me anymore?" I asked, the words slipping out before I could stop them.

He didn't answer immediately, and for a moment, the world seemed to pause around us, as if waiting for him to say something profound. Instead, he simply looked at me, his gaze steady and unwavering, and then he gave me a small smile, not an answer, but a promise.

"We'll figure it out together," he said. "One step at a time."

And somehow, with those few simple words, I felt the last of the weight lifting from my shoulders. It wasn't about knowing exactly who I was or where I was going. It was about the fact that I wasn't alone anymore. That was enough.

The path we followed seemed to stretch on forever, the world around us bathed in the soft glow of the evening sun, its rays filtering through the last remnants of the rain. The earth smelled like wet stone and grass, fresh and rich with life. It felt like we were walking into a story that wasn't mine, or his, but ours—something entirely new that had yet to be written.

Connor's fingers laced through mine again, and I realized that for the first time in what felt like forever, I was starting to feel like I could breathe without constantly looking over my shoulder. The air didn't weigh me down anymore. It felt lighter, almost like I could fly if I let myself, if I could just trust the wind to hold me.

I glanced at him, caught by the way his eyes were fixed ahead, the lines of his jaw set in determination, but there was something soft there, something quiet and knowing. He was my anchor, but he was also my compass, and the realization hit me all at once: maybe he was guiding me as much as I was guiding him. Maybe it wasn't just about me letting go, but about us both finding a way to start over, to be something different than the versions of ourselves that had existed before.

I opened my mouth to speak, but just as the words started to form, I heard it—the distant sound of something crashing, followed by a sharp yelp. My heart skipped a beat, my instinct to protect rising like a wave in the ocean. Without thinking, I tugged on Connor's hand, pulling him in the direction of the sound.

"What the hell was that?" I asked, my voice breathless, already quickening my pace.

Connor didn't say anything, but I saw the flash of determination cross his face. He didn't question me, didn't ask what I thought was happening. He simply followed, his hand gripping mine, steady and strong.

We rounded the bend of a small hill, and there it was—at first, just a shadow, and then clearer as we drew closer. A figure. A woman, her knees buckled beneath her, her back arched in a way that made the hair on the back of my neck stand on end. The woman was hunched over, gasping for breath, her hands clutching her side as if something was squeezing the life out of her.

I didn't hesitate. My feet were already moving faster, pushing forward, driven by something deep inside me that I couldn't name. It was only when we got closer that I noticed the blood—dark and spreading quickly across the woman's dress, soaking into the grass beneath her.

Connor swore under his breath, crouching beside me as I knelt down beside the woman, reaching out instinctively, despite the voice in my head screaming that I shouldn't touch her. But there was no time for hesitation.

"Hey," I said, my voice gentle but firm. "Hey, you're going to be okay. We're here. We've got you."

The woman's head turned toward me, her eyes wide, terrified. She tried to speak, but her voice came out in a ragged rasp, barely a whisper.

"Please... don't let him... find me," she gasped, the words barely escaping her lips before she passed out, her body crumpling into a heap against the ground.

My heart was hammering in my chest, and I could feel Connor beside me, tense and ready. His hand was still on mine, but he was already scanning the area, his eyes darting around, looking for any sign of danger.

"Who is she?" he asked, his voice low, almost too calm for the situation.

"I don't know," I whispered back, my gaze fixed on the woman's pale face, her lips pressed together in a grimace of pain. "But we can't just leave her here."

Connor didn't argue, didn't say a word. He just nodded, moving with purpose as he pulled out his phone. "We need help. I'm calling an ambulance."

I glanced at the woman's dress again, and then at the blood pooling around her, and the sharp instinct in my gut told me that this wasn't an accident. This was intentional. The blood had been deliberately spilled, and the woman was still alive, but barely.

"What happened to you?" I whispered, my hand resting lightly on her arm. The feel of her skin beneath my fingertips was icy, far colder than it should have been.

Connor was still speaking urgently into the phone, his brow furrowed, and I could see his jaw working, muscles tensing with each second that passed. I didn't know what had happened to this woman or who had hurt her, but I knew one thing for certain. This wasn't just a random act. The urgency in her plea, the terror in her eyes... there was something far more sinister at play.

The more I looked at her, the more I felt like I had seen her before, though I couldn't place where. Her face was so familiar, yet I couldn't connect the dots. Was she someone from my past? Someone from a story that hadn't quite finished being told?

The voice on the phone started to fade into the background, the sound of the dispatcher offering their reassurances, but they seemed so distant now, so far away. The only thing that mattered was the woman in front of me, the way her breathing was shallow and erratic, her pulse weak beneath my fingers.

"Connor," I said suddenly, my stomach dropping. "There's something wrong. We're too late. We have to—"

Before I could finish, there was a sound, sharp and sudden—footsteps. Coming toward us. Heavy, deliberate.

I looked up, my heart stalling in my chest. Connor's grip tightened on my hand as he scanned the horizon, eyes narrowing. And then, just as I opened my mouth to ask him what was happening, a shadow moved through the trees, tall and imposing, with a silhouette I could barely make out in the fading light.

It wasn't the relief of help that was coming toward us.

It was something much worse.

"Get her out of here," I whispered, panic rising in my chest, but it was too late. The figure was already too close. And the voice that followed it sent chills down my spine.

"You're not supposed to be here," the man said, his voice low and menacing.

Chapter 37: The Burned Road

I woke up the next morning, the sun slicing through the half-open blinds, painting the room in golden streaks that felt almost too peaceful for the storm brewing in my chest. My eyes lingered on the pillow where Connor had slept, the faint impression of his head still there, as if he'd left a piece of himself behind.

But the sheets were cold now, and the quiet was different—hollow. The hum of the air conditioner seemed louder somehow, filling the space where his laugh used to echo. He was gone. The transfer had come through, the paperwork finalized, and just like that, Connor was heading to another city for a new position. I had known this was coming. He had warned me weeks ago that the offer was on the table. I had nodded and smiled, all while secretly hoping it would fall through, that something would hold him back, that we would find some way to make this work without the looming shadow of distance stretching between us.

But that was before. Now, with the last of his things packed into a suitcase and the weight of the unspoken words between us, I knew there was no turning back. He had to go. And deep down, I understood. The choice wasn't really his either. He wasn't leaving because he wanted to. He was leaving because he had to. His career was at a crossroads, and this was the path laid out before him, no matter how much we both hated it.

I rolled over, staring at the ceiling as if it would somehow offer a solution, a way out of the mess we'd gotten ourselves into. But the only thing staring back at me was the light fixture, familiar and indifferent, like everything in my life had become since he left. The absence of him, so tangible now, gnawed at my insides.

I could still hear the sound of his voice in my head, low and steady as we talked late into the night. We had danced around the inevitable, both of us reluctant to say what we knew needed to be said. The weight of our unspoken words hung in the air, thick and suffocating, but there was no escaping it. It had to be done. It had been done, but neither of us was ready to call it quits.

"Do you think this is it?" I had asked, knowing full well it wasn't a question I could answer. It wasn't really about that. It was about the sinking feeling that clawed at me when I thought about how long we would go without each other, how many hours would stretch between our conversations, how many mornings I would wake up alone without him beside me.

His answer had been a soft chuckle, the kind that was bittersweet in its familiarity. "We'll figure it out. We always do."

But as I lay in the bed now, the echoes of his voice fading into the stillness, I realized that figuring it out didn't seem as simple as he made it sound. It wasn't about being strong. It wasn't about finding some grand solution. It was about the spaces between us, the ones that had already begun to grow before he even left.

The phone buzzed on the nightstand, pulling me from my thoughts. I grabbed it, seeing his name flash across the screen.

Connor: "Hey. I miss you already."

I pressed my hand to my mouth to stifle the lump that rose in my throat, a mixture of longing and frustration swirling inside me. I missed him too. I missed everything about him—the way he would smile in the mornings, all sleepy and disheveled, the way he would joke about my obsession with coffee as if he didn't drink three cups himself before noon. I even missed the way he would steal the covers at night, his feet somehow always managing to end up in the most inconvenient places.

But I knew I had to be strong for both of us. He needed to go. We needed to let this play out, to see where it would take us. I wasn't sure if I believed in fate, but if I did, I couldn't ignore the feeling that this was one of those moments, the kind where you either take the leap or let it slip through your fingers.

Me: "I miss you too. But you're doing what you have to do. I get that. We'll figure this out."

I didn't want to say the words out loud, but they hovered in the back of my mind, pressing against my ribs, aching to be released.

The reality of it all felt like a weight in my chest, but somehow, I couldn't bring myself to delete the message. Instead, I left it there, sitting in the air between us, holding onto the fragile thread of what we were.

I could hear the sounds of the city below me—cars honking, people shouting, the faint hum of traffic—and for the first time in what felt like forever, I felt small. Like I didn't belong in this city anymore, like everything I knew was about to slip out of my grasp. I had never thought of myself as someone who depended on someone else, but in that moment, I realized I had come to depend on Connor more than I cared to admit.

But there was no denying it now. He was gone. The apartment was quieter, the streets outside seemed less vibrant, and the whole world felt a little bit colder. I stood up, brushing my hand over the counter, touching the objects around me, each one a little more distant, a little more irrelevant without him here to make them feel like home.

I wasn't ready for this. But sometimes, we have to face things we're not prepared for.

The clock ticked, the minutes stretching out longer than they should have, a mockery of time itself. I stared at my phone, willing it to ring, to buzz, to remind me that Connor was still out there somewhere, still thinking of me. But nothing came. Not that I expected it, not really. I was trying to be strong, trying to convince myself that this wasn't the end. But a gnawing emptiness had taken root in my stomach, and I was failing at pretending it wasn't there.

My apartment felt like a tomb—quiet, uninviting, as though it had somehow absorbed the absence of his laughter, of his quiet

FLICKER

presence that had once filled the space with warmth. I had left the blinds open, the morning sun spilling in, but the light seemed wrong, harsh even, as if it were mocking me for not being able to let go. It illuminated the small, insignificant things—the chipped mug on the counter, the stack of papers he had left behind in the rush of leaving, the empty spot on the couch where he had always sat.

It wasn't like I had been blind to the inevitable. I had seen it coming long before the paperwork arrived on his desk. His phone calls had started to sound more distant, his texts clipped. He was busy. He was consumed by the weight of his future. But I had buried it all under the soft, warm blanket of denial. Because I wanted to believe that we were different, that love could outlast everything—distance, time, even the quiet despair that had been creeping into my chest.

I had gone to work that morning, mechanical in my motions, numb to the world around me. My coworkers noticed, of course. They always did. Everyone had their theories—something had happened between Connor and me, they whispered. Maybe he was a little too tied up in his career. Or maybe I was the one pulling away, hiding behind the mask of independence I had so carefully cultivated. But none of them understood. None of them could feel the weight that hung in the air between me and Connor, the delicate tension that neither of us knew how to undo.

"So," said Max, leaning against the doorframe of my office as I stared at the spreadsheets in front of me. His voice was light, like he was trying to keep it casual, but I could hear the undertones of concern in his words. "How's the... boyfriend situation?"

I didn't look up. "He's gone," I said simply, as if the words didn't pierce me every time I said them.

Max whistled low under his breath. "That sucks. You're not the 'long-distance' type, are you?"

I shifted in my chair, finally lifting my eyes to meet his. "Neither is he."

Max's face softened, his eyes narrowing as though he could see right through my tough exterior. He pushed off the doorframe and took a step closer. "It's okay to be upset, you know. You don't have to bottle it all up. I've seen you do it before."

I didn't want to admit it, didn't want to acknowledge the fact that the last few days had been an emotional hurricane I couldn't navigate. But Max was right. I had done it again—smiling through the ache, pretending it was all fine when inside, I was crumbling. It felt like I was being pulled in a thousand different directions, all of them equally impossible to follow.

"I'm fine," I lied, a little too forcefully.

Max didn't buy it. He never did. "Yeah? Fine? That's why you look like you're going to fall asleep on your keyboard?"

I could feel the tears threatening, a thin line between me and the emotional breakdown I had been avoiding. I could hear Connor's voice again in my head, that quiet reassurance that everything would be okay, that he'd be back soon enough. But the longer I thought about it, the more it felt like an empty promise, a hope that would burn out like a match, its glow fading too quickly to last.

Max's presence in the room was comforting, if only for the fact that he was the one person I knew would never ask too much of me. He had seen me through bad breakups, terrible decisions, and life's general chaos, but he was also the kind of friend who knew when to give space and when to push.

I forced a smile. "Thanks, Max. Really. I'm fine."

"Whatever you say," he said, backing out of the room but pausing at the door. "But just so you know, I'm here if you need to vent. Or, you know, drink a bottle of wine and eat an entire pizza. Your call."

I chuckled, despite myself. "I think that's a little too close to your regular Wednesday night routine, but I'll keep it in mind."

Max grinned, and I could tell he wasn't fooled, but he respected my silence. "You know where to find me."

With a soft click, the door shut behind him, and I was left alone with my thoughts again. But his words lingered—you know where to find me. And for the first time since Connor left, I wondered if I could be that person for myself. If I could stop pretending everything was fine and allow myself the space to feel all the things I'd been running from.

I had spent so much of my life convincing myself I didn't need anyone, that I was stronger alone, that it was safer to keep people at arm's length. But now, with Connor's absence pressing down on me, I wasn't so sure anymore. Maybe I needed people. Maybe I wasn't as invincible as I thought.

I closed my eyes for a moment, allowing myself the luxury of grief, of missing someone who had been a part of my life for so long. But as the weight of it all settled over me, I couldn't shake the nagging feeling that I was letting myself drown in something that wasn't even real. That this version of me—sad, broken, aching—wasn't me at all. And it was time to start being the person I used to be. The one who didn't let herself be defined by what she lost.

The apartment was quieter than usual, the hum of the refrigerator the only sound in the room. I sat in the armchair, my fingers drumming restlessly against the armrest, the space where Connor had once been still fresh in my mind. The weight of everything—of him leaving, of the future we had tried to plan slipping through our fingers—pressed down on me like an anchor. I had told myself I wouldn't let this break me, that I would stand tall and strong through it all, but I hadn't expected the hollow feeling that followed him out the door.

I took a deep breath, willing my mind to focus. I had my job to do, my life to get back to. This wasn't the first time I had to pull myself together and carry on when life got messy. But this time felt different. There was a rawness to it, a fragility I hadn't been prepared for. I glanced at the clock—mid-afternoon already, and the day had gone by in a blur. The emails, the calls, they had all felt like noise, distractions from the real weight I couldn't escape.

My phone buzzed again. I knew who it was before I even checked—Connor. My thumb hovered over the screen for a moment. Should I? Should I let him invade this carefully constructed space of mine? I didn't want to be the one holding us together over a thousand miles of distance, but neither did I want to let go. So, I opened the message.

Connor: "I've been thinking about you. It's crazy how quiet this place is without you. Can't help but miss you already."

A small smile tugged at my lips. Despite everything, he still cared. I had known he would, but knowing it didn't make it easier. It made it harder, actually. Because it meant he was struggling too. And for once, I didn't want to be the strong one. I didn't want to pretend that I was fine when all I wanted was to be next to him, to hear his voice, to feel like the space between us didn't stretch endlessly into some unknown future.

Me: "I miss you too. But we both knew this was coming. It'll be okay, Connor. I'll be okay."

I hit send, watching the words on the screen for a moment before I put the phone down, refusing to acknowledge the twist in my stomach that said otherwise.

But I wasn't entirely convinced.

The next few hours passed in a fog, the weight of his message and the lingering ache inside me hard to shake off. I tried to focus on work, on the things that normally occupied my mind, but everything felt like it had been put on pause. It was almost as if the universe had pressed the reset button on my life, and I had no idea what came next.

I had made plans to go out with friends later that night—some kind of distraction, I suppose, though I wasn't sure it would work. But when I stepped into the bar, the noise, the chatter, the laughter, all of it felt like too much. I'd always been the one to keep the party going, to make sure everyone was having a good time, but tonight, I was the one who felt like an outsider.

My friend Zoe spotted me as soon as I entered, a wry smile lighting up her face. She raised her drink in my direction, and I couldn't help but smile back. "There you are," she said, leaning in close so I could hear her over the music. "I was starting to think you'd wimp out on me."

"I almost did," I replied, my voice not quite matching the smile I was forcing. "But I figured I needed to stop moping."

"You need more than one drink for that," Zoe said with a laugh, pulling me toward the bar. "You've been holding it together for way too long. You're due for a meltdown."

I laughed, though it felt hollow. "I'm not really the meltdown type."

Zoe arched an eyebrow. "Then tell me why you look like you want to crawl under a rock and never come out?"

I could feel the familiar walls I'd built around myself starting to crack. Zoe had always been perceptive, far more than I liked. But I couldn't do it—not here, not now. I wasn't ready to let the dam break in front of a crowd.

"I'm fine, Zoe. Really. Just a little... tired."

She didn't buy it for a second. "Uh-huh. Sure. Just make sure I have a front-row seat when the tears start falling."

I couldn't help but smile at her persistence. It was exactly what I needed. Someone who wasn't going to let me bury my feelings under layers of sarcasm and work.

"You're insufferable," I muttered, but there was affection in my tone.

"And you're going to get drunk and tell me everything, whether you like it or not," she shot back with a wink.

I rolled my eyes but decided to play along. We ordered drinks, and soon enough, the noise of the bar, the warmth of the alcohol, and the presence of friends started to dull the edges of my thoughts. I didn't realize how much I needed the distraction until it wrapped around me like a blanket, softening the sharp edges of my reality.

Hours later, the night was winding down, and Zoe was still buzzing with energy, but I felt like a deflated balloon. My phone buzzed again. This time, it was a call.

Connor.

I stared at the screen for a moment, the sound of the crowd swirling around me as I debated whether to answer. Was I ready to hear his voice? Was I ready to dive back into that complicated space we shared? But when I saw the message below it, I knew I had no choice.

Connor: "I'm sorry. I should've never left. This feels wrong. I don't know what I'm doing."

I swallowed, trying to fight the wave of emotions crashing over me. I couldn't—no, I wouldn't—be the one to fix this. Not tonight.

I took a deep breath and answered. "Connor."

And for the first time, there was a hesitation in his voice that made my chest tighten. "I don't want to lose you," he said, his words like a fragile thread, reaching out to me through the static of a long-distance line.

Chapter 38: Reignite the Heart

The scent of fresh coffee hangs in the air, mingling with the earthy undertones of rain outside. I lean back in my chair, fingers tracing the rim of my cup, lost in thought. The rhythm of my life has settled into a pattern—work, calls with Connor, the rare but treasured moments of stillness. I've grown accustomed to the quiet hum of distance, and yet, every time his voice echoes in my ear, it's as if he's right here with me.

The days have stretched and folded into one another, like the pages of a well-worn book, each one offering something new, a deeper layer of connection. There are nights when I fall asleep to the soft glow of his face on my screen, his words lingering in my mind as I drift into dreams. It's almost as though his presence is woven into the fabric of my daily life, a constant that I can't imagine living without. The text messages, the late-night calls, the little snapshots of his world—his life, though distant, feels so close. We speak about everything and nothing, the mundane and the extraordinary. I've come to treasure even the small moments—the way his voice softens when he tells me about his day, the pause before he says something that he knows will make me laugh.

But there are days when the silence between us feels too heavy, when I find myself staring at my phone, waiting for a message that might not come. Those moments are rare, though, fleeting like a passing storm. And just when I start to doubt, just when the thought creeps in that maybe this isn't enough, the phone lights up with his name, and the worry fades away like a shadow at sunrise. It's the little things, the details, the reassurance that we're both still here, still present, even if we're miles apart.

And then, finally, the day comes. The one I've been waiting for since the first time he left—when Connor steps off the plane, and it feels like I can finally breathe again. The moment he walks through the door, my heart stutters in my chest, a leap of joy so powerful I almost stumble forward. He's taller than I remember, his smile more radiant, his presence even more intoxicating than before. Time hasn't changed him, but the years we've spent apart have made this reunion feel like a long-awaited reward. He's here. Right here.

His arms wrap around me before I can even think, pulling me close in a way that's both familiar and new. I laugh, the sound shaky, because I realize that for the first time in months, I'm not talking to a screen, not imagining what it might feel like to be near him. I'm here, and so is he, and the world has never felt smaller, or more perfect, than in this moment.

"I missed you," he whispers, his breath warm against my ear, and I can feel the sincerity in his voice, the weight of everything we've been through just to get to this point.

I pull back slightly, studying his face, wanting to memorize every inch of him. His eyes, the ones that have haunted me during sleepless nights, are even more mesmerizing in person, their warmth pulling me in like an unbreakable tide. "You're really here," I say, my voice barely more than a breath, as if I might wake up and find this all a dream.

He smiles, his lips curling into that easy grin I've missed so much. "Did you think I'd forget?"

"No," I answer, though the uncertainty in my voice betrays me. "But it feels unreal. Like you should be a phone call away, not standing right in front of me."

"Maybe we've gotten used to this," he says with a shrug, his gaze softening as he brushes a strand of hair from my face. "But now, I'm not going anywhere."

His words hang between us, and for a moment, there's nothing but the hum of the world around us—the sound of feet shuffling on the tile, the faint clink of luggage being wheeled by, the distant murmur of voices. But here, in this moment, everything else falls away, leaving just the two of us, standing together at last.

I laugh softly, a sound that feels so foreign after so many days of talking through screens. "You better not be," I say, teasing him lightly, but there's a truth in my voice, a promise that I can't hide. "I've waited too long for this."

He steps back slightly, the warmth of his touch lingering on my skin. His eyes flicker with something unreadable, a glint of mischief and longing all wrapped up in one. "You know, we've got a lot of time to make up for."

"I know," I reply, my heart racing in my chest, a mix of excitement and anticipation flooding my veins. This is the start of something new, something I can't quite name, but I know it will change everything. It already has. And I'm ready. Ready for whatever comes next, ready for him. For us.

Connor grins, that slow, assured smile that always makes my pulse skip. "So, where do we begin?"

I step closer, my gaze locking with his. "Let's start with dinner. Then we'll see what happens after that."

And as I speak, I realize that in that moment, with him standing before me, there's nothing left to figure out. We've already begun.

The days in the city have settled into a kind of quiet rhythm since Connor arrived. I've taken to leaving the blinds open in the mornings, letting the golden morning light pour in like a welcome guest, instead of the harsh artificial glare I'm usually accustomed to. It's a small thing, but the presence of sunshine has made the space feel warmer, more alive. I've always thought of myself as someone who preferred the soft glow of evening, but now—now, I find myself lingering in the daylight, soaking it in as though I might forget what it feels like.

And Connor—well, he's something else entirely. Every moment with him is a reminder that we were never truly apart. His laugh still has the ability to make everything around us blur, and when he looks at me, really looks at me, it's like a promise. Not just a promise of now, but of forever. It's in the way he lingers when he touches my arm or how he grins after making a joke, as if he's waiting for me to join in, to get it. We fall into old patterns with ease, the kind of familiarity that feels like slipping into a favorite book, where every word, every sentence, is something you already know but somehow surprises you all over again.

"Do you ever get tired of this?" he asks one evening, his voice low, the question unexpected but not unwelcome. We're curled up on the couch, my feet tucked beneath his legs, a bowl of popcorn between us that neither of us has bothered to touch for the past few minutes.

I tilt my head, studying him. "Tired of what? You?" I tease, nudging his shoulder with mine.

He laughs, but there's a slight edge to it, something that tells me he's asking more than he lets on. "No, tired of us," he clarifies, his fingers tapping a rhythm against the side of his glass. "Of doing this long-distance thing. Are we just putting it off? Is this just... a nice way to pass the time until we can figure out what we're really doing?"

The question hangs in the air, almost heavy enough to change the mood. I don't answer right away. Instead, I take my time, thinking about what he's really asking. I'm not surprised by the question—it's been a while since he left, and we both know that the distance between us has begun to weigh on him as much as it's weighed on me. But sometimes, it feels like he wants more than a simple answer. Sometimes, I think he's looking for permission to stop worrying, to take that leap into something we both know is already there.

I reach for his hand, pulling it into my lap. "What do you mean by 'really doing'?" I ask, playing coy, though the question itself is anything but.

He looks at me, and there's something in his gaze that says he's no longer just joking. He's serious now, but not in the way that makes me anxious. Serious in the way a person is when they're ready to face the truth. "I mean… I know we've both said we're figuring things out, but how long are we going to keep saying that? I want to know what we're building. I want to know if you're as serious about this as I am."

There's a small knot that tightens in my chest at the weight of his words. I exhale slowly, setting the glass down on the coffee table, the crystal cool beneath my fingertips. It's not that I don't know the answer; it's that sometimes, saying it out loud makes it more real, and real has always been a little scary.

"I'm serious, Connor," I say, finally looking at him, letting the words fall between us like a promise. "But I'm not sure what you mean by 'building.' We've already built something. It's just not in the way you might think. This"—I gesture between us—"this is already ours. We're not starting from scratch."

His brow furrows slightly, and I can see the confusion flitting across his face. "Then what are we waiting for? Why can't it be something real? Something we don't have to tiptoe around anymore?"

I swallow, feeling the pulse of uncertainty flicker somewhere deep inside me. There's so much I want to say, so many things I wish I could explain, but it's hard when you're still figuring out the exact shape of your own heart. I know that Connor's ready for more, but I can't help but wonder if we're both missing something. Maybe we're both just too eager to cross the finish line without realizing that we've already been running the race all along.

"I think you're rushing us," I say, my voice gentle but firm. "We've been doing this long-distance thing for months, and now you're asking for the next step. It's not that I'm not ready, it's just... this feels like more than just a next step. It feels like a leap, and I'm not sure I'm ready to take it just yet."

His eyes soften, the challenge slipping from his face. "I'm not asking for a leap. I'm asking for something that feels real. Something we don't have to question every day."

And just like that, I realize it. The tension between us isn't about love, or distance, or timing. It's about how we've been playing the game of "what if" instead of living the "what is."

I smile then, a small, self-assured smile. "Okay. Let's make it real then," I say, my heart steadying in my chest. I have no idea where this will take us, but I know one thing for sure—whatever it is, I want to be with him. "But no more questioning. No more wondering what's next. We just take it as it comes, one day at a time."

He grins, the tension evaporating as he pulls me closer. "Deal."

And for the first time in a long while, I believe it.

The days since our conversation have unfolded with a quiet kind of intensity. Every morning I wake up to the sound of Connor's voice in my ear, his words wrapping around me like a blanket. We talk about the mundane—what he had for lunch, whether I remembered to pick up milk—but there's always an undercurrent of something more. He's here, really here, and yet we are still discovering what this next phase looks like, how it feels.

Some days, it's perfect. We slip back into old rhythms as though no time has passed, and every glance, every touch, feels like a reunion of sorts. There's something undeniably comforting in the way we fit together, in the way his laugh fills the spaces in my apartment, as though it was meant to be there all along. Other days, though, the reality of it hits me harder than I expect. The uncertainty. The weight of the future. How do we keep this up? How do we make it work when the distance is still there, when we both know that one day, he'll be gone again?

"I can't believe we haven't been to that bakery down the street yet," he says, a teasing smile on his face as he takes another sip of his coffee. The café is bustling around us, the sound of clinking cups and laughter filling the air.

I laugh, reaching across the table to steal one of the pastries he hasn't touched. "You know I'm not really the breakfast pastry type," I say, nibbling at it despite myself. "But I'll go with you. I'm a sucker for an adventure."

He raises an eyebrow, the playful glint in his eyes unmistakable. "That's not what I thought you'd say."

"Well, life with me is full of surprises," I retort, a wry smile tugging at the corners of my lips.

The teasing fades, though, as he watches me for a long beat. It's as if he's trying to find something in my expression, something more than what's on the surface. I can't help but wonder if he's still trying to decipher me, trying to figure out if the smile I wear is as genuine as the words I say.

"You still haven't told me what you're thinking," he says, voice softer now, more earnest. "What's going on behind those eyes?"

I shift uncomfortably, the words I've been dancing around suddenly too real to ignore. "I'm thinking that I wish we could freeze time. Just for a little while, so I could have you here like this without wondering what's coming next."

His expression softens, and he reaches across the table, covering my hand with his. "I'm not going anywhere," he says, but I see the flicker of doubt behind his eyes. "Not unless you tell me to."

I shake my head, the flicker of fear settling in my chest. "I'm not telling you to leave. But you have to understand, Connor—this is... this is big. We're talking about more than just a visit now. We're talking about the future. And I don't know what that looks like."

"You don't have to know everything right now," he says, squeezing my hand. "I just need you to know that I'm here. For now. For whatever comes next."

It's a promise, simple and steadfast. But there's something in his voice, the way he says "whatever comes next," that makes the weight of his words sink deeper. It's one thing to be here together now, but what happens when the next visit ends? What happens when we are faced with the question of what to do with the rest of our lives?

Later that evening, as we walk along the riverbank, the lights of the city casting long shadows across the water, I feel the same unease creeping in. The night is beautiful, the air crisp and cool, but inside, I can't shake the feeling that something is about to change. We've been dancing around it, avoiding the conversation we both know needs to happen, but neither of us seems willing to pull the trigger.

Connor stops walking suddenly, turning to face me, his eyes serious in a way that makes my heart race. "What are you afraid of, Rachel?"

I blink, thrown off balance by the directness of the question. "Afraid?" I laugh, but it comes out too high-pitched. "I'm not afraid."

"You are," he insists, stepping closer. "You're afraid of what happens when it's not just about the fun, the connection. You're afraid of making a decision. Of deciding whether or not we can actually make this work."

I try to take a step back, but my feet are caught in the gravel, and I stumble slightly. He reaches out, steadying me, his hand warm against the small of my back.

"You're right," I admit, the words feeling like they've been trapped inside me for far too long. "I am afraid. But I don't know how to make this work when I can't even see what it's supposed to look like. I can't make promises I'm not sure I can keep."

He looks at me for a long moment, his face unreadable. "So, what happens now?"

The question hangs between us, thick and heavy. I want to tell him that I'm ready to take the leap. I want to throw caution to the wind, trust that we can make it work no matter the distance, no matter the obstacles. But something inside me holds back, a nagging doubt whispering in my ear that maybe I'm not as ready as I thought.

"Rachel," he says softly, "I'm not asking for everything right now. Just... a little bit of trust. Can you give me that?"

I open my mouth to respond, but before I can form the words, a loud crack splits the night air, followed by a series of hurried footsteps. My heart skips in my chest as I turn toward the sound. My stomach drops when I see the figure approaching in the distance—familiar, too familiar.

"Connor..." I whisper, my voice barely audible. The world around us seems to freeze as he steps into the light.

Chapter 39: Trial by Fire

The door swung open with the same smoothness as a curtain parting to reveal a new scene, and I was there, standing in the threshold of Connor's office. The light of the mid-afternoon sun spilled in like liquid gold, wrapping itself around the sleek leather chairs, the polished mahogany desk, the tall windows overlooking a city skyline that seemed more distant now than it ever had before. It had been a week since everything had shifted—the whispers, the uncertainty—and now, there was a figure standing at the very edge of everything we had built. His name echoed in the room, as if spoken aloud would make the past come alive again.

"She's here," Connor said, his voice low but filled with the weight of something heavier than dread. "That's who's here."

I felt my stomach tighten. Of course, it had to be her. The woman from the past who could unravel everything.

I glanced up at him, eyes narrowing. The confusion in his voice seemed to be more about himself than anything else, more about the fact that the past had, at long last, come back to haunt him. I could feel the electricity crackling between us—an unresolved tension that demanded to be dealt with. "Are you going to let her walk in here and tear you apart?"

Connor didn't answer, but the tightness around his jaw told me everything. It was a question he had yet to answer for himself.

The woman who had arrived was no mere shadow of some previous fling. She was a force, an undeniable presence that had slipped through the cracks of the past and now stood in front of him, tall, confident, and undeniably certain of her purpose. I recognized her in an instant, the confidence in her step a reminder of everything Connor had once been—and still was, despite all he'd tried to bury.

Her eyes met mine with the sharpness of someone who was used to cutting right through to the heart of things. "You must be Emma," she said, her voice smooth like melted velvet, but beneath the silk, there was a deliberate edge.

I stood taller, pulling the strands of tension tighter across the room. "I am. And you are?" I said, with just the right amount of sweetness to make it clear that I wasn't buying whatever she was selling.

The woman didn't even flinch. "I'm the one who's going to get Connor back to where he belongs. Not just as your little sidekick, but as the man he used to be."

Connor's hand tightened around the back of his chair, his knuckles blanching under the pressure. He said nothing, but there was a definite shift in the air—something dark, something unresolved. He had never told me the full story, the parts that this woman seemed to know too well.

I took a step forward, standing between her and him, my voice steady but edged with challenge. "If you think that you're going to waltz in here and take him from me, you've underestimated us both."

Her lips curled slightly, amusement flickering in her gaze. "Oh, darling, I'm not here to take anyone. I'm just here to remind him of his place." The words were clipped, final, as if they carried some hidden weight that neither Connor nor I had the privilege of fully understanding.

I locked eyes with Connor then, not allowing myself to look away, even as the fire in the room began to build. This wasn't just about her. This was about the crack in his armor she had come to exploit, the chink in the chain of everything he thought he had conquered.

"I told you," I said quietly, "I'm not going anywhere."

There was a pause. The tension in the room thickened, stretching long and tight, until even the air seemed to hold its breath. Connor's eyes shifted from the woman to me, a flicker of gratitude hidden beneath layers of guilt, regret, and something that looked very much like fear. I wanted to reach out to him, but the moment we were in was fragile, delicate, and neither of us could afford to break it.

"You're right," he finally said, his voice low and almost hesitant. "You shouldn't have to deal with this." His gaze softened as he took a step forward, his hands finding mine in the silence between us.

But then she laughed, a sound that felt like a crack in the ice of an otherwise calm pond. "Oh, but she's already dealing with it, isn't she? She's already here, in this world you've made. The one where you pretend to be someone you're not."

I could feel Connor's muscles stiffen beside me. The words were a poison, each one designed to burrow into his mind, to chip away at the foundations he had so carefully rebuilt.

But I wasn't going to let it happen.

"You think you can just walk in here and rewrite the narrative, don't you?" I asked her, my voice cutting clean through the venom she spat. "But the truth, the one that matters, is that Connor's here with me. He's here because he wants to be. Not because of you, or anything you think you can offer."

Her eyes narrowed. For a moment, I thought I could see a flicker of uncertainty behind that cool facade, something that almost resembled fear—or perhaps regret.

And just as quickly, it was gone. "We'll see about that," she said, turning on her heel and walking out the door, her exit as graceful as her entrance.

The room was silent again, save for the faint sound of Connor's breath, a little shakier than before.

I turned to him, giving him space to speak if he needed to. But the only words that came were the ones I had been waiting for him to say, the ones that carried with them all the weight of what had come before.

"I don't want to go back there," he whispered.

I took his hand, squeezing it tightly. "Then you won't."

The door closed behind her with a soft click, leaving behind a quiet that felt much too loud for my liking. I could feel the tension in the air like the residue of a storm, every second pregnant with something unsaid. But it wasn't just the weight of her words that lingered—it was the look on Connor's face. The way his jaw was set, his eyes darkened by thoughts I couldn't reach, even if I tried.

He turned slowly to face me, as though the world outside the walls of the office had disappeared entirely. And maybe it had, for a brief moment.

"Are you alright?" I asked, the words tumbling out more softly than I intended. I already knew the answer. He was anything but alright.

Connor sighed, rubbing the back of his neck, his posture sagging as the weight of the moment settled in. "I didn't expect her to show up here. Not like this."

I stepped closer, careful not to crowd him, but close enough that my presence could offer some measure of comfort. "It's just a visit from the past, right? You don't have to let it unravel everything." My voice held a confidence that I didn't entirely feel, but he needed it. He needed me to be strong. And I would be, even if I had to fake it until the moment passed.

He looked at me, really looked at me for the first time since the door had opened, and I saw the faintest flicker of something behind his eyes—a mix of relief and gratitude, with just a hint of something darker, as though he'd been expecting to face this storm alone.

"I thought I could leave it all behind," he said, his voice quiet, almost to himself. "But some things—some people—don't let go so easily."

"I know." I said it with a steadiness I hoped would reassure him. "But you're not alone in this. You're never alone."

There was a pause, heavy with everything that neither of us said. Then, with a slight exhale, he pushed himself away from the desk, moving toward the window that overlooked the city below. The glass caught the fading light of the day, a soft golden hue that made everything outside look almost dreamlike. But inside, the air had thickened with unsaid words, and it wasn't just the woman from his past hanging between us.

"I don't even know what she's here for. I thought… I thought she was gone for good. The things she could still know about me," he said, trailing off as if the very mention of it caused some distant memory to surface, a memory he wished to leave buried.

I couldn't blame him. Some ghosts had a way of clawing their way to the surface, no matter how deep you buried them.

"Then let's find out," I said, the words feeling like a declaration rather than a suggestion. "We'll handle this together, step by step. One thing at a time."

He didn't answer right away, but his posture softened. A small shift, the kind that only happened when he was starting to trust again. Trust me, specifically.

"I should've told you," he muttered, more to himself than to me. "About her, about everything."

"I'm here now," I reminded him. "And you don't have to face it alone. You're not responsible for what she knows. But you are responsible for what comes next. We decide that together."

Connor looked at me then, eyes searching, and for a moment, I thought he might say something more. But all he did was nod, a small, almost imperceptible motion, and it was enough. Sometimes silence spoke louder than words, and in that moment, we both understood.

But that didn't make what was coming any easier.

"We're going to have to meet her," I said after a long pause, as if the words themselves were enough to bring the storm back into the room. "If we don't, she'll just keep trying to pull you back. We confront this now, before it gets worse."

Connor's eyes darkened with something close to resolve, a flicker of the old fire that had drawn me to him in the first place. "I'm not going to let her tear us apart."

His words were simple, but they carried weight. I could hear the edge of something deeper in his voice—a promise that neither of us had ever spoken aloud, not in these terms. It was a turning point, a pivot that, once made, would irrevocably change everything.

"We'll go together," I said firmly. "I'll be there. She won't have the power to destroy what we've built." I meant it, and somehow, saying it out loud made it more real, more certain.

But that certainty was fleeting, the sound of the world outside too loud, too invasive. There was no going back now. The battle was about to begin in earnest, and there was no telling what we would find when we finally faced the truth.

As we stood there, side by side, staring out at the city below, I couldn't shake the feeling that things were about to shift. The calm before the storm was a deceptive thing, and as much as I wanted to believe everything would resolve itself with some quiet confrontation, I knew better. The truth had a way of coming out, no matter how much you tried to keep it buried.

Connor's voice broke through my thoughts. "You really think we can clear the air with her? That we can make all of this go away?"

"I think we can. But we'll have to face it head-on. No more hiding, no more running."

He turned to face me, a faint smile tugging at the corners of his lips, but it didn't reach his eyes. "We're going to need a plan."

"Already ahead of you," I replied, returning the smile with one of my own. "We start by confronting her with everything. The truth, no matter how ugly it might seem."

Connor raised an eyebrow, clearly intrigued. "You always did know how to handle a crisis."

"Survival instincts," I said with a grin. "I'm good at getting us out of trouble."

And just like that, with a breath of resolve in the air between us, I knew this fight—whatever it was going to be—was one we could win together.

The next morning, the weight of everything that had been said the day before hung in the air like a thick fog, not quite lifting. Connor and I had spent the better part of the evening talking in circles, hashing out what we knew and what we didn't. There was little in the way of resolution, only a sense of inevitability that this confrontation was coming, and we couldn't put it off any longer.

I woke up to the sound of rain tapping against the windows, soft and persistent, the kind of rain that washed everything clean, or so it seemed. I stretched lazily, feeling the weight of the night settle in my bones. The calm before the storm. But no matter how much I willed it, there was no escaping what was waiting for us. Connor had already left for work, but I knew he was avoiding looking me in the eye, as if by doing so, he could somehow ignore the inevitable.

When I arrived at his office later that morning, it was impossible to ignore the change in the air. There was an edge to everything, a tautness that suggested no one dared to breathe too deeply, as if the space between us and the door leading outside held a secret no one was brave enough to ask about. I didn't want to ask. But I couldn't help myself.

"I talked to her," Connor said the moment I stepped into the office, his voice flat, like someone reading a script they'd memorized but wished they hadn't.

I raised an eyebrow. "You did? And?"

He scrubbed a hand over his face, dragging his fingers through his hair in a way that was so unlike him I almost didn't recognize it. "She came in, told me everything. I didn't say much. Couldn't. I wasn't sure what would set her off, what she might still have over me." He paused, his gaze drifting to the window. "She has a way of making you feel like you owe her. Like you always will."

I could feel the pulse of frustration building inside of me, the urge to shake him out of his silence, but I resisted. He was hurting. I could see it in the way he was holding himself, the way his eyes lingered on that patch of sky outside, as if looking for an escape.

"What did she want?" I asked, my voice softer now, the words careful.

Connor's laugh was bitter, a sound without humor. "It's not what she wants. It's what she wants to make me feel. She's going to keep coming back, trying to pull me into her web, Emma. And I—"

"You don't have to fall for it," I interrupted, taking a step forward, my fingers brushing the back of the chair he had been leaning on. The touch was brief, but it felt like grounding us in something solid, something real.

His eyes met mine, and for a fleeting second, I saw something in them—a rawness, a vulnerability. "I know. But it's not that simple."

I shook my head, refusing to let him spiral. "You're not going to let her control you. Not anymore. We deal with this together, step by step, but you need to remember who you are."

Connor took a deep breath and exhaled slowly, as if trying to summon the strength he so often kept hidden beneath layers of stoic detachment. The room was still, and for a moment, everything seemed to quiet down—the sound of the rain, the soft hum of the city outside.

"I'm scared," he confessed, his voice barely above a whisper. It was the first time I'd heard him admit that. Not just about this situation, but about everything. And in that moment, I realized just how much he had been carrying all on his own.

"You don't have to be," I said, crossing the room in two strides, my hands reaching for his. "You're not alone in this. I'm right here. Whatever happens, we face it together."

For a moment, I thought I saw him relax, but then his phone buzzed on the desk, interrupting the fragile moment of connection we had built. He glanced at the screen, and his expression shifted instantly—his shoulders tensing, his eyes narrowing with a mixture of frustration and dread.

"It's her again," he muttered under his breath, grabbing the phone as if it were a lifeline he wasn't sure he wanted to hold onto. He didn't even look at me as he answered.

"Connor," she said, her voice too smooth, too practiced. I could almost hear the smile in it, the kind that sent shivers down your spine. "I was hoping we could finish our conversation from earlier."

I didn't need to hear the rest. I could see it in his face—the way he clenched his jaw, the way his fingers tightened around the phone. There was nothing left for us here, no more room for hesitation. This was the confrontation, and it wasn't going to be pretty.

He ended the call without a word, the silence in the room oppressive.

"Are you sure you want to do this?" I asked, keeping my voice steady even as I felt the knot in my stomach tighten. This was no longer about trust. This was about survival. His. Ours.

Connor didn't answer at first. He just stared at the phone in his hand, the weight of it seemingly unbearable.

"I have to," he finally said. "There's no other choice."

And just like that, everything shifted. We were no longer in the calm before the storm. The storm had arrived, and we had no choice but to face it head-on. I took a deep breath and nodded, willing myself to be the calm that he needed, even if I wasn't entirely sure I could be that for him.

But when the door opened with the familiar creak, it wasn't just the woman from his past who stepped inside.

A man followed her.

And in his eyes, I saw the one thing I hadn't expected.

Recognition.

Chapter 40: Embers of Peace

The fire crackled softly in the fireplace, the only sound filling the room, a gentle reminder of the night that had fallen over the world outside. I could hear Leo's quiet breaths, a soft rhythm as he slept on the couch, his little form tucked under the blanket Connor had draped over him hours ago. The low hum of the wind against the windows was almost comforting, a constant, like the heartbeat of the earth itself.

Connor, however, was still awake. He sat in the armchair across from me, staring into the flickering flames with a sort of quiet contemplation that seemed to absorb the very essence of the room. His hands were clasped loosely in his lap, the sleeves of his worn flannel rolled up to reveal forearms marked with faint scars, lines of past battles, both literal and metaphorical. I had learned so much about him in the last few weeks—how the hardness in his gaze had once been a shield, how the easy charm he carried had been a mask, and how, beneath it all, he was something rare. Something I was beginning to believe I could trust entirely.

"Do you ever think about what comes next?" I asked, breaking the silence.

He turned his head slowly, as if pulling himself from some faraway place, before his gaze settled on me. There was a glint in his eyes, something soft and knowing. "I think about it all the time. About what it could mean for us, for Leo."

I nodded, though the weight of the question pressed on my chest. "It's strange, isn't it? To feel like everything's finally... safe. Like I can actually start thinking about things without wondering if we're all going to fall apart again."

He leaned forward slightly, his voice quiet but sure. "I know what you mean. I've never been good at this—good at just living. But I think... maybe I'm getting better at it."

The words were simple, but there was an honesty in them that made my heart give a little jolt. A crack of light breaking through the shadows we'd carried for so long. I had always been a planner, a woman with a thousand lists and a thousand ideas about how life should unfold. But with him, sitting across from me now, I realized I had no plans left. I didn't need them. All that mattered was the quiet, steady rhythm we were finding together. One day at a time, one moment at a time.

Leo shifted slightly on the couch, mumbling in his sleep. Connor's eyes softened as he glanced over at him. There was a kind of tenderness in the way he looked at the boy, something that wasn't forced or out of obligation, but simply... true. Leo had become his as much as he had become mine, and in that moment, I couldn't think of anything more beautiful.

"I always thought... I don't know, that it would be different," I said after a moment, my gaze following Connor's. "That it would be hard to step into this whole... family thing. You know? It's not like either of us expected it. But it feels right, doesn't it?"

He smiled, the edges of his lips curling in a way that was completely his own. "It feels right. I think I always knew it would, even if I didn't want to admit it."

There was something in the way he said it, something deeper, like he was finally acknowledging the truth of the life we were building. The walls he had kept up for so long were starting to crack, and I could see the man I had always known was there. The one who wanted to build something real. Something lasting.

"I guess... I guess I'm just still surprised," I continued, my voice catching slightly. "Surprised that we ended up here. After everything."

His gaze softened, and for the first time in a long while, the hardness in his eyes seemed to fade entirely. "Life has a funny way of surprising us," he said. "But maybe... maybe that's the point. The surprise is where the good stuff is hiding."

I let out a small laugh, shaking my head. "You're getting all deep on me, Connor."

He raised an eyebrow, the mischievous glint returning. "I can get deeper if you'd like."

I playfully tossed a pillow in his direction, but he caught it with ease, grinning like he always did when he was in his element. We had found a kind of peace in the chaos, a balance that didn't feel forced or fragile but solid. The connection we shared wasn't about perfection; it was about the understanding that we didn't have to be perfect. Just real.

"I think," I said, my voice growing a little more serious, "that maybe this is what I was meant to do all along. To help him—help both of you. Be what you needed, even if we didn't know what that was."

His expression softened, his eyes glistening with something I couldn't name. "You already are. More than you know."

The fire crackled again, and for a moment, there was nothing but the steady, comforting sound of the flames. I let myself bask in it, in the warmth that surrounded us, the peace that had settled into the corners of the room. We had come so far, and yet, in this quiet, it felt like we had just begun.

Connor's voice broke through my thoughts, low and thoughtful. "What do you think we'll do next? With all this time we've found."

I looked at him, really looked at him, taking in the man who had once seemed so distant, so untouchable, and yet here he was, right in front of me. No longer a stranger, but someone whose future was now intertwined with mine. With Leo's. "I think we'll figure it out," I said, my voice firm but full of the trust I had come to place in him. "Together."

Connor's laugh, low and genuine, was the first sound I had heard in hours that felt like it came from a place of complete ease. It had taken me a long time to get used to the rhythm of his life, the unsaid things that lingered beneath the surface, but here—this quiet house, the fire, and Leo snuggled up with his toy car next to the couch—it felt like we were finally building something steady, something we could claim as our own.

"I swear, you're determined to torture me with those books," he said, tossing a playful glance my way. I had been sitting at the small table in the kitchen, poring over a new set of blueprints for a community outreach program I'd been designing, a way to give back, to build something real in this quiet town. It had started as an idle thought one evening over takeout, but now, after months of finally feeling like my feet were planted firmly on the ground, it was turning into something more. Something I could take pride in.

I glanced up from my notes and met his eyes. "You never know when a little community outreach might save your skin one day."

"Not if you keep making me work with kids," he muttered, his voice tinged with exaggerated reluctance. "I'm barely getting the hang of this whole 'father' thing, and now you want me to mentor the entire elementary school?"

I raised an eyebrow at him, an impish smile curling my lips. "It's not just the kids. It's about teaching them how to stand up for themselves, how to be part of something bigger. They need to know that they have a place in this world, just like you've found yours."

He exhaled dramatically. "You're really laying it on thick tonight, huh?"

"I'm serious," I said, my tone softening. "Sometimes, it's the small things—the right words at the right time—that make all the difference. That's how you build a family, you know. Not just the one you're born into, but the one you choose."

The silence that followed was comfortable, like the hum of the refrigerator or the sound of a distant car passing on the road outside. Connor didn't respond immediately, and I didn't need him to. Sometimes, it was enough just to be in the same room, the same space, with nothing else to prove.

"Do you ever wonder how long this... peace... will last?" His voice broke through my thoughts, quiet and contemplative, as though he had been mulling it over for some time.

I was quiet for a moment, choosing my words carefully. "No," I said finally, meeting his gaze. "I used to, but not anymore. I think we've earned this. All of us." I gestured toward Leo, still asleep on the couch, his face peaceful in a way only children's faces can be. "We've fought too hard to be here. And the world may try to throw curveballs at us again, but I think we'll be ready."

His eyes softened, the tension I hadn't noticed before in his shoulders easing. "You really believe that?"

"I do." The words felt solid on my tongue. I did believe it. In this moment, there was no question. We had found something rare, something worth fighting for.

Before he could respond, a loud yelp echoed from the living room. Connor and I both turned to see Leo sitting upright on the couch, his little face scrunched up in confusion, the blanket half-draped over his legs. I sprang to my feet, but Connor was already there, moving with that fluid grace that always seemed so effortless, like he was born to be a protector.

"What's wrong, buddy?" Connor crouched down beside him, his voice soft but full of concern.

Leo rubbed his eyes and yawned. "I heard a noise... like a... like a big rumble," he mumbled, his words still slurred with sleep.

I froze, my pulse quickening slightly. A rumble? The town was quiet, too quiet, with nothing more than the occasional sound of a car or a dog barking in the distance. But I had learned by now that Leo's instincts were sharp. He might not always have the words to describe what he sensed, but I couldn't ignore the unease in his voice.

Connor and I exchanged a glance. I saw the same thought flicker in his eyes—the same unease that had been building ever since we had settled here. As much as I wanted to believe that danger was behind us, I knew better than to assume that things could never go wrong again. The world had a way of throwing curveballs when you least expected it.

"Maybe it's just a dream," I said, forcing a calm smile as I crouched down next to Leo. "You know, sometimes your brain just plays tricks on you."

But Leo shook his head. "No, Mommy. It wasn't a dream. It was... a rumble. Like the ground was shaking." He frowned as if that should have been obvious to everyone in the room.

I exchanged another glance with Connor, this one longer, filled with unspoken understanding. He stood up slowly, brushing his hands against his jeans. "Alright, Leo. We're going to check it out, okay? But you stay here. We'll be right back."

Leo looked uncertain but nodded, his eyes wide. "Promise?"

"I promise," Connor said, his voice firm and steady.

I moved to follow Connor as he made his way toward the front door, my heart pounding in my chest. What had Leo heard? What had he sensed that we had missed? The world around us had been quiet, almost too quiet, for too long. And as much as I wanted to believe that our little slice of peace would last forever, I couldn't help but wonder if we were about to discover that the world wasn't done with us yet.

The crisp night air hit my skin like a splash of cold water, sending a shiver down my spine as Connor and I stepped outside. The porch light flickered once before casting a steady glow over the yard. Leo's worry still clung to me, his words echoing in my mind. A rumble. The kind of thing you don't just ignore.

Connor adjusted the collar of his jacket, his gaze scanning the street with a mixture of caution and something else—something protective, a readiness that was as much a part of him as his broad shoulders. I could feel his pulse quicken as he took a few steps down the porch, his boots scraping against the wooden planks.

"Keep close," he muttered, as if it was more for him than me. We'd never been great at voicing our fears, not even now, not with everything we'd gone through. But I knew. The weight in his shoulders, the way his jaw tightened—it wasn't just about Leo's nightmare. He felt it too. Something was off.

I followed him, my footsteps quiet in the gravel driveway. We both turned toward the horizon, where the faint outline of the town lay, peaceful and still. The kind of calm that felt too perfect, too much like the eye of a storm.

"Do you hear that?" Connor asked, his voice low, barely above a whisper.

I strained, listening for any sign of disturbance, but there was only the gentle rustling of the trees in the distance. I shook my head. "Nothing."

"Exactly." His tone was sharper now, his instincts kicking in, and I could almost feel the shift in him. His posture had become more alert, as if he were waiting for something to jump out of the shadows. I knew that feeling all too well. It was the same one I'd had when I first moved here—when I still thought I could outrun my past.

We moved closer to the edge of the yard, our eyes scanning the area. There was a feeling in the air, something thick and heavy, like a storm was waiting to break. The world seemed to hold its breath, just before chaos erupted.

The sudden sound of a distant growl made my heart leap into my throat. It was low, a rumbling that could have been mistaken for thunder if not for the sharpness in it. But this wasn't a natural sound—it wasn't the wind, and it certainly wasn't a wild animal. The hairs on the back of my neck stood up, and I could see the same realization dawn on Connor's face.

"What the hell was that?" I asked, my voice barely above a whisper, as if speaking any louder would bring it closer.

Connor didn't respond immediately, his eyes narrowing. Instead, he pulled his phone from his pocket, quickly scrolling through the screen. I watched him, waiting for some sign of confirmation, some explanation, but none came. He shoved the phone back into his pocket with a grim expression.

"Stay here," he said, his voice firm, but not unkind. "I'll check it out."

I reached out, grabbing his arm before he could take another step. "You're not going alone."

He turned to look at me, a flicker of surprise crossing his face. "We don't know what's out there. You need to stay inside, where it's safe."

I shook my head, the urgency in his tone sparking something in me—a need to not be left behind, to stand beside him, to face whatever was coming head-on. "No. If this is something... anything... I'm not sitting this one out."

There was a long pause, and for a moment, I thought he might argue, but then his eyes softened. He nodded once, briefly, before glancing back toward the darkened street. "Alright. Just stay close."

Together, we started walking toward the edge of the town, each step heavy with a mix of anticipation and fear. The lights from the houses seemed to fade as we moved further from the center of it all. The growl grew louder, closer, and I realized with a sickening certainty that it wasn't thunder. The ground beneath our feet was still, not even the faintest vibration from what was approaching.

We turned a corner, the darkened alleyway stretching out before us like a mouth waiting to swallow us whole. The streetlights overhead flickered once before going out entirely, leaving us in near-complete darkness.

The growl came again, but this time it wasn't just one sound. It was a chorus, as if something was stirring in the deep shadows, something too large to ignore.

Connor stopped dead in his tracks, his eyes wide, staring into the abyss ahead. "Did you hear that?" he breathed, his words barely audible.

I couldn't even respond. The growl had become a cacophony, a series of sharp, guttural noises that seemed to vibrate through my very bones. And then, just when I thought I couldn't take any more, I saw it.

A figure moved in the shadows, slow and deliberate, its shape unnaturally large. It wasn't human. It wasn't anything I'd ever seen before. The way it shifted through the dark—it was as though it didn't belong to this world at all. My heart hammered in my chest, every instinct screaming at me to run, to get Leo and Connor to safety.

But Connor didn't move. His gaze was locked on the figure, his body tense, prepared for whatever was about to unfold. I took a step closer to him, my voice shaky as I whispered, "What the hell is that?"

His lips barely parted as he murmured, "I don't know. But I think it's here for us."

And just as the figure stepped into the dim light, a monstrous face with glowing eyes locked onto ours, everything around us seemed to collapse in on itself.

Chapter 41: Blazing Future

It had taken months for us to settle on a place. I don't mean the house or even the land, though that was a decision we made together after many weekend drives through towns I couldn't pronounce, crisscrossing rural roads with nothing but fields and the occasional mailbox to guide us. I mean the feeling of home—what it would look like, what it would feel like, and how it would fit us, like a pair of well-worn jeans, comfortable and slightly frayed at the edges but strong enough to carry us through the long haul. I never imagined I'd stand here, hand in hand with Connor, on the dirt of land we now owned, watching him dig into the earth with the same quiet determination he always carried. He had a way of making everything seem possible, like everything we needed was already out there, buried beneath the surface.

The land was wide, stretching out in all directions, with wildflowers dotted along the edges and a sky so big it felt like it was swallowing us whole. There was no noise, no constant hum of traffic or the distant chatter of the city. Just silence, the kind of quiet that allows you to hear your thoughts with a clarity that almost feels unnerving. And yet, standing here with Connor, I felt nothing but peace.

It was a kind of stillness I hadn't known before. The kind that held so much potential, like we were standing at the beginning of something that hadn't yet fully taken shape, but we were ready to make it ours. A house wouldn't just be a structure of walls and rooms; it would be an extension of everything we were together—an intimate reflection of the days we had shared and the ones we hadn't yet lived.

Connor looked over at me, his face softened by the late afternoon sun. He always looked like that, as if life itself was softer in his presence. The edges of his jaw, the way his eyes crinkled when he smiled—it all felt like home. No matter where we went, he made sure I never doubted we were exactly where we were meant to be.

"Do you see it?" he asked, his voice low, tinged with excitement. His eyes weren't just looking at the land, not really. They were looking beyond it, seeing something no one else could yet.

I squinted against the sun, following the line of his gaze. There was nothing but dirt, grass, and a few scraggly trees. But somehow, I could see it, too.

"I see it," I said, and I meant it. It was more than the wood and nails and mortar; it was the laughter, the late-night talks, the quiet mornings when we'd sit on the porch, sipping coffee in the kind of silence that felt like an old song. "I see us."

Connor smiled, and for a moment, I wondered if maybe he'd read my mind. He stepped closer, closing the space between us until we were standing so close I could feel the warmth of his skin pressing against mine. His fingers brushed the edge of my hand before slipping a small, cool metal band onto my finger. It caught the light, gleaming like the promise of everything we'd ever wanted.

I stared at it for a beat, the weight of the moment hitting me like a wave. I hadn't expected it, not this soon. But Connor never played by anyone's rules but his own.

"You're not just getting a house," he said, his voice steady, but there was something in his eyes that made my heart skip. "You're getting me. All of me. For as long as you'll have me."

The world shifted, expanded, or maybe it contracted, and all I could hear was the sound of my heart beating loudly in my chest. This was it. The moment that changes everything. The kind of moment you look back on and wonder how it ever seemed anything but inevitable.

I hadn't realized how badly I needed to hear that from him until the words left his mouth. But as they did, I felt a warmth spread through me. Something deeper than the sunburn I was likely to have later. It was a promise—simple, profound, and forever.

I looked at him, seeing all the ways he had already woven himself into my life, the quiet support he gave me without ever asking for anything in return. He was a force of nature, a whirlwind of laughter and fire, and yet when it came to me, he was patient, kind, and steady.

"I think I'm going to hold you to that," I said, my voice a little rough, but not from doubt—just from the enormity of what it meant.

He chuckled, low and confident. "You can hold me to it all you want."

I laughed, the sound light, but rich with the truth we had both been building together for so long. "It's a good thing I'm not in the habit of letting go."

And just like that, the ground beneath us felt firmer, steadier. This land, this life we were about to create, would hold us. It was more than just a physical place; it was a testament to everything we'd already survived, a home where we'd make a future that was all our own.

I stood there, looking at Connor—this man who had promised me forever with nothing more than a simple ring—and realized that I had no doubt, not a single shadow of uncertainty. With him, everything was possible. Everything.

It wasn't the ceremony, or the grand gestures that sealed the deal—it was the quiet moments that followed, the way life settled into a rhythm I hadn't known I was missing until it was already here. It was the way the days began to shape themselves around us. First, there was the house. And then there was everything else—the daily, small things that felt as monumental as the structure itself.

Connor was a man who didn't care for many things beyond what was necessary. He didn't ask for much, and even less in return. But building this life together, this home that wasn't just a place but a possibility—well, that was something he could sink his teeth into. He became a man who had ideas that stretched beyond just the walls of our house. He wanted every part of it to feel like us—like it had always been meant to be that way.

We spent weekends with our boots in the dirt, scouring lumber yards and testing paint samples like it was a new kind of adventure we were embarking on. His hand was always in mine, guiding me through each decision, whether it was where to put the front door or what shade of cream would give the walls that perfect, lived-in look without making it feel too sterile. I let him take the lead, finding comfort in how he carefully considered each move. And when it came to the kitchen, well—he let me take over. I suppose I wasn't going to let him dictate what kind of cabinets we would have. But that's what I loved about us—our ability to coexist in a space that was just as much his as it was mine.

"Imagine this," he said one evening, his voice low, eyes sparkling with the kind of enthusiasm that had become a hallmark of our new life. "A big kitchen island in the center, and we'll make dinner together. You and me. We'll have wine, music playing, and the scent of rosemary and garlic drifting in from the stove. Maybe we'll even burn something on purpose, just for the fun of it." He grinned. "A little imperfection never hurt anyone."

I couldn't help but laugh. "Is that supposed to be your idea of romance? You just listed out the most chaotic dinner party I've ever heard of."

"Maybe. But that's what life's going to be like with us—messy, fun, a little off-kilter, but exactly where we're supposed to be."

I thought about that for a moment, my fingers tracing the edges of the ring he'd given me, now worn slightly from where I played with it absentmindedly, while our plans and dreams twined around us like ivy creeping up a fence. There was something about him, about us, that made all of this seem not only possible but inevitable. There were no doubts anymore, only days ahead of us that would unfurl with a promise as solid as the foundation we were laying down.

It wasn't all perfect, of course. Life never really is. The uncertainty of it all wasn't lost on me. There were nights when the future felt as heavy as the world itself, and the weight of everything we hadn't yet lived, of the mistakes we hadn't yet made, pressed down on me in the dark. But then there were mornings like this one, when I woke up to Connor standing in the kitchen, his back to me as he poured coffee into two mugs. I could hear the way his boots shuffled on the tile, the clink of the spoon against the ceramic, and when he turned around, a grin stretched across his face like a secret only he and I shared.

"We've been at this for hours, and I'm still not sure we're getting it right," I said, eyeing the plans he'd spread out across the table.

He raised an eyebrow, crossing his arms. "I don't know what you're talking about. I think it's going perfectly."

I couldn't help but chuckle. "You're just saying that because it's your plan. But you're right, we don't need everything to be perfect. Just enough to keep us going."

Connor took a step closer, his expression softening as he reached for my hand. "And we'll keep going. All of it. Together. We've built something that can't be broken." His thumb brushed lightly over the palm of my hand, and for a moment, everything else melted away. It was just us—no plans, no house, no future except the one we were building with each other.

"You're right," I said quietly, squeezing his hand in return. "And maybe that's enough."

The house wasn't just a structure—it was an anchor. A symbol. But it was also a promise, one that only made sense because of the life we had already built together. There were no false expectations, no grand illusions. There was just a shared certainty between us. We didn't need everything to go smoothly, or for each detail to align perfectly. Life would still have its bumps—there was no way around that. But we had the foundation, the strength, and the desire to keep moving forward no matter what came next.

But even with all of this certainty, there were moments of doubt that crept in, hidden beneath the surface like a shadow. We hadn't talked about the harder things yet, the stuff that was still too fragile to touch. The things we were afraid to say out loud. We hadn't spoken about how, once the house was finished, we might start to think about bigger things. The kind of things you only start imagining when your feet are firmly planted in the ground. Marriage. Children. A life together that spanned beyond just a couple of rooms and a few acres of dirt.

I could feel the tension between us, though unspoken, as we took each step forward. Connor was a man of few words, and when he spoke of the future, it was with a certain casualness. But there were days when I wondered if the unspoken questions between us were the things that would make or break us. Would we be able to handle all the unknowns that still lay ahead? Would we both be brave enough to face them, together?

For now, though, I didn't want to dwell on it. There was a sweetness in the uncertainty, in the fact that we didn't yet know all the answers. For now, I was content with the life we were creating. The rest, I thought, would come when it was ready.

The days passed with the rhythm of an orchestra tuning itself. There were moments of dissonance, like when we argued over whether to paint the living room a muted sea green or something bolder, but those moments passed, and the music resumed. Our lives, once jagged and sharp, began to smooth out, note by note, as we built this home with our own hands and hearts. We worked on weekends, planning, measuring, even laughing at our own mistakes. It was all part of the process, I realized—the building and the learning and, yes, even the failing. It was a kind of dance, one where we never fully knew the next move, but trusted each other enough to stumble together.

Connor's insistence on doing things himself sometimes amused me. He wasn't a perfectionist by any stretch, but he was a man who liked to know how things worked, even if it meant staying up late with a hammer in one hand and a cup of coffee in the other, cursing under his breath when things didn't line up as they should.

"Don't look at me like that," he said one evening, catching me staring at him from the doorway, his forehead glistening with sweat and a piece of wood precariously balanced on his shoulder. "This is part of the charm. Every perfect house has a few crooked boards."

"Uh-huh, right," I replied, my lips twitching with suppressed amusement. "You know, you're not going to convince me this place is charming when you end up getting a splinter in your thumb again."

He grinned, a mischievous gleam in his eyes. "It's all part of the experience, babe. Besides, a splinter here and there builds character. And we've got a lot of character to build."

It wasn't just the house that was shaping us; it was everything around it—the quiet moments, the glances that spoke more than words ever could, the soft touches when we passed each other in the hallway. I had learned, over the course of our relationship, that our love wasn't built on grand gestures. It was built on the small, often unnoticed things—the way he always left the last piece of pizza for me, how we shared a laugh over stupid jokes that no one else would find funny, or the way he listened when I talked about something that made my heart race, even if it was the most trivial thing in the world.

Our connection was something I couldn't describe easily. It was more than just love; it was a trust that ran deeper than the roots of the oak tree that stood in the backyard, its gnarled branches reaching toward the sky like silent witnesses to everything we had already endured. There were moments when I wondered if the universe had conspired to make sure we found each other, but even in those moments, I didn't dwell on it. What mattered was that we had found each other, and everything else had fallen into place after that.

But of course, life had a way of reminding us that we weren't done yet.

One night, when we were sitting in the kitchen, the light from the overhead lamp casting a soft glow over our coffee mugs, I felt the weight of something unspoken in the air. Connor was quiet, more so than usual. His usual playful banter had faded into a silence that pulled at my thoughts. I couldn't help but notice the tension in his jaw, the way his fingers tapped the edge of his cup with a rhythm that didn't belong.

"What's going on?" I asked, leaning forward, the weight of the question heavier than I intended.

Connor's gaze flickered toward me, a flicker of something—guilt, maybe—passing through his eyes. He opened his mouth as if to speak, but then closed it again, as if deciding against it. He took a long sip of his coffee, his gaze steady but not quite meeting mine.

"I've been thinking," he said slowly, carefully. "About everything. About us. About... the future."

A knot tightened in my chest, and I braced myself for whatever was coming next. I knew him well enough to know when something was weighing on him. "What about the future?"

He shifted in his seat, clearly uncomfortable. "I don't know how to say this... I've just—sometimes, I wonder if we're doing this right. If we're rushing into things. If we're ready for it. All of it."

The words hit me like a sharp gust of wind, knocking me off balance. I blinked, trying to process what he was saying, trying to grasp at the shifting ground beneath me. "What do you mean, 'rushing'?" I asked, my voice quieter than I meant it to be.

Connor ran a hand through his hair, his gaze distant as though he were seeing something far beyond the walls of our little kitchen. "I mean everything. This house. Us. It's all happening so fast, and I don't want to mess it up. I don't want to screw it all up because we're moving too quickly."

I felt the breath leave my chest, a sudden chill creeping through me. Had I been moving too fast? Had I missed something? Was this whole thing, this life we'd been building together, too much for him?

The silence between us stretched out, heavy and unyielding, until I couldn't take it anymore. "Connor, if you're having second thoughts—"

"I'm not," he interrupted, his voice sharp, almost too sharp. "I'm not having second thoughts about you. It's just... this. All of it. I want us to be ready, you know? Really ready. I want to know that we're not doing this because it's the easy thing, or because it's what we're supposed to do. I want to know we're doing this because we're both completely sure."

The knot in my chest loosened slightly, but there was still a raw edge to his words that made my heart ache. He wasn't pulling away from me. He was just... pulling back. Trying to make sense of something, trying to piece together a future that, even now, felt uncertain.

I sat back in my chair, taking a deep breath. "Connor, we've been through so much already. If we can get through that, don't you think we can handle anything?"

He looked at me then, really looked at me, his eyes softening. For a moment, I saw everything he felt, everything he feared. "I hope so," he whispered, his voice almost breaking.

And just when I thought I might say something to reassure him, to calm the storm that was rising between us, the doorbell rang—loud, insistent, cutting through the tension like a sharp knife.

Connor's face went pale, and I felt the blood drain from my own cheeks.

"I wasn't expecting anyone," I said, standing up, my pulse quickening.

Connor stood too, his eyes wide with something I couldn't quite name. "Neither was I."

Chapter 42: Everlasting Flame

The air smells like rain, even though there hasn't been a drop in the sky all day. It's the kind of scent that lingers in the soul, the way old wood smells when you walk past a house with a fireplace burning. Warm, nostalgic, and yet filled with the thrill of something new. I'm standing in the small courtyard of an old stone church, its bell tower looming like a watchful guardian over the garden that holds the few who have stayed with us through thick and thin. The kind of people who don't flinch when life gets messy, the kind of people who show up and stay long after the shine of new beginnings has worn off.

Connor stands next to me, his hand warm against my palm, the steady beat of his pulse as familiar as my own heartbeat. I glance up at him, our gazes locking, and his smile tugs at the corners of my lips, a quiet confidence in his eyes that makes everything feel right. As if, for once, we don't need to prove anything to anyone. Not today. Today is ours.

I want to say something witty, something that will make him laugh, but all that comes out is a small breathless sound, a barely-there whisper that matches the flutter in my chest. His thumb moves in slow circles against my skin, the only gesture needed to tell me he understands. He always does. It's a strange sort of magic, the way we've come to know each other. Like we were always meant to be two halves of a whole, but never quite in the way you expect.

I glance around at the guests, my heart swelling. My best friend Sarah is tucked at the back, her smile as wide as I've ever seen it, and beside her, her husband Peter is doing his best to look composed, though the twinkle in his eye betrays the mischief that lurks beneath. My mother stands to the side, tears streaming down her cheeks as she watches her only daughter finally take a step forward in life—into something that isn't just the next phase, but a choice. A choice to let go of the past and embrace a future that looks brighter than any of us dared to imagine.

But even as I take in all these faces, the one I'm most attuned to is Connor's. I'm trying so hard not to stare, not to let my emotions spill over like an untamed river, but it's hard not to. The way he looks at me, like I'm the only person in the world. Like no one else could ever compare. It's a look I used to dream about when I was younger, the kind of gaze that promises safety and passion all at once.

The ceremony is brief, the vows simple but profound, a reflection of what we've already shared—a lifetime compressed into a few short sentences. The words roll off my tongue, steady and clear, though my insides are a jumble of nerves and wonder. I can feel the warmth of Connor's hand as it tightens around mine, and it steadies me, anchors me in the moment.

When it's time to say "I do," it's not just words. It's the accumulation of everything that's come before. The late-night conversations where we revealed our deepest fears and hopes. The quiet mornings spent wrapped in blankets, the sound of rain drumming against the window, the silence between us never awkward, always comforting. And the times we've fought, too. The moments where we've stumbled, tripped over our own baggage, but always found our way back.

There's no doubt in my mind as I speak those words, no hesitation. And when the officiant pronounces us husband and wife, the world seems to hold its breath for a beat—just a beat—before it explodes with cheers and applause. But even as everyone around us erupts into joyous noise, all I can hear is the sound of my own heartbeat, steady and sure, echoing in my chest.

Connor leans in then, his lips brushing against my ear, warm and soft. "You're mine now, forever," he whispers, and the heat of it lingers long after he pulls back, his grin wide and knowing.

The words send a shiver down my spine, a thrill so sharp and unexpected it makes me dizzy. Forever. It's a word we toss around lightly in conversation, but it feels so heavy in this moment, this moment that belongs to us and only us. We're standing on the precipice of a life we've built together, and I know, with every fiber of my being, that we're not just surviving anymore. We're living.

The reception is a blur of laughter and clinking glasses, everyone basking in the happiness we've somehow managed to carve out for ourselves. I steal glances at Connor as the evening wears on, watching him talk with my family, his eyes lighting up as he gestures animatedly. There's a quiet assurance in the way he carries himself, as if he's never been anything but comfortable in this world he's created with me. I've always admired that about him—the way he walks into a room like he belongs, no matter the circumstances.

But there's one moment, as the night deepens and the candles flicker low, when it's just the two of us standing alone in the garden. The sky above us is dark, the stars little pinpricks of light in a sea of black, and I feel the weight of it all—the years we've spent navigating our way through life, through love, and through loss. The struggles we've faced, the way we've learned to trust each other even when the world seemed to be falling apart. And still, here we are, standing on the edge of forever.

Connor's hand slips into mine once again, and I can't help but smile. "I never thought I'd get here," I admit softly, my voice barely louder than a breath. "Not like this. Not with you."

He turns to face me, his eyes searching mine with a quiet intensity that's all his own. "Sometimes the best things in life come when you least expect them," he says, his voice low and full of meaning.

I nod, feeling the truth of his words settle in my chest. We've walked a long road to get here, but the journey was worth it. Because now, standing in the quiet of the night, I know that this is just the beginning. The flame between us isn't just a spark—it's an everlasting blaze that will light our way for the rest of our lives.

The reception is an explosion of sound and movement, as though the whole world is exhaling a collective breath. People are laughing, glasses are clinking, and there's an energy in the air that I can almost taste, sweet and effervescent. The soft hum of music swirls around us, and every now and then, I catch the flutter of a dress or the sparkle of a perfectly polished shoe, the kind of little details that add to the magic of the moment. I catch myself wondering if, somewhere in the universe, there are two alternate versions of this day: one where I stayed in my apartment, buried under a pile of books, alone and safe in the predictable chaos of my life; and the one I'm living now, with Connor beside me, his laughter mingling with mine as we weave our way through a crowd of our closest people. I know which version I'd pick a thousand times over.

I grab a glass of champagne, feeling the bubbles dance on my tongue. The glass is delicate, the crystal thin and light against my fingers, and I think about how everything—everything—has led us to this moment. The stumbles, the mistakes, the pieces of my life that once felt like they didn't fit together but now, in the soft glow of tonight's celebrations, fit perfectly.

"Careful," Connor teases as he slides up next to me, his voice playful but warm. His hand grazes mine, and for a brief second, I feel the sharp intensity of his touch all the way down to my spine. "You're going to end up drunk before we even cut the cake."

I roll my eyes at him, trying—and failing—to hide a smile. "I'm not the one getting sloshed off of champagne," I point out, though I'm aware the gleam in his eyes suggests he might already be a few sips in.

He raises an eyebrow, a gesture so full of cheeky charm it could be a sin. "Who, me?" he says, his voice a mix of innocence and mischief. "I'm just here for the company, love."

"Uh-huh," I reply dryly, though my heart skips a beat as he takes my hand and gently pulls me toward the dance floor. It's funny, I always imagined our first dance would be this grand, picture-perfect moment, some slow waltz with hundreds of eyes on us, a moment that would define the start of our forever. But the reality is much more us—no spotlight, no choreography, just a soft sway to the music, his hand at my waist and mine on his shoulder as if we've done it a thousand times before.

I lean in close, my cheek brushing against his, and for a moment, everything falls away—the crowd, the noise, the world—and it's just us, surrounded by the kind of quiet that can only exist in the most tender of moments. His breath is warm against my ear when he whispers, "I still don't know how you talked me into wearing this tux."

I laugh softly, pulling back just enough to meet his gaze. "You look ridiculous in it," I tease. "But I'll keep it to myself. You're much more handsome than I imagined in a tux."

Connor smirks, the playful glint in his eye making it clear he's enjoying every moment of this banter. "I knew it. You're secretly in love with the idea of me in a tux. You can't get enough of this handsome face, can you?"

I roll my eyes, but the truth is—he's not entirely wrong. There's something undeniably magnetic about him, especially when he gets that glint of mischief in his eyes, like he knows something no one else does. It's an edge that pulls me in, a little dangerous, a little unknown, and yet, somehow comforting. He's never been afraid to speak his mind, to tell me exactly what he thinks, but there's a softness in him that I've come to rely on. A steady anchor, even when everything else seems to be drifting.

"I think you're just trying to make me blush," I say, raising an eyebrow, the hint of a smile playing at my lips.

His smirk widens, and then, without warning, he spins me out, twirling me under his arm before pulling me back in close. "Is it working?"

I laugh, feeling the tension in my body melt away. He's always had this ability to make me laugh at the most unexpected times, and right now, with everyone around us caught in their own little worlds, I'm struck by the simplicity of this—this life we're building, the love that has been tested and tried, but that, in the end, is undeniable.

As the song shifts and the tempo picks up, the room seems to shift too. The chatter grows louder, and people start breaking off into little groups, but Connor and I are still here, still dancing, still lost in the quiet rhythm of our own world.

"You know," he murmurs, his eyes tracing the delicate line of my jaw, "I think we're the luckiest people in the room."

I stop moving, my feet stilled for a moment as I process his words. "What do you mean?" I ask, my voice steady but curious. "I thought we were supposed to be the happiest."

He chuckles, the sound low and warm. "No. Not the happiest," he says, brushing a stray lock of hair from my face. "The luckiest. The world doesn't always hand out second chances. And here we are, having one."

I blink, feeling a sudden lump rise in my throat. "Connor, don't—"

"No, listen to me," he interrupts softly, but with conviction. "I know we've had our moments, our struggles, but we found our way back, didn't we? It wasn't luck that brought us together—it was us, our choices, our resilience. And I'd pick you, every single time. No matter how many wrong turns we had to take along the way."

I can feel the sting of tears behind my eyes, but I blink them away quickly, determined not to let them fall. Not tonight. Not when everything feels so perfect.

"You're right," I whisper, my voice trembling slightly. "We really are lucky, aren't we?"

He grins, the playfulness returning to his eyes. "The luckiest," he repeats, dipping me low in a dramatic flourish that makes me laugh out loud, the sound ringing through the room.

And just like that, all the tension, all the weight of the past, vanishes. It's just us again, swirling in the quiet joy of what we've built, our hearts beating in time with each other, our future as uncertain and infinite as the stars above us.

The night lingers in the air, soft and velvety, like the kind of evening that stretches its arms and refuses to let go. We've danced, we've laughed, and now, as the last of the guests trickle out of the courtyard, the sounds of their chatter fading into the distance, a peaceful silence settles over us. The candles flicker gently in their holders, casting long, warm shadows on the stone walls. I stand there, hand in Connor's, our fingers laced together like puzzle pieces that have always belonged.

He pulls me into his arms again, the familiar comfort of his embrace anchoring me, and I rest my head against his chest, listening to the steady rhythm of his heartbeat. The world feels smaller now, quieter, as if everything outside of this moment has receded into the background, leaving only the two of us standing at the center of our own little universe.

"Are you happy?" he asks, his voice low, full of that soft rasp that always makes my stomach flutter. There's something about his tone, about the way he looks at me now, as though we're the only two people left in the world, that makes my heart skip a beat. It's not the first time he's asked me this, but there's something different tonight. Something that feels more urgent, more raw.

I take a deep breath, savoring the warmth of the night, the joy that's still bubbling in my chest. "I am," I reply, my voice steady but full of the unspoken truth. "More than I ever thought I would be."

Connor's grip on me tightens, his fingers pressing into my back, and for a moment, the only sound is the rustle of the leaves overhead, stirred by a breeze that feels like a whisper. "Good," he says, his lips brushing the top of my head. "You deserve it. All of it."

I glance up at him, my heart swelling with something close to gratitude, close to wonder. He's not perfect, not by a long shot. But then again, neither am I. We've both fought for this—fought for each other, for the chance to build something real. Something that's ours, built on the rubble of all the broken parts of our lives.

We stand there in silence for a while, watching the last few guests leave, their cars disappearing down the winding driveway, and when it's just us, alone in the courtyard, Connor's hand slides down my back, brushing against the fabric of my dress, warm and intimate. I shiver slightly at the touch, the sensation rippling through me like a wave of heat.

"I was thinking," he says suddenly, his voice light, as though he's testing the waters. "Maybe we should leave tonight. Go somewhere—anywhere. Just us."

My heart races at the thought, a thrill rising in my chest. I should be the responsible one, the one who says we can't just run away, that we have responsibilities, places to be. But there's something in his eyes, a spark that dares me to break free of the rules, to be wild with him, just this once.

Before I can respond, a loud crash interrupts the moment. My body stiffens instinctively, and Connor's arms tighten around me. We both look toward the sound—something heavy, something